Soon after arriving in the Bay Area, Amparo had fallen in the habit of meeting her uncle for dinner after his meeting ended. Over the years, the pair had developed a hybrid relationship of father/daughter/brother/sister, one forged as much by blood as by the fact that both came to California after having been expelled from the clan. Curiously, neither one ever talked about the reasons for their expulsion. Amparo's reticence was born of shame, Aldo's, of guilt. . . .

* * * *

Cocking an eyebrow, the doorman leaned into the door's levered handle and swung it wide. "Ahhhh—mail-order bride *siguro*."

Beverly ignored his smirk and stepped into the wide lobby, its gleaming marble floors reflecting the scuffed soles of her sandals. Straightening her shoulders and lifting her chin, Beverly walked up to a massive mahogany console manned by a woman in a dark suit. A discreet black tile on the woman's lapel proclaimed her name in gold: *Felicidad*. Even the concierge had a fancy name for joy. . . .

OTHER BOOKS BY MARIVI SOLIVEN

Suddenly Stateside

Spooky Mo

MARIVI SOLIVEN

NAL ACCENT

NAL Accent
Published by the Penguin Group
Penguin Group (USA) Inc., 375 Hudson Street,
New York, New York 10014, USA

USA | Canada | UK | Ireland | Australia | New Zealand | India | South Africa | China

Penguin Books Ltd., Registered Offices: 80 Strand, London WC2R 0RL, England
For more information about the Penguin Group visit penguin.com.

First Published by NALAccent, an imprint of New American Library,
a division of Penguin Group (USA) Inc.

First Printing, May 2013

LIBRARY OF CONGRESS CATALOGING-IN-PUBLICATION DATA:
Soliven, Marivi.
The mango bride/Marivi Soliven.
p. cm.
ISBN 978-0-451-23984-6
1. Filipinos—California—Oakland—Fiction. 2. Women immigrants—California—Fiction. I. Title.
PS3619.O4327M36 2013
813'.6—dc23 2012039084

Printed in the United States of America
10 9 8 7 6 5 4 3

Set in Bell MT
Designed by Spring Hoteling

PUBLISHER'S NOTE
This is a work of fiction. Names, characters, places, and incidents either are the product of the author's imagination or are used fictitiously, and any resemblance to actual persons, living or dead, business establishments, events, or locales is entirely coincidental.

The publisher does not have any control over and does not assume any responsibility for author or third-party Web sites or their content.

For the indomitable Vega clan, and for my husband, John

ACKNOWLEDGMENTS

The Mango Bride was conceived in one frenetic month during NaNoWriMo 2008 and then labored on and finally delivered after a two-year gestation in Judy Reeves's magical Wednesday Writers group. The perceptive comments of Kathy Bucher, Zoe Ghahremani, Greg Johnson, Chau Matser, Jim Ruland, Gary Seiser, Sandra Younger and Ken Zak proved invaluable in refining each chapter. As I wrote, workshops with Drusilla Campbell, Lisa Shapiro, Tom Spanbauer, Sage Ricci and Butch Dalisay at San Diego Writers, Ink honed my craft. At the end of this journey, Sandra Harding at Penguin offered suggestions for revision and polished my words until they sang.

I owe these amazing writers and editors the very deepest debt of gratitude.

Many thanks as well to Taryn Fagerness, who first read the manuscript and sparked a chain of enthusiasm that eventually led to my peerless literary agent, Jill Marsal, who in turn engineered the publishing deal with Penguin.

Hedgebrook holds a special place in my heart for bestowing the luxury of two weeks' undisturbed writing, enabling me to revise the manuscript and continue work on my next novel. Nancy Nordhoff, Amy Wheeler, Vito Zingarelli, Kathryn Preiss, Cathy Bruemmer, Denise Barr and Katie Woodzick have created a haven for artists like no other, and I wrote more in those fourteen days than I had in the last six months.

Special mention must be made of the more than a little help I got from my friends. Lila, Maral, Heather, Elizabeth, Nicole, Dave, Courtney and Rachel at Pilgrimage of the Heart Yoga Studio helped me work through writer's block and sundry kinks. Wendell Capili and Lawrence Tan helped me remember what the Hotel InterContinental looked like in the 1990s. Nancy Kwak conjured a lovely author's photo; Candy Gourlay showed me how to develop a blog and John Barron designed my author's Web site. My best friend, Grazia Goseco, proofread the entire draft on her cell phone. When all else failed, my neighbor Cindy MacCallum offered alcohol.

Finally I would like to thank my family. My mother, Tita Tess and the incomparable Vega clan inadvertantly provided some of the best lines of dialogue and all the elegant smoking gestures in this story. Above all, my husband, John, and daughter, Sofia, kept me sane and grounded through these long years of writing. I could not have completed this novel without their unfaltering humor, kindness and love.

"All human beings have three lives: public, private, and secret."

—Gabriel García Márquez, *Gabriel García Márquez: a Life*

THE MANGO BRIDE

Prologue

December 17, 1995

Marcela was barely thinking when she took a knife from the plate of mangoes and stabbed Señora Concha in the chest. Her thrust lacked direction, so the blade glanced off the collarbone and tore a shallow groove down her capacious bosom before coming to a stop two inches above the right nipple.

The wound was messy but hardly fatal.

For once, Señora Concha was speechless, not just because there was a knife wobbling under her nose, but from utter disbelief that her longest-suffering servant had attacked her. Feeling faint at the sight of her own blood, she fell back against her chair and gazed up at the chandelier. Through the fog of pain, she could see that the chandelier's crystal teardrops desperately needed a good dusting. She'd have a less surly maid dust it later.

Meanwhile, her hand scrambled over the table like a demented tarantula, toppling a glass of *calamansi* juice and a coffee cup in its wake while groping blindly for the servants' buzzer that sat on the table next to the ashtray. Wandering blindly onward, it pushed the *capiz* ashtray off the table, which was slowly drowning in blood, caffeine and citric acid. Finally her fingers found the buzzer.

She pressed hard.

DING-DONG . . . hello? It was the best buzzer a Manila matron could buy and the one with the least vulgar summons: a doorbell followed by the suggested reply. *Ding-dong . . . Hello?*

Trining the laundress emerged from the kitchen and shrieked upon seeing the lurid stains on the newly ironed table linens.

"*Diós ko,* what happened to the señora?" She looked from her stricken mistress to the cook. "Marcela, what did you do?"

Marcela ignored her, staring fixedly at the señora's lavender peignoir, where the knife had grown a rapidly blooming corsage of roses.

Trining was something of a recluse who preferred scrubbing soiled underwear to serving at table, because Señora Concha habitually mocked her lazy left eye. The eye strayed from its pair whenever Trining was tired or agitated and given the frequency with which her employers changed into fresh clothes, drifting was a daily occurrence.

Seeing Señora Concha in such disarray made Trining's wayward eye swing like a pendulum, so she clung to the doorframe, dazed. The view from her one good eye suggested that Marcela, standing so calmly amid the gore, was caught up in some sort of trance.

"*Kinulam siya,*" Trining gasped, declaring to no one in particular that the cook had been bewitched.

The señora looked already dead.

Addled by her fickle eye and an apparent murder, Trining fled screaming to the servants' quarters.

Her shrieks penetrated the air-conditioned confines of the bedrooms upstairs, interrupting *Yaya* Esther's attempts to dress Señora Concha's two grandchildren. The nanny had herded three-year-old Nico into his older sister's room, intending to get both children dressed and fed before the family driver came to take them to school. Barely five feet tall and bony, *Yaya* Esther flitted about her young wards with the nervous energy of a sparrow.

"Listo" was Señora Concha's assessment of the *yaya* she had hired shortly before her first grandchild was born.

"The girl is alert, never mind that she's nothing to look at," the señora had whispered to her daughter-in-law, Lilliana, at the baby shower, before announcing she would pay the nanny's first year of wages as a gift to the impending parents. "She will serve you well for decades."

Esther had made good on the señora's promise until that Monday, when the laundress's hysterics ruptured the morning calm.

"*Yaya* Esther, why is Trining yelling?" Pia asked, twisting her head in the direction of the noise and undoing the braid the nanny was weaving. "Is *Mamita* scolding her again?"

"Iwannasee, Iwannasee!" Nico scrambled for the door. "She's not *supposed* to talk back to *Mamita*!"

"*Hayy naku!* Nico, if you do not stop yelling, I will tell you to your mama." Esther grabbed the boy's pajama pants, halting his leap for the door. She pulled him in so close that Nico could smell the dried fish she had eaten for breakfast. "You and Pia stay here. No going outside, promise? Only your *yaya* Esther can find out why that Trining is making *iskandalo* downstairs."

The children giggled as the nanny wrinkled her beaklike nose at them and pursed her lips in the direction of the bed. Under Esther's relentless glare they retreated to the pillows and promised to stay put till she returned.

Jamming bobby socks and hairpins into her pockets, the nanny flew out of the nursery room, ready with a few choice words for the scandal-making laundress. She leaned over the banister and nearly fell headfirst onto the steps below upon seeing the señora sprawled in her armchair at the head of the dining table.

Señora Concha's mouth sagged open as though she were snoring. Hennaed hair cascaded from her widow's peak, standing in stark relief against the pallor of her skin. Only the Castilian nose remained unchanged—stuck up in the air, as usual.

Clutching the banister, *Yaya* Esther hollered for the only male resident in the Guerrero home. "*Kuya* Javier, come quickly, the señora is hurt!"

Amid the hysteria erupting around her, Marcela remained uncannily serene. Seeing that the señora had fainted, she dislodged the knife from the heaving chest, wiped it clean on her checkered uniform and returned it to the plate of mangoes.

Deep in a calm born of blood loss, Señora Concha drifted through the nether land of unconsciousness. The trill of a fan flicking shut announced her mother's presence. The fact that her mother had died several years earlier hardly perturbed Señora Concha, for Doña Lupita was fond of making theatrical entrances, and death enhanced drama. Smoke drifted into a languid halo above Doña Lupita's bouffant as she sucked on her cigarette, leaving a scarlet rim round its filter.

"Sit up, Conchitina. Slouching does not become you." Even death had not mellowed Doña Lupita's caustic tone. "And by the way, your chandelier needs dusting." She swept an arm skyward, the cigarette twirling gray ribbons at the ceiling. "Just as I suspected: Marcela is as wicked as her elder sister, that slut." Doña Lupita clucked her tongue. "Now look what she's done to you. *Susmaryosep*, it's impossible to find good help these days!"

The sudden sensation of weight upon her chest prevented Señora Concha from replying. She opened her eyes in time to see a chubby man pressing a napkin to her breast. "Javier, have you no shame? Why are you touching my *pitso*? You should not be so fresh with your own mother!" Indignation caused her to forget her wound.

"Shhh, Ma, don't move," Javier murmured. "I need to stop the bleeding."

She grimaced at the damp curls that clung to her younger son's forehead. Javier had always been so moist. At puberty he'd grown a moustache to hide the perpetually humid upper lip, but over a decade later, this only made him look like an anxious, untenured assistant professor. Which, unfortunately, he was.

Fearing his mother's uncharacteristic silence meant she'd gone into shock, Javier yelled for his wife. "Lilliana, call Miguel! We can still catch him before he leaves for the hospital." The burble of children's voices alarmed him. "And tell Esther to keep the kids upstairs."

A pale woman in curlers came halfway down the stairs. "What on earth has that maid been babbling about? I had to slap her when she told the kids their *lola* was dead." Lilliana drew her dressing robe tightly around bony shoulders and peered at her mother-in-law. "She doesn't look dead yet."

"*Punyeta*, can't you see she's bleeding? Just call my brother already!"

"Watch your language, Javi!" Señora Concha chided.

"My language is the least of your worries." Javier put more pressure on her chest.

Señora Concha shook her head impatiently. "*Qué scandalo*—Javier, the neighbors must not hear about this. No police, no hospital. Miguel has to treat here. And Pia and Nico must not see me like this. Take me to my bedroom."

Seeing the napkin was nearly soaked through, Javier called over his shoulder to the cook. "*Nanay*, please get me another rag."

When Marcela did not respond, he turned, then recoiled at the sight of the cook's bloodied hands. "*Por Diós, Nanay*. Did you stab *Mamá*?"

Marcela shrugged and stared at the mangoes. "I just wanted her to shut up."

Anyone else would have been slapped for insolence, but Marcela was no ordinary servant. Decades ago, when Señora Concha made clear that she could not be bothered with motherhood, Marcela had been compelled to take on the role of "*Nanay*." Javier could hardly have struck the only true mother he had ever known.

. . .

A scant half hour later, three short horn blasts outside the Guerrero garage summoned Trining away from the servants' room and sent her running down the wide driveway to unlatch the heavy wrought iron gates. Like all the servants who worked in the homes on Hermosa Street, she recognized arriving family members by the way they honked their horns. These three beeps stood for Dr. Miguel Guerrero, Señora Concha's eldest child.

Miguel's work usually kept him too busy to visit during the week, but he could not refuse Lilliana's plea, not when Señora Concha had paid for his medical studies and the initial outlay for his clinic.

Miguel emerged from his car, towering over the diminutive laundress. In his bespoke suit and an oxblood leather satchel in hand, Miguel looked more like a banker than the cosmetic surgeon who had built his career on the vanity of Manila's richest women.

"Saan si Nanay?" Miguel asked Trining, looking for the cook he called Mother. Like his two siblings, he sought Marcela first each time he visited his childhood home.

"She's feeling ill." The laundress looked away uneasily.

Miguel forgave the evasion, knowing someone would eventually give him the full story; it was impossible to keep secrets in a home full of servants. As he hurried through the dirty kitchen, he savored the familiar aroma of fried garlic and pork fat but gave a wide berth to the cabinets lacquered by decades of cooking grease.

Beyond it lay the clean kitchen, where he had eaten most of his childhood meals. These days it served as a showcase for Señora Concha's lesser china and a yellow stand mixer, its never-used beaters laced with cobwebs. From there stretched a hallway lined with the abstract paintings that had fallen from Señora Concha's favor. He counted five oils by Veneración and Vinlúan before reaching the formal dining room, with its bloodstained tablecloth and toppled glasses.

Trining had been following him all this time, wringing a dishcloth and murmuring about how Señora Concha needed to be tended by the only doctor she trusted.

"Your brother took the señora to bed, *Kuya* Miguel," she said when he paused by the dining table.

"Pia and Nico will be frightened by this mess." Miguel nodded at the bloodstained tablecloth. "Lay out a clean one before they come to breakfast."

Miguel crossed the large sala, where lived various porcelain shepherdesses and milkmaids, converted urns that wore lampshades like bonneted English matrons and a covey of overstuffed peau de soie sofas upon which none but the most distinguished rumps had ever sat. The room was suffused with an aggressively floral air freshener, which failed to hide the fact that a feral cat liked to pee behind the couch whenever it could sneak inside.

Miguel had laughed out loud when *Nanay* Marcela first told him about the cat. *That's* Mamá's *karma for not letting us play there when we were kids,* he had joked at the time.

Was his mother's stabbing also karma? he wondered now as he strode through the hallway to the master bedroom.

Entering with the calmness of a doctor jaded by countless emergencies, Miguel waved his younger brother aside and lifted the sodden towel.

"Good thing *Mamá* postponed her breast reduction; that extra flesh probably saved her life." He handed Javier the towel. "I should be able to suture the laceration here."

"Perfect. *Mamá* is more worried about causing a scandal than scarring her cleavage. She doesn't want the neighbors to hear about it." Javier swabbed his clammy forehead with a handkerchief.

Miguel glanced up at his younger brother as he laid out his tools. "What happened?"

"*Nanay* had something to do with it, but she hasn't said a word since I sent her to the maids' room."

"We'll talk to her after I've stitched *Mamá* up."

Señora Concha's eyelids fluttered. She smiled as Miguel's silk paisley necktie came into focus. No matter the crisis, her favorite son never left home without being perfectly turned out, a habit she loudly encouraged. After all, Miguel was an eminent plastic surgeon, guardian of the most artificially enhanced complexions in Manila society. It would not do for him to look like some low-class *bugoy*.

"Migo, can you believe, Marcela did this to me! *Qué cara!* That woman owes me her life. . . ."

"Sssh, *Mamá*, plenty of time to talk later . . ." Miguel swabbed the cut with antiseptic and pulled a syringe out of his bag. "Hold still and let the local anesthesia do its thing. You're lucky I still make house calls." He slipped the needle under her skin.

Señora Concha relaxed. This son never broke a sweat, not even when operating on his own *mamá*. Humming Señora Concha's favorite *kundiman* to calm her, Miguel sutured and bandaged with impersonal efficiency. When in his professional surgeon's frame of mind, skin—even his mother's—was nothing more than skin.

"*Basta* you promise me there will be no scar, okay, Migo?" She gazed at Miguel's face, marveling at how much he resembled her brother, Aldo. Thank God good looks were the only thing the two men had in common. "You have a reputation to uphold among my *kumadres*, you know."

Señora Concha took great pride in the fact that many of her friends' faces had gained second and third lives under Miguel's scalpel. Matrons fawned over him like groupies whenever he walked in on their mah-jongg parties.

"Shhsshh, of course, *Mamá*, I'll do the best I can. . . . You just rest for now." Miguel took a glass of water from her bedside table and pulled a bottle from his satchel. "This will make you drowsy, but you need to rest after this ordeal."

Señora Concha swallowed the tablet, with uncommon docility.

"Ahh, Migo, *qué suwerte tengo.* I'm so lucky you're such a good doctor."

"Try to rest, *Mamá.* . . . Javi and I need to talk before I go to the hospital." Squeezing her hand, Miguel nodded at his brother. "Let's go outside. I have a face-lift scheduled for ten thirty, so this will have to be quick."

The brothers returned to the dining room, where Trining had replaced the linens and reset the breakfast table. An innocent box of cereal stood in place of the mangoes; knives were not in evidence. Pia and Nico were bickering over who would get the first glass of chocolate milk but stopped when their father and uncle joined them.

"*Tito* Miguel, what happened to *Mamita*? *Yaya* Esther said she has a big *owie* right here." Nico pointed at his chest with a teaspoon, smearing his kindergarten smock with milk.

"Stop talking like a baby, Nico. Your *mamita* has a wound, not an '*owie*,'" Lilliana chided. "I'm sure she's feeling better now that your *tito* Miguel has taken care of the wound."

She smiled rather too brightly at her brother-in-law, who never failed to eclipse her husband. "How is *Mamá* doing?"

"She'll be fine. It was only a flesh wound, thank God." Miguel took the cup of coffee she offered. "She said something about *Nanay* Marcela . . . ?"

"Not in front of the children." Javier raised a warning hand. "Lilliana, it's nearly eight o'clock. Don't Pia and Nico need to leave for school? Don't tell me Ernesto is late again."

"He texted *Yaya* Esther—the police confiscated his license the other day when he ran a red light."

"Lilliana *naman.* Did you forget to give him extra cash for bribes, like I told you?"

"Don't you start with me." Lilliana's voice was deceptively smooth as she glared at Javier over the children's heads. "Every time I give him extra cash, he squanders it on God-knows-what. You cannot trust these people. Give them an inch and they'll take . . ."

"Ehem," Miguel cleared his throat. "Lilliana, could you drive the children to school just this once? We need to find out exactly what happened between *Mamá* and Marcela."

Lilliana's resistance crumbled under Miguel's cajoling tone. "Of course. Pia, Nico, come along, we'll be late if we don't leave now."

The children left in a flurry of backpacks, lunch bags and whining as Miguel and Javier turned their attention to breakfast.

"What happened to your *longaniza* and fried-egg breakfasts?" Miguel teased, shaking a box of oat bran.

"Lilliana claims she won that war, but cholesterol did me in." Javier handed his brother a pitcher of skim milk. "Your cardiologist friend Dr. Luciano said I was really pushing the envelope on sodium and fat." He dabbed at his damp brow with a napkin. "I'd have ignored him, but Lilliana was there too. I'd never have heard the end of it if I ignored the doctor's advice. Do you know how long it's been since I've tasted *patis*?"

"So you'll live a salt-free life. Worse things have happened."

Before Javier could reply, the servants' buzzer sang its inane summons. *Ding-dong . . . Hello?*

"Looks like your sedative wore off." Javier chuckled.

"Doesn't *Mamá* ever let go of that thing?"

"There's another by her bed." Javier shrugged. "She recently decided it's déclassé to yell for the servants."

The nanny emerged from the kitchen hallway and nodded at them as she hurried to the master bedroom.

"*Teka muna*, Esther." Miguel waved a hand to catch her attention. "Wait a minute—how is *Nanay*?"

It no longer startled the other servants to hear the Guerrero children call Marcela "Mother." Marcela's elevated role in the family was a long-standing tradition, one she made immediately clear to every maid, driver and gardener who came to work at the Guerrero home.

"She's resting in our room, *Kuya.*" Esther lowered her eyes, but whether for respect or evasion, Miguel couldn't tell.

"After you help *Mamá*, could you tell *Nanay* to come out? We want to know what happened."

"Yes, *Kuya,*" Esther murmured. Thin slippers flapped against the maid's heels as she scurried off, the susurrant rhythm reminding Miguel of a bird in flight.

The brothers waited while the nanny returned to the kitchen, then reemerged bearing a silver coffee service and a fresh pack of Señora Concha's Salem Menthol Lights. Their mother never ingested anything but caffeine and cigarettes before noon; not even Miguel could make her switch to a healthier breakfast.

The brothers were sipping their second cups of coffee when Marcela walked out of the kitchen. She had replaced the bloodstained uniform with a faded floral skirt and white blouse. The cook's hair had turned silver and her large hands were calloused, but she stood stiff-backed and grim, with the mutinous dignity of a deposed queen.

Her eyes softened at the sight of Miguel. "You wanted to see me, *anak*?"

Even after the stabbing, Miguel could not bring himself to rebuke the only woman who had ever called him "child."

"I hear you stabbed *Mamá* this morning. Why would you do such a thing?"

The cook gazed at the man she had loved since infancy, the first of three children that Señora Concha had abandoned to her. She shook her head slightly but remained silent.

"Miguel, don't you think I asked her the same thing before you got here? She simply will not talk." Javier swabbed his forehead with a napkin. "*Ano ba, Nanay?* Should we just call the police? Do you want us to have you arrested?"

Miguel shot a warning glance at his brother. "Javi, you don't have to threaten her."

He leaned over and tugged at the cook's hand, forcing her to look at him. "Please, *Nanay*, I know you would never intentionally hurt Mama. We are your family. Just tell me why you did it. We can settle this without having to go to the police."

Marcela looked from Javier to Miguel, eyes red with unshed tears. She hesitated and seemed about to relent when her gaze fell upon Señora Concha's favorite piece of art. A stylized Madonna and Child were rendered in ochre and persimmon tints on an enormous glazed plate. The señora had purchased it from an old friend shortly before he died and was posthumously named a National Artist.

"Ask the señora, *anak*. She knows why." Jerking free of Miguel's grasp, Marcela turned and walked out through the swinging door.

"So, what do we do now?" Javier asked.

"Keep an eye on her." Miguel frowned into his coffee. "I don't think she'll attack *Mamá* again, but she's clearly suffered some sort of psychotic break. I'll lend you my cook, Isang; she can take over the kitchen for a few days—makes a killer *cocido*. Let's just allow both women to recover—apart from each other. We can try again when they've both had some time to calm down."

Miguel got up and straightened his tie. "I hate to leave you with this mess, but Mrs. Tesoro's crow's-feet need lifting."

"Can you come back tonight?" Javier pushed his chair back but made no move to get up. "I'm done with my last class by five thirty. Why don't we all have dinner together? It will make *Mamá* happy to see all her children home."

"You're forgetting Amparo," Miguel said. "Does she even know what happened?"

"Punyeta!" Javier slapped his forehead. "I forgot to call her. I'll get on it as soon as you leave."

Señora Concha's plan to keep the neighbors from hearing of her morning assault was foiled before noon, for keeping secrets in a house with servants was like carrying water in a sieve.

The first leak was sprung by Ernesto the driver, who sauntered into the Guerrero kitchen an hour after the children had gone to school. Surprised that Marcela was not there to offer up the remnants of the family's breakfast, he poked his head out to the laundry porch. The slab of cement that marked the outdoor laundry area was shaded by yesterday's clothes hung in rainbow rows above Trining, who squatted by a tin basin, wrestling with a stained tablecloth.

"Oy Trining, saan si Marcela?" he asked, looking for the cook. "Has she gone to the market already?"

Trining looked up at the heavyset man with pomaded hair, jingling car keys at the hip. Ernesto wore a short-sleeved *polo barong* that Lilliana had weeded out of her husband's wardrobe. Extra helpings of Marcela's food had swelled his belly till it tried the patience of the shirt's middle buttons.

Trining glanced at her fingers, wrinkled by a lifetime of soapy water, and scowled to think that Ernesto's smooth hands never suffered such abuse on the job. Like all drivers, he was paid more but worked less than the housemaids. *"May sakit si 'Cela*—'Cela is sick," she muttered, hoping Ernesto would accept the cook's indisposition as a good enough excuse to forgo his usual hot breakfast. "There are some mangoes on the table you can eat."

Ernesto watched Trining scrub at the red blotches. *"Mangga lang?"* The family had to have eaten more than just mangoes.

"E bakit may ketchup *pa sila?* What was the ketchup for?" He pointed his lips at the stains, hoping he could have whatever it was the family had eaten with ketchup that morning.

"Sira ka ba? What, you crazy?" Trining snorted. "That's blood!" She waggled the stained linen under his nose. "I should have soaked this before the blood dried, but Marcela was crying like a *telenovela* widow and the señora kept ringing her damn buzzer. *Hayy naku!"*

Exasperated, she rubbed a damp cheek on her wrist. "Now I'll have to bleach it."

Trining's rapid-fire Tagalog confused Ernesto, who spoke only Cebuano and the idiosyncratic English he had picked up from *Law & Order* reruns. *"Ano—?"*

It took the laundress a moment to realize she had to spell out the morning's events in simpler language for this cretin to understand the gravity of the situation.

"Marcela stabbed Señora Concha, but she did not die, *awa ng Diyos*!" Trining remembered to thank a merciful God for sparing the señora's life and tried—in vain—to direct both eyes heavenward.

"Baliw ba siya?" The notion of a maid attacking her employer struck Ernesto as so implausible that only insanity could explain it. He himself had fantasized about shoving a tire jack down Señora Lilliana's throat, whenever she scolded him from the backseat as though the morass of traffic on EDSA were his fault. *But an actual stabbing* . . . Ernesto pictured the assault, turning it over in his mind like a shiny coin.

"Stop dreaming, the señora is not dead, and Marcela is not in jail—yet." Trining was mortified by Ernesto's half smile. "The only bonus you get out of this is less work. *Kuya* Javier and *Até* Lilliana went to work already, so you have nothing else to do but pick up the children after school."

The laundress eyed Ernesto's belly peeping through the strained buttonholes. "Why don't you mow the front lawn? You could use the exercise."

"You calling me fat?"

"I'm saying if those buttons pop, you'll have to sew them back on yourself. Besides, I'll be doing the cooking while Marcela is sick. Unlike her, I do not feed the lazy."

"Sige na nga," Ernesto conceded. He had to make up for coming in late to work and it would be easy to slack off outside the Guerreros' tall walls.

Ernesto dragged the manual lawn mower out the gate to the

wide rind of grass that hemmed the Guerrero mansion and spotted Paéng, the burly security guard, sitting at his post by the Tuazons' home next door. Ernesto was sweet on Paéng's cousin Cristeta, who tended the Benitez baby across the street, and he sucked up to the guard whenever he could.

A massive fire tree shaded the guardhouse and sprinkled the Tuazon driveway with scarlet petals. As with many of the grand mansions on Hermosa Street, granite slabs surrounded the Tuazons' home. Coconut husk baskets pinned sprays of magenta orchids and scarlet bromeliads like brooches to the wall's gray expanse. The guardhouse barely contained the crew-cut Paéng, whose presence pointed to the elevated status of the army general and his socialite wife who lived in their fortress of a home.

Walking over to the small guardhouse, Ernesto held up a pack of Camel Lights. The security guard grinned his thanks, flashing a silver tooth.

"You the gardener now?" Paéng jerked his head at the lawn mower.

"Just for today. Strange things going on at the Guerreros'." Ernesto bit his lips and shook his head in the manner of a TV detective surveying a crime scene.

"Talaga?" Paéng exhaled at the sky, but his eyes stayed on the driver. "Like what?"

"*Inday* Marcela stabbed Señora Concha."

"*O?* She dead?"

"Suwerte siya." Ernesto smirked. "She got lucky."

"Ahhh . . . so that is why Dr. Miguel came so early this morning." As one who slung a rifle over his shoulder at work, it was beneath Paéng's dignity to admit that he too was shocked. "I thought maybe she had a heart attack or something." He sucked on his Camel. "What happens now?"

"*Alam mo naman*—you know how it is." Ernesto shrugged. "With rich people, things never turn out the way you expect."

. . .

That day proceeded like any other on Hermosa Street. At nine thirty, gardeners hopped off jeepneys at the far end of the subdivision and hiked twenty minutes along wide, acacia-shaded streets to reach the bougainvillea and hibiscus bushes they coddled. An hour later the junkman rolled his cart through the neighborhood yodeling *"BOT-E-DYARYO!"* to collect the used bottles and newspapers that he sold for centavos on the pound; a knife sharpener hollered *"Ha-saaa!"* inviting cooks to bring him their dull cleavers and shears.

After wasting a few more minutes trading jokes with Paéng, Ernesto gave the lawn mower a few halfhearted turns around the grass, then retreated to the relative coolness of the Guerrero garage. By then, Hermosa Street was sweltering in midday humidity and servants moved in slow motion at their chores or simply stopped altogether for a half hour's nap.

As the long afternoon stretched out its tired legs, a procession of food strolled through the neighborhood. But for the ice cream man shaking a desultory bell, each vendor sang long drawn-out syllables that echoed far ahead to announce the approaching edibles: *"PU-U-U-to . . . ta-HO-O-O! . . . ba-L-U-U-U-t!"*

When their favorites drew near, maids, drivers and the fortunate child whose parents permitted street food ran out to buy their afternoon snack. They chose from banana-leaf-wrapped rice cakes perfumed with anise, warm tofu curds topped with molasses and tapioca, and boiled duck eggs with a thumb-long cone of rock salt, the interrupted chicks suspended bone-beak-feathers in a savory broth.

The one thing that set this day apart from all others was the deliciously shocking story that meandered, as persistently as the ambulant vendors, from one home to the next. After Ernesto left to fetch the Guerrero children, Paéng the security guard shared *suman* and the stabbing with Peping, the Singsons' houseboy, who rushed inside to tell his *tía* Anita, the family cook.

Anita gave her pot of *adobo* a final stir before waddling out to join a gaggle of maids from houses up and down the block who had come to squat on the Guerreros' front lawn, pretending to pluck weeds, as they picked over the meager grains of Marcela's feat like famished hens in an abandoned farm.

PART I

Smoke and Mirrors

CHAPTER 1

Amparo

"Good evening, this is Amparo, your Filipino interpreter, how may I help you on this call?" Amparo automatically switched on her professional interpreting voice whenever she answered the phone. After so many years, it had become virtually second nature to her.

"'Paro, cut it out. It's me, Javier." The voice of her brother jarred her out of work mode and she pulled her long hair over to the opposite shoulder, clutching the phone to her ear.

"Javi! What time is it in Manila? I was going to call. There's something I need to tell you and Miguel—"

"Save it for later. Mamá's hurt."

"Ano? What happened?" She threw an alarmed glance at Seamus, who had looked up from the book he was reading as soon as he realized she was talking to her brother.

"Nanay stabbed her this morning."

"Madré de Díos," Amparo gasped, color draining from her face. She raised a hand to her cheek as though she'd been slapped. "Is she okay?"

"Yes, luckily. Miguel stitched her up here. She refused to call an ambulance because she was afraid the neighbors would talk."

"Just like her to worry about that." Amparo would have laughed, had she not been so concerned.

"We're still trying to find out why Nanay attacked her, but neither of them want to talk."

"I think I know why—"

"How could you know anything? You haven't been home in years."

"You can't blame me for that—Mama made me leave, remember?"

"Water under the bridge. Look, my first class starts in five minutes. Miguel and I just need to know: are you coming home?"

"I'll let you know as soon as I talk to Tito Aldo. Maybe we can all come home."

"Don't you mean 'both'?"

"Don't get all English professor on me, Javi. I meant what I said."

Amparo hung up and turned a worried gaze on Seamus. "It's finally happened. After all these years, listening to my mom's rants, Nanay 'Cela snapped."

"But you know it was more than just your mother's scolding that pushed her over the edge." Seamus raised an eyebrow.

"Yes, of course. This is why we need to make sure we do right by Nanay 'Cela and her family."

CHAPTER 2

"They Are Not Like Us"

March 1995—nine months earlier

The phone rang just as Amparo sat down to a late breakfast. Taking a sip of coffee, she grudgingly punched the call button and raised the headset's microphone so it came level with her mouth.

"Good morning, this is interpreter number 6817, my name is Amparo, how can I help you today in Tagalog?"

"Interpreter, this is Lavonnya over at Triple A." The voice was deep and honey-thick, the voice perhaps of an African-American woman, chin-length bob sleek and immotile, turning slow crescents in her swivel chair.

Putting faces to callers and imagining the rooms they occupied helped Amparo focus on interpretation even as she minced onions, folded laundry or slogged through any of the other chores servants had spared her in Manila. Mindful of the irony, Amparo wore her headset like an ersatz tiara, cordless phone slung like a gun in a hip holster, as she multitasked. *Domestic Goddess, not maid* had been her operative mantra these last four years.

"Our member Josefa Santos is complaining about the way Triple A serviced her car yesterday. I couldn't understand why she's so upset."

"Happy to help." Amparo tried to salvage breakfast by draining the milk out of her cereal bowl. *"Gandang araw po, Miss Josefa*—how can we help you?"

She greeted the woman with a chirpy good morning, taking pains to show respect. Amparo had learned early on that addressing clients with the honorific *po* often compensated for the offense of being told their English was incomprehensible to the American ear.

"Ay salamat!" Josefa's querulous gratitude evoked a frail, old woman hunched over her telephone.

"Help me, please," the woman bleated. "I want to report what one of your mechanics did."

Amparo interpreted this, intrigued despite her mounting hunger. Disgruntled old people sometimes provoked the most volatile exchanges.

"Sure thing, Miz Santos," Lavonnya purred. "Could you give me your member ID number so we can find out which mechanic helped you out?"

"Ay ayoko—I don't want to. Can you not take my complaint without it?"

Amparo imagined Josefa peering out her window from behind lacy curtains.

"All right, then. Why don't you just tell me what happened?" Lavonnya cooed.

"Ayaw umandar ang kotse ko," Josefa explained how her car wouldn't start that morning. "That first mechanic came to my house, but after he left, the car still would not start. Worst of all, he stole from me. I kept some pin money in the glove compartment. After he left, it was gone."

Josefa's tone had sharpened noticeably, but Amparo kept hers calm, knowing that Lavonnya would pick up on the woman's irritation.

"So I called Triple A again and the second one fixed my car. But I want to complain about that first mechanic, the thief."

"We'd be happy to open an investigation. Could I have your member ID number? We'll need it to find out who serviced your car."

Amparo imagined Lavonnya tapping a pencil on her desk like a metronome as her patience dwindled.

"I cannot tell you. What if that mechanic finds out I complained? He knows where I live—" Josefa's voice dropped to a whisper. "... you know, I am scared because he is of another *color*."

Amparo rolled her eyes as she interpreted this last bit. One of the first things she had learned upon moving to Oakland was that for many Filipino immigrants, the only "other color" was black.

"I see...."

Was that a smile Amparo heard in Lavonnya's voice?

"But even if he *is* another color, *Miz* Santos, that won't make it any easier for us to track him down. You must understand, we have many employees with so many *other* colors working at Triple A. I doubt this mechanic would risk losing his job by harming one of our clients. After all, wouldn't he be the prime suspect if anything happened to you?" Lavonnya's tone carried the honeyed threat of a cat splaying its claws before swiping at an unsuspecting mouse.

Amparo grinned as she interpreted. Customer service reps rarely had fun at their clients' expense. Josefa seemed as oblivious to sarcasm as she was to Lavonnya's ethnicity.

"*Ay huwag na lang*—never mind, just you never mind," Josefa huffed. Amparo imagined the old woman standing in the middle of her apartment, afraid now to approach the window. "I did not lose so much money. If that mechanic found out ... I am so afraid what might happen—I already had a bad experience with these ..." Josefa lowered her voice "... It is because they are from another culture, they are not like us, don't you know?"

Amparo relayed this to Lavonnya, stifling a giggle.

"We are *all* from other cultures, Miz Josefa," Lavonnya sighed. "But without your ID number, we can't open that investigation. I'm sorry."

"Ohhh . . . that's okay." Josefa sounded deflated. "I cannot afford to lose my life over so little money. So many people are depending on me—my mother is old, my husband is sick. Who will take care of them if someone kills me?"

Amparo bit her lip to keep from going off script and berating Josefa for her paranoia. *C'mon, woman—you're making us look bad!*

"All right, then, Ms. Santos. I'm sorry we couldn't help you, but we do appreciate your business. . . ." Lavonnya was cordial but detached. Amparo imagined her pulling out a pocket mirror to retouch her lipstick, having already written off the old lady as crazy.

How strange, Amparo thought later, eating soggy bran flakes. Back in Manila, if Josefa Santos had been anything like her own mother, she would not have thought twice about haranguing a lowly mechanic for bungling the car repairs. Here, the idea of confronting a man with a wrench terrified her. Oakland really was a step through the looking glass.

The kitchen timer rang just then, reminding Amparo that two loads of laundry needed to be transferred to the dryer in the basement three floors below. If she waited, another tenant would likely cut the line and dump his wash in the dryer first. It was the inevitable consequence of having four washing machines and two working dryers in a building with fifty tenants.

She grabbed dryer sheets and a fistful of quarters and headed downstairs.

As she loaded up the dryer with damp laundry, a belt loop snagged on the Santo Niño charm hanging from Amparo's bracelet. The flaring robes and tiny crown on the Christ child figurine caught on sweater sleeves regularly, but Amparo gladly bore the inconvenience, for it reminded her of Nanay. Marcela had given it to her as a last-minute present just before Amparo left Manila. Señora Concha had been too angry that day to see her daughter off, but had allowed the nanny to join Amparo on the hour-long drive to the airport.

Years of oxidization had darkened the figurine till only the Santo Niño's halo and feet glinted bronze. When her American friends teased her about the oddly shaped charm, Amparo humored them, not caring to explain why Filipinos venerated the child Jesus.

Amparo tossed the last of the damp clothes into the dryer and counted out four quarters. *Now to make the bed and thaw some chicken for dinner*... She wondered what her mother would have made of this scene. Javier once told her that when Señora Concha heard about this weekly routine, the matron had thrown up her hands and sighed, "*Santa Maria*. My daughter was not raised to wash her own clothes!"

"And where would I keep maids in this place?" she asked aloud.

The rustle of clothes churning in the dryer was the only reply. Raking fingers through the tangles in her dark brown hair, Amparo trudged upstairs.

Stepping into the quiet apartment, she grimaced at the dirty beige carpet. Vacuuming was her least favorite chore, but one she knew was long overdue. Señora Concha would be mortified to see the sparsely furnished living room, with its beat-up futon that doubled as a bed for overnight guests and the scratched coffee table Seamus had snagged at a garage sale. Amparo suspected her mother never visited because she was afraid to discover exactly how far her daughter had fallen from grace; this was nothing like the expansive Guerrero mansion in which she had spent her childhood. The one-bedroom apartment she shared with Seamus was on the top floor of a three-story walk-up just beyond Berkeley's southern border, on the seamy side of Alcatraz Avenue. Realtors euphemized this neighborhood as "transitional" because it was three blocks distant from the restaurants and cafés that put Rockridge's posh rentals beyond the couple's reach.

Telegraph Avenue marked the western border of that stylish district. As Alcatraz crossed that larger road, the street's downhill slope seemed to portend the neighborhood's decline. Chic boutiques gave way to small homes whose paint flaked like sunburnt skin, and a one-legged crack addict patrolled the block in her wheelchair. Amparo had grown accustomed to the moldy scent of old carpet that infused her building's dim hallways, and was no longer startled by the occasional homeless person slumped in the front-door alcove.

Amparo had inherited her mother's alabaster skin, fine narrow nose and pronounced widow's peak, a currency of beauty with which she could have acquired a wealthy husband, servants and a Manila mansion as large as the one she'd grown up in. To Señora Concha's everlasting frustration Amparo's willfulness had disrupted that equation.

Amparo was not one to dwell on these much reduced circumstances, concluding that housework was a small price to pay for freedom from the constricted life she might otherwise have led as a Manila matron. And yet despite her determined optimism, melancholy sometimes set in. On cold nights when Seamus worked late, she longed for her large childhood home, fragrant with Nanay's cooking, lively with the banter of maids as they passed one another in the hallways. When she wasn't working on the phone, the apartment was largely silent, and the voices she heard drifted up from people on the street three floors below. In America even cars remained silent.

But of all the things she yearned for in Manila, Amparo missed Nanay Marcela the most. Marcela had served the clan for so long that Amparo could not imagine childhood without her surrogate mother.

Concha and her older brother, Aldo, were mere teenagers when Marcela came to work in the Duarté kitchen. Growing up, Amparo hungered for stories about Señora Concha's youth, hoping to find a commonality between her and an emotionally opaque mother. But Señora Concha never volunteered anecdotes and even Nanay Marcela remained tight-lipped about those early years.

Nor was her uncle Aldo any help; Amparo kept a running tally of the times he had deflected questions about his Manila childhood by reminiscing about more recent shenanigans in San Francisco. Amparo thought it the greatest irony that in the land of Oprah's confessional tales, her nearest of kin remained secretive about their own family.

"Maybe I'll get lucky tonight," she murmured, glancing at the calendar on the refrigerator door. It was the first Friday in March. On the first Friday of every month, her uncle boarded the 2:41 train at Sixteenth Street Mission BART station and crossed the bay to spend an afternoon in Berkeley with a group he referred to as his "flock of fallen angels." The half-dozen men in this covey had been Aldo Duarté's mates in rehab homes and halfway houses at various times during the decades he'd spent battling alcoholism. Each a veteran of his own personal war, the men met every month to see how well or poorly they had managed to stay sober.

Soon after arriving in the Bay Area, Amparo had fallen in the habit of meeting her uncle for dinner after his meeting ended. Over the years, the pair had developed a hybrid relationship of father/daughter/brother/sister, one forged as much by blood as by the fact that both came to California after having been expelled from the clan. Curiously, neither one ever talked about the reasons for their expulsion. Amparo's reticence was born of shame, Aldo's, of guilt.

The rising crescent moon reflected gold off the setting sun as Amparo walked up Telegraph Avenue to Le Bateau Ivre. It amused her uncle to dine at a restaurant named *The Drunken Boat* after his Alcoholics Anonymous meeting. *I am perversely fond of tempting fate*, he liked to say.

Aldo Duarté was waiting for her at a patio table, nursing a cup of tea. His ash-colored hair still swept low across his forehead as it had since he was a teenager, but wrinkles now ringed the playful eyes, giving him the air of a reformed roué. "They let me wait for you out here, but saved the best table for us inside."

"I don't know how you manage to get the best service all the time." Amparo kissed him on the cheek. "Tell me, Tito, what's your secret?"

"It comes from growing up in Manila." Aldo winked. "I know how to treat the help." He got up with a soft popping of knees, scuffed leather jacket hanging loose on his lean frame. "Let's tell Madeleine we're ready for our table."

Dressed in a black turtleneck and peplum skirt, her hair swept up in a French twist, the hostess resembled a Parisian schoolmarm. She ushered Aldo and Amparo inside, her greeting unctuous with Gallic tones, and led them to a table by the fireplace, its bricks faded and chipped from a century's use.

"Even Seamus with all his Irish charm can't get that woman to crack a smile and here she is, greeting you like an old lover," Amparo teased as she surveyed the menu. "Perhaps he should take a few lessons from you."

"Ahh, but charm is a double-edged sword, *hija*. In my life it's been both blessing and curse." He waved away the question in Amparo's eyes before she could find words for it. "Enough philosophizing, we must decide on dinner."

After they'd placed their orders, Amparo leaned across the table. "So how are your friends doing?"

"Not so well. One of them's just been diagnosed with cirrhosis." Aldo pinched the stem of his goblet, swirling the water as though it were wine. "He's divorced, you know. His ex won custody and moved the kids to Oregon. Poor guy's got to face this alone." Sorrow dragged on Aldo's laugh lines, making him look suddenly old.

"Don't worry, Tito Aldo. If you ever got sick, I'd be here for you." Amparo reached over and squeezed her uncle's hand. "I'm the closest thing you've got to a daughter here."

"But I—" Aldo swallowed the rest of his thought with a long gulp of water. He set the glass down with an inaudible sigh. "What I meant to say was, I have a mind to try the dessert this time."

"Really, Tito Aldo?" Amparo sensed he was dissembling. "Weren't you about to say something else?"

"*Ay hija*, what else can a man hope for in life but a sweet finish?" Aldo's flirtatious tone returned. "Now if you remind me to eat only half my cassoulet, I will definitely have room for dessert. Our hostess, Madeleine, said the lemon tart *est très magnifique.*"

Amparo smiled at Aldo's parody of the maître d's accent, and the moment passed.

As they strolled back to her apartment after dinner, the inevitable wistfulness for home crept over Amparo. Nostalgia always hit after she'd spent time with her sole link to the family in Manila. "Do you ever wish you could go home, Tito Aldo?"

"Every time I did, I drank a toast to staying put—and look where that got me." He threw an arm around Amparo's shoulders, staring pensively into the navy sky. "My punishment—penance perhaps?—is that I will always be recovering: from alcohol and Manila."

They had arrived at Amparo's door by then, but curiosity prickled kitten claws on her head.

"I wish you'd tell me what happened in Manila."

"If I did, I'd have to kill you." Aldo's chuckle was mirthless. "Lord knows it nearly killed me." He checked his watch. "Now I really must run to catch that eight-thirty train."

"Tito, you know a train comes every twenty minutes."

"Try to understand, *hija*, I control this unfortunate tendency to dissipation by living within very precise parameters. Train schedules just happen to be one of them." He wrapped her in a hug fragrant with chamomile and lemon curd. "Why don't you come visit me Sunday after next for *merienda cena*? We'll have tea."

"All right, then." Amparo pouted. "But you know I'll keep asking."

"The thrill is in the chase, *guapa*. Always in the chase." With a rakish grin, Aldo Duarté turned on his heel and loped down Alcatraz.

Amparo watched his retreating figure, her thoughts a jumble of fond confusion. Her uncle was a master of the double entendre, but she sometimes sensed that he was speaking to another person entirely. But who would that possibly be?

CHAPTER 3

Athens, Georgia

April 1995

"Hello, this is Ashley Perkins and I'm a social worker callin' from the Athens Regional Medical Center in Georgia? I'm fixin' to do an intake interview before we send this lady off to a shelter. Monina here understands English, but she's been through a lot today, bless her heart, so I thought it be easier for her to speak her own language. I put you on speakerphone. Would you introduce yourself to Mrs. Monina Patterson?"

The broad vowels that fanned across Ashley's Southern drawl made it difficult at first to decipher, but Amparo understood enough catchphrases to construct a context for the request. The rest was a matter of winging it. Amparo was rinsing lunch plates when the phone rang. Wiping hands on a dish towel, she punched the talk button.

"Gandang hapon po, Miss Monina—" Amparo set her rinsed lunch plate on the rack and dried her hands. A cautious "Good afternoon" was usually the most neutral way to open the conversation. One never knew what crisis was being managed when a social

worker called. "Ashley called me to help out in your interview, *okay lang?*"

"*Salamat naman.* Thank you. I cannot think in English now. . . ." The hoarse voice conjured a woman slumped in a chair, sallow beneath fluorescent lights.

"Interpreter, could you ask Monina how she's feelin'?" Ashley asked.

"Okay lang." Despite claiming to be okay, the woman sounded exhausted.

"Monina, d'you know why you're here?"

"Of course. The policeman took me here." The reply was a verbal shrug, as though this sort of thing happened to her all the time.

"But why'd the police take you out of your home?" The social worker's tone was calm, conversational. Amparo imagined a blue-haired, pale-eyed professional in a shirtdress and sensible pumps, balancing sympathy with professional detachment.

"Because my husband was beating me. I was afraid Trent would hurt my baby."

"Baby? What baby? Did you leave a baby back there?"

"I'm four months pregnant." Amparo could almost hear multiple fissures crazing the woman's bravado. "I'm not showing yet. The doctor said that was normal for first babies." Monina cleared her throat, sounding somehow ashamed.

A knife slid into Amparo's heart and twisted. She put down the dish she had been drying, knuckles white against the counter tiles. Shame was something she remembered, after all these years.

"Well, I'll be darned . . . ," Ashley said under her breath.

Amparo heard the dried-leaf rustle of pages being flipped. She guessed the social worker was resorting to what bureaucrats did when caught off guard: retreating behind documents.

"Hold on a minute while I look over your chart again, hon," Ashley said. "I clearly missed the part about your pregnancy. . . ."

"That's okay. . . . I must look like a mess," Monina whispered.

Amparo imagined the woman combing fingers through tangled hair, but Monina provided something more explicit.

"The doctor who sewed up my cheek said the scar would fade eventually. I don't believe him. It feels like a really big cut. There was so much blood."

For once Amparo faltered, stumbling over English as she fought to block out the image of Monina's torn face.

"Oh honey, don't you worry about all that—Dr. Moore cleaned you up good."

The social worker's reassurances sounded unconvincing even to Amparo. She recalled how her brother Javier had split open his forehead on their pool's diving board when he was nine years old. The gash had spouted a geyser of blood, but their mother seemed more upset over the pool water turning pink than about consoling her son, who she dispatched to a local clinic with Nanay Marcela.

Ashley's voice reeled the interpreter back to the current crisis. "Well anyway, I aim to keep you and your baby stay safe from now on. I'd like to set you up in a shelter for women. I just need you to answer a few questions before sending you there. . . ."

"I can't afford it." Monina's voice quavered. "The policeman made me leave so quickly. He wouldn't even let me find my purse or put on shoes. . . ." She caught her breath. "It was raining but he forced me to run outside in my bare feet. . . . *Nakakahiya.*"

Amparo translated the Filipino word for shame, wondering if the social worker could fathom the depth of Monina's humiliation. The indignity of being herded out of her own home by the police like a criminal, bloody and unshod, her dishevelment witnessed by American neighbors, the same people who must have looked askance at the dusky bride when she first arrived in the Deep South.

Nakakahiya.

It didn't sound as though Ashley had any time to squander on cultural nuance. Amparo could tell from the social worker's briskly efficient manner that she wanted Monina processed and sent on to the next stage of bureaucracy before the woman fell through the cracks like so many others before her.

"I spoke with Officer Ruland, the police officer who drove you to the emergency room? He said his partner done chased your husband down. Trent is in police custody now. Mind my askin' why he flew off the handle like that?"

Monina's laugh sounded like a lament. "Mayonnaise. *Akalain mo ba*—can you believe it? That's what started it. When Trent got home from work today, he said he wanted a sandwich. I said we were out of mayonnaise and could I use mustard instead. 'This is what I get for marrying a stupid Filipino,' he said. 'You think you can use mustard in place of mayonnaise.' He said I was useless, that I didn't know how to do the groceries. . . . *Hayyy naku* . . ." Amparo imagined Monina shaking her head, weary of words.

"Go on, honey," Ashley urged.

"I should have kept my mouth shut, but I was fed up. I had been throwing up all day from morning sickness and the last thing I wanted to do was make a sandwich. So I said maybe if he gave me enough money to do the groceries, we would never run out of the damn mayonnaise. That's when he punched me."

"Why didn't you call the police?" Ashley's question was matter-of-fact. This was what decent people did in Athens, Georgia. Let the police put things in order.

"Our neighbors would have been scandalized. *Nakakahiya*."

The scene playing out in Amparo's mind as she interpreted this exchange was one she'd heard before on similar calls: a woman cowering behind a table or a door, or nothing more than her own small hands, while a man pummeled her with shoes, skillets, belts and a river of profanity that drowned her cries. Sometimes while her children or in-laws watched. These things never ended well.

Meanwhile, Monina continued her wretched narrative.

"Trent wears this big square ring with diamonds on his left hand. He was so proud of that ring. It was from his first marriage—

'kept the ring but ditched the bitch,' he liked to say. When he punched me, I felt my cheek rip."

"How did you get away from him?"

"It was that ring. He was going to punch me again, but when he saw blood all over his precious ring, he stopped to rinse it under the kitchen faucet. I ran and locked myself in the bathroom. *Takot na takot ako*—I was terrified. . . ."

"Who called in the police?"

"Mrs. Dupree, probably. Our kitchens share the same wall. She saw me once in the laundry room with a black eye. She must have heard Trent yelling."

"This wasn't the first time your husband hit you?"

Monina snorted. "First time this week."

"Can you tell me when he began beatin' you?"

"Nothing happened while I was getting settled here those first few months. But I couldn't just stay home all day. Except for Mrs. Dupree, none of our neighbors were friendly. I thought things would improve if I got a job—make friends at work, you know? But Trent wanted me to stay home."

"Did he try to stop you from working?"

"He wouldn't take me anywhere. He wouldn't even give me money for bus fare."

"Did he give you any money at all?"

Again the sad laugh.

"The only money I got was what I found in his pants pockets when I did the laundry. A few quarters, sometimes a dollar if I was lucky. Never enough for a full fare. That's when we began fighting."

"Is that when he began hittin' you?"

"No. That didn't come until after I got back from the Philippines. When Trent found out I was pregnant, he said I should visit my family one last time before I got too big to travel. He said he couldn't leave work just then, that I should go ahead."

In halting sentences, Monina explained that she had flown

home to Manila, then taken the two-hour bus ride south to Lipa in Batangas province. Amparo smiled when she heard the city's name, for it brought to mind a favorite Catholic tale she had heard in third grade. Sister Mary Bernadette had told her Christian Life class how, on a clear September Sunday in 1948, the Blessed Virgin had showered thousands of rose petals upon the Carmelite convent in Lipa. Villagers gathered the fragrant petals, claiming later that the sacred roses had cured them of various ailments: deafness, appendicitis and a near-fatal hernia.

Amparo wondered if Monina had scanned Lipa's skies for petals from the Virgin, or a plane from America bearing her absent husband. One vision no less miraculous than the other.

The defeat in Monina's voice made it clear she no longer believed in miracles. "Two weeks passed and I did not hear from him. Every time I called, I got the answering machine. After a month I decided to fly back."

A heavy sigh. "That's when I found out he had bought me a one-way ticket."

"Now, that takes the cake." Ashley sounded incredulous. "Are you sayin' you didn't know this when you left?"

"I was so excited to be going home that I didn't check the ticket. *Ang tanga ko*—I was so stupid. I only looked at it again to confirm my return trip." Monina's voice caught on a sob. "There was none."

"Did you ever think about just stayin' there, least until the baby was born?"

"*Susmaryosep!* Why on earth would I do that?" Monina snapped. "There is nothing for me in Lipa!"

Amparo heard the slap of a palm on the desk. "My family is poor—how could they support me and my child? My parents were hoping *I* would send for them one day, that *I* could give them a home in America. *Awa ng Diyos*—merciful God—what will happen to me and my baby now?"

When logic fails, one turns to God, Amparo thought, as she translated the outburst, raising her voice above the uneven cadence of Monina's sobs.

Amparo could not explain the subtext to Monina's grief without offending Ashley. No man in Lipa would have wanted a *separada*—much less one pregnant with a white man's spawn.

"Here, honey, have yourself some Kleenex. You don't want tears messin' up those stitches." If Ashley's composure seemed shaken, she recovered quickly. "Give yourself a moment to settle. Can I get you a Coke or somethin'?"

Amparo stared into the kitchen sink, wondering at the second chance she herself had claimed. Monina and all the others she had helped on similar calls were not so lucky.

Eventually the weeping subsided.

"Feelin' better now? Could you tell us how you made your way back to Athens?"

"I borrowed money from everyone I knew to buy the return ticket."

"Was your husband happy to see you when you returned?"

Monina sighed, as though her heart were deflating. "What do you think?"

"What did Trent think?" Ashley seemed impervious to sarcasm.

"The night I returned was the first time he hit me. He kept saying I had wasted his money. He said I'd wasted the free trip home by coming back." Monina's voice turned dead calm. "Trent said if I tried to find work, he would have me deported. Then he took away my passport and green card. That's when I knew our marriage was over."

"So I take it you haven't become an American citizen yet?"

"We've only been married a year and a half. That means I have . . . *Ano bang tawag diyan*—what do they call it? A conditional green card. The lawyer said I would become permanent only if we stayed married for two years." Monina swallowed a sob. "But how can I go back to him after this?"

"Honey, you don't have to." Ashley's tone turned steely. "Don't ever believe you have to stay in an abusive relationship just 'cause you're afraid of bein' deported."

"You mean I can leave Trent but stay here?" For the first time Monina sounded hopeful.

"You have every right to do so. After you get settled at the shelter, I'll set you up with a lawyer who can help with your immigration papers."

Amparo imagined Ashley stretching out her hand, giving Monina a reassuring pat on the shoulder. Chair legs grated on the floor.

"Now if y'all could 'scuse me a few minutes, I'm gonna call the women's shelter to see if they have a room for you tonight. I'll be back directly to explain a few more things to Monina." A door swung open, then clicked shut.

Amparo kneaded her tense shoulders. Trying to erase the chaos of Monina's life, she looked around her own small kitchen and ticked off each point of calm domesticity: the bottle of Pinot Noir she'd shared with Seamus the night before; eight mismatched plates, bowls, cups, stacked neatly in glass cupboards; mayonnaise and mustard coexisting peacefully in the fridge.

All safe.

"Excuse po, Até Amparo, saan kayo ngayon?" Monina wanted to know where Amparo was. She called Amparo her big sister and whispered the question, even though she was alone in the room. "Are you in a call center in Manila or here in Georgia?"

"I'm in California."

"That's so far away. . . ."

The sigh suggested shoulders sagging with disappointment. Amparo knew from past calls that women like Monina clung to anyone who reminded them of home.

"Até Amparo, ganito ba talaga—is this how it really is?" Monina whimpered.

"What do you mean?"

"Is this what marriage is like here? I really loved Trent. I didn't marry him just for the green card like all my friends said."

Amparo's company forbade private conversations between interpreters and what it referred to as the *English-Challenged Individual*, but Amparo broke the rules for Monina.

"How did you meet him?" Amparo asked.

"I was a waitress in the coffee shop of his hotel. He was a big tipper—and he came to breakfast every day for a week."

The whoosh of a door opening cut off their conversation.

"I'm back, thank y'all for waiting." Ashley sounded cautiously upbeat. "Come to find out the shelter can't take you this evening. The shelter's full up for tonight. Seems when the economy sags, men start takin' it out on their wives."

Amparo sensed Monina's trepidation in the silence that followed.

"Are you sending me home?" Monina's voice shrilled with anxiety. "What if Trent is waiting for me?"

"Oh, honey, we would never send you back to an unsafe situation." Ashley put on her take-charge tone. "We got you a motel room for this first night. I'll have a taxi carry you there free; you won't have to pay for anythin'. No one but me and the shelter director know where the motel's at. There'll be room for you at the shelter tomorrow night, and God willin', there'll always be someone close to help you out."

"How long can I stay at the shelter?"

"However long it takes to get you back on your feet, honey. There's one condition to your staying there—and, interpreter, please make sure she understands this—the shelter's location must be kept secret. You can't tell anyone where you live. That's to protect you and the other women from bein' tracked down by the men y'all left. Understood?"

Ashley ended their interview by promising to send Monina off with a bag of sandwiches for dinner, a change of clothes, a pair of shoes—just enough to get through that first night on her own, truly alone in Athens.

"*Ingat*—take care, Monina." Amparo ended the call, knowing they would never speak again. She took off her headset and massaged her temples, feeling suddenly exhausted. How many times had she heard Monina's story? America was an ocean whose restless inhabitants floated from one city to the next, dissembling, reinventing, ultimately forgetting what they'd left behind. Its vast anonymity made the country unnavigable for women like Monina.

Amparo's mother used to say people migrated to America only when they had nothing to lose. "Look at us," Señora Concha would declare, raising a hand to her dinner guests as if all of "us" sat on one smooth palm. "We live like kings here. Over there you would have to do your own housework."

Five years earlier, Señora Concha had sent Amparo to America to avoid disgrace, declaring at the time that her daughter had nothing to lose. Now Amparo wondered if some grievous scandal had also compelled her uncle Aldo to leave Manila. Señora Concha had warned Amparo not to waste her time with ". . . that *laseng*o brother of mine . . ." but in truth she had only ever seen her uncle Aldo sober. He was just now drying out from another episode of what he called his *habitual fall from grace*, and she was glad he'd invited her to visit that Sunday. Perhaps this time he would tell her about this other fall from grace.

Chapter 4

Lingering Mistakes

Sunday afternoon Amparo walked up to an old Victorian home whose gilded eaves and lavender facade marked it as one of San Francisco's painted ladies. Her uncle Aldo greeted her at the door, dressed like an aging graduate student in boat shoes, khakis and a faded flannel shirt that had long forgotten its original color.

"Come in, *hija*, I made us some tea." Aldo ushered her into a large salon that smelled faintly of sandalwood, a room completely devoid of angles. A large bay window rounded out the front end of the sala, and rose-hued velvet sectionals stretched across the back corners, gathering around an oval wicker coffee table. It was a room designed to provide a soft landing for the home's four residents, all men recently released from rehab and at least momentarily free of their respective addictions. Aldo had returned here several times over the last decade and considered it his second home.

"Shall we sit by the window?" Aldo gestured at a circular table upon which he had set a tea service.

"I brought you dim sum from Oakland, Tito Aldo." As they sat down, Amparo handed him a bag, still warm from the Chinese bakery.

Aldo broke open a pork bun, inhaling the hoisin-scented steam as though sniffing a rose. "Let's eat this with our tea. Will you do the honors?" He took a large bite of *siopao* while Amparo poured tea. "I hope you don't mind that it's herbal: we're not allowed any caffeine in rehab."

"I remember, Tito." Amparo watched her uncle set a half-dozen shrimp dumplings on a saucer. "But are you sure MSG isn't a stimulant?"

"Only by Marcela's standards." Aldo smiled. "How is your old cook anyway? Your mother treating her well?"

"Nanay is fine." Amparo nibbled on a dumpling. "I spoke with her for a few minutes when I called home last Friday to greet Mama. You remembered it was Mama's birthday, didn't you?"

Aldo took a long sip of tea before replying, his shoulders tensing. He set his cup down with exaggerated care, delaying his reply. "I toasted her with a mug of chamomile. There was no need to call."

"Are you ever going to tell me why you don't speak to each other? I bet Nanay Marcela knows, but she won't tell me anything." Amparo remembered the dour expression that would come over the cook's face whenever, as a child, she had asked about her uncle. "I don't understand why you all have to be so secretive."

"Haven't you learned that Manila's families are built on secrets? People like my mother and sister guard their secrets like jewels to protect the family's good name." Aldo scowled out the window at the Muni trolley rumbling past. "Better to live here, where no one knows the damn name to begin with."

"Is that why you haven't been home in thirty years?

Dimples deepened into parentheses when her uncle smiled, as though happiness were no more than an afterthought in his old age. "*Déja lo, hija*—let it go. Why bring up ancient history?"

"Because maybe it would help me understand why—"

"There is nothing to understand, and everything to forget. That should be the immigrant's motto." Aldo stood up abruptly, his tea napkin falling to the floor. "It's such a nice afternoon, why don't we go outside? Do us good to get some fresh air."

Perplexed, Amparo followed her uncle down the hallway and through a small kitchen whose back door opened out to a pocket garden. A weeping willow drooped over a weathered park bench, and wind chimes hung silent in the still air. Aldo was examining a tall bush in the far corner when she caught up with him.

"See these fuchsia?" He pointed to fairylike flowers whose scarlet petals flared like peplums around the lilac cups within. "Hummingbirds go crazy for their nectar. I come out here every afternoon just to watch them feed."

"I didn't know you liked birds." The idea of Uncle Aldo sipping tea and watching hummingbirds contradicted all the stories her grandmother Lupita used to tell about her son's party-hectic youth. "Last time we spoke, Mama said she would visit me this year. When she does, maybe I could bring her here."

"Don't bother, *hija.* No point upsetting the old girl." Aldo turned to Amparo, a hard look in his eyes. "I broke away from the Duarté clan decades ago, you know that."

"But why, Uncle Aldo? What were you all fighting about?"

"Haven't you been paying attention? We bickered over family. I was too young and foolish at the time to realize I'd lost."

"You can always change your mind, can't you?"

"Too late for that, I'm afraid. Some decisions are irrevocable." A soft clicking sound distracted Aldo. Moving slowly, he pointed at a blur of emerald wings just beyond Amparo's shoulder. "That hummingbird could have taught me something about women back when it mattered," Aldo murmured. The thumb-sized bird flittered about, inserting its needle-thin beak into each flower for a scant second before going on to the next one. "See, he knows if he lingers, he'll kill the bloom." Aldo riffled gray bangs. "That was my mistake: I *lingered* thirty years ago. Probably ruined her. Regretted it ever since."

"But, Tito Aldo, who did you—" The question died on Amparo's lips when she saw the sorrow in her uncle's eyes, three decades of disappointment etched into his forehead.

"Enough talk of old sins, it's time to do penance." Aldo gestured toward the house. "I hate to send you away, *hija*, but I've got an AA meeting to attend."

Amparo left reluctantly, her mind whirling with even more questions than when she had first arrived. With whom had Uncle Aldo lingered, and how had he ruined her? She would not have expected her mother to gossip, but even Nanay Marcela, the longest-serving cook of the Duarté-Guerrero clan and de facto keeper of family secrets, had never offered the slightest hint that her uncle had ever been involved with a woman.

Amparo passed a man and woman arguing loudly in front of another apartment. The woman stormed into her home, closing the door just as the man sagged against the banister, heaving with frustration. Stepping carefully around the wreck, Amparo reconsidered: what if it had been the other way around? Had some long-ago catastrophic affair so shattered her uncle that he had been driven to drink? Was he making penance for lost love?

CHAPTER 5

Old-timer

The afternoon was waning as Amparo walked back to the BART station, but she was reluctant to leave the city. She had not expected the visit to end so quickly, and with Seamus gone to Nevada on a weeklong Ayurvedic retreat, she did not relish spending the evening alone. Such solitude was next to impossible in Manila and unheard of on weekends. Marcela habitually cooked larger meals on Sundays, for friends or relatives often dropped in at the dinner hour, and everyone was welcome.

Amparo wandered past stacked pyramids of fruit at the Mexican grocery, the steamed-up windows of a *pho* restaurant and Roxie Theater's scarlet facade, seeking a reason to linger. On slow weekend afternoons like this, when wayward sons wandered home to doze on their parents' sofas and matriarchs claimed playtime with grandchildren, she yearned to feel less alien.

At the Sixteenth and Mission BART station, a pair of street performers opened violin cases upon a spread-out blanket, their attire unconventional even by the Mission District's bohemian standards. The man offered a study in black: his face shadowed by a fedora, a thick plait of hair hanging down the back of a dark oxford shirt that tucked into a pleated black miniskirt. A cuff of brass bells jingled from each ankle. Costumed as his polar opposite, the woman had powdered her face to a skeletal pallor that matched her ivory pompadour; her dress was the palest pink of a baby's bottom. She too wore anklets of bells above her silver shoes. "Welcome everyone. We are the Tribal Baroque, come to you from the concrete canyons of New York." The man's voice rang deep as a gong. "If you like our mad music, we urge you to take it home." He gestured with the bow at the row of CDs stacked in his violin case.

Casting beatific smiles upon onlookers, the pair began to play. The music was unlike anything Amparo had ever heard: the man growling a guttural chant set in counterpoint to his frenzied fiddling and jingling stomps. Every now and then his pallid partner released a full-throated cadenza, her soprano swooping like a fleet-winged swallow above the noise of traffic. The crowd thickened and Amparo gladly made space, grateful for the company of strangers.

Dusk was falling when the duo concluded their performance, and Amparo tossed a few dollar bills into the fedora the man held out. Still hearing bells and violins, Amparo rode the escalator down into the station and boarded a half-empty train to Richmond. She chose a seat close to the door and counted through three more stops before the train rushed with an ear-popping whoosh through the tunnel beneath the bay. How frightened Nanay Marcela would have been if she were riding the train right now, she thought. The cook had never flown in an airplane, let alone traveled beneath water. She wondered if she could persuade her mother to allow Nanay Marcela to visit her in Oakland one day.

"Miss? Hello, miss? You Filipina?"

The question drew Amparo out of her reverie. She glanced up at a short, bald man smiling at her from across the aisle. He resembled a brown gnome in his rumpled chestnut jacket and corduroy slacks, but his eyes and gap-toothed grin sparkled with the liveliness of a much younger man. The two-wheeled cart beside him was filled with well-worn chess sets.

Amparo replied with cautious courtesy. "Yes, Filipina."

"I knew it!" The man cackled. "The prettiest girls are always Filipina. Me, I am also Pinoy." He stretched an arm across the aisle. "I am Wendell Moreno. You call me *Manong* Del for short."

Amparo hesitated at the sight of nails stained yellow with nicotine, but shook the hand anyway, calloused knuckles scraping against her own smooth fingertips. "Nice to meet you, Manong Del."

"Will you not tell me your name, *kabayan*?"

She briefly considered inventing a name, but could not bring herself to lie to someone who called her "countrywoman." *Probably a lonely old-timer; indulge him.* "Amparo. Amparo Guerrero."

Manong Del's eyes lit up. "I knew a Guerrero once in Santo Domingo—Ilocos Sur, you know. Purificación Guerrero. Puring was the town beauty and we were in love—ahh, so much in love! But I left her to come to America. What kind of fool was I? . . . Heehee, that was a song! Sammy Davis, you know." Noticing Amparo's bafflement, he leaned across the aisle. "But really, no joke. You look just like my Puring, so I had to say hello."

In spite of her misgivings, Amparo smiled. "Why didn't you bring her with you?"

"Ahh, in those days we could not bring women to America." Manong Del released an extravagant sigh. "So what did I do? I spent all my money at taxi dance halls."

"You rode taxis? I'm sorry, I don't understand." Amparo was relieved that they had by then emerged from the tunnel. Night had fallen and Oakland's lights twinkled in the distance.

"*Ahhaay*, you young people!" Manong Del slapped his thigh. "*Women* were our taxis. We paid their fare for every dance. Can you imagine: ten cents and you could choose from all these pretty ladies—many of them blond."

Amparo frowned, wondering if "dance hall" was a euphemism for "bordello." Perhaps he was an old lecher after all. She smiled politely and looked out the window, counting the stops remaining before hers.

When she heard the announcement for the Ashby station, she nodded a good-bye to Manong Del and went to stand by the door. Down by the far end of the car, another man got up as well, glancing over his shoulder at Amparo.

Amparo stepped out on the platform and hurried upstairs to the street level, leaving Manong Del to struggle with his unwieldy rolling basket. Mulling over which leftovers to nuke for dinner, she walked through the darkened parking lot, but paused when she heard a hoarse *hello*. Amparo turned, composing a polite brush-off for Manong Del, just as someone grabbed her bag.

"Let go!" Amparo jerked away, her heels skidding on the pocked cement as a man, his face obscured by his hooded sweatshirt, tried to wrench away her satchel. A straggle of people were walking out of the station, but none looked her way. "Somebody help me," she screamed.

A punch in the eye sent her reeling, but Amparo refused to let go of her purse. Suddenly a whistle blast ripped through the night. Startled, the man dropped Amparo's bag and sprinted to the far end of the parking lot, disappearing into darkness. Amparo fell to her knees, clutching her purse like a lifesaver.

"Miss? Miss Amparo, you okay?"

Amparo raised a hand to her tender cheek, feeling the beginnings of a bad headache. Someone helped her sit up and guided her to lean against something that creaked under her weight. She opened her eyes to Manong Del's concerned face.

"I saw you with that guy when I came out. First I thought you were arguing with your boyfriend. But then he hit you. *Ineng*, a pretty girl like you should never go out alone at night. You should have waited for me to escort you."

Amparo doubted little Manong Del could have held his own

against the mugger, but she was grateful nonetheless. "Okay *lang*. I should have been more careful. The whistle scared him away."

Manong Del held up the whistle hanging from a chain round his neck. "The policemen don't even use these anymore, I don't think. But those bad guys, they still get scared when they hear it. Good thing he did not have a gun. Did he take anything?"

Amparo quickly went through her purse, and found its contents intact. "Thanks so much, Manong Del. I can get home okay from here." She stood with difficulty and would have fallen again from dizziness had the old man not caught her.

"Let me walk you home. You cannot even cross the street, you are so unsteady. Come, put your arm around my shoulder." Keeping a hand on her back, Manong Del took hold of his cart and urged her to take a step.

"Too many bad men, not enough cops." The old man shook his head. "Not safe for you young ladies."

"Have you lived in this neighborhood long?" Amparo asked.

"Ever since they kicked us out of the I-hotel, back in—oh, it must be almost twenty years now."

"The I-hotel?"

"All the old-timers lived there. Used to be on Kearny Street." Manong Del hoisted his cart up on the sidewalk as they turned onto Alcatraz.

"Did you forget to pay rent?"

"No, no. Nothing like that." He rubbed thick white eyebrows. "I tell you all about it next time. Bad enough you have a headache, don't need to give myself one too."

When they reached her apartment, Amparo gave in to impulse. "Why don't you come upstairs, Manong Del? I can heat up some leftovers for dinner."

"*Talaga?* I don't want to bother you." Manong Del peered up at the building.

"My boyfriend is out of town. I couldn't face going into an

empty apartment, after this attack." Amparo unlocked the lobby door. "Mind keeping me company for a little bit?"

"Okay, then. Thank you." He rolled his cart into the foyer. "We have to go slow, so I can bring this up."

She would have tried persuading him to leave it in the lobby, but Manong Del was already dragging the cart toward the stairs. Without a word she picked up the bottom end of the cart and they trudged up the three flights.

"This is a nice place, Amparo," Manong Del panted. "You are lucky to live here."

Amparo looked skeptically at the faded wallpaper and threadbare carpet. "I guess it was nice enough, thirty years ago."

"You would think better of your home if you saw mine." Manong Del stopped on the third landing to catch his breath. "Next time you come over to my place, okay? No stairs there."

Amparo let him in and put last night's lasagna into the microwave. As the food warmed, she ducked into the bathroom to survey the damage. A large purple bruise darkened her left cheekbone. *I look just like a battered wife.* She ran cool water over her face and hoped it would heal by the time Seamus returned.

Manong Del had gotten busy while she was gone. When she emerged from the bathroom, the table was laid with clean napkins and cutlery. He looked up from pouring water into wineglasses as she came to the table. "You don't mind, I set the table already? I was a valet for twenty years until poor Mr. Pemberton died. Old habits, you know." He pointed at a bundled-up dish towel on the counter. "Here, you put some ice on that bump. Make the swelling go down."

Holding the ice pack to her cheek, Amparo sat down to dinner as her guest served her a generous cube of lasagna. She glanced over at his cart, standing like a sentinel by the front door. "Could you tell me why you carry all those chess sets around?"

Manong Del's eyes crinkled when he grinned. "Mr. Pemberton,

my employer, he taught me how to play. He left me a chess set in his will. I bought five more and rent them out. I give the old-timers something to do, make a little money. Everybody happy."

Amparo sat back, surprised that someone his age was still hustling for what must have been a pittance. "But where do you play?"

"Over by the Powell Street BART station. I used to bring tables, but it was too hard to bring them on the train all the way from Oakland. Now my friend Dionisio brings the folding tables. He is only fifty-five."

"Only fifty-five? How old are you?"

"*Aba*, I am seventy-two years old." Manong Del pulled his sweater sleeve up and flexed a bicep the size of a crab apple. "Yes, seventy-two years young and still going strong."

"But do you earn enough to live on?" Amparo picked at her food. She realized how much she disliked reheated lasagna.

"How it is, I get a little bit of social security, a little bit of food stamps, little bit from chess: all add up to just enough." Manong Del made pinching motions as though plucking grains of rice to put on his plate.

He chuckled at Amparo's look of skepticism. "Why don't you come see me sometime? See my chess tables all in a row, the other *manong* waiting their turn to play." He ran his fork across his plate, making a neat line in the tomato sauce. "Sometimes there are hotheads. They argue about cheating, start to mess up my chess pieces. I just blow my whistle and everyone calm down."

Amparo smiled at the idea that anyone could live on chess rentals and food stamps. If this old man could get by on so little, she had no right to feel sorry for herself.

Manong Del cleaned his plate and took a long gulp of water before smoothing his napkin back on the table. "Next time, you come to my place, okay? Is on the other side of the Ashby BART station. Not far."

"But you don't have to rush off, Manong Del." Amparo set her fork down. "Stay. I can make us some tea."

"No, thank you. I go home now. They say the weather tomorrow will be good. I want to set up my chess tables first thing in the morning. The other *manongs* are counting on me." He leaned across the table to squint at her purple cheek. "Looks better already. You see? Everything heals fast when you are young."

He stood with a subtle creaking of joints. "How about you come visit me next Saturday? Bring your young man too. I serve him a good Filipino dinner."

Amparo blushed. "Seamus won't be back yet, but I'm happy to visit."

"We have a date then, just you and me." Manong Del pulled a pen and a small pad out of his back pocket and scribbled his address. "You come at five next Saturday night. I make you the best *adobo* you ever had."

As she walked her guest to the door, Amparo felt nostalgia well up in her throat, blurring her gaze with unexpected tears. Not since Nanay Marcela had anyone offered to cook her a Filipino meal. Who would have known she so desperately missed home?

Manong Del gave her shoulder a gentle squeeze. "I know, I know. It is hard to be so far away. That is why the *manong* come to me every day: not for chess. For their *kababayan.*"

A week later, Amparo parked in front of a run-down cottage six blocks from her apartment. She was about to walk up the stairs to the front porch when a door opened just beyond the bushes on the right side of the house.

"Amparo! There you are. Good thing I caught you before you knocked. My landlady does not like to be bothered. Come, come this way. I live in the basement."

Manong Del ushered her down a short flight of stairs into a studio no larger than the servants' quarters in Amparo's childhood home.

"Go ahead, look around." Manong Del gestured at the room. "Not much to see, but it is home, sweet home for me."

Ten steps took Amparo to the opposite wall, against which huddled a chest-high refrigerator, a sink and an old gas stove, all bearing the shabby patina of age. To her left, a window at eye level offered a view of the front yard's crabgrass and the wheels of her car. Across from the kitchenette stood a bunk bed with a single mattress on the lower level, its upper section filled with a row of old paperbacks and folded clothes.

The room's only other furnishings were two folding chairs and a card table upon which Manong Del had set steaming bowls of chicken stew and fried rice. He spread his arms like a conjurer, his face turned copper by a *capiz* lamp hung above the table. "You like my place?"

Amparo inhaled the aroma of fried garlic; if she closed her eyes, she could almost imagine she'd returned to Nanay Marcela's kitchen. "I like it fine."

The old man beamed. "Smells like home, no? Rent is cheap because there are no closets." Manong Del nodded at the back wall.

Amparo walked past the table and saw cardboard boxes stacked like bricks along the wall, each one neatly labeled in Manong Del's childlike script. The top row offered *Sweaters, Towels, Life Magazine, Tools, Sinatra.*

Amparo remembered Señora Concha playing Frank Sinatra records one after the other in the living room, sipping scotch and plowing through a pack of Salems as she waited for her husband to come home from work. Ever afterward Sinatra's ballads would remind Amparo of late nights, thick with longing and cigarette smoke. "You like Sinatra?"

"Been a fan since his first record. My friends and I, we used to take out the record player and sing until the old lady"—Manong Del jerked a thumb at the low ceiling—"banged on her floor. I would put on Old Blue Eyes for dinner, but my player is broken."

Amparo looked around the room, trying to imagine a bunch of old-timers yodeling along with Sinatra. A framed picture by the stairs caught her eye, and she walked up for a closer look. In it, two couples stood arm in arm beneath a brightly lit marquee: *Rizal Dance Hall.* The women wore cinch-waisted, full-skirted dresses that bared alabaster shoulders; the men stared into the camera with onyx eyes, dark-skinned dandies in double-breasted suits and brilliantined hair, parted down the middle like silent-film actors.

"Manong Del, did you know those people?"

"*Aba*, of course, the man on the right was me!" Manong Del squared his shoulders and angled his face, miming the young man's pose. "I was *handsome* when I was young. Hard to believe now, eh?"

Amparo stared hard at the photo and saw he was right. "So was that your girlfriend?" Amparo pointed at the blonde on Manong Del's arm.

"Ahh, I was just one of her many admirers. Most popular taxi dancer in town, that Judy Reed." The old man stared at the photograph, his eyes soft with fond remembering.

"All day I picked asparagus, one hundred pounds for ninety cents. At night I spent it on tickets to dance with Judy. Heehee!" He slapped his forehead, laughing. "My money all gone by midnight—but my golly, she was worth it!"

"She must have been flattered." Amparo smiled. "You looked like a movie star."

"Heck, I danced like Fred Astaire. Come, I show you." Stepping around the table, the old man took Amparo's hand in his and hummed "In the Mood" as he twirled her through a mincing swing routine.

Swaying in stately loops around the dinner table, Amparo pictured young farmworkers dressed to the nines, blowing a day's worth of dimes on a chance at love. Had any won out?

"*Tama na*—enough." Manong Del released her hand, panting. "All this excitement makes me hungry. Sit, sit. Let me serve you."

Waving Amparo to the chair opposite his, he spooned rice on her plate, then drizzled adobo sauce over it with a flourish.

Amparo raised her spoon, but could not resist teasing. "Tell me the truth, Manong Del: were you and Judy in love?"

"Maybe so, maybe so." He dabbed at his forehead with a handkerchief, neatly folded it into a square and returned it to his breast pocket. "But I was only eighteen—what did I know about love? Besides, we stopped dancing after Pearl Harbor." He let out a low whistle. "Big trouble, that war. I worried about my parents back home. Then Roosevelt promised we Pinoys could become citizens if we fought for America. So I enlisted."

He raised an eyebrow at Amparo, his ladle hovering over the adobo. "You want white meat or dark?"

"Dark, of course."

Manong Del put a chicken thigh on her hill of rice and picked up his story. "Me and my buddies left the fields and signed up soon as we heard the news. First Filipino Infantry Regiment, that's what we joined. From everywhere more Pinoys came: cannery workers from Alaska, laborers, waiters from New York. If you were over eighteen but under forty, you went to San Luis Obispo and trained for war."

"Were you sent to Manila to fight?" Amparo stirred the adobo gravy into her rice until every grain turned glossy, then ate with rapt attention.

"No, my regiment went south to Leyte and Samar. There I was, the dashing soldier from America"—he winked at Amparo—"and those pretty native ladies could only speak *Waray*. My best *Ilocano* jokes were useless. Ahhh, I was not destined for love." He chewed thoughtfully before continuing.

"After the war ended, I looked for Judy, but the Rizal Dance Hall had closed down, and she was gone. Maybe better that way." He shrugged. "Back then it was illegal for Pinoys to marry white women."

Amparo drove home after dinner in a pensive mood. The loneliness she felt in America was unlike any she had known growing up in Manila, yet somehow Manong Del and her uncle Aldo had endured it for decades. She knew the old man had come to America hoping to escape poverty. Manong Del was a prime example of the "immigrants with nothing to lose" of whom her mother had spoken. But how did that apply to Uncle Aldo? What had he hoped to escape when he left home?

PART II

Love and Death

CHAPTER 6

Zero Sum

September 1995

"Interpreter, this is Patricia Haynes, the registered nurse-practitioner who works with Dr. Soames. I'd like to discuss test results with my patient Inés Molina, but she's having a hard time understanding me. Could you please introduce yourself before we proceed?"

Amparo set the watering can back down on the windowsill. Oakland was simmering through an unseasonably warm September, but the geraniums could stand to go thirsty while she took this call. "*Gandang araw po*—good morning, Inés. This is Amparo and I'll be interpreting for you today."

"Hello? *So ano ba?* What is it?" Amparo could barely hear the woman's voice over the wailing of her child. From the sound of it, Inés was balancing a baby on one hip and holding the phone with the opposite hand, neck craned as far away as possible from the crying infant.

"Ask Mrs. Molina if she can put the baby down," Nurse Patricia said. "I can barely hear her."

Before Amparo could interpret this, she was interrupted by a chortle.

"I love you! You love me! We're a happy family . . . !"

"Jordan! Turn that Barney off right now! You want me to throw it in the *basura?*" Inés yelled, not bothering to cup her hand over the receiver. "Can you not see? I am talking on the telephone!"

"But, Mama, I'm singing—" Jordan whined.

The baby gurgled, distracted by the toy.

"Won't you say you love—me—too! Hwehweyyy!"

"That's it! I told you already so many times! *Ay buwisit mga batang 'to!*" The rising shrillness of the woman's voice reminded Amparo of the last argument she'd had in Manila before fleeing to America. She remembered staring at her right hand, splayed on the floor like a spider fallen from its web. She remembered wondering how the wood could be so cool on such a hot, sticky day. Her mother's red toenails flashed dangerously close to Amparo's fingers and she jerked away.

"How could you do this to us?" Señora Concha raged, standing over the daughter she'd slapped. "What were you thinking, *ha,* Amparo? Did you even consider the scandal you would bring to our name?"

Amparo remained on the floor, too stunned to cry until Nanay Marcela gathered her up in a protective embrace. Only then did tears come.

"*Tama na.* Leave her be, señora. It's done. No one has to know about this." Marcela stroked Amparo's cheek, still red from her mother's hand.

"Isa ka pa. Kunsentidor!" Accomplice, Señora Concha hissed.

Nurse Patricia's voice yanked Amparo back to the present. "Interpreter? Are you still there? Normally I would call back, but every other time it's been like this." The nurse sighed. "Let's wait a few moments and see if things settle down."

"No problem, I'm happy to wait."

There was murder in Inés's voice as she argued with the little boy. "No buts, Jordan! You go to your room right now! I said NOW!" A distant door banged. The baby resumed yowling.

"Interpreter, we're just going to have to make do. Could you please tell Mrs. Molina that her pregnancy test came back positive?"

When Amparo translated this information, she heard a sharp intake of breath.

"No. No. *Imposiblé!*" Inés sputtered in furious Tagalog. "I'm still breast-feeding this baby, and that Jordan, the day care will not take him until he is potty-trained. *Diós ko,* I'm going to kill Gary! That bastard wouldn't leave me alone long enough to recover from my C-section. . . ."

"Mrs. Molina, calm down, please," Nurse Patricia pleaded.

"I cannot. I cannot have another baby." Inés's voice turned desperate. "Please *lang* Amparo, tell the nurse I cannot go through with this pregnancy."

Amparo shut her eyes to another memory as she conveyed the request.

"Is she saying she would like to terminate the pregnancy?" Nurse Patricia seemed unwilling to say the word over the phone.

"Yes."

"In that case she'll have to come in and talk with Dr. Seiser. . . ."

When Amparo ended the call, she was clammy with sweat. She continued watering the geraniums but succeeded only in drenching the windowsill; her hand was shaking so badly. She stared out the window, not really seeing old Mrs. MacCallum ambling down Alcatraz with her terrier or the kids skimming the curb on skateboards. Instead she saw Inés, shackled by two children, frantic to avoid a third. Needing a distraction, Amparo yanked the pot of flowers off the sill and began to deadhead the spent geraniums, her tears watering the soil.

Years ago, Amparo had played the same zero-sum game with pregnancy. She had never recovered from the loss.

Chapter 7

Amparo and Matéo, 1988

Señora Concha had warned Amparo about boys like Matéo, but as happens with most mothers of eighteen-year-old girls, her advice fell on deaf ears. Amparo first noticed the boy in her Thomas Hardy class. It was impossible not to: he was the only straight male in the gaggle of women and gay men.

Earlier, the class had been momentarily interrupted by sounds of a scuffle down the hall, but Professor Valoria commanded her students to remain seated. Through thirty years of teaching at the University of the Philippines she had survived humiliating, often murderous constrictions under martial law; she would not allow a mere brawl to disrupt her class. Ignoring the distant yells, she returned to the original question.

"Mr. Madrigal, could you explain how religion and social class contributed to the tragic events in *Jude the Obscure*?" Professor Valoria peered over her bifocals at the brown-haired teenager in the front row whose long limbs looped around his desk like a paper clip. As in most of the old university's classrooms, the thirty desks in A.S. room 413 were crammed together like floor tiles, their occupants acting as human spacers. The girl beside Matéo had somehow managed to wedge her desk away from his, her coyness a sure sign of infatuation. Matéo smiled at the girl, who giggled and scribbled something in her seatmate's notebook. He was clearly used to the attention.

Professor Valoria rolled her eyes. *Another Lothario trawling for dates in Upper Division English.* She had one in every class. "Mr. Madrigal? Any thoughts before noon?"

"Sorry, I'm just getting my ideas together." Matéo sucked on the tip of his pen. "Religion and class, hmmm . . . I'd say that would be the easy answer."

"I'd like to see how those concepts could be considered 'easy.'" Professor Valoria crossed thin arms over her pigeon chest and locked eyes with the nineteen-year-old, a challenge in the tilt of her chin.

Matéo never took anyone seriously enough to be intimidated. "Religion and class would be the obvious *intellectual* answer, but from a practical point of view I'd say unprotected sex caused the guy's bad luck."

A wave of murmurs swept through the class and washed up against the lecturer's platform. "Now, let's not oversimplify Thomas Hardy—"

"But think about it—if Jude hadn't gotten those two women pregnant, Little Father Time wouldn't have come along to kill his other kids, would he?" Matéo punctured air with his pen. "Dude was too prolific for his own good."

The girls burst into giggles and a pair of gay English majors in back commenced whispering behind a flurry of fingers. Amparo squinted at Matéo from the opposite end of the front row. The Basquiat T-shirt, tattooed forearm and ripped jeans suggested fine arts major, but the pristine indigo high-tops gave him away: no paint splatters. Amparo decided he was a poseur, a *coño*-kid preppy pretending to be punk. At that moment Matéo looked up from his doodling and caught her staring at him. He winked, dimples bracketing his smile.

Amparo scowled and looked away, hoping he didn't see her blush. *What an ass. He probably thinks I have a crush on him like everyone else here.*

Matéo got away with being cheeky because he was among the smarter students in class, a pretty boy with a working intellect. Even Professor Valoria, jaded by decades of teaching, could not ignore catnip. "If you could stop flirting long enough to focus on historical context, Mr. Madrigal, you will recall that Jude lived in 1895. Birth control wasn't as common or effective in those days."

Matéo twirled a pen around thumb and index finger like a whirligig. "I'll give you that. But if Jude weren't crippled by his scruples, I bet he'd have found a way out of those pregnancies. Abortion's been around for centuries, hasn't it?"

The students burst out laughing and Nening Valoria gave up. She had run overtime as usual and students waiting for the next class were already chattering in the corridor outside. "You are all Philistines, the lot of you!" She brandished an eraser at them. "Go, then, but remember your reaction papers are due next Tuesday."

Amparo was the first to slip out the door. Being nearsighted and mildly claustrophobic, she always sat in the front row, closest to the jalousied windows that flanked the door. The windows looked out on the fourth-floor breezeway, which offered an aerial view of mature acacias; their foliage obscured prewar buildings aging ungracefully around the academic oval.

Trees were far from Amparo's thoughts as she rushed out of the classroom, tacking back and forth along the corridor to avoid students spilling out of the other classrooms. The thicket of bodies parted as she neared the stairs and she broke into a sprint. Suddenly she slipped on something wet and began skidding to the edge of the stairs.

"I got you!" An arm encircled Amparo's waist and she fell back against a broad chest. For the briefest moment she felt another heart thumping between her shoulder blades. She startled at the snake swallowing its own tail on the muscled forearm that steadied her. She'd seen that tattoo before. . . .

"Gotta watch your step in a war zone. Rumble's not over yet."

Amparo glanced back to find herself caught in Matéo Madrigal's arms. "I'm fine." She pushed free, irritated that he of all people had come to her rescue.

"You're welcome!" Matéo raised both hands in mock surrender. "You'd be walking around with dirty jeans all day if I hadn't caught you." He nodded at the floor. She was standing in the middle of what looked like dark red paint.

"*Punyeta*. Is that blood?" Amparo stepped away from the smear, leaving vermilion footprints on the floor. "Whose?"

"Another casualty of war. *Boss, basá pa rito,"* Matéo hollered to a gray-haired man on the landing, drawing his attention to the wet floor. Amparo noticed the custodian was mopping up an even larger pool of blood. A river of students eddied around his pail, barely glancing at the mess.

"So that's what all the noise was about." Amparo grimaced at the splotches on her espadrille heel.

The yelling had echoed loudly enough to break Professor Valoria's train of thought midway through her lecture. Motioning for her students to remain seated, the professor had looked down the hallway, wrinkled fingers smudging the doorjamb with chalk. "*Hoy mga bugoy!* You hooligans, I'm trying to teach here. Stop it already before I call the police!"

It was an empty threat, for none of the classrooms had telephones.

The sounds of scuffling continued a few more minutes, but Professor Valoria pressed on, raising her voice over the shouts and thuds. Her noninvolvement was born of fear, not indifference. It was only two years after People Power had unseated the dictator, not long enough for those who'd survived martial law to shed old habits: when trouble brewed outside, it was best to lock the door.

Looking now at the dark smear, Amparo shuddered involuntarily. Nothing in her hermetic all-girl high school had prepared her for this. She instinctively moved closer to Matéo as they walked downstairs. "Who's fighting now?"

"The usual—Upsilon and APO. I hear someone from APO insulted an Upsilonian's girlfriend in the parking lot yesterday. Somebody's car got keyed. Things escalated." Matéo edged Amparo close to the banister in case she tripped again.

"So that's why that guy was walking around with a baseball bat this morning," Amparo said. "Is that how you settle all your disagreements—with baseball bats?"

"Don't look at me—I never joined a frat." Matéo stopped at the bottom of the stairs and looked out across the first-floor lobby. Students strolled through the ballroom-sized space or sat on long benches that lined the lobby's right wall, the garble of disparate conversations amplified by granite columns and grimy windows that stayed shut even on the hottest days.

"Oh . . . okay." Amparo smiled. Wide-set almond eyes and a prominent widow's peak marked her as Señora Concha's daughter, but she had also inherited her father's narrow nose and slender frame. Absent the scowl, she was actually quite pretty.

"I have about two hours before my poli-sci class. Are you hungry?" Matéo nodded toward the tall front doors of the lobby. "There's this place called the Beach House behind the library. Serves the best barbecue on campus.

"C'mon, you can at least have lunch with the guy who saved your butt."

Amparo blushed. "Okay. As long as we leave the war zone."

She followed him across the lobby and down the front steps that spanned the middle third of the Arts and Letters building. As they waited for the crush of jeepneys and cars to ease up, Amparo gazed up at the acacias' boughs, which arched high overhead to touch leaves with their neighbors across the street. She wondered if, when they were courting, her parents had strolled beneath the same verdant canopy.

When Matéo reached for her hand to cross the street, she did not pull away. They walked past vendors frying fish balls in murky oil, urchins selling cigarettes by the stick and *Manang* Anacélia with her *biláo* of spring rolls and hip-slung bottle of coconut vinegar. As they strolled, they chatted about mutual friends, tracing common lines of family that bound their lives as closely as plaits on a wicker chair.

Matéo's father had preceded Amparo's by just a few years at the same Jesuit high school; they had later studied and partied together in the same college fraternity. The two men would have continued along the same parallel track indefinitely but for the innate restlessness of Matéo's father, Vinicio. Over the course of his peripatetic career in diplomacy, Matéo's father had moved the family from Brussels to Madrid and then Los Angeles before returning to Manila. Had Matéo not spent the first seventeen years of his life abroad, Amparo would surely have met him in grade school, so small were the circles in which their families moved.

"Here we are—the Beach House." Matéo pointed to a huddle of warped wooden picnic tables fronting the Quonset hut from whose roof a plume of smoke rose.

"I don't see a beach anywhere, do you?" Amparo whispered, as Matéo held the rickety screen door open for her.

"They might've misspelled it." Matéo winked. "I hear the owner's really mean."

"You're terrible!" Amparo slapped his arm, but couldn't help grinning at the bad pun.

As in many of the makeshift eateries on campus, food sat in a row of battered chafing dishes warmed by halfhearted burners. The air inside smelled of old grease, but the barbecue looked almost appetizing. Matéo selected a half-dozen skewers, each with five gobbets of dark red pork, sticky from a cola–soy sauce marinade. The plump woman in a stained housedress swiped her moist forehead with the back of a hand before tamping garlic rice into a mug and unmolding the cone on each plate. Waving away the flies dive-bombing into the condiments, she ladled pickled green papaya *at-sara* alongside the barbecue.

"*Balik kayo ha?* Come back," she urged, flashing the wide gap in her teeth.

Amparo and Matéo took their plates and sat across from each other on one of the picnic tables, hoping a breeze would stir the sultry air. Matéo chomped down and slid a mouthful of pork off the skewer, the blackened bamboo leaving a thin line of charcoal across his cheek.

"You've got a smudge on your face." Amparo offered a paper napkin, but Matéo leaned across the table, waiting to be swabbed. She dabbed gingerly, unsettled by the intimate gesture.

"Can't eat barbecue without making a mess. Go ahead, try it!" He nodded at her plate.

Amparo eyed the rim of fat glistening the edge of her barbecue, wondering how best to separate it from the meat with her flimsy plastic fork. She stood the skewer up on its point and pushed down on the barbecue, but the bamboo was gummy with caramelized marinade and it wouldn't budge.

"Are you always this finicky?" Matéo reached into his back pocket and brought out a Swiss Army knife, unfolding the largest blade. "I don't generally use this on food but—" Before Amparo could check if the knife was clean, he began sawing pork off the stick, the shaved meat forming a hill beside her cone of rice. The dish looked sloppy yet strangely endearing.

When Amparo was much younger, Nanay 'Cela had often sliced meat off chicken wings and thighs to protect her from choking on bones. Señora Concha considered it one of a servant's many chores, but Amparo had always seen it as an act of love. She looked now across the table at Matéo and wondered what Nanay would think of him.

Late that afternoon, Amparo arrived home and headed straight for the kitchen. Like her brothers, she habitually sought out Nanay 'Cela before greeting her mother.

"Ay, anak!" Marcela looked up from carrot and bean sprout cakes she was frying. "Want to try my *okoy*?"

The cook looked on fondly as Amparo nibbled on the vegetable fritters. With each passing year the girl looked more and more like Señora Concha, but her naturally sweet disposition softened the mouth and kept the sharpness out of the eyes. Marcela had cared for the girl since Señora Concha had brought her home from the hospital, a squirming, colicky infant with skin so pale it was virtually translucent. Señora Concha had refused to hold, let alone nurse, her daughter and it had fallen to Marcela to nurture the newborn, even as she tended the two older brothers.

Marcela no longer remembered who had begun calling her *Nanay*, but "Mother" seemed an appropriate title. After two decades, she knew Señora Concha's children as intimately as if she had carried each one in her womb. "You look different, 'Paro. Something happened today. Who is he?"

Amparo sucked on fork tines. "Just a classmate. His name is Matéo Madrigal. I had lunch with him today."

Marcela raised her eyebrows. "You ate at the university? Was it clean?"

"Nanay, *naman*! I don't look sick, do I? Not everyone cooks in a kitchen as nice as yours."

Marcela nodded, acknowledging her fiefdom. "I could always cook in a smaller kitchen. But I would not be as happy."

The Guerrero kitchen was significantly larger than the one in which Marcela had first learned to cook decades earlier. Señora Concha's husband, Federico, had wooed Marcela away from Doña Lupita's home with promises of a six-burner gas stove, an extra-large refrigerator and an extravagant expanse of marble countertop. To encourage Señora Concha's sporadic forays into baking,

Federico had also designed a "clean" outer kitchen, to which the children were exiled whenever the elder Guerreros entertained.

The door to the clean kitchen swung open just then, held ajar by a pale bejeweled hand. "Marcela! Was that Amparo who arrived? You need to feed the driver early tonight. I'm meeting friends for dinner at seven." Señora Concha stood in the doorway, peering past the half wall that separated the two kitchens. She rarely ventured into Marcela's domain, not wanting her clothes to catch the smell of food.

"Hi, Mama, I'm home." Amparo emerged from the dirty kitchen with a forkful of *okoy*.

"What are you eating? You'll get fat if you snack between meals." Señora Concha paused for the obligatory peck on the cheek. Amparo knew to aim for the soft spot just above her mother's jaw, avoiding the swath of rouge that contoured the cheekbones.

Out of habit, Señora Concha took a step back and appraised her daughter's appearance. "When was the last time I bought you shoes? Those espadrilles are filthy."

"We can go shopping this weekend." Amparo avoided telling her mother about the frat war, aware that it would only have bolstered Señora Concha's conviction that allowing her to study at U.P. had been a mistake. "Where are you going tonight?"

"I'm having dinner at Minggoy's with your *tita* Carina and *tita* Charito. It's Tita Charito's birthday, and she wants paella."

"Is Papa meeting you there? I didn't see his car in the garage."

"Your father is working late again. He said he had to dine with prospective . . . clients."

A look of understanding passed between Señora Concha and the cook, who was listening from the border of the clean kitchen. A night out with clients meant Marcela would have to sweep the car seats when Kuya Federico got home, no matter how late he arrived that night. Months earlier, Señora Concha had instructed Marcela to clean out her husband's car, searching for specific items: a restaurant matchbook perhaps, or a fragment of lipstick-smudged tissue—anything that might tell her what sort of clients her husband had consorted with. Muttering about the late night ahead, Marcela left to prepare the driver's dinner.

Amparo followed Señora Concha out to the living room. She'd learned to snare her mother's attention by talking about the children of Señora Concha's wide circle of acquaintances. It would be the easiest way to dig up information on Matéo, for her mother had a nearly encyclopedic knowledge of Manila's prominent families.

"You know, there's a Madrigal in my class. Matéo said his dad's name is Vinicio. When you see her tonight, can you ask if they're related?"

Señora Concha motioned Amparo to join her on the sofa. She pulled out a Salem Light from the silver minaudière Doña Lupita had given her after her third C-section. Tiny lines radiated from coral lips as she sucked on the cigarette. "Vinicio . . . do you mean Vinchy Madrigal? Of course—I've known him nearly as long as I've known your *tita* Carina. I had a crush on him in high school. Such a charming man, and so *guwapo.* His grandmother was Basque, you know. That's why he and Carina are super *mestizo*: *balbón*—hairy with pale, pale skin. Vinchy was an ambassador in America until recently, no?"

Amparo nodded, suppressing a smile. She could always rely on her mother for social histories, if not much else.

"Yes, Vinchy Madrigal is her first cousin. Carina says he came home to run for Congress." Señora Concha gazed at her only daughter, noticing the way Amparo's eyes lit up.

"So you met one of his sons? He has three, two by the first wife. Pachot Madrigal died in a car crash, *pobrecita.* If I remember correctly, Vinchy was still in Belgium at the time—" Señora Concha rubbed her forehead, her cigarette making lazy whorls of smoke that floated toward Amparo, who leaned away, wrinkling her nose. Amparo was the only female in her mother's family who did not smoke.

". . . Ahh, now I remember. Yes, Pachot crashed into a streetlamp in Antwerp when the two older boys were still in grade school. Died instantly. Then Vinchy married a Belgian woman and had one more son with her. Your *tita* Carina was so excited about flying to Brugge for that wedding." Señora Concha exhaled twin streams of smoke from narrow nostrils, and cocked an eyebrow at her daughter.

"All of Vinchy's sons are good-looking, but the youngest is the cutest *daw—mestizo*-Belgian *kase.* Is he your classmate?"

Amparo plucked at a tasseled throw pillow, wary of the direction their conversation was taking. When it came to personal matters, she confided only in Nanay.

"Do you like him? I'll ask Tita Carina to find out if he has a girlfriend."

"Mama!" A look of horror erased Amparo's smile. "She'll think I have a crush on him!"

"Well, don't you?"

Amparo's cheeks were burning. "Matéo and I had one lunch. It was cheap and I paid for my own barbecue. Don't jump to conclusions."

"Nobody's jumping, *hija.* I will ask Carina about her nephew tonight. Maybe I'll invite the Madrigals to our next party. Would be nice to meet the wife." Señora Concha stood up and smoothed her dressing gown. "*Pués.* I have to get dressed. The driver should be done eating by now—can you check?"

Amparo shook her head in exasperation, alternately pleased and appalled that her mother's social gears had already begun to spin. If there was one thing Señora Concha excelled at, it was throwing a party.

CHAPTER 8

Liaisons

Federico Guerrero returned home in the small hours of morning, his horn blasts prompting a roll call of barks from the neighborhood dogs. Ensconced in air-conditioned rooms, Señora Concha and her children slept undisturbed, but the noise roused Marcela, who opened her eyes with a start, searching the room for her sister. Years after Clara's accident, it was still the first thing she did upon waking.

She rolled off her mattress, jostling three other cots as she ran barefoot to open the gate. The sedan coasted into the driveway and slowed to a stop beside the two other cars. Federico got out and shut the car door with a stealthy click, waving thanks at the cook.

One hand on the car's warm hood, Marcela waited for the squeak of the clean kitchen's swinging door, which signaled that Kuya Fico had passed into the living area. Then she opened the front passenger door and squatted down, eye-level to the seat. Squinting in the dim glow of the dome light, she ran her palm over the fine-grained leather, then dug fingers into the crevice between seat and chairback. Nothing.

She fished out a flashlight from the glove compartment and

aimed its beam underneath the seat and across the floor mat. In the far corner beneath the air-conditioning vent, something glinted.

"Ayan." With a melancholic *tch-tch,* she tugged at the small object that had snagged on the carpet. The flashlight's beam revealed a pendant earring whose lozenge-sized stone gleamed scarlet amid a circle of *diamantítas.* Marcela was certain this did not belong to Señora Concha, for her mistress wore only white gems.

The cook stood with some difficulty, shaking her head over this latest artifact, the third in nearly a year. Thus far, Marcela had found a matchbook from the Hobbit House in Ermita and a crumpled piece of tissue imprinted with lipstick in a shade her mistress dismissed as "whorish." As instructed, the cook surrendered everything to Señora Concha, who had instituted the searches when her husband began spending too many late nights at the office. Although Marcela liked the genial adulterer, her first loyalty would always belong to the woman whose children she considered her own.

Marcela habitually synchronized her movements to the rhythms of the Guerrero household, having observed the individual habits of her employers for over two decades. She knew that no matter how late Kuya Fico had come home the night before, he invariably left for work at six forty-five a.m. to avoid rush hour traffic. At seven fifteen Señora Concha would emerge in her dressing gown to have coffee and her first cigarette of the day as she waited for Amparo and Javier to come down to breakfast. After Miguel had left for medical school in San Francisco, she had taken a more active—if belated—interest in her remaining children.

Marcela knew her mistress would have a good half hour alone. A half hour was what Amparo took to assemble an outfit from her own and her mother's closets. A half hour was how long Javier took for the first of two daily showers, so self-conscious was he of his propensity for sweat.

Marcela decided that Señora Concha's brief period of morning solitude was the best time to deliver bad news, because she would have limited time in which to brood before the children arrived to distract her. Accordingly, the cook walked out of the kitchen at seven seventeen, her breakfast tray weighed down with *longganiza*, fried eggs, garlic rice and the bauble she had discovered the night before.

"I found this in Kuya Fico's car," Marcela murmured, laying the earring on the place mat next to Señora Concha's ashtray.

"On the seat?"

"The floor."

If Señora Concha suffered any grief at that moment, she buried it well with disdain. She dangled the earring from her fingertips as though it were an exotic beetle. "Cabochon ruby. So big it looks fake. But it's probably authentic, if Fico bought it. He never skimps on jewelry."

"It didn't look like one of yours."

"I would never wear something so *baduy*." Señora Concha wrinkled her nose. "Fico must have picked it up at some wholesale store when he flew to Sydney last month with that junior associate, Candida what's-her-name. I noticed them flirting at his office Christmas party last year." She flicked the earring onto the table and reached for her minaudière.

Marcela straightened a napkin on the table. "You know who she is?"

"Who else could it be but Candida? He'd never risk the business by seducing a client, and all the other women in that office are too old and too married." Señora Concha's eyes narrowed as she tapped the earring with her cigarette. "I call her Miss False Eyelashes. Too much lip gloss, legs to the armpit, and *Madré de Díos*—such breasts. You could serve high tea on them." Señora Concha picked up her lighter. "She must buy all her bras in America."

She busied herself with lighting her cigarette. Looking up, she saw what looked like pity in Marcela's eyes. "*Hayaan mo na*—never mind. It's my cross to bear. You will get a little extra in the next paycheck for finding this. *O, sige na.*" Señora Concha dismissed her cook with a swirl of smoke. "We're done for now."

Marcela paused at the sight of Señora Concha's drooping shoulders, the frown that pleated the skin between those perfectly plucked brows. "Do you ever think of leaving him?"

Her mistress's laugh was short and bitter. "And where would I go, *ha*, Marcela? Who else would give me a home like this?" She gestured toward the sala, adorned with furniture and art acquired over two decades with her husband's money. "Even if I kicked him out, then what? Who would have me? No man wants a *separada*—especially not one my age."

A clatter of steps on the stairs ended the conversation. Javier set his overstuffed book bag on the far end of the table and sat down. "Ma, can I borrow your car tonight? I'm taking Lilliana to a movie after dinner." Javier grinned at Marcela. "Nanay, is there any *embutido* left from last night? Can you make me two sandwiches for lunch?"

"*Siyempre*, Javi." Marcela nodded and headed for the kitchen.

"Going out with Lilliana again?" Señora Concha wagged her cigarette at Javier, scattering ash across her plate. "Looks serious."

"Ma, *naman*. We've been dating for over a year." Her son dabbed at his dewy forehead. Javier had inherited his thick frame and florid skin from a paternal ancestor, a farmer of German extraction. Rudolf Stendhal had left Idaho to establish a trading company in Manila three generations earlier; while the business had flourished, his Teutonic genes had never made peace with the hothouse climate of his adopted home.

"Go ahead, take the car, I'm staying in tonight." Señora Concha ground a fleck of ash into the earring with the tip of her thumb. "Why don't you take Amparo?"

"Amparo doesn't have a date on Friday night? *Milagro.*" Miracle. It was usually Javier who stayed home, hunched over his desk behind ramparts of books, while his younger sister held court at Café Adriatico with a half-dozen friends. "Hasn't she gotten over Pipo yet? They split up months ago."

"Yes, but no one's come along to fill the void." Señora Concha reflected on her children, the son solid as earth, the ephemeral daughter. Miguel, her eldest, had been the axis mediating the two extremes; in his absence it fell to her to restore equilibrium. "Maybe you could organize a double date."

"Bad idea." Javier snorted, jabbing a spoon into the platter of rice and piling its load onto his plate. "Amparo thinks all my friends are nerds."

"What do I think?" Amparo walked into the sala just then, her mother's new Fendi purse dangling from a slim forearm.

"That you're too cool to date any of my friends."

"Got that right—" Amparo sat down. "Besides, I might have a date tomorrow night."

Señora Concha gazed at Amparo's smooth forehead and felt a prickle of envy. The girl did not yet have to spackle multiple layers of foundation to affect flawless skin. "Still dreaming about the Madrigal boy? How do you know he doesn't have a girlfriend already?"

"If he did, he wouldn't have asked me out for coffee today, would he?" Amparo blotted the grease on her fried egg with a paper napkin.

"*Naku*, Amparo. You have so much to learn."

"That's right, Ma. Tell 'Paro men can't be trusted," Javier teased, mashing molten egg yolk into his garlic rice.

"What's the rush? She'll find that out on her own." Señora Concha pursed her lips, aiming a jet stream at the chandelier, where a fly lay in one of the dusty globes. Dead, like her marriage.

"You're too cynical, Ma." Amparo nodded at her brother. "Look at Javier. He's never cheated on Lilliana—right, Javi?" As she dipped a slice of chorizo in the saucer of garlic vinegar, she noticed the earring. "Is that new? I want to try it on."

Señora Concha snatched the earring off the table and leaned away, fist clenched.

"Calm down, Mama—I just wanted to look at it."

"Don't bother. It would make you look cheap. It's just a sample from your *tita* Salomé's latest collection. I'm not buying this time—the design is so déclassé."

"I thought you liked Tita Salomé." Javier skewered the last sausage.

"That doesn't mean I agree with her poor taste in jewelry." Seeing the puzzled looks Amparo and Javier exchanged, Señora Concha realized she sounded unreasonably harsh. "If you want to borrow my good earrings, just ask."

"Maybe next time." Amparo sliced her egg into neat strips.

The matron looked at her two children, a vague remorse gnawing at her. All through their early years she'd been too busy attending soirees and gallery openings to pay any mind to them. Marcela had spared her the tedium of motherhood's chores—the meals, homework and mucky infections that never made for interesting dinner conversation. Now that they were nearly full-grown, she recognized the need to make up for lost time. After all, at least one of them would have to like her well enough to remain in the Guerrero home. She tried another tack.

"I asked your *tita* Carina last night about her nephew Matéo. Did you know he and his brothers speak four languages? Besides English, Vinchy's boys are fluent in French, German and Spanish."

"Make that five languages. Matéo also speaks Tagalog—," Amparo began.

"Oh, that doesn't really count. Anyway, she was delighted to hear that you and Matéo are classmates. She's throwing a party at her house next week. We're all invited and of course, so are Vinchy and his family."

"What's the occasion?" Javier asked.

"Haven't you heard?" Señora Concha smiled. "Tita Carina's engaged!"

"Women her age still get married?" Javier dropped his spoon, looking scandalized.

"*Puwede ba*, she's as old as I am—" Señora Concha caressed her cigarette lighter. "So maybe she won't be wearing white, but who says she's too old to fall in love?"

"Well, I have a paper due next week, so count me out." Javier set a rumpled napkin on the table and made to get up. "Besides, how do you know this one will stick? Hasn't she broken off three engagements?"

"So maybe she avoided three broken marriages." Señora Concha's knuckles were white around the earring she clenched. "Your *tita* Carina likes to do things in her own time. She's not as"—the matron searched for the polite word—"conventional as the rest of us."

"I'm happy for Tita Carina." Amparo stirred sugar into her coffee, trying to imagine a man who could keep up with her glamorous aunt, a gallery owner whose flamboyant show openings dominated the society pages. "I didn't even know she was dating anyone."

"They've been very discreet. She's been seeing him for years, but it took forever for Tom Di Palermo's wife to give him the divorce. He and your *tita* Carina will be married in Hong Kong before the end of the year."

"Why there?" Amparo's lips were a thin line of disappointment at wasted opportunity. "*Sayang naman*. I could have been her bridesmaid here." Carina Madrigal was her favorite aunt, the godmother who'd slipped her a glass of Prosecco on her sixteenth birthday.

"There are no bridesmaids at civil ceremonies." Señora Concha's tone was patronizing. "Until the pope recognizes divorce, they'll never be married in a Catholic church." She shrugged. "*Pués nada*. At least she can finally marry the man. He'll be a useful addition to our circle: Tom's the vice-consul at the American embassy."

"No wonder you're so excited. You're going to pump him for a ten-year multiple-entry visa, aren't you?" Javier raised his coffee cup, toasting his mother. "Mama, *talaga*. I bet you're already planning to visit Miguel in San Francisco."

"Nothing wrong with wanting to see my eldest child. If you lived abroad, wouldn't you want your mother to visit you?" Señora Concha stubbed out her cigarette in the tray. "But that's not the only reason I want to meet him. Tita Carina is like a sister to me and we should welcome her fiancé into the family. You can start by calling him Uncle Tom."

CHAPTER 9

Eve Wasn't Hungry

Carina Madrigal's engagement party was unlike any other Amparo had ever attended. Waling-waling orchids floated amid tea lights in shallow crystal bowls that adorned the dozen round tables on the hostess's sprawling lawn. A string quartet played Vivaldi's *Four Seasons* beneath a frangipani tree ablaze with fairy lights, and white-jacketed waiters wandered among the guests bearing trays of champagne and jewellike hors d'oeuvres.

"*Ay punyeta*, there go my Choos." Señora Concha cursed under her breath as her heels sank into the grass. "I've never understood Carina's obsession with garden parties."

"They're just shoes, Concha. Have the maid clean them tomorrow." Federico Guerrero cupped his wife's elbow, steering her to the end of the receiving line. He glanced over his shoulder. "Come along, Amparo. Let's meet this guy your *tita* Carina's mad for."

Teetering in her mother's stilettos and trying not to scratch at the itchy straps of her raw silk dress, Amparo wondered if she could ever be as self-assured as the glamorous women swanning around the garden, if men in sharply cut suits would ever rush to take her elbow or replenish her drinks.

The impending bride received her guests in a silvery frock, gleaming with South Sea pearls that adorned her neck and ears, freshly hennaed hair cascading over her shoulders. Women half her age would have killed to look as good as she did that night. "Concha, Fico, so glad you could come! This is Tom—" Carina smiled up at the tall gray-haired man in the rumpled *barong* standing beside her. "Finally he's going to make an honest woman of me."

"I've heard about you for years." Señora Concha extended her hand. "So nice to meet you at last."

"Do you know what you're in for?" Fico grinned at the American. "If you don't watch out, Carina could take over your embassy."

"In my dreams." Tom Di Palermo smiled. "Most of our work is so tedious I wish someone with more patience could take over."

"And I know all about patience, *no, amor?"* Carina squeezed her fiancé's beefy hand. "Did I not spend these last five years displaying the patience of a saint?"

"Patience, perhaps—but a saint? *Exagéra.*" Señora Concha cocked an eyebrow at Carina. The women were practically sisters, but their relationship was framed in the brittle veneer of rivalry. That Carina's betrothal had trumped Señora Concha's long-held advantage of marriage was a fact both women recognized, but would never discuss.

Carina turned to Amparo, who was contemplating her newly polished toenails. "*Santa Maria*, Amparo, you've grown into such a pretty young lady!" Carina chucked Amparo's chin as though she were six years old. "A little bird tells me that you and my nephew have been spending a lot of time together. Tell me, *guwapa*, is Matéo your new *novio*?"

"Of course not, Tita! Nothing's going on. We're just classmates." Amparo flushed.

"Don't embarrass Amparo with Concha's gossip. That'd be one more thing to blame on her mother." Fico slung a protective arm round his daughter's shoulder. "Not that she doesn't deserve it," he whispered.

Amparo elbowed her father's ribs, grinning.

"*Pués,* don't waste your time with us." Carina winked at her godchild. "Go find him."

While Tita Carina regaled her parents with plans of a honeymoon in Bali, Amparo wandered over to the string quartet. The cool October air bore a complex bouquet of Chanel No. 5, trampled grass and kerosene from the line of torches rimming the lawn. As she watched the elegant guests eddying around the betrothed couple, exclaiming delight in a dozen foreign accents, Amparo began to fear she was out of her depth. Middle-aged men in *Barong Tagalog* and dark suits thronged the bar, but Matéo was not among them. The women, with their glossy chignons and conspicuous jewelry, made her feel like a child in hand-me-downs.

"Some party, huh?"

Amparo turned, nearly knocking the champagne flute out of Matéo's hand. He looked uncharacteristically formal in a charcoal shirt with French cuffs and black linen trousers.

"Look at you, all dressed up." Matéo's gaze wandered over Amparo's bare collarbones, noting the subtle promise of cleavage, the narrow waist, the sheer skirt that floated just above the knee. He offered her his glass. "Have you been here long?"

"Just arrived." Amparo sipped the champagne, pretending it was something she'd done many times before. The bubbles tickled her throat and she took another gulp.

"So what do you think of Tita Carina's fiancé?" Matéo gestured at the American, trailing after Carina like a docile giraffe.

"I don't know. He's a lot older, but he seems like a nice guy." Feeling reckless, she drained the glass, tilting her head so that her hair swung below her shoulders, brushing the lilac bow that cinched the low back of her dress.

"Look around, that's the template for couples at this party: the white guys are at least a decade older than their Filipina dates."

When Matéo leaned close to whisper, Amparo took a half step

back, overwhelmed by the scent of musk. Her left heel sank into a moist spot of soil and she would have stumbled but for Matéo's steadying hand on her arm.

"You okay?"

"Why am I always off-balance around you?" Amparo tried to sound flippant as she pulled on the strap that was slipping off her shoulder. The champagne had turned her knees fluid as unset flan. "I didn't mean to finish your drink."

"I'll get us another round. Shall we?" His fingers tickled her elbow.

Amparo felt instantly more mature as she sauntered back toward the other guests, holding the champagne flute like a long-stemmed rose, level to the meridian of her heart.

"What do you know about Tita Carina's fiancé?" She steadied herself with an elbow on the bar while Matéo got her a second glass of champagne.

"My dad says he's probably CIA." Matéo took a glass of red wine from the waiter. "But he says that about everyone at the American embassy."

"So what if he's a spy? Why should it matter?" Amparo looked across the garden at the betrothed couple, encircled by laughing friends. "They're obviously in love."

"Not everyone believes in fairy tales like you do." Matéo smiled down at Amparo. "Let's go sit somewhere away from this crowd."

"Of course."

Drink in hand, Amparo followed Matéo past the blazing hem of torches and down a long flagstone-lined pathway that led to the other end of Tita Carina's estate. Here the grass narrowed to a corridor the breadth of a car, bordered on the left by crimson bougainvillea espaliered against the house's wall, and on the right by a dense thicket of bamboo, whose fronds obscured the full moon. Knee-high lanterns pooled light on either side of the path at yard-long intervals, forcing Amparo to slow down.

"Have you seen this part of Tita Carina's house?" Matéo turned to Amparo as he stepped off the last flagstone. They had arrived at the public side of the mansion, which Carina had converted into a suite of art galleries.

"Tita Carina hasn't had us over in months. She said she was going through another one of her renovating moods and didn't want to entertain until the workers were done." Up to that point, Amparo had been too busy watching each step to notice much else.

"I think the renovations were a success." Matéo raised his drink. "Look."

Amparo caught her breath, delighted. They stood on the edge of a tiled patio lit by *capiz* lamps that hung from two plumeria trees. She walked up to a familiar shale grotto on the far wall. "This used to be a fishpond—my brothers and I would catch tadpoles in it every time we came to visit," she exclaimed. "It's so much prettier now."

In place of the original plaster statue of the Virgin was a bronze Thai Buddha, who sat cross-legged and serene in the back-lit niche. A single white lotus floated in the pool below. As Amparo leaned over to touch its waxy petals, she caught the scarlet flash of a carp.

"I bet the fountain over there is new too." Matéo pointed up and beyond her left shoulder.

Halfway up the wall in the patio's left corner, water streamed from a bamboo spout, burbling down seven gradated saucers that spiraled into a Talavera basin.

"This is so lovely!" Amparo let the cool water dribble over her fingers before pressing them against her hot cheek.

"Ready for another drink?" Matéo called from the cabana set in one corner of the grotto. A creamy gauze canopy draped over the wooden crossbeam, creating the appearance of an airy tent. Amber light from a Moroccan lantern glimmered upon the daybed upon which Matéo sat. He patted the overstuffed ivory pillow beside him. "Come sit with me. Most of Tita Carina's guests are diplomats—or, as Dad calls them, professional drunks. I'm guessing dinner won't be served for at least another hour."

Amparo looked back at the torches glinting from the end of the bamboo corridor. Her aunt's party seemed miles away, its clamor hushed by the murmur of falling water. She walked to Matéo, Buddha's smile on her lips.

"Tita Carina said she wanted to create a meditation space, but I bet she uses it for smaller parties too." Matéo pointed to a mini refrigerator tucked beneath the narrow console table on which he had set his glass.

Amparo perched on the edge of the daybed, reluctant to slide back and lean against the pillows, for that would have involved shedding her shoes. She was tipsy, but had yet to reach the point of capitulation.

She looked across the patio to where wide glass sliding doors opened into the sculpture gallery. The room was dark but for one pin light trained on a nude that stood in profile, head flung back, breasts defiant, left arm reaching for the sky.

"I bet the model got the worst cramps, holding that pose." Amparo stretched her fingers up to the milky gauze and tilted her head back, miming the statue's arabesque. She dropped her arm at the sound of Matéo's chuckle.

"That piece is called *Eve Wasn't Hungry.* I heard the feminists loved it." Matéo eyed the deep scoop of Amparo's backless dress, the curve of her fingers resting lightly on the cushion next to his shin. "Tita Carina discovered the sculptor fresh out of UP's fine arts program. For the show's opening, the artist swung a fresh apple from the ceiling. The next day it was swarming with ants. Tita Carina had the sculptor make her a wooden apple instead. Like it?"

"It's beautiful, but Mama would never buy it. She thinks most nudes are too scandalous for private homes." Amparo nibbled the rim of her glass, wondering how many hours the artist's model had had to pose naked. "I never understood how my mom and Tita Carina could be best friends, they're so different."

"It just took her longer to settle down." Matéo stroked Amparo's fingertips. "I've never seen the point in rushing to marry."

"Well, people said unkind things after she left the second fiancé. I already had the flower girl's dress for that wedding. Mama let me wear it to my sixth birthday party so it wouldn't go to waste." Amparo smiled, remembering a confection of white tulle and ballerina slippers. "I'm glad Tita Carina finally found the right man."

Matéo leaned forward and tickled Amparo's bare back. "Let's not worry about her anymore. Why don't you scoot back and get comfortable?" He patted the oversized pillows against which he lounged. "Don't be afraid—I don't bite."

"You don't call either." Amparo swiveled to look at him, her knee brushing up against his ankle.

"You could have called me. Girls call boys all the time in Europe."

"This isn't Europe." Amparo drained her glass. "We do things differently here."

"Then maybe you should teach me." With one deft movement, Matéo slid forward, coming abreast of her. He took Amparo's empty glass and set it on the table, then stretched an arm behind her.

Floating in a heady, alcohol-induced languor, Amparo gazed upon Matéo's blond-tipped eyelashes, the clean sweep of his jaw, the dimples indenting his cheeks. "I think you know enough tricks to get by."

"And which one should I try on you?" Matéo was so close now that Amparo felt his breath on her cheeks.

Amparo opened her mouth to reply but was cut off by a kiss, a kiss that, to her surprise, she was unwilling to interrupt with words. Matéo moved with practiced ease, unhooking, unzipping, unraveling restraint, seducing his Eve beneath the gaze of Buddha, God of second chances.

Chapter 10

Siblings

The second sandal was dangling from Amparo's toes when a woman's giggle caused her to stiffen and pull away. "Who was that?"

"Merde." Matéo rolled off Amparo and straightened his shirt, pulling the front of it out farther so that it hung loosely over his hips, obscuring the bulge that subsided with excruciating slowness beneath his belt.

In a panic, Amparo fumbled with her zipper and shrugged dress straps back in place, her left foot searching the floor for its shoe.

"So this is where you've been hiding." The speaker was a stocky man who stood on the edge of the flagstones, arm in arm with his tittering companion. A meticulously trimmed Vandyke framed full lips, parted now in a smile that did not rise to predatory eyes. "I wanted to show Roxanne the meditation garden." The man tried to see behind Matéo. "But maybe you've been doing more than just meditating, eh, 'Téo?"

Amparo slipped her foot into the sandal just as Matéo turned to introduce her.

"Amparo, come meet my oldest brother." Matéo stared at his brother, refusing to be embarrassed. "You can call him Dick."

"Nice to meet you, Di—"

"I prefer Richard." Matéo's brother shook Amparo's hand, his gaze lingering over her wrinkled skirt. Straightening up, Richard smirked at his younger brother, muttering in French, *"That the new flavor of the month?"*

"There you go again, Richard, showing off your foreign languages. It's too sexy." Richard's date wedged a thumb into her skin-tight bustier, yanking it up over flesh that had muffin-topped beneath her armpit. "What did you just say?"

"Nothing. I was applauding his taste in women." Richard leered at Amparo, ignoring the flush that darkened Matéo's face.

"I thought so!" Roxanne winked at Matéo. "Aren't you going to return the compliment?"

"Of course." Matéo contemplated the large silver hoops peeking out of Roxanne's Farrah fringe, her talonlike coral nails, knees dimpling five inches below the hem of her purple taffeta mini. "Richard's taste in women has always been"—he sighed—"exceptional."

Roxanne giggled, lurching slightly against Richard.

"You'll have to excuse Roxanne, she never lets a bar go unattended." Richard squeezed her shoulder. "Tita Carina sent us to find you because they've begun serving dinner. Dad and Chantal are holding a table for us." Richard turned back to the flagstone path, his thick fingers enclosing Roxanne's nape. "*On y va.* Let's go."

"Who's Chantal?" Amparo whispered, as she and Matéo followed the couple back to the party.

"My mom. Dick was thirteen when his mom died and he never forgave Dad for remarrying."

After the patio's calm, the party seemed almost cacophonous, with the quartet's Mozartquartet providing a restless cadence for the prattle of a hundred guests. A troupe of waiters pirouetted around each table, balancing wheel-sized trays of food. Tita Carina stood by the bar with her fourth martini, opening and shutting her Spanish fan as though conducting a personal orchestra. "There you are, you young people! Richard, your table is the one closest to the cellist."

She tapped Amparo's shoulder with the fan as her niece walked by. "Hold on a minute, *hija.* Your dress needs fixing." She leaned over to reattach the bow, which had fallen off its hook on the back of Amparo's dress. "Every detail counts, *guwapa*: I want you to look perfect when you meet the parents." Carina squeezed Amparo's elbow. "Go. Make your godmother proud."

Señora Concha and her husband were chatting with another couple and Amparo waved at them as she walked by. She caught up with Matéo and the others as they reached the farthest table, where a man in a *jusi barong* was sipping scotch beside a woman with hair the color of butter.

The woman looked up as they approached, her face breaking into a smile identical to Matéo's. "*Voilà, mon fils!* We thought you had left the party, Matéo—you just disappeared."

"I was showing Amparo the new meditation garden." Matéo put his hand on Amparo's back, nudging her gently forward. "*Maman*, Dad, this is Amparo Guerrero. Tita Carina and Amparo's mom are old friends."

"You're Concha's daughter? I've known your mother since she was a teenager!" Matéo's father set down his whiskey tumbler, rubbing moist fingers on a napkin. "I took her out once or twice, before Fico stole her from us all. Good to meet you, *hija.*"

Mr. Madrigal stood, reaching over his wife's leonine tresses to shake Amparo's hand.

"I've always been curious about Vinchy's childhood. It's amazing how many of his old girlfriends we've run into since we moved to Manila." Chantal Madrigal tapped the chair next to hers. "Have a seat, you must be famished."

Amparo sat down, smiling shyly at his mother. She noticed that Richard and his date had taken seats directly opposite his parents, even though the two seats beside Ambassador Madrigal remained unoccupied. As the evening progressed, Amparo noticed that conversation in the Madrigal family operated on two levels: benign chitchat and pugnacious sparring. Matéo's parents excelled at the former, keeping up a constant patter with the Galician couple from the Spanish embassy, who claimed the last seats at their table. While the older couples traded anecdotes on expatriate life, Matéo and Richard kept up a desultory conversation.

"So, Amparo. How did you like Tita Carina's meditation garden?" Richard's lips spread tight across his large teeth in a wolverine grin that unnerved Amparo.

"Oh, it's beautiful, of course. My brothers and I played there when we were little, and Matéo showed me all the changes Tita Carina made: the fountain, the Buddha . . . that cabana. . . ." Amparo paused, blushing. She hadn't intended to give Richard another chance to taunt his younger brother.

"Don't be fooled by Matéo's charm, Amparo. He can be quite fickle when it comes to his interests." Richard held up his empty wineglass, index finger raised to hail a waiter walking by.

Amparo noticed Matéo crosshatching the tablecloth with the tip of his butter knife and realized it was time to redirect the conversation. She'd seen Tita Carina do the same thing whenever the dinner chatter turned peevish. "Don't you have another brother? Where is he?"

"Last I heard, Luca was somewhere in Mexico, learning Nahuatl on a postdoc." Richard watched the waiter refill his wine goblet. "He's the intellectual among the three of us, a professional student. With Matéo still at university, I'm the only one helping Dad with his campaign."

Matéo's reply was interrupted by a shriek two tables away. Even the musicians squeaked to a halt as Señora Concha got up so quickly she overturned her chair. The target of her fury was a slender waitress clutching a tray smeared with syrup from mango crepes that now lay upon the grass between them.

"How could you be so clumsy? This is a Halston!" Amparo's mother dabbed at a claret stain that spread across her cream halter like a stab wound. "I didn't want dessert, I asked for coffee! *Santa santisima,* don't you people ever listen?"

"Excuse me, I need to help Mama." Amparo hurried to her parents' table.

Carina Madrigal got there ahead of her. "Concha, I'm so sorry! How did it happen?"

"This idiot was serving dessert and jostled me just as I was sipping my wine." Señora Concha scowled at the cowering waitress. "Didn't you know you're supposed to serve from the left and take away from the right? *Baliktad ka kase!* You did it the other way around." Señora Concha demanded the waitress's name. *"Sino ka ba?"*

Amparo took her mother's arm. "Ma, you're scaring her."

"Good!" Señora Concha shook off her daughter's hand and repeated the question. *"Ano'ng pangalan mo?"*

"Beverly *po.* Beverly Obejas." She hung her head, displaying a prominent widow's peak that marked all the women in Señora Concha's family. The coincidence only fueled Señora Concha's rage. "What kind of name is that?" She sneered. "Beverly like the *Hills*? Your mother had some imagination."

Beverly's dark brown hair was pulled back in a tight bun; it quivered now with each silent sob. The headwaiter approached Beverly, but even he froze under Señora Concha's glare.

"Fire her." Carina Madrigal snapped her fingers at the headwaiter. "I won't tolerate incompetent servers at my party."

"But, Tita, it was just an accident—" Amparo began, but was immediately silenced by her mother's thunderous look.

"Carina *naman,*" Fico Guerrero spoke up. "It's just a dress, nothing worth losing a job over."

"Easy for you to say," his wife hissed.

"It wouldn't kill you to be the bigger person, Concha." Fico lowered his voice, jerking his head in the direction of the other guests. "Consider how bad it looks. Not everyone grew up with servants."

Señora Concha glanced around, suddenly realizing that a large contingent of the expatriate community and many prominent Manila hostesses were staring, transfixed. Lifting her chin, she shrugged. "Fine. Don't fire her. But send her home. I don't want to see her face again tonight."

Smiling for the sake of the other guests but murmuring in her native Ilonggo, Carina Madrigal sent the headwaiter off with a honeyed threat. "Expect the dry-cleaning bill for Mrs. Guerrero's dress next week. Make sure you take it out of that girl's pay."

Cradling Señora Concha's elbow, she cajoled her friend. "Come. Let's get you into a new outfit. We still wear the same size, don't we? You're going to *love* the Chanel knockoff I bought in Hong Kong last month."

As Señora Concha stalked back to the house, Carina Madrigal turned and nodded at the string quartet to resume playing. Spreading her arms with a magician's flourish, she flashed a brilliant smile at her other guests. "Everybody, get your toasts ready. When we return, I'm breaking out the Dom Pérignon!"

Chapter 11

Beverly

While Carina Madrigal's guests polished off their mango crepes, Beverly Obejas took her leave of Voltaire Solito, Carina Madrigal's caterer. They stood by the kitchen sink, amid a constant stream of waiters emptying and replenishing their trays.

"*Ay naku,* darling—why are you crying *pa*? *Tigilan mo na 'yan.* Stop already. You may be a waitress, but you're as pretty as any of those women outside. *A ver—*" He lifted Beverly's chin with a finger and assessed her tearful face. "Look at that widow's peak, that pale skin. In better clothes you could pass for Señora Concha's daughter."

This brought forth a fresh stream of tears from Beverly, who was unaccustomed to compliments. Voltaire fluttered his fingers to shoo away the eavesdropping dishwasher. Lowering his voice, the caterer continued, "*Sa totoo lang*—to be totally honest, I would have fired you if you were ugly."

The caterer held Beverly's uniform neatly over one forearm and waved his free hand like a traffic policeman, directing servers to the rows of champagne flutes waiting to be carted out with chilled bottles of bubbly. Turning back to Beverly, he grimaced at the waitress's appalling lack of style: a chartreuse fake La Coste T-shirt turned her skin sallow; unhemmed acid-washed jeans pooled around dirty clogs. Such a waste. Voltaire considered Beverly a diamond in the rough, with her heart-shaped face, large brown elvish eyes and straight nose. If Voltaire had met her at eighteen, he could have conjured a beauty queen makeover, a personal hobby of his that had yielded a few finalists and one Miss Philippines World. Unfortunately Beverly was twenty-four and too old to compete; she would never be more than an attractive waitress.

"Beverly, *palangga*, did you hear me? Your job is safe. I can't afford to fire you because pretty waitresses are so hard to come by these days. Girls with half your looks just want to be Japayukis in Tokyo. Lucky for me, you can't sing or dance to save your life. So, enough *na*. No more crying over spilled wine."

"*Opo, Kuya* Voltaire." Beverly balled up the soggy tissue in her fist, trying not to gawk at the wad of money Voltaire pulled out of his clutch bag. The caterer always paid his employees in cash, knowing they would spend their meager earnings almost immediately on food, beer or cigarettes.

He calculated her wages, deducted half in anticipation of Señora Concha's dry-cleaning expenses and handed her a few bills. "*Ayan*. Here you go. You understand, even though I'm not firing you, I can't call you for any more parties until December. The ladies need time to forget."

"*Opo, Kuya* Voltaire." Beverly nodded, staring at the caterer's patent leather shoes. "Sorry again, *po*."

"*Sige na.*" Voltaire dismissed her with a quick nod, frowning at a speck of tomato sauce on the cuff of his *barong*. "The manager at Ma Mon Luk owes me a favor. I'll ask him to put you on double shifts at the restaurant through November. Slinging pork buns is not as glamorous as serving pâté, but at least you won't go hungry. I'll call you when office Christmas party season gets going in December."

"*Kuya* Voltaire, Señora Carina wants you outside," a waiter called from the door. "The chocolate fountain is clogged."

As the caterer hurried off to his next crisis, another waiter slipped Beverly a plastic bag filled with leftover paella. "Voltaire said you can't have a share of tonight's tips, but at least you'll eat as well as those bitches."

"Salamat naman." Beverly smiled her thanks, tucking the food into her pleather purse.

Laughter and applause faded in the background as she trudged down the circular driveway and out the gate held ajar by the uniformed security guard. The wide avenues were dark but for lamplit corners every twenty yards. Walking past each mansion, Beverly wondered which one housed her godmother. If she only knew where *Ninang* 'Cela worked, she could have at least sought out a sympathetic ear, perhaps a cup of ginger tea to take the sting off her humiliation. Instead she swallowed her misery and hiked fifteen blocks past estates as grand as the one she'd left, the Manila Polo Club, and the Santuario de San Antonio before reaching the freeway where she could catch a bus back to Cubao.

At the corner of McKinley Road and Epifanio de los Santos Avenue Beverly joined a less elegant assemblage of people: clutches of chattering shopgirls, newly released from department store jobs; office boys scratching at the collars of their rumpled button-down shirts; and urchins selling waxy garlands of sampaguita, the blooms' cloying scent muted by diesel fumes. Clenching her shoulder bag, the waitress squinted at the hundred-eyed beast of Manila traffic, searching for a ride home. Cars, trucks and buses hurtled down the highway, their drivers chiding or challenging one another with horn blasts and sudden swerves. Some commuters danced a two-step in the bus lane, hopping back scant seconds before being run over, but Beverly stayed well clear of the sidewalk's edge. It was a caution she'd adopted after her mother's death.

Just then, a blue air-conditioned bus careened to a halt a hundred yards beyond its designated stop, drawing hordes from the curb like metal filings to a magnet. Beverly took one look at the people cramming into the narrow door and decided to wait for the next bus. The last thing she wanted was to stand through the ride to Cubao, lurching against a wall of bodies.

Not long after, an un-air-conditioned bus screeched to a halt within sprinting distance. Ducking under the pungent armpit of the conductor hanging from its accordion door, Beverly scrambled in ahead of everyone else.

"O Cubao, Crossing, Aurora, Monumentoooo, sakay na!" The conductor hawked the bus's destinations, ushering passengers on board. Beverly found an empty spot beside a window, pouting at the crude heart scratched into the wooden seat frame in front of her that declared *JAYJAY LOVES JEMMA*. In her despair, even graffiti made her feel excluded.

The conductor rapped on the side of the bus and it lunged forward. A breeze gusted nonstop through glass-free windows, sweeping away her tears, replacing them with soot. Beverly sighed, already dreading her monthlong exile from Forbes Park.

Beverly lived for Voltaire's events, which allowed her access to a parallel universe that was cleaner and more fragrant than her own. She would carry her tray across marble floors or manicured lawns, bedazzled by ivory-skinned ladies in shimmering frocks and languid men whose hands looked smoother than her own. When no one was looking, she would sneak a taste of their rich food and during slack moments, she pretended to be one of the glitterati, humming along to melodies never heard on a public bus. It was like acting a minor role in a movie: Beverly was an extra who dreamed of being the star.

Resenting the sudden end to this glamorous fantasy, Beverly glowered at the plebeian landscape of her real life. Gray concrete office buildings and gap-toothed neon signs lined the sides of the freeway like mah-jongg tiles, squeezed more tightly together the closer they got to Pasig River, which marked the end of Makati. Beyond the bridge rose a gaudy forest of billboards touting poultry feed, soft drinks and skintight jeans. Bile rose in Beverly's throat as the bus carried her up the hill, speeding beneath a row of denim-clad buttocks. It would be another month before she could return to that wealthier, happier world on the far side of the river.

Minutes later, the bus swerved to a stop in front of a mall, cutting off a car whose driver responded with a tirade of beeps. The noise jolted Beverly from her reverie. Hooking fingers on the rusted iron railing, she gaped at the sleek brick of a building whose windowless walls contained innumerable shops, food courts and a basement video arcade: an amusement park for consumers. Beverly repressed the urge to hop off the bus. She couldn't afford to squander her diminished wages, for Ma Mon Luk's manager underpaid his waiters, and his patrons were niggardly with tips.

A dozen gray-faced commuters clomped down the bus aisle and a large woman squeezed in beside Beverly, sealing off escape. The greasy odor of cheeseburgers filled Beverly's nostrils as the woman rolled open a paper bag and unwrapped a half-eaten quarter-pounder. Beverly looked out the window, dreaming of the paella in her purse.

Some time later, Beverly got off at Aurora Boulevard, zigzagging between other buses and taxis that barely paused or pulled over before regurgitating their passengers. She flagged down a jeepney that looked like it could squeeze in one more person. Stooping chest to knee, she stepped into the jeep's tight aisle, which was hemmed in on both sides by the shins of other commuters. Taking care not to trample toes, Beverly ran her fingers along the jeep's low ceiling to keep balance until she found an empty spot directly behind the driver.

GOD KNOWS JUDAS NOT PAY proclaimed a laminated card dangling from the rearview mirror. Ignoring the tired pun, Beverly passed her fare to the boy beside the driver, who counted out her change from the cashbox on his lap. A Santo Niño statuette bobbled on springs atop a dashboard upholstered in scarlet fur as the jeep began its herky-jerky route through Cubao. Beverly's eyes welled up again, irritated by smoke from the driver's cigarette.

"*'Wag kang iiyak, papangit ka*—don't cry, or you'll get ugly," teased the drunk sitting across from her, but his eyes were fixed on her chest. Biting back a retort, Beverly kept her eyes on the road and counted down the city blocks till they reached her stop at New York Avenue.

One tricycle ride later, Beverly walked down a dim alley silvered with snail trails and ripe with the odor of moldering garbage. Rutting cats yowled from the neighbor's tin roof, wailing like abandoned children. Tears prickled Beverly's eyelids as she remembered the perfume of night-blooming *dama de noche* and the silken shushing of wind through acacia boughs in wealthier homes. She knew full well the rich were different, but did even flowers know this? Did cats?

It was past eleven o'clock, but a silver flicker through the curtains meant her landlord was watching TV in the living room. *Manang* Charing was a widowed mail clerk who had begun renting out her spare room to bedspacers after her two sons left to join the construction boom in Dubai. Beverly shared the room with Nelia, a second-year nursing student who monopolized the single desk that separated their iron cots.

Beverly noticed the lamp was still on in their second-floor bedroom. Exam week. Turning the key, she lifted the knob to release the misaligned dead bolt and pushed, only to be foiled by the chain lock. Sighing in exasperation, she leaned her forehead on the door. "*Manang* Charing, it's me, Beverly."

"*'Tay muna.* Wait." Manang Charing unhooked the chain, then opened the door wide. She nodded a greeting at her second bedspacer, her round face framed by its nocturnal helmet of pink curlers, threadbare housedress dimpling at the navel. "*Naku naman*, Beverly, it's practically midnight. What were you doing out so late?"

"Sorry *po.* I waitressed at a catered party in Forbes Park." Beverly froze as the words left her mouth, realizing she had trapped herself. Manang Charing knew she usually brought home leftovers and would expect to share her precious paella. Beverly couldn't aggravate someone who charged so little rent, but she was not feeling generous that night.

"*Siya nga?* Is that right?" Tattooed sable eyebrows rose on Manang Charing's pale forehead, and thin lips curled into her jowls, giving her the appearance of a grinning sow. "And what treats did Voltaire give you this time?"

"Just rice. The guests ate everything else." Beverly feigned indifference, but her stomach growled as she trudged to the kitchen, landlady waddling close behind. "I need a drink before going to bed."

"Go ahead, water is cheap." Manang Charing drummed the faded oilcloth on the kitchen table with her stubby fingers, calling Beverly's bluff. "Don't bring that glass upstairs."

At that moment, a thumb-sized brown cockroach crept out from behind the jar of turbid corn oil on the counter beside the stove. Manang Charing picked up her rubber slipper and nailed the insect as it scurried across the cracked tile. Brushing the flattened roach to the floor, she turned back to Beverly. "We're out of Raid. I'll get more after you and Nelia pay next month's rent. Until then, remember my rule about no food on the second floor."

"*Opo*, Manang." Beverly took a tumbler from the cupboard and filled it with tap water. Searching for a way to rid herself of the old woman, she glanced at the wall clock. "*Naku*, it's eleven thirty already! Don't let me keep you, *Manang*, you may not wake up in time for your early-morning mass. *Sige na*, we're both home now. You can stop worrying and go to bed." Beverly faked a yawn, knuckles white against the shoulder bag concealing her dinner.

Manang Charing was thinking of a rejoinder when the variety show's closing theme song started up. "You're right. We all need our beauty sleep, don't we? Make sure you wash that glass." She shuffled back to the sala to switch off the TV, her broad rump jiggling under the orange duster.

Beverly waited for the bedroom door to creak shut before undoing the knot on her plastic bag. Slipping a spoon from the drawer, she ate straight out of the bag, not bothering to sit down. The paella had grown cold during the hour-long commute, but she was afraid that reheating it would rouse her landlord and roommate with the scent of saffron. It had been a difficult night and she refused to share her solace.

When she was done eating, she tiptoed upstairs and hoped her roommate would be too busy studying to want more than minimal chitchat. Nelia lay snoring on her bed, an anatomy textbook tenting her flat chest.

Beverly opened the closet at the foot of her bed, stepping out of her clogs. "Hello, Ma." She smiled at the faded baby picture set eye-level on a shelf that held her undergarments. The photo had been taken around her first birthday: Beverly in a frothy pink dress, perched on her mother's lap, both of them smiling at the photographer. *Clara and Beverly, 1964* was scrawled across the bottom of the yellowing margin.

Beverly reminded herself to ask her godmother about All Souls' when they met at Megamall the following afternoon. It was the tenth anniversary of her mother's death and she wanted to spend the day with Ninang Marcela by her mother's grave.

Marcela was pacing in front of the fast-food restaurant's bumblebee mascot when Beverly arrived at the mall. She lifted her cheek for a kiss, and smiled at her lissome niece. "Look at that face. Every day you look more and more like your mother. If only I had kept my looks, I could have passed you off as my sister in Banate." She laughed at her own joke, smoothing down the knit blouse that kept rolling up over her haunches. At forty, the spinster's figure had filled out to approximate that of a woman who'd had multiple pregnancies. Twenty years of hunching over stoves and hefting large pots had rounded Marcela's shoulders and thickened the arms. Nothing in Marcela's appearance reminded Beverly of her mother, but she loved her aunt with the ferocity of an orphan.

"*Kumusta na,* Ninang 'Cela?" Beverly linked arms with her godmother, asking how she was, even though she already knew the answer.

"*Okay lang*." Marcela was so even-tempered that her days seemed to be an endless succession of "just okay." Apart from her job, the cook's only concern was the niece whom she had mothered since Clara's death. "What about you, *anak*? You look like you haven't been getting enough sleep. Why the eye bags?"

"Voltaire had me do another catering job last night in Forbes Park." Beverly steered the older woman around torrents of shoppers as they strolled down the mall's avenue of boutiques. Mall Muzak blurred the yammer of a thousand other conversations, its bland melodies interrupted every few yards by Madonna tunes blaring from individual boutiques.

Beverly tilted her head toward her aunt. "You see, if only you'd told me which house in Forbes Park you worked at, I could have visited you on the way home."

Marcela dismissed the topic they'd debated for so many years that it had evolved into a running joke. "Stop needling me, I don't know why you think I'll ever tell you. It doesn't matter where I work."

"So then why won't you tell me?" Beverly had always resented her aunt's inexplicable reticence.

"Because my employers are very private people. They asked me not to discuss my job outside of their home and I must respect their wishes." Marcela pulled out her trump card. "If they'd fired me, how could I have supported you after your mother died?"

Marcela referred to her dead sister whenever she wanted to shut down an argument. Clara's death had been so sudden, so unspeakably violent, that mentioning it never failed to divert the conversation.

"I'm not ungrateful, Ninang." Beverly pouted at her godmother, picking at ragged cuticles. "I just wanted to see you last night."

Marcela stroked her niece's arm. "*Naku,* those fancy parties always go on past midnight. Even if you knew where I was, it would have been too late for you to stop by afterwards."

Beverly pulled her aunt to the side, distracted by an elaborate window display. Tinfoil stars and crepe streamers hung above three mannequins in jewel-toned dresses who stared blankly at her, as though she'd interrupted a cocktail party. "Actually, Voltaire sent me home early. I had an accident."

"Did you hurt yourself?" Marcela clutched her goddaughter's hand, forcing Beverly to look at her. "Tell me what happened."

"I spilled some wine on a guest. Someone named Señora Concha. She wanted Voltaire to fire me, but he said I was too good-looking to let go." Beverly shrugged, still skeptical of her good luck. "He likes pretty servers."

"Did you say Señora Concha?" Marcela's eyes widened, but she was careful to keep her voice even. "What did she look like?"

"I don't know, she was yelling at me in front of all the guests and I was afraid to look at her." Beverly rubbed her forehead, still smarting from the humiliation. "I wanted to disappear.

"Voltaire was trying to console me, so he said I looked like Señora Concha because our foreheads were shaped the same way." She traced a finger along her widow's peak. "Isn't that funny? What do you think—if I bought that dress, could I pass for a rich señorita?" She pointed at the mannequin in a claret confection, its diaphanous overskirt shimmering with bugle beads. Pressing her fingers against the glass, she tried to imagine herself in the dress, missing the look of dismay that crossed her godmother's face.

"Did she lay a hand on you?" Marcela whispered.

"No. She was too upset about her dress to slap me." Beverly glanced at her godmother. "Why—you know who she is?"

"She has visited the family I work for. A real witch—but the daughter is a sweetheart." Marcela stepped back from the window, rubbing sweaty palms on her skirt.

"That must have been the girl who came up to us. She tried to save my job." Beverly tore herself away from the window and caught up with her aunt.

"Lucky you didn't get fired." Marcela squeezed Beverly's shoulder. "You should thank your mother for giving you a pretty face."

"How do you know my father wasn't handsome too?" Beverly teased, knowing that her godmother would never take the bait. Her father was another topic Ninang Marcela refused to discuss.

"I can't remember. He died before you were born."

Beverly shrugged, knowing there was no point pursuing that mystery either. Both her mother and her aunt had been so tight-lipped about her father that one would think Clara had been blessed with an immaculate conception. "So can you come with me to Mama's grave? All Souls' falls on Tuesday this year, but maybe you can ask your *amo* for extra time off. Just tell her it's Mama's tenth-year death anniversary."

"Don't you think I know that?" Marcela sighed. She led Beverly to a vendor selling freshly baked *ube ensaymada*, which had been Clara's favorite snack. Marcela bought two and peeled back the wax paper on hers, inhaling the aroma of whipped butter. These *ensaymada* were a step up from the cheaper buns slathered with salty margarine that Clara used to buy from the corner bakery. "Too bad we don't have hot chocolate to dip this in."

"But you haven't answered my question, Ninang. Can you come with me to the cemetery?" Beverly swiped a fingertip into the sugared butter and sucked on it. When she was little, her mother would cut the bun in half and let her pinch out the swirls of purple yam.

The memory made it hard for Beverly to eat, and she put the bun back in its paper bag.

"I can take the afternoon off, but not the entire day."

"Then you can catch up with me there. I'll buy *siopao* from Ma Mon Luk and we can have a picnic after cleaning the grave, just like all the other families. Mama would like that." Beverly looked across the aisle at the department store display of silk flowers. "I'll save all my tips these next two weeks and buy fresh flowers too. Mama loved flowers."

Marcela turned her back on the gilded buckets of fake orchids and poinsettias, crushing the *ensaymada* in her fist. Clara had been shopping for plants the day she died.

CHAPTER 12

Araw ng Patay—Day of the Dead, November 1978

A decade had passed since her older sister's death, but as she stood now in the mall, remembering that horrific day, she could not help raising a hand to her mouth as though to stifle the scream that escaped it when she first saw her sister's mangled body.

But up until Clara's accident, the Obejas sisters had never celebrated the Day of the Dead in the traditional manner. While Doña Lupita reluctantly dragged her family to Manila North Cemetery along with thousands of other Manileños to commemorate their deceased loved ones, Clara and Marcela occupied themselves with an entirely different celebration, for they had no graves to visit. Four years earlier, stormy seas off the southern island of *Maestro de Campo* had swallowed their parents, along with the *MV Mactan*'s entire cargo of lumber and bananas. When it became clear the bodies of Fortunato and Consolacion Obejas would never be recovered, the sisters had spurned tradition and spent the holiday organizing a party for Clara's only child, who had crowned in the final minutes of November 1, 1963, foiling the midwife's valiant efforts to delay the birth.

Marcela remembered, with a bitter smile, how the midwife had insisted her sister hold off pushing, hoping in vain to prolong her labor. Despite her best efforts, the baby had slipped out anyway.

"*Naku, anong malas*—what bad luck to be born on the Day of the Dead," 'Nay Socorro muttered, as she cut the mewling infant's umbilical cord.

"Nonsense. I will name her Beverly, like the hills where American movie actors live." Clara whispered into her baby's damp fontanel, "Your life will be better than mine."

Marcela remembered hugging her sister as much to congratulate her as to defy the midwife's warning, which had chilled her heart.

To her dismay, Marcela soon realized that the niggardly amount that Doña Lupita had her deliver to Clara each month was insufficient to keep the child housed, fed and educated. In keeping with a covenant forged years ago, she insisted Clara avoid seeking work as a servant and instead take on a job as a salesgirl.

Even though Clara no longer asked about Aldo, Marcela now and then came across signs that her sister still savored the scraps of news that came her way. When Concha had been married in an elaborate society wedding, Marcela had arrived at Clara's small apartment to find the Sunday paper open to the full-spread photo coverage of the event. As her two-year-old daughter toddled about the kitchen, Clara sheepishly explained how she'd looked in vain for his face in photos of the bridal entourage only to read that the bride's only brother had been too busy with graduate school in California to attend the wedding. Over the years, despite Marcela's silent disapproval, Clara had maintained her abiding fascination, which frequently turned nostalgic around Beverly's birthday.

Unable to dissuade Clara from such an unhealthy interest, Marcela had devoted herself to her niece, who by her fifteenth birthday had grown into an unusually pretty teenager. Never mind that she was technically a bastard, for Beverly had been blessed with her mother's up-slanted almond eyes and the Castilian pallor of ancestors on both sides. Beverly had inherited her father's height; she would be just tall enough now for him to kiss her forehead without stooping.

Beverly, for her part, had always believed that she owed her looks entirely to her mother, whom she considered as pretty as a movie star. On the eve of Beverly's fifteenth birthday, her mother had come home from work flashing a movie star smile, for she suddenly had more than just her daughter's birthday to celebrate. When Beverly opened the door of their tiny apartment, she found her mother balancing a boxed cake in one hand and a bag of groceries in the other.

"*Anak*, I have some good news."

Beverly happily relieved her mother of the cake. "A Goldilocks cake? Did you get your bonus early this year?"

"Better." Clara beamed at her daughter.

Clara had spent years tossing boxes down a chute at Grace Shoes in response to the cryptic merchandise codes yelled into the PA system by sales associates on the floor below.

"Oy Miss Clara, MarikinaShoeExpo Model PF1763 patent red stiletto, size 6plus6andahalf *nga!"* Each announcement triggered a frenzied hunt for the requested shoe. Salesgirls working the floor lorded it over stock clerks, and Clara hated the imperious voices nearly as much as the dusty storeroom in which she toiled.

"You know that Bingbing Banson? I could never tell if she was saying *P* or *F* when she called out the codes. Mr. Tan shouldn't have hired a Pampangueña." Clara set the grocery bag on the kitchen table. "Well, today Miss Bingbing was flirting with a customer and didn't look up when Susana dropped a box down the chute. Size ten wood wedges—bull's-eye on Bingbing's cowlick. Knocked her out cold."

Beverly gasped. "Did she die?"

"No, but she had to go on sick leave—the boss said she suffered a concussion. When they cleaned out her locker, they found a pair of silver T-straps with the price tag still attached."

Beverly's eyes grew round. "Bingbing stole them?"

"They suspect so. But that's not all. This happened just before the lunchtime rush hour and they were short one salesgirl." A wide grin lit up Clara's face. "Since I was the only one who knew the codes, the manager asked me to fill in for Bingbing." Clara shook her head, still dazed by her good luck. "Can you believe it—I got to work the PA system all day! Mr. Tan liked my pronunciation so much that he promised to move me to sales."

"You were promoted?" Beverly bounced on her heels, and would have tripped on the uneven floorboards had her mother not caught her in time.

Clara smoothed a lock of hair off Beverly's forehead. "By November two I will be a salesgirl on the main floor."

"With the pretty blue uniform? Wow!" Beverly hugged her mother, inhaling Nenuco, a Spanish cologne that Clara had splurged on. Her mother already smelled like success.

"Tomorrow we'll have a double celebration: my promotion and your birthday."

"Can we ask Ninang 'Cela to make spaghetti for long life?" Beverly said.

"Yes, of course." Clara gazed at their sparsely furnished apartment, remembering the gilt-framed paintings and brocade furniture of the home in which she'd worked as a maid so many years ago. Remembering how her toes had curled when she had first stepped barefoot upon those pristine marble floors, she grimaced now at their apartment's scuffed linoleum. "I think it's time we decorate this place."

She glanced at the single window, bare but for thin curtains she'd sewn herself. "That spot could use a tall houseplant." She recalled the palm trees that framed the entrance to her employer's dining room, behind which she had sometimes been pulled for a quick kiss. The memory brought a wistful smile to her face.

"We're lucky the store is closed for *Araw ng Patay*—we get to spend your whole birthday together. What if we buy a plant in the morning and ask your *ninang* 'Cela to cook something special for your birthday dinner?"

"Anything you want, Ma." Beverly smiled. "This will be my best birthday ever."

The next day, while others decorated family gravestones and filled the November air with the drone of novenas, Clara and Beverly wandered through a makeshift garden rimmed by shanties along the West Bicutan railway. The cheapest plants could be found at these ragtag nurseries, which backed all the way up to the tracks, their ornamental grasses and potted ferns flicking at commuter trains with jaded tendrils. Clara was determined to find a palm tree like those in the mansion where she had worked so long ago, wanting to offer her child the one signifier of wealth she could afford. Unaware of her mother's quest, Beverly grew restless after the first half hour. In the distance she heard the tinkle of shells and a contrapuntal clip-clop of bamboo. "Ma, there's a store that sells wind chimes up ahead. Can I wait for you there?"

Clara peered at her daughter through the fronds of an areca palm and waved. "*O sige*, but make sure you don't go any further." She noticed a larger tree in the row closest to the tracks. "Manang Geny, *magkano dito?*" she asked for the plant's price, poised to haggle.

"Three hundred, best price!" Manang Geny, owner and namesake of the improbably named Genoveva's Green Acres, emerged from a thicket of *azucena* spikes, her gaunt face stretching into a professional smile. Twenty years in this business and she knew all the bargaining ploys. Pretty women were the worst: they were used to getting what they wanted.

"Can you do better than that? *Buena mano naman*," Clara wheedled, hoping Manang Geny would accept a lower price on her first sale to ensure good luck the rest of the day.

"You can have a smaller one for a hundred fifty. *'Tay muna*—wait. My son will bring it out." The skeletal woman waved at a man smoking by a shanty on the edge of her garden.

Clara nodded her head, pouting. For such a discount she would wait for the palm to grow to the size of the one beneath which she had enjoyed her first kiss. The sudden memory of illicit caresses made her blush. Over the years other suitors had come along, but only the first had set her heart pounding with frantic exhilaration, as though joy and terror could not be contained in one bosom. Clara ran her fingers along one slim green spear, remembering a Beatles tune he used to sing to her. After over fifteen years, she could really only recall the chorus: "I wanna hold your hand . . ."

The roar of traffic seemed uncommonly loud that morning, but Clara ignored it, lost in wistful daydreams of her first, most profound love. Suddenly a whirring bullet of a bug zoomed up from the greenery: an irate *salagubang* as thick as her thumb hovered inches from her nose. Clara scrambled backward to avoid the beetle, her sandals slipping on the slick soil. Letting out an embarrassed giggle, she grabbed the nearest tree to steady herself, but this threw her even further off-balance, the mess of green limbs thrashing across her face, its plastic pot tipping over the thrumming tracks. The train approached with lethal swiftness, but Clara saw only the clear blue sky through palm fronds, her mind brimming with memories of first love and Beatles songs, as she fell backward upon the tracks.

Her scream had no time to escape before PNR Train #817 crushed Clara's throat entirely, dragging her body and the palm she clutched another fifty feet before it shrieked to a halt in front of Jhefferson Air Play. Beverly was stroking a row of brass wind chimes at that store when she heard a chorus of screams above the screeching lament of brakes. A cadaverous woman ran to the front of the train, pointing at something by the tracks.

"*Sino 'yan, sinong' nasagasaan?* Who was hit?" Jhefferson himself bolted past Beverly, the lavender bandanna flying off his forehead as he ran to meet Manang Geny. Beverly wandered up to the tracks, curious to see what the half-dozen men and women were huddling over. She pushed into the crowd and saw a familiar pair of scuffed sandals, slender fingers tinted the same shade of pink she wore on her nails. What remained after the train was done with Clara Obejas.

The first unbelieving wail was hers, but Beverly after that surrendered everything else to a world with which she had lost all connection: her knees to the mud, her tears to crumpled palm fronds, her hands to the arm that had not been severed. When Beverly tried to crawl onto her mother's mutilated chest, Jhefferson picked her up and carried her back to his store. Others gathered what they could of the corpse, borrowing a sheet to cover the tattered pieces, laying the body on a woven mat beneath bamboo chimes.

Someone searched Clara's purse as Beverly sat frozen in shock, ignoring the glass of soda that Jhefferson offered. Someone else ran to the corner store and paid a few pesos to call the number scribbled on a card in the dead woman's wallet. The rest sat and waited with the new orphan, who until that day had never been touched by death.

Chapter 13

Day of the Dead, 1988

On the Day of the Dead Beverly kept to the routine she had begun a year after her mother's death: she rose early, putting on her newest pair of jeans and a blouse in the pale pink her mother favored. She took her baby picture from the closet, giving Clara's image a quick kiss before tucking it into an inner pocket of her backpack. Then she spritzed herself with the Spanish cologne her mother had loved and walked out the door.

The holiday was acutely bittersweet for Beverly, marking as it did two milestones in her life. She had been born in the final hours of November 1, and on her fifteenth birthday, a train had ended her mother's life. As Beverly turned twenty-five, it occurred to her that her mother had been gone for ten years. She had mourned long enough; it was time to seek joy.

Her first stop was Ma Mon Luk, where she bought half a dozen pork buns, their ivory skins still sweating from the steamer. Her hour-long journey through the city grew progressively more cramped as people squeezed into the elevated train and the jeepney Beverly rode to reach Manila North Cemetery. It was midmorning by the time she arrived at the edge of the wide river of people flowing to the cemetery's entrance and swirling around the barriers. Beverly hugged her backpack defensively against her chest, mindful of pickpockets but thoroughly enjoying the carnival atmosphere that infused the picnic-cum-vigil with which Filipinos celebrated their dearly departed. Before entering the cemetery, she paused at one of the many sidewalk stalls that sold candles and flowers. Candles hung from uncut wicks like slim yellow foot-long sausage links, flanking large tubs filled with chrysanthemums, calla lilies and daisies. Beverly took her time browsing before selecting one flawless shell pink rose and a white taper as long as her forearm.

"*Yun lang*—is that all?" the vendor asked, smiling at the pretty young woman counting out her money.

"*Opo, Manang*. It's my mother's tenth death anniversary but I can't afford more than this." Beverly offered an apologetic smile as she paid.

"*Naku anak*, the tenth deserves more than one rose." The woman pulled out two red gerbera daisies and a few sprigs of baby's breath, wrapping the modest bouquet in a page from an old tabloid. She handed the flowers to Beverly with a gap-toothed smile. "No extra charge. Just make sure to come back to me next year, *ha*?"

"Salamat po, Manang." Beverly nodded thanks before plunging back into the crowd. After her mother's death Beverly had often been visited by the kindness of strangers, their generous acts as delightfully random as butterflies landing on one's head. Ninang 'Cela said it was God's way of making up for taking her mother away so early in her young life.

Security checkpoints marked the final hurdle before the cemetery gates. Crowds puddled around long tables, where volunteers poked through every purse, basket and cooler, confiscating plastic forks, metal nail files, crochet needles and anything that might even remotely have been conceived as a weapon. Like most holidays involving crowds with access to alcohol, *Araw ng Patay* carried the usual risk of drunken brawls. The police were bent on preventing sudden additions to the one million people already interred at Manila North Cemetery.

Past the inspection tables Beverly took her time strolling through the roads that dissected the necropolis. She enjoyed mingling with these anonymous multitudes, imagining that they all belonged to one larger family if only because their dead were neighbors. There were new visitors every year, but over time Beverly had come to know some of the cemetery's full-time residents, impoverished families who had transformed the necropolis into a rent-free suburb of Manila. She waved as she passed the makeshift school where, on regular days, Teacher Ipat gathered the neighborhood children around a blackboard propped up against the marble tomb of her mausoleum. After school hours the tomb did double duty as dining table and bed, and today Ipat sat cross-legged atop it, reading a dog-eared paperback. Down the road, the enterprising *Aling* Nening had converted her family crypt into a *sari-sari* dry goods store that sold everything from packets of laundry detergent to instant coffee.

Off to one side of the road, youngsters clutching their coins watched as a wizened vendor twirled a bamboo skewer round and round a whirring vat, magically spinning a pink cloud of cotton candy larger than their heads. The Day of the Dead always meant brisk sales for the living, and vendors hawked salted duck eggs, barbecued pork and rice cakes up and down the cemetery's labyrinth of streets.

As Beverly drifted down the cemetery road with the crowd, she looked out for her favorite monuments, silently greeting each like an old friend. Here was the alabaster sphinx guarding a pyramid-shaped mausoleum, its caretaker wiping down the marble with a soggy rag. Further along, the pergola that encircled a life-sized crucified Christ offered scant shade to a trio of crones flapping palm fans. In the distance she could see the weathered back of *The Thinker* eternally hunched atop his boulder, contemplating the section reserved for Jews. It was the only part of the cemetery not crammed full with visitors that day. A slight breeze riffled the leaves of the fire trees and shrubs, which softened the bleached landscape of limestone angels and marble tombs. Seeking relief from the collective heat of the shuffling masses, Beverly lifted her face to catch the wind.

Clara did not lie in this gracious memorial park but farther out, in a humble section reserved for those who could not afford to buy an individual grave and all the sky above it.

Nearly an hour later, Beverly arrived at her mother's final home: a microwave-oven-sized niche tucked between many others in a five-story condominium for the dead, each unit identical to the next but for the birth and death dates that set the margins of its occupant's life. Dozens of mourners were already there, chanting novenas, lighting candles and arranging flowers in small vases. Beverly nodded greetings to each of them. There would be time to chat after everyone was done with prayers.

Beverly unwrapped her humble posy and laid it upon the narrow ledge beneath Clara's niche, then lit the candle, dripping melted wax to anchor it to the pocked cement. Standing back to assess her little tableau, she whispered the promise Clara had made to her at bedtime all through childhood: *One day my life will be better.* This was the one item of faith Beverly clung to, the closest thing to a prayer she'd learned from her mother, who had never been a conscientious Catholic. Without the anchor of traditional invocations, Beverly felt isolated as she watched families all around her murmur into folded hands. She glanced at her watch: it was half past noon. With the heavy traffic, Beverly estimated it would be another two hours before her godmother arrived.

She was about to wander off to visit the larger tombs when little fingers tickled her arm.

"Happy birthday, *Até* Beverly!" Tintin, the six-year-old daughter of Cresencia Jurado, smiled up at her. She had lost two front teeth since the last Day of the Dead.

"Ay, Beverly, happy birthday *pala!"* Tintin's mother, Cresencia, walked up to Beverly, leading with her belly. A little boy in a grimy tank top and low-slung diaper toddled behind her. Cresencia's family had lived in the same mausoleum for two generations, gaining a home in exchange for daily prayers for the soul of a Realtor whose descendants had migrated to Queens. "Tintin still talks about the birthday cake you shared with her last year."

Beverly had met Cresencia as a newlywed, but in the last decade she'd hardly ever seen her friend without an ongoing pregnancy or suckling infant. *"Pang-ilan mo na 'yan?"* Beverly nodded at the woman's belly. She could no longer remember how many children her friend had.

"Six if you count two miscarriages." Cresencia sighed, her face prematurely aged by fecundity. "At least I know Nardo isn't sleeping with anyone else—where would he find the energy?"

"Where do you find the time?" Beverly teased. Stooping to look Tintin in the eye, she pulled one pork bun out of her bag. "If I give you this, will you promise to share it with your little brother?"

Tintin skipped away, holding the pork bun high above her brother's head, his cries disrupting the hum of prayers. Beverly watched Cresencia waddle after the children and hoped that the better life Clara had wished on her would include a daughter as adorable as Tintin.

Beverly was in the middle of adding a tall, attractive husband to the fantasy of her future life when a petite matron got up off her knees and tucked a plastic rosary into her purse. She whispered final prayers, bowing slightly to each of three niches, before turning to Beverly.

"Ay, Beverly! Kumusta na ba?" Alfonsa Pison had tended the graves of her parents and twin brother for decades and was an old hand at caring for the newly bereaved. A decade earlier, she happened to be making her weekly visit when cemetery workers arrived to settle Clara's broken body into the niche beside that of her

own mother. When Marcela and Beverly became too distraught to deal with the laborers, the spinster had overseen the rest of the work, placating the two mourners with coffee and boiled eggs.

Now Alfonsa looked Beverly over, her gerbil-like nose twitching with perennial allergies. "You look like you haven't had breakfast. *Heto*—this *pan de sal* was made fresh this morning." She held out a bag of rolls. "You look like you've lost weight. Are you in love?" Alfonsa's large eyes twinkled above a raisin-sized mole perched on her right cheekbone. "Who is your *novio*?"

"*Wala*. I don't have a boyfriend." Beverly blushed, anticipating the usual jokes about her uneventful love life. "Mama taught me not to trust men, you know."

"*Hija naman*, they're not all bad," Alfonsa clucked. "All you need is one good—" A minor commotion at the far end of the columbarium stopped her midsentence, her mouth forming a startled O. Turning around, Beverly was surprised to see a vaguely familiar girl smiling as she walked toward them. The girl wore a canary yellow sundress and silver hoop earrings; she carried a sheaf of long-stemmed roses in one arm like a newly crowned beauty queen.

"*Diós me salve*—God save me—can it be?" Aling Alfonsa whispered. "Yes—it's Lisa, Lisa Patané."

The girl in question had been orphaned seven years earlier, when her parents had perished in an apartment fire. Their charred remains had been buried together in an extra-wide niche just above the one that Clara occupied. Like Beverly, Lisa had been forced to forgo a college education and find a job after the tragedy. The two orphans had quickly bonded and Beverly looked forward to their annual reunions, when the irrepressible Lisa would spend hours describing her latest romantic escapades.

Today Lisa seemed different—regal, almost. She sauntered forward, a clear path opening before her as people stepped aside to gawk at the man following in her wake. The gray-haired foreigner stood a head taller than everyone else, long of chin and short of neck, mirrored sunglasses perched on a bulbous nose. As the couple neared, Clara noted the sweat crescents that darkened the armpits of his Hawaiian shirt, the Bermuda shorts that bared thick calves covered in pale fur. She wondered where Lisa, who worked the cosmetics counter six days a week at Shoemart, could possibly have met him.

"Behhh-ver-lyyyyy, long time no see!" Lisa's voice was higher-pitched than usual, her English broadened by an accent Beverly only heard in American movies.

"*Kumusta na*, Lisa?" Beverly greeted her friend, insisting on Tagalog. "Who's that old man? Was he a friend of your parents?"

Lisa's giggle pealed like a church bell run amok. "Of course not! *Ikaw talaga*—" Lisa pinched Beverly's arm, switching to Tagalog as well. "You know the *'kanó*—they always look older than they really are."

"Honey, what did we say about talking TAG-alog when I'm around?" The man's tone was petulant.

"Honey *naman*, it's so hard to do that when we're in Manila." Lisa offered the man a pout, crimson lips just level to his chest. "Don't you worry, love, when we get to America, I promise to speak English all day every day, just for you. 'Kay?" As she winked at Beverly, her eyeliner left a blue smear upon her cheekbone. "Beverly, I want you to meet my fiancé, Lydell Kinkade the Third."

"Fiancé?" Beverly could barely hide her disbelief. How could Lisa have found a *novio* to provide the "happily ever after" ending Clara had promised her? Did her friend's two dead parents pull greater weight among the gods than her never-married mother? "You didn't even have a boyfriend when I saw you last year."

Lisa shrugged, slinging an arm around Lydell's hips. "When it's true love, there's no point waiting. Right, hon?" She looked up at Lydell, who puffed out his barrel chest.

"You betcha, sweetheart." Lydell jerked his head at Lisa and clicked his tongue. "This here's m'girl. I knew it the minute I saw her standin' there, holdin' all my letters tied with a red ribbon."

"Lisa, *talaga.*" Beverly grinned. "You stole that trick from an old Sharon Cuneta movie, didn't you?"

Lisa let out a delighted yelp, and for the briefest moment reverted to the giddy teenager Beverly remembered. Recovering quickly, she chirped, "Beverly's being silly. She thinks magic only happens in the movies."

Lydell took off his glasses, looking Beverly over as though she were a used car. "I wish you'd told me you had such pretty friends, Lisa. If I'd known, I'd've brought Hank along." He leaned close enough for Beverly to smell mint from the gum he chewed. "Hank's newly divorced too. Could've been a love match!" His grin bared teeth the color of weak tea.

"Ay sayang!" Lisa waggled her eyebrows at Beverly. "Never mind, when I meet Hank in Naples, I'll tell him to start writing you."

"That's Naples, *Florida*, to you." Lydell made the clicking sound again. "Wouldn't want people to think I was some kinda mafioso." He chuckled at his own joke while the women traded puzzled glances.

Beverly stared at the oddly matched couple. Lydell looked to be twice Lisa's age and more than double her weight, and yet she had never seen her friend so ecstatic, nor, for that matter, so vividly made-up. Plum rouge conjured cheekbones on Lisa's round face, and her crimped lashes glinted indigo in the morning sun.

Quelling skepticism, Beverly asked, "So how did you meet?"

"We were pen pals for six months on Filipina Sweetheart. Then he came to visit three weeks ago and it was instant magic. He took me to dinner, bought me flowers—he even chose this dress for me. Can you imagine?" Lisa gushed. "And it was so easy—I gave my pictures to this international dating service and in two weeks, I got letters from three different men." She pinched her beau's forearm.

"But Lydell's letters were special. He's a stenotype reporter. At court, you know. Stenotype reporters have to write all the time."

"Wow." Beverly fixed a smile on her face, unsure what exactly a stenotype reporter was. "So when's the wedding?"

"We'll do it in Florida. I wanted *sana* to have a church wedding here, but it's too complicated. Did you know you have to ask permission from the archbishop of Manila to marry a foreigner?"

"It's like you Catholics never left the Middle Ages." A sunburst of laugh lines deepened around Lydell's green eyes. "'S'why I'm a Mormon."

"Just like Donny and Marie Osmond! You know, Lydell promised he'd take me to Utah one day. Can you believe it?" Lisa squeezed Lydell's arm, her nails like cherry lozenges on his papery skin. "After he proposed, the agency took care of everything, including my fiancée visa. I quit my job so I could show Lydell around the country before we leave. You know, when Lydell asked me to marry him, he showed me pictures of his house in Florida. *Biro mo,* it has three bedrooms, two bathrooms and a big living room! One bathroom even has a whirlpool tub. There's a garden in back and a lawn out front. . . . I could get lost in that house." Lisa leaned her head into Lydell's shoulder, oblivious to the murmurs of bystanders who'd abandoned prayers to eavesdrop. "I can't wait to see it."

"*Suwerte mo naman,* what luck. Looks like you're moving into a palace." Beverly was surprised at the sudden pang in her gut, as she thought of the tight bedroom she shared with her roommate, the mossy shower stall, the roach-ridden kitchen. "When are you leaving?"

"In two weeks. This is the last time I get to visit *Tatay* and *Nanay* until we come back to Manila. Who knows when that will be? *Oo nga pala,* I brought this for them." Lisa looked at the narrow ledge below her parents' niche as though seeing it for the first time. "Oh, but, honey, our flowers won't fit on that small space! What should I do?"

Lydell scratched his hairy nape, unconcerned. "Figure it out quick so we can leave. This heat is making me thirsty."

Lisa stood the bouquet on the ground and propped it up against the wall of niches, accidentally knocking over Beverly's candle.

"*Hayaan mo na*—leave it alone, I'll fix it." Biting her lip, Beverly pulled her mother's modest posy out from behind Lisa's roses, then relit the candle on the farthest end of the ledge. Clara's niche seemed to recede in the shadow of the gargantuan bouquet.

"Beverly, favor *lang*, can you take our picture?" Lisa waved an Instamatic camera, pulling Lydell to the side of her parents' niche. "This is the closest I'll get to introducing *Tatay* and *Nanay* to Lydell. *Sayang* they didn't live to see this. They could have come to America."

Beverly peered through the camera lens, motioning for Lydell to stoop so that she could fit both faces in the same frame.

"Say green card!" Lydell teased. Lisa giggled, baring lipstick-smeared teeth.

Beverly handed the camera back to Lisa with a mournful smile. "So is this my last birthday with you?" She felt a keen melancholy at the prospect of losing her friend. It was ungenerous to be envious, but she felt that too.

"O my Ghad, how could I forget? Happy birthday, *pala* Beverly!" Lisa opened her arms wide for a hug, accidentally jostling Aling Alfonsa, who had been listening the entire time. "How old are you now? Twenty-five, *di ba*?" She looked at Lydell. "Beverly is three years older than I am, hon."

"Well, aren't you ripe for the pickin'?" Lydell leered at Beverly. "Why don't you come have lunch with us somewhere nice 'n' air-conditioned? Graveyard's no place for a party."

Beverly was on the verge of accepting their invitation when she remembered her godmother. "*Ay*, I'm sorry but my *ninang* Marcela is coming. We always spend the whole day here. *Inay* was her favorite sister." She looked at Clara's niche, pinching her lips together in disappointment. It was the first time she regretted having to see her godmother.

"Then why don't you come to dinner with us *kaya* tomorrow? We're staying at the Hotel InterContinental in Makati. *Sige na*, come see us there."

Beverly perked up at the mention of Makati, city of her dearest fantasies and home to the parties at which she loved to serve. "*O sige*. I'll ask my boss if I can work the day shift tomorrow at Ma Mon Luk and get the evening off."

"Ma Mon Luk? Is that where you work now?" Pity shadowed Lisa's eyes. She bumped hips against Lydell's thigh. "We'll show Beverly a good time tomorrow night, right, hon? I may not see her again for a long time."

"Sure you will. We'll get her signed up at Filipina Sweetheart, just like you did. If she plays her cards right, she could wind up in Naples too." Lydell clapped a beefy arm around his fiancée's shoulders, squeezing hard enough to elicit a squeal. "Now let's go someplace I can get an ice-cold San Miguel. It's hotter'n Key West out here."

Lisa whipped out a business card and scribbled on its back. "This is our room number at the InterCon. Can you be there by six? Lydell likes to eat dinner early, don't you, hon?"

"Not even a month together, and already she reads me like a book." Lydell clapped his sunglasses back on, flashing his tea smile at Beverly. "I'd never get this spoilin' from an American gal, tell ya that. Give me a traditional woman any day of the week." Lydell nodded good-bye to Beverly. "Come along, now, Lisa, we're all done here."

The couple left, cutting a wide swath through the crowd.

Beverly took a second look at the lavender card Lisa had given her and examined the script embossed in gold:

FILIPINA SWEETHEART

Let us introduce you to the Love of your Life!

"I think you should take her advice." Aling Alfonsa's voice startled Beverly. She was peering over Beverly's shoulder at the card. "*Sige na,* just call and put your name in. Maybe you'll get lucky like Lisa did. I know you will. Even with all that makeup she'll never be as pretty as you are."

"I can't flirt with men the way she does," Beverly protested, the image of Lisa in the yellow sundress still burning in her mind's eye. Lisa exuded the same glowing self-assurance that had lit up Señora Carina at the engagement party weeks earlier. Perhaps this was what happened when a wealthy man pursued a woman, lavishing roses and clothes and hotel holidays on his beloved till she turned fairly incandescent at the thought of marrying him.

Aling Alfonsa took Beverly's silence for indecision. "*Hija,* be practical. You're not getting any younger. A chance like this may not come up again." The lone black hair that grew from the mole on Aling Alfonsa's cheek quivered as she argued her case with rising passion. "*Tignan mo ako*—look at me. I should have searched for love instead of waiting for it to show up on my doorstep. *Naku hija,* learn from my mistake! Do you want to spend your life sitting by your mother's grave?"

Beverly glanced at Clara's niche. The candle had gone out again and the flowers had begun to droop. "No, I suppose not. But promise you won't say anything about this to Ninang Marcela. I don't want to worry her over nothing." Smiling at the first real secret she'd kept from her godmother, Beverly tucked the business card into her backpack next to the picture of her mother.

Beverly was eating her second pork bun by the time Marcela arrived, perspiring profusely and grousing about the traffic.

"*Susmaryosep!* I thought I was going to have a heart attack trying to get a ride—the jeeps were so crowded. I should have asked for the whole day off." She set two bulging plastic bags on the ground, then made a quick sign of the cross, kissing her fingers before laying them upon Clara's name for a long moment. "Can you believe it's been ten years?" When she turned to Beverly, her eyes were moist with the rumor of tears.

Thinking back on that day ten years past, Marcela now recalled that telling Doña Lupita and Don Rodrigo of Clara's death had been almost worse than the accident itself. From experience she knew that Doña Lupita and her husband would return that evening from the cemetery feeling out of sorts, wanting only a cold beer and a shower to wash away the trying day. From where she waited in the darkened hallway, she had heard Doña Lupita stroll into the large living room.

"*Madré de Diôs*, every year more and more people cram into that cemetery. It's enough to drive one insane." From the shadows on the floor, Marcela could tell that the matron was stretching her arms wide, as if pushing away the memory of the perspiring pious multitude. Marcela chose that moment to enter the sala. It was a route she had traveled thousands of times over the years, bearing trays of food and drink. Her hands were bare now, but she walked as though wading through wet cement, slumped beneath an unseen burden.

"What are you doing here? Shouldn't you be cooking dinner for Concha's family?" Doña Lupita gripped her hips, resisting the urge to scratch. Mosquitoes had earlier feasted on every inch of exposed skin, drawn by the copious amounts of perfume she'd sprayed to block the miasma of sweat and urine that pervaded the cemetery on such high-traffic days.

"I have bad news." Marcela raised her head with effort, eyes red and heavy-lidded, her moon face glistening with snail trails of tears.

"Tell me quickly and go. Concha's family left the cemetery when we did. They should be getting home just now." Doña Lupita cast a withering look at her former cook. Over a decade earlier, Concha had been incapacitated by the first of three bouts with postpartum depression and persuaded her mother that she needed Marcela to run her household and care for her infant.

"Señora Concha gave me the day off to celebrate my godchild's birthday." Marcela noticed Doña Lupita stiffen and lean away, as though a large dog were sniffing at her ankles. Remembering the rules, Marcela avoided mentioning names.

"My sister was run over by a train." Marcela stared at her bare feet. Even in grief she had remembered to take off her shoes before entering the sala. "She died instantly."

"Good Lord! How can this be?" Don Rodrigo dropped his cigarette. "I remember your sister as though it were just yesterday. . . ."

"And do you recall, Digoy, *why* the memory is so clear?" Doña Lupita raised an eyebrow, daring him to recount that last confrontation with their former servant.

"Why bring that up now?" Don Rodrigo fiddled with the flint on his lighter.

"We are sorry for the loss." Doña Lupita conceded a modicum of sympathy. "I will tell Concha you need to be with your niece tonight."

"Yes, go to the child, Marcela. *Nakikiramay kami.*" Don Rodrigo offered his condolences. "If I may ask, how did it happen?"

"They say she was shopping for plants. She slipped and fell in front of the train."

"Did she not hear it coming?" Bizarre deaths had fascinated Don Rodrigo since a rearing horse had trampled his own father.

"No." Marcela shut her eyes to the memory of Jhefferson pointing to the earth furrowed by Clara's body. She had taken a fistful of dirt, dark with her sister's blood, warming it in her palm until someone offered her a plastic bag. Her nails were still black with soil.

"What a tragedy." Don Rodrigo resumed lighting his cigarette. "And how is the child?"

"She is destroyed." Marcela lifted swollen eyes to the Señores Duarté. "Now she has no one else except—"

"You. You are the only one she can depend on." Doña Lupita's gaze was pitiless. She had never learned the name of the bastard, had banned any mention of the child in her house. "My son has made a decent life in San Francisco. I forbid you to disrupt it."

"Of course." Marcela dug her fingers into her palm. "I will care for my niece as my own daughter. But I must ask a favor. For Clara's sake."

Doña Lupita flinched at the name she had not heard in over a decade. "What is it?"

Marcela straightened her shoulders, affecting a dignity she did not feel. "I need money for a niche in North Cemetery." Fresh tears traced now-familiar paths down her plump cheeks. "There is no point in having a wake, no one at the *funeraria* can fix what's left of . . ." Marcela smothered a sob with her fingers. "Clara needs to be in a grave I can visit on *Araw ng* . . ."

"Enough!" Doña Lupita held up a hand. Repulsed as she was by the thought of the servant in the same cemetery as her own ancestors, she detected an opportunity. "You realize that burial plots are expensive. It would take you years to pay back that loan."

Marcela's shoulders sagged and Doña Lupita knew to dangle bait. "But there is a way. We will pay outright on the condition that this ends our support of that child. Let this be the final settlement for Aldo's indiscretion."

"I underestimated you, Lupé." Don Rodrigo swirled ice cubes into his scotch. "You're a bigger bitch than I gave you credit for."

"Then I suppose you got what you deserved, didn't you, Digoy?"

"We both did."

The Duartés regarded each other with companionable hostility, before retreating to the usual estranged indifference. It had been a long day and after thirty-five years of marriage, they no longer cared to resurrect old arguments.

Sighing, Don Rodrigo turned back to the cook. "Marcela, how old is the girl now?"

"She turned fifteen today."

"*Pues* we've done fifteen years' penance. Is that not sufficient,

Digoy?" Doña Lupita was enjoying the stupefied expression on her husband's face; she had seen it so infrequently in recent years. "I'll throw in a little extra so she can finish high school. That should be sufficient reparation. Are we agreed?" Doña Lupita looked from husband to cook. Both nodded, but neither would meet her gaze.

"*A ver*, let us know how much you need. Given the condition of—" Doña Lupita cleared her throat, refusing after all these years to say the name. "You probably want an immediate burial."

"Yes, Doña Lupita. *Salamat po.*" Marcela left, bitterness encrusting her heart like burnt rice on the bottom of a pot.

Ten years later, her insides still itched with that burnt-rice feeling whenever she thought of the hateful pact she had made with Doña Lupita. But Marcela had done it for Beverly. Beverly, who now leaned her head against Marcela's, sighing. "I miss her as much as ever. But I have much less time to think about her these days. How did we get so busy?"

"I don't know about you, but I'm busy cooking, raising other people's children and spying on a *palikero* husband. I might as well have married the man, considering all the work I've taken over from his wife!"

"You? Married?" Beverly laughed. Despite the fact that she had spent most of her life serving a woman, Marcela was too strong-willed to submit to any man.

"Tell me again, what else you do for the señora and her family? Maybe you should tell me where you work so I can come help sometime."

Marcela wrestled with a knot on one of her plastic bags. "Nothing to tell. They're all alike, those señoras. They expect you to do the dirty work so they can keep their nail polish perfect." She pushed the tight knot away, exasperated. "*Ay*, Aling Alfonsa—your fingers are smaller than mine, can you help me with this? I made chicken barbecue to celebrate Beverly's birthday."

"You missed the big event this morning, Marcela." Alfonsa

began picking at the knot. "Remember Lisa Patané? She came earlier, dressed all fancy and showing off her *novio*."

"That little flirt?" Marcela snorted, pulling paper plates and glasses out of the other bag. "Who is it this time? Wasn't Cresencia's husband, Nardo, giving her the eye last year?"

"Cresencia's pregnant again, you know." Alfonsa pulled the sticks of barbecue out of the plastic bag and began piling them on a paper plate that Beverly held.

"Better her than Lisa. So who is Lisa's new boyfriend?"

"Not a boy, Ninang, an old man." Beverly shot a warning glance at Alfonsa. "He's *'kanó*. Looks old enough to be her father, but they're getting married."

"She's marrying an old American? *Linting yawa*," Marcela cussed with a phrase more profane than her usual Jesus-Mary-Joseph. "He just wants someone to take care of him in his old age. *Maniwala ka*, in ten years she'll be changing his diapers."

As Alfonsa told Marcela about Lisa and Lydell Kinkade, Beverly watched her godmother in vain for the slightest signs of approval.

"I cannot believe that girl would go to another country with a complete stranger," Marcela sputtered. "If her parents were still alive, they would never have allowed it."

"But, Ninang 'Cela, Lisa is of age—and she said she's in love." Beverly's envy of Lisa's engagement grew stronger. The more her godmother protested, the more attractive a life abroad seemed. After all, an older husband seemed a fair price to pay for three bedrooms and a garden, for a new life in a town with the glamorous name of Naples.

"Who says you cannot find love in Manila? Those who run to America are only trying to escape their lives here." Marcela glanced at her sister's grave. "But you never really escape those left behind. You only abandon them." Tearing off a last mouthful of meat, she stabbed the skewer into the soil.

Surprised by her friend's bitterness, Alfonsa sought to change the subject. "Beverly, *anak*, go buy some soft drinks for us, will you?"

Beverly was only too grateful for an excuse to leave. "I'll visit Cresencia. The *sari-sari* store next to her place sells cold drinks."

Wandering through the crowds, Beverly wondered if her Ninang 'Cela's rage was somehow related to Clara's death, but could not understand why it extended to America. Pushing the mystery from her mind, she paused to get her bearings. To her left stood the cavernous mausoleum that did double duty as a beauty salon; Aling Marsha bent over the gnarled toes of a middle-aged man who was flipping through his newspaper, nodding reflexively as he read headlines out loud to her. The sound of singing drew Beverly farther down the road to another crypt turned karaoke house. Under the gaze of a concrete angel, a skinny teenager performed a George Michael burlesque of "Father Figure" before a giggling female audience. The off-key singing faded as Beverly continued walking to Cresencia's home. Sleeping mats were stacked in rolls to one side and an oilcloth was spread upon the tomb on which Cresencia's family sat, slept and ate. She was setting out plates of chicken adobo and sautéed long beans when Beverly arrived.

"*Ay*, Beverly, you're just in time for dinner," Cresencia welcomed her, ignoring the little boy sucking on the hem of her skirt. "We're celebrating Nardo's Overseas Contract Worker permit. It just came through. He leaves for Qatar next week."

"Where is Qatar?"

"Somewhere in Saudi." Cresencia shrugged. "He has a year's contract and if he does well, they could renew him."

"But if he leaves, who will help with the other children when you give birth?"

"*Naku*, Beverly, he never helps care for them—" Cresencia's voice dropped to a stage whisper. "He only helps *make* them!"

The two women were still laughing when Nardo walked up,

carrying a plastic bag of cold beer. It was rumored that Nardo had once stabbed a man in a drunken squabble over roast pig. The short man could have been a killer drunk, but he was unfailingly mellow when sober.

"Beverly, *halika* have a beer with me." Nardo waved a bottle at her, his sparse moustache stretching into a smile.

"*Mang,* Nardo, *naman,* you know I don't drink." Beverly had a soft spot for the man who had helped lay her mother's body in the niche, then refused payment for his work.

"Never too late to start." Nardo took a long swig. "I'm celebrating the new job in Qatar." He looked fondly at his bottle. "I have to drink as much as I can before leaving—they don't allow alcohol over there *daw.* Muslim *kase.*"

"Think of all the money you'll save." Cresencia rubbed her belly. "Maybe you'll save enough to move us out of here; maybe we'll buy a real house."

"I'll need more than one year abroad to get us out of here." Nardo frowned at his bottle. "My friends have been working in Saudi for four, five years now; their families still live here."

"Couldn't Cresencia and the children go with you?" Beverly stroked the tomb's cool marble.

"To America maybe, but not Qatar." Nardo nailed a snail on the dirt with a gob of spit. "A Muslim country's no place for my family."

The mention of family reminded Beverly of her original errand and she excused herself to buy soft drinks for her godmother. Walking back to Clara's niche, she daydreamed about starting a family in America. Perhaps Filipina Sweetheart would lead her to a good American man. Perhaps he would even be handsome.

CHAPTER 14

Intercontinental Interlude

As soon as she was done with the lunch and *merienda* service at Ma Mon Luk, Beverly hurried home for a quick shower. Wanting to look her very best, she slipped into her least faded pair of jeans and an embroidered blouse Marcela had given her the previous Christmas. She smiled at the photo of her one-year-old self on Clara's lap back in its usual spot in the closet as she buttoned up her shirt. "I look nice, don't I, *Inay*? You promised I would have a good life. Maybe things will begin to get better tonight." Spritzing herself with baby cologne, she shut the closet door and set off for Makati.

The Hotel InterContinental glowed amber in the slate sky, honeycombed with hundreds of lamplit windows that looked out on the molten stream of rush hour traffic on Ayala Avenue. In all her twenty-five years, she had never dared enter its imposing doors. As she walked up its circular driveway that evening, her stomach churned with nerves. Daunted by the languid swoosh of the central revolving glass door, she decided to enter through a smaller side entrance.

"Excuse me, miss?" A doorman in a black and maroon uniform adorned with epaulets intercepted Beverly. He grinned with the playful wariness of a guard dog as he asked where she was going. *"Saan ang punta niyo?"*

"I'm seeing friends here," Beverly replied in Tagalog. Anywhere else she would have laughed out loud at the carmine fez perched on the doorman's head, but here it suggested an extravagance so far removed from Beverly's life that it made an exotic country of the InterContinental Hotel, a country to which he belonged, and she did not.

This made Beverly even more determined to gain entry. If her mother had taught her anything, it was that she deserved as much respect as the next person, poverty notwithstanding. "I'm meeting friends for dinner."

"Are they guests at this hotel?" The doorman draped a forearm along the door's bar, holding it shut. "What are their names?"

"Lydell Kinkade the Third." Beverly gave special emphasis on *the Third* because it made Lydell sound more important.

Just then a lady in pearls and a silk mini sauntered up to the revolving doors. The doorman turned to her with his best smile and nodded like a bobblehead doll. Indignation rose through Beverly's neck, warming her earlobes and turning the tip of her widow's peak pink.

"Mr. Kinkade is engaged to my friend Lisa. They're getting married next month. In *America.* They want to see me before they leave."

Cocking an eyebrow, the doorman leaned into the door's levered handle and swung it wide. "Ahhhh—mail-order bride *siguro.*"

Beverly ignored his smirk and stepped into the wide lobby, whose gleaming marble floors reflected the scuffed soles of her sandals. Straightening her shoulders and lifting her chin, Beverly walked up to a massive mahogany console manned by a woman in a dark suit. A discreet black tile on the woman's lapel proclaimed her name in gold: *Felicidad.* Even the concierge had a fancy name for joy.

"Can I help you?" Sizing up the dowdy cotton blouse and naked face, Felicidad surmised Beverly was not a working girl. "Are you here to see someone?"

Beverly pulled out Lisa's card and squinted at the number scribbled on its back. "My friends are staying in room three-two-zero. Lydell Kinkade and Lisa Patané."

Felicidad noted the Filipina Sweetheart logo on the opposite side of the card and leveled a cool smile at Beverly. "I see. Let me find out if Mr. Kinkade is expecting you." She punched in the numbers on the phone, hoping no one would answer so she could send the girl packing.

"Yes, this is Felicidad Yñiguez at the front desk, may I speak with Mr. Kinkade?" Felicidad frowned as she listened to Lisa mangle the American accent she herself had perfected. "Good evening, Mr. Kinkade. This is Felicidad calling from the front desk? You have a—*another* lady friend here to see you. Yes, of course. I'll have her wait in the lobby." Felicidad looked down her nose at Beverly, underlining her disdain with professionally polite Tagalog. "You may have a seat over there while you're waiting. It's best you don't wander off. Mr. Kinkade and his girlfriend are coming down right now."

As Beverly headed for a cluster of large armchairs off to one side of the lobby, the concierge turned her attention to a redhead in rumpled linen who'd walked up with several shopping bags. "*Bonsoir*, Madame Calcoen! I see you've been busy at the boutiques. Let me call a valet to help you with those bags."

Feeling as though she'd been sent to detention by the school principal, Beverly flopped into a chair so deep that she could not lean back without lifting her feet off the floor. She was slouched that way when Lisa and Lydell stepped out of the elevators.

"*Ay*, Beverly! Do you like our hotel?" Lisa spread her arms like a game-show presenter, delighted. "Are you hungry? Lydell's taking us to dinner at the Café Jeepney."

Beverly gaped at Lisa's magenta minidress. It seemed vacuum-sealed to her figure, emphasizing how much smaller she was than her fiancé, whose turquoise golf shirt clung to a formidable gut with less flattering results.

Lydell cocked his head, scrutinizing Beverly's clothes as she climbed out of the armchair. "You'd better take Beverly shopping before she sends any pictures to Filipina Sweetheart, honey. Her photos need to look as good as yours did if she wants anyone to write her."

Beverly pouted, smoothing down her blouse. "What's wrong with these clothes?"

"Don't be upset, Lydell means well." Lisa put a placating hand on Beverly's arm. "He's right, Filipina Sweetheart's manager made me wear a dress for photos. You know, to show off your legs."

"You want to put your best foot forward, don't you?" Lydell raised his eyebrows. "It's the same advice I'd give my own daughter if she were going to a party. I mean look at my Lisa here—" Lydell stroked Lisa's arm. "When I saw her photo in that snappy red dress, I thought to myself, 'This girl's a contender, no question.' I wrote her a letter that same day."

"Look how he flatters me." Lisa squeezed Lydell's beefy thumb. "None of my Pinoy boyfriends ever said that." She beamed up at Lydell, who tucked a stray strand of hair behind her ear. It dawned on Beverly that, despite the age difference, these two seemed genuinely fond of each other, flirting like lovers in the romantic films on which her mother had raised her. Beverly wondered if a man would ever treat her with the same adoring tenderness.

"Napaka-sweet naman ninyo! You two are too sweet. *Ka-inggit naman."* Beverly admitted envy, knowing it would flatter Lisa.

"Don't worry, you'll find Prince Charming at Filipina Sweetheart, just like I did." Lisa winked. "I'll lend you one of the dresses Lydell bought me. *Tara na*—let's go. I'm hungry."

Lisa led them across the lobby to the Café Jeepney, where a

gray-vested waiter snapped to attention, greeting the couple and pulling out menus. Beverly stopped in her tracks, stunned to see three immaculate jeepneys parked against the left wall of the restaurant. Chrome horses polished to a high shine pranced on each hood, lemon fringe trimmed the long windows and plastic pink and red tulips sprouted from the dashboard. The waiter ushered them into the nearest jeep, which housed a narrow table. As they slid onto the long benches, Beverly smiled at the absurdity of eating a swank dinner in the poor man's carriage.

"Can you imagine—Lydell and I only take taxis around Manila, but here we are, back in a jeepney! *Kaloka!*" Lisa ran her fingers over the immaculate salmon-colored vinyl seats, an upgrade from the cracked upholstery of working jeeps.

"So is this the closest I'll get to a jeepney? Looks like it'd be a fun ride." Lydell stretched his arms along the back of the bench and leaned his head out the window, so that the fringe hung over his forehead. "Hey, Beverly, d'ya think I look better with bangs?"

"*Pasensya ka na lang*—don't mind him." Lisa smiled indulgently, tugging at Lydell's sleeve to make him sit up. "He loves to make people laugh, *kahit* corny." Lisa sipped water, leaving a crescent of lipstick on the glass's rim. "Let's see what they serve in these fancy jeeps."

Beverly envied the couple's easy intimacy. She wondered if Lydell would teach Lisa how to drive in a country free of jeepneys. Anything could happen in America. "You think you'll miss Manila?"

"No. With Nanay and Tatay gone, there's no one left to miss here." Lisa tickled her fiancé's formidable chin. "You're my family now, right, hon?"

"Mmhmm." Lydell peered at the menu through reading glasses. "Soon's you meet Dorothy and Bernard, they'll be your family too."

"Those are Lydell's children by his first wife." Lisa smoothed a snowy napkin on her lap. "I'm sure we'll get along—Dorothy's my age and Bernard just turned nineteen."

"Will you have your own kids right away?" Beverly asked.

Lisa opened her mouth to reply, but Lydell spoke sooner. "Been there, done that. Not sure I want to start over again at my age. Heck, I'm due to retire in five years. About time someone babied me for a change, right, hon?"

Lisa smiled, but the sharpness in her eyes could cut glass. "We're still talking about kids. I know I'll want at least one." She walled him off by raising the large menu.

How could they have already argued over the question of children in under a month of dating? Beverly wondered. Did things develop this quickly with foreigners? The menu Lisa continued to hold up dissuaded Beverly from asking her friend such questions, even in Tagalog. Lydell ducked behind her menu, cajoling her with endearments.

Beverly looked around for their waiter, who was just then escorting a well-dressed couple and two small children to a table by the glass wall opposite them. That seating offered a panoramic view of the garden that led up to the softly lit pool. The mother took a seat next to the glass, pulling her small son into the chair next to hers, but the boy looked longingly at the jeepneys. "Mommy, why can't we sit in the jeepneys too?" he whined.

The matron glanced at the heavyset American with his diminutive dates, lips puckering as though she'd swallowed a slice of soursop. Filigreed silver earrings swung above her mandarin collar as she leaned across the table, whispering to her husband.

Their daughter piped up just then, her high voice echoing across the restaurant. "Mommy, what's a *puta*?"

"Puta-puta-puta!" the little boy chanted, until his mother pinched his chubby arm.

Whore. Beverly stiffened. Lisa had lowered her menu and was too busy murmuring in Lydell's ear to have heard, but Beverly's cheeks burned. She waved the waiter over and nudged her friend's foot. "Lisa, ready to order? Let's eat so we can take Lydell somewhere else."

"What's the rush? This is the prettiest jeep I've ever ridden." Lisa snuggled into the crook of Lydell's arm.

Beverly wondered if she was the only one feeling unwelcome at the InterContinental. "Did you know I had a hard time getting in? The doorman wouldn't open the door until I told him my friends were hotel guests."

"*Ganyan talaga*—that's just the way they are with security." Lisa shrugged. "I never have that problem because I'm always with Lydell. That doorman's always nice to us."

"He better be, considering what I tip him." Lydell spread his hands across the table.

"*Sa totoo*, he must think we're already married. The doorman began calling me Mrs. Kinkade after Lydell passed him a five-dollar bill for carrying my shopping bags!"

Something clicked in Beverly's mind. *Access*. That was what being with a wealthy man guaranteed. Access to the better life her mother had promised.

When it was finally served, dinner turned out to be mercifully brief. Lydell inhaled his steak in noisy mouthfuls, and Lisa abandoned her utensils in short order, sucking each chicken bone clean with parsimonious zeal. Beverly, on the other hand, had spent many catered events watching society ladies at table and was eager to practice her borrowed manners, slicing fish into dainty morsels and dabbing at the corners of her mouth after each bite. She was only halfway done with her dish when Lydell pushed his plate away.

"Servings here are a tad smaller than in Florida, but boy are they tasty." He swiped his mouth with the napkin. "Where to next?"

Lisa sucked on a toothpick. "Let's go to a karaoke house. Bar Bibliotek is really fun, it's in Malate. Other side of Manila, closer to Roxas Boulevard."

"Isn't that where we went for our interview at the American embassy? What an ordeal." Lydell set his crumpled napkin on the table. "I hear people start lining up outside for tourist visas at midnight. When we went in to get Lisa's fiancée visa, the line stretched a country mile down the boulevard."

"Oh, honey, don't scare Beverly, she might not join Filipina Sweetheart." Lisa pulled out a tube of shimmery red gloss and freshened her mouth, smacking her lips for emphasis. "Anyway, Bar Bibliotek is on the *fun* side of Roxas. I haven't taken you to a karaoke bar yet. You like to sing, don't you, darling?"

"Good idea! Lydell should see other parts of Manila before you leave." Beverly had never been to a karaoke house but jumped at the chance to escape the hotel's snide inhabitants.

Moments later, they strode out the revolving doors and had the parking valet summon a taxicab. Discomfited by the couple's incessant cuddling, Beverly slid into the front passenger seat. The taxi sped out of Makati's glass maze of skyscrapers and carried them to Malate, a seamier section of the metropolis veined with narrow, potholed streets. The only remnants of the gracious prewar neighborhood it once was were a few moldering mansions whose grilled windows peered over cracked cement walls. Dusty acacias stretched across electric light poles, their roots kneeing up through sidewalks littered with cigarette butts and dried leaves. Beyond this somber residential border blazed Malate's red-light district, which drew tourists and navy men to its souklike warren of discos, bars and brothels. Converted homes and storefronts sat like old vaudeville queens in tight, neon-lit rows, belching cigarette smoke and disco every time a door opened. Jeeps, taxis and ambulant vendors crept around bar-hoppers, who jaywalked with a nonchalance born of alcohol. A block down from the main drag, Lisa directed the driver to pull up by a low building whose wrought iron frontispiece read BAR BIBLIOTEK.

As Lisa counted out Lydell's cash, Beverly gazed about her, fascinated by the party atmosphere pervading the streets. She had never been to this part of the city so late at night; it seemed nearly as exotic as the InterContinental. Just then, a pair of foreigners emerged from a nearby club with their dates. The women could have been members of the same salacious sorority, dressed identically in shrunken candy-colored tank tops and silver bangles. Their dark hair hung like veils below their hips; denim miniskirts extended not much farther beyond. They chattered in Tagalog while their dates joshed with each other in broad Australian accents. As they passed Lisa and Lydell, one of the women caught Beverly staring and nudged her friend. "*Oy, Tara, tignan mo 'yung matanda, nakadalawa pa siya.* Look at the old man—he's got two."

Tara smirked at Lydell, teasing in Tagalog, "Too bad, they'll have to split his tip."

Dissolving into giggles, the two women teetered away on icepick heels.

Beverly choked down indignation, coughing on the fog of cigarette smoke that greeted them as Lisa ushered her into the bar. She followed her friends down a short hall and into a crowded room that was dark but for a single spotlight trained on the stage at the far end. In keeping with its name, Bar Bibliotek was tarted up to approximate an old-fashioned English library. Frayed armchairs huddled around small round tables where low-slung banker lamps cast a green glow upon the faces of those who hunched over them. Shelves crammed with leather-bound encyclopedia sets and a collection of wooden globes lined the walls leading up to the stage. The bartender greeted Lisa like a homecoming queen as they took stools by the counter. Beverly gawked at the deer head hung between liquor shelves, its antlers garlanded with fairy lights.

Lydell and Beverly huddled close on either side of Lisa so they could talk over the throbbing bass of "Like a Virgin" and the yelps of a transvestite impersonating Madonna for the rowdy audience.

"You like this place, hon?" Lisa yelled into her fiancé's ear.

"Durnedest thing I ever seen," Lydell hollered back. "Order us a pitcher of beer from your pal, will ya? Madonna always makes me thirsty."

Beverly, who did not drink, hoped that a better amateur would seize the mike after Madonna was done. No such luck. The next three rounds were sung by a couple who channeled Sonny and Cher until the DJ pried the microphone out of the woman's hands.

"What do you think of this place, Bev?" Lisa breathed beer into Beverly's ear. "It used to be a gay bar, but everyone is welcome now."

"Okay *lang*." Beverly shrugged. "Maybe you should have told Lydell it's mostly gay. I don't think this is his kind of music. At least not for his generation."

"We're getting married. He'll have to get used to my music too, *di ba?*" Lisa took a long swallow of beer and squeezed Lydell's chubby fingers.

Despite Lisa's unconcern, Beverly noticed Lydell becoming increasingly restless as one bad singer followed another. A dreadlocked teenager was wailing through "Do You Really Want to Hurt Me" when Lydell leaned across Lisa's lap and declared, "I've had it with these faggots! Time someone showed them how it's done." With some difficulty he squeezed between the tables and made his way to the stage. Beverly watched him flip through the thick song binder and hold a page up to the DJ. The DJ shook his head, but the American loomed over the smaller man, his face reddening as he talked.

"What do you think they're arguing about?" Beverly asked Lisa. "Do you think Lydell's song isn't on the list?"

"*Imposiblé.* Neil has all the best songs, even the golden oldies. Maybe he doesn't like the one Lydell picked. But Lydell always gets what he wants." Lisa winked. "Just watch."

As the last chords of Boy George faded away, the DJ raised hands in surrender and stuck another CD into his machine. Lydell picked up the microphone and propped reading glasses on the tip of his nose as the opening bars of Sinatra's "My Way" unfurled.

Beverly didn't know whether to laugh or cheer. Apart from being half a beat off-tempo, Lydell was singing in tune. It soon became apparent that Lydell wasn't the only one who wanted to sing the song. Midway through the second verse, a wiry Filipino by the bookshelves got up and began singing along. Raising a beer bottle like an ersatz microphone, the man swung his other arm wide and belted *"And MORE much MORE than this, I did it MY WAY . . ."* The last phrase wavered in an off-key vibrato that drew jeers from the audience.

Beverly shifted uneasily, noticing that some men in the audience were lobbing peanut peels at the interloper. The parties she'd served at had never been this boisterous.

"Upó, upó, upó!" Two men at the table beside the drunk yelled at him to sit down. The man responded by singing even louder, his brays drowning out Lydell's crooning.

Lydell frowned over his glasses. "Can we start over? This guy's ruining it for me."

"What you mean I'm ruining? I know the words, *putrés kang puti."* The drunk waggled his bottle, pitching forward as he gave Lydell the finger.

"'Hoy, wag kang bastós—" A man beside the drunk berated his rudeness. "Shut up so we can do another song!" Standing up, he grabbed the drunk's free arm and tried to yank him back into his chair.

"'Tangina naman." Cursing loudly, the drunk swung his bottle but missed, managing only to drench his attacker in beer. Bellowing rage, the other man lunged at the drunk and threw him off-balance. The drunk grabbed onto the bookshelf to break his fall, jostling it so violently that a bust of Shakespeare crashed into the margarita pitcher on the table behind him. Three frat men who'd been cheated out of their third round of drinks got up, pissed off and ready to rumble.

"Away!" The minute someone hollered "Fight," the rest of the

audience, emboldened by alcohol and Sinatra's anthem, swarmed around the drunk and his assailant. In the dimly lit bar, Beverly heard rather than saw the scuffle, an alarming succession of grunts and profanity, the velvet thud of bodies colliding with fists and furniture.

"Leave now!" the bartender warned the women as he vaulted over the bar, a two-by-four in hand.

"Lydell, get back here NOW!" Lisa shrieked over violins and trumpets soaring to the song's histrionic finale. Lydell stepped gingerly around brawling men, upturned tables and broken glass. Beverly grabbed Lisa's hand and pulled her out the door.

The women pushed through curious passersby and street urchins who'd gathered around the bar's door and ran toward Remedios Circle trailed by Lydell.

"Son of a bitch—I lost my reading glasses," Lydell panted.

"Don't worry, we'll get you a new pair tomorrow."

"Should've listened when the DJ said 'My Way' was a risky song," Lydell muttered. "But I couldn't stand any more of that gay music."

"It wasn't your fault that fight broke out, honey." Lisa stroked his back. "People get crazy, drinking."

"Got that right. But why didn't anyone call the cops when the trouble started?" Lydell scanned the street as though he expected a police car to come careening up to the bar. "Folks back home always call 911."

"That's not how things work here. The police expect a bribe in exchange for not shutting the bar down. My friends can't afford to have that happen."

"All's I'm saying is, this would never happen in Naples."

"We'll be there soon. Let's enjoy our last days here, okay, hon?" Lisa patted Lydell's arm.

"All right, then. How 'bout setting me up for a round of golf tomorrow? Maybe the hotel concierge can find someone to walk a few holes with me."

Sweat glistened on Lydell's forehead as he looked at the small circle of restaurants that surrounded them. "Too bad we left without finishing our drinks."

"Maybe tonight we were just *malas*—unlucky." Lisa straightened her dress, touching earlobes, neck and wrist to make sure all her newly acquired jewelry was intact. "We can order a drink somewhere else. Plenty of bars nearby."

"Nahh. I'm done with this ghetto." Lydell ran his hands through his sparse hair. "How 'bout we just go back to Café Jeepney?"

Beverly checked her watch. "I should go home. It's nearly eleven and I work the morning shift."

Lisa pursed her lips, reluctant to end the evening on a sour note. "So will you join Filipina Sweetheart? I can lend you a dress and we can take pictures by the pool at our hotel. There's still time. Lydell and I don't leave for Boracay until after the weekend."

Beverly looked over her shoulder at the men stumbling out of Bar Bibliotek, one of them holding a bloody kerchief up to his nose, others pausing to light cigarettes before lurching off to the next bar. She dreaded the long ride back to Cubao, the narrow iron cot that awaited her. She imagined Lisa sinking into fluffy hotel pillows, the lights of Makati glittering through a picture window just beyond her lacquered toenails.

Someday my life will be better than it is now. It was time to make good on the promise her mother had made.

"Okay. I'll do the pictures. Let's talk about it in the taxi back to your hotel."

CHAPTER 15

Filipina Sweetheart

For the remainder of the week, Beverly worked double shifts at Ma Mon Luk so that she could take Saturday off to get her pictures done. As she loaded pork buns on trays and swabbed plum-sauce-splattered tables, she dreamed about the better life her mother had promised. Thanks to Lisa, she could see everything more clearly now: a big house in America, a husband more handsome than Lydell, pale-skinned children with high-bridged, perfect noses. Was it mere coincidence that she had learned about the matchmaking service on the anniversary of her mother's death? Surely not. The more Beverly thought about it, the more convinced she became that Filipina Sweetheart was no less than *hulog ng langit*—fallen from heaven.

A cool November breeze raised goose bumps on her arms that morning as she got off the bus in Makati. Christmas followed quickly on the heels of All Souls' Day in Manila, and window displays in the shopping arcade beside the hotel already glistened with tinsel and fake snow. Beverly believed this augured well for the day's endeavor: one day she would live in a country where real snow drifted from the sky and covered the ground like cake frosting. She resolved that no one, not a doorman nor a concierge nor even an impudent child, would prevent her from claiming the life she deserved.

Without the lamp-lit windows that gilded it at dusk, the Inter-Continental Hotel looked rather unremarkable in the midmorning glare, just one of many other concrete buildings along Ayala Avenue. This time Beverly strolled up to the revolving middle door, ignoring the doorman's chortled *Good morning.*

"Beverly, over here!" Lisa hopped out of a lobby armchair, looking like a lemon Popsicle in her jumpsuit and matching espadrilles. "Lydell left to play golf half an hour ago, and I decided to wait for you here. I get lonely up in our room when he's gone."

"Salamat naman," Beverly thanked her, glad that she would not have to dodge the concierge so early in the day. "Is this outfit good enough for pictures?"

Beverly had been blessed with long legs, a narrow waist and breasts that were the pride of Duarté women, but none of these gifts were evident in her dowdy outfit.

Lisa grimaced at her friend's calf-length denim skirt, loose floral blouse and bedraggled canvas backpack. "Why don't we look at the clothes Lydell bought me the other day?"

The women stepped into the elevator, where an attendant glanced at their reflections in the mirrored console. The friends were polar opposites: the short dusky one a lushly made-up Lolita, and her pretty, barefaced friend a nun escaped from the convent.

"Mr. Kinkade is out *po*?" the attendant asked Lisa with pointed respect.

"Playing golf. My friend is keeping me company today." Lisa nudged Beverly. "Efren works the elevator shift during the day. We talk whenever there aren't any foreigners in the elevator."

"Kasi naman po, it's against the rules to talk to guests." Efren flashed them a grin over his shoulder. "But Miss Lisa is very kind."

Beverly smiled at the floor, happy to know Lisa hadn't lost the common touch despite the prosperous life she'd won.

Moments later, Lisa ushered Beverly into her hotel room, which contained a wall-sized picture window and the largest bed Beverly had ever seen. "Four people could sleep on this bed." Beverly ran her palm across the quilted bedspread.

"Lydell likes to stretch out. I always sleep on the very edge, but take most of the pillows." Lisa opened the closet and began pulling out dresses, tantalizing confections of cotton, satin and voile. Tossed across the bed, they resembled brightly colored flowers. Beverly looked each one over, feeling fabric and studying necklines, marveling at clothes she'd only ever seen through department store windows. She didn't have the nerve to try on the tight pink sheath Lisa had worn to Bar Bibliotek, and the yellow sundress her friend had worn to the cemetery looked too short.

"What about this?" Lisa held up a blush pink frock with little bows at the top of its straps. "I haven't shortened it yet."

Beverly smiled; that shade of pink had been her mother's favorite color. "Let me see if it fits." She slipped on the dress and knew from the sudden envy in Lisa's eyes that it flattered her figure, its scooped neckline and snug bodice displaying curves she had always been too modest to show off.

"Good choice." Lisa nodded. "Now let's get some color on your face." Directing her friend to a stool by the vanity, Lisa began pulling out little pots of cream, variegated palettes of eye shadow and a fistful of brushes and pencils. "Chin up, eyes closed. This will go faster if you stay perfectly still."

"Do you wear this much makeup every day?" Beverly tried not to squirm as Lisa painted a thin black line along one eyelid. She was happy it was just the two of them that day, chattering freely in Tagalog as they had since girlhood.

"*Aba, siyempre!* I would never let Lydell see me without makeup. A girl needs to look good *all* the time for her man."

"Ganoon ba?" Beverly was skeptical. "Really? Even in bed?"

"Especially in bed." Lisa deepened the arch in Beverly's eyebrow with a sable pencil. "When you're lying that close to a man, the last thing you want to offer him is a naked face."

"But is everything else . . . naked?" Beverly was glad she had to keep her eyes shut.

"Bastos!" Lisa pinched her friend's shoulder. "Eventually, yes."

"What does it feel like"— Beverly was torn between curiosity and discretion—"to be naked with a man?" She opened her eyes, hoping Lisa would not take offense at such a personal question.

Lisa met her friend's gaze in the mirror, twirling a mascara wand as she composed a reply. "*Noong una*, I thought I would suffocate—Lydell is so big, you know. But it only hurts in the beginning. And every time we—" Lisa hesitated. The only words she knew were too vulgar to say out loud. "*Ewan ko ba*. I can't explain it. All I know is afterwards, I feel small and warm and very tired. Like a baby."

Beverly's mouth formed a surprised, silent O as her gaze traveled from Lisa's distracted smile to the bed and its meadow of dresses. "Do you think it will always be like that with him? Even in America?"

"Especially in America." Lisa unscrewed a tube of pink lipstick. "*Dalawa lang kami*—it will be just the two of us over there. Who else would I depend on?"

Half an hour later, Beverly could barely recognize the image in the mirror. Lisa had accentuated her eyes, cheekbones and lips with kohl, rouge and lipstick, making her more emphatically pretty. She looked like a boldfaced version of her old self, Beverly with an exclamation point.

"*Para ka nang* movie star!" Lisa stepped back to admire her handiwork. "Let's go take photos by the pool before the mascara smears."

Wobbling on heels taller than any she'd ever worn, Beverly walked across the lobby, drawing a glare from the concierge and admiring stares from a trio of Japanese tourists. Lisa led her past a gallery of jewelry and perfume boutiques and out through wide glass doors to the pool area. In contrast to the lobby with its air-conditioned bustle, the hotel's garden simmered with a tropical languor. An apron of verdant grass led up to the swimming pool, where three foreign women, generously oiled and basting under the blazing sun, reclined on lounge chairs. The pool was empty but for a pair of teenagers swimming leisurely laps. Apart from two waiters huddled in the shade of the poolside bar, Lisa and Beverly were the only fully clothed people in the area. It was past eleven a.m. by then, and the sun made Beverly squint.

"How about we go over there?" Lisa pointed to the shallow end of the pool. Just beyond the pebble wash periphery rose a border of bird-of-paradise plants, spiky purple and orange blooms craning above a sea of emerald blades. The chairs on that side were unoccupied, being in the shadow of palm trees.

"There's some shade there, and those flowers make a great background," Lisa said.

Beverly hesitated. "Can't we do this in your room instead? I don't want to pose in front of all these people. *Diyahe naman*—how embarrassing."

"Don't be so self-conscious," Lisa murmured to her friend in Tagalog as they walked past three pairs of pale feet, long-toed and bony as rabbit paws. "These women are too busy tanning to care about us. Come on, now: stand by those flowers and smile."

Stifling self-consciousness, Beverly followed Lisa's directions to set a hand on one hip and tilt her head so that her hair cascaded over one shoulder. The photography session was not what Beverly had anticipated. She had thought she could emulate the elegant grace of a society lady standing straight and tall like a champagne flute, but these poses Lisa instructed her to hold seemed almost insistently cute. But Beverly knew better than to contradict the friend whose dress she was wearing, in whose hands she had placed her dreams.

"Now sit on this chair. YES! Lean back, push your chest out, big smile. Ready? *Ganda mo!* Beautiful! One more just to make sure. Look at me and smile. . . ."

Lisa's frenetic stage directions caught the attention of the young couple in the pool. Intrigued, they wandered over to sit half-submerged on the pool's wide steps, eavesdropping.

"What do you think they're doing?" Amparo whispered to Matéo. "I thought only Koreans dressed up to swim."

"Maybe they're tourists from Davao." Matéo leaned against the top stair and stretched his left arm so that it rested on the tiles just behind Amparo's bare back. This allowed him an optimal view of her bikini-clad figure, of virgin knolls and hollows, of lissome legs stretched alongside his own.

"But what a weird place to be taking pictures." Amparo twirled her hair into a loose braid down her back and cast sidelong glances at the women.

"Why don't we just enjoy the show?" Matéo raised his hand and drizzled a few drops of water down Amparo's shoulder, making her jerk forward with a surprised squeal. She would have pushed off from the steps, but he tugged on her hair.

"Stay and pretend we're talking, so we can spy on them," he whispered.

"Only if you promise to behave." Amparo leaned back, barely noticing that Matéo had shifted closer, so that the length of his thigh pressed against hers each time he leaned over to whisper. They'd gone on several group dates since Carina Madrigal's engagement party, but this was the first time they'd been truly alone. The absence of the usual crowd of friends made Amparo feel uncharacteristically shy, and she was grateful for this unexpected diversion.

"I really shouldn't criticize—we have no more right to be here than they do. How exactly did you sneak us in? I thought only guests were allowed here."

"My brother Richard used to date the concierge." Matéo

winked. "I think Felicidad's still hoping to get back together with him, because she gave him a year's pass to the pool and executive lounge. I borrowed it from Richard."

"You Madrigal boys are too charming for your own good," Amparo chided, secretly pleased that he'd gained them special access.

Meanwhile the little photographer scampered about, giggling when she wasn't talking, demonstrating poses for her friend to imitate. Lisa was just then instructing Beverly to lean forward so that her face hovered above the spiked purple plumes of a bird-of-paradise. "Turn your head so I can get a three-quarter view."

"You said we were only taking a few photos." Beverly smiled through a clenched jaw.

"We need to take as many as we can. Filipina Sweetheart's catalog displays full-length, three-quarter and close-up shots of every girl." Lisa pointed with her lips toward the edge of the pool. "Let's try a shot over there."

Amparo giggled into Matéo's shoulder. "Haven't these people ever seen a hotel pool?"

"People get excited about all kinds of things." Matéo concentrated on quelling his own excitement as he gazed upon the creamy expanse of flesh, naked but for a few frivolous triangles of scarlet Lycra. "Besides, aren't you glad we have something to watch? If we'd gone to Polo Club, we'd be the ones on view. Everyone goes there on the weekend. Your mom would have heard all about our date before you got home."

"But you can't avoid gossip; it's the Manila way. Uh-oh!" Amparo clapped a hand over her mouth. The girl in the pink dress had backed up to the rim of the pool and nearly lost her balance. Had the photographer not grabbed her wrist, she would have tumbled into the water.

"*Tama na*—that's enough!" Beverly was breathless, her face burning with embarrassment. "You've taken enough pictures to fill a whole album."

"Sige na nga!" Lisa laughed. "Let's get you out of my dress before you ruin it. There's a place at the mall that develops pictures while you wait. After lunch we'll take the photos to Filipina Sweetheart's office on Buendia. They're open on Saturday."

"What's Filipina Sweetheart?" Amparo adjusted her bikini top.

"Sounds like one of those mail-order bride places." Matéo willed himself to look at the retreating figures, grateful that the water was just cool enough to calm an incipient bulge. "My dad had to deal with those women all over Spain and the East Coast when their marriages went sour. Lots of deportations, a few deaths."

Amparo's eyes widened. "You're kidding."

"Wish I were, but Dad told us about the worst cases. He said anyone who had to import a wife was bound to be a loser." Pushing off from the stairs, he flicked water at Amparo. "Show's over. Race me to the end of the pool?"

Beverly's makeup was melting in the midafternoon heat by the time she and Lisa walked into the gray building that housed the offices of Filipina Sweetheart. A creaking elevator delivered them to the third floor, where linoleum floors bore the odor of bleach. Lisa led her friend past a closed notary public's office and a travel agency plastered with posters of rice terraces and white sand beaches, all the way to the end of the hall. The Filipina Sweetheart logo was emblazoned above glass doors, through which Beverly could see a sallow-faced receptionist burrowing through a bag of Clover Chips.

"*Kumusta na,* Miss Connie?" Lisa greeted the receptionist. "Is Carmelo here? My friend wants to sign up. We brought photos."

Slightly nauseated by the lavender-scented air freshener, Beverly scanned wedding photos displayed like so many diplomas on the wall beneath a lavender banner touting Mango Brides Make the Sweetest Wives! Several photos had dedications scrawled across their bottom corners. *Mabuhay from Melbourne! Happy in Hawaii! Auf Wiedersehen aus Berlin!* The brides were uniformly dressed in frothy white gowns and gossamer veils, fresh as the flowers they clutched. Most looked decades younger than their graying husbands, who towered over their petite brides, somber as undertakers in dark suits. She imagined herself dressed in ivory lace, wrapped in the embrace of an American groom, beaming down from the walls of Filipina Sweetheart.

Connie wiped her hands on tissue, casting an appraising gaze on Beverly. "Sir Carmelo went to Cebu yesterday. He's hosting a party weekend for ten German and Australian clients who joined our end-of-the-year Lovefest: '*Thrilla in Manila* doubled with *Rendezvous in Cebu*.'" She sucked on her teeth. "*Biro mo,* we invited four girls per man at every soiree. Those foreigners just can't make up their minds!" Connie nodded at Lisa. "*Suwerte ka,* Lisa, you're lucky Mr. Kinkade chose you right away."

"I didn't know I'd have to compete against three other girls. What if I'm not chosen?" Beverly pouted. "*Naku,* I've never even had a boyfriend. How would I know how to flirt with a foreigner?" Beverly wanted to kick herself. She had been naive to think a husband could simply be delivered to her door, like letters in the mail.

Connie cooed with practiced empathy. "Don't worry. A pretty girl like you could easily have three men fighting for a date."

"Connie knows what she's talking about." Lisa nudged Beverly. "She says in the seven years she's worked here, she's seen hundreds of couples fall in love."

"Oo naman," Connie agreed, waving at the wedding pictures. "These foreigners pay expensive membership fees just to see the Sweetheart catalog; then they spend even more money to fly here and meet the girls. No one wants to leave empty-handed. With Filipina Sweetheart, *garantisado ang* sweetheart! The girls are all so sweet that we call them our Mango Brides."

Connie's staunch guarantee bolstered Beverly's resolve. With a shy smile, she took the packet of photos out of her backpack. "I hope these are good enough to put in your catalog."

Connie looked from Beverly's photos to the woman standing before her. "You should wear short skirts more often—look how pretty you are in these pictures. *Sayang naman*—why hide your legs under that old-lady outfit?"

Connie took a sheet of paper from a folder on her desk and passed it to Beverly on a clipboard. She smiled, chapped lips stretching above purplish gums. "Fill in this questionnaire and tell us what you're looking for in a man. Take your time—true love is forever." Connie cackled as Beverly and Lisa retreated to a red couch covered entirely in plastic.

With Lisa looking over her shoulder, Beverly scanned the questionnaire, bewildered by a menu of options that listed everything from age and height to faith and political affiliation.

"How did you answer this?" Beverly asked.

"*Basta*, don't be picky." Lisa traced a finger down the sheet. "See here where it asks about age? Check all the age ranges—twenty to thirty, all the way up to sixty."

"That's what you did?" Beverly held pen above the paper, afraid to commit her future to boxes on a page.

"*Puwede ba*, Bev—Lydell is fifty-five, no? Do you think he was this rich at twenty-five? Don't you want someone who's already made his fortune?"

"Sige na nga," Beverly conceded, remembering what Lisa had told her about Lydell's home. *Three bedrooms, two bathrooms and a garden.* "I don't care if he's not rich, as long as he has a good job. Anyway, I want to work, at least until I start having babies." Beverly nibbled on the tip of her pen, wondering what her half-American child would look like.

"Bagal mo naman." Lisa poked Beverly in the ribs, chiding her slowness. "You won't have babies at all if you don't finish the questionnaire!"

With Lisa's repeated admonitions to cast her net wide, Beverly specified her preferences for religion (none), educational attainment (high school) and profession (any). She had almost reached the end when she paused, stumped, by a section for *"Special Requests."* Wasn't wishing for a husband in itself a special request? If her *inay* were alive, what would she want for her only daughter? Beverly wondered. Finally, the answer presented itself. Pressing down so hard that her pen nearly gashed the sheet, she scribbled: *"Must love kids."* A father was the one thing that would instantly have made life better for her and her mother.

Beverly signed the form and handed it back to Connie, who put it into a lilac folder along with the photos of the newest Filipina Sweetheart.

"Salamat," Connie thanked her. "Just you wait. Your life will change. *Garantisado'yan.* Guaranteed."

Putting her love life in the hands of a stranger made Beverly feel light-headed. She'd felt the same terrified euphoria when Clara took her on a Ferris wheel for the first time at age six. As the wheel swung them high in the evening sky, Beverly held her breath, frozen between a wail and a giggle. Was this the way love would feel?

"How long before I get a pen pal?" She was six years old again, holding her breath.

"Don't worry. *Maganda ka naman.*" Connie was skilled at offering reassurance. "Pretty girls like you get letters almost as soon as we put the pictures up on our Web site. *Maniwala ka,* even ugly girls have found husbands with our help." Connie raised an eyebrow. "If only you'd signed up with Lisa here, you two might have had a double wedding, no?"

"*Eh ikaw*—what about you?" Beverly couldn't help asking, noticing the receptionist's ringless hands. Connie's narrow eyes, pug nose and thin lips made her plain, but she was hardly ugly. "Have you put your own application in, just to see who'll write?"

"Me?" Connie snorted. She stood up with some difficulty and took a few crooked steps to the watercooler. Only then did Beverly notice that the receptionist's left leg was distinctly shorter and thinner than the right one. Connie filled her paper cup and turned to catch Beverly staring at her shrunken leg.

"I would have been married and living in America long ago, if not for polio. I can't hide the leg in the photos, so no one's written me yet. Mr. Carmelo said Americans have no patience for imperfection." She shrugged. "*Pero* okay *lang*. I just help other girls and keep praying to Saint Joseph." Connie straightened up as best she could, given her asymmetrical hips. "One day, Saint Joseph will find me a good husband. I know it."

"Oo naman," Lisa agreed. She'd already heard this story; Connie told it to every girl who enlisted at Filipina Sweetheart. Tugging at Beverly's sleeve, she backed up to the door. "*O sige,* Connie, Lydell is waiting for us back at the hotel."

On the way to the elevator, Beverly glanced at the travel agency posters of Boracay's white sands. *Voted best beach in the world!* the caption proclaimed. Unless she found a rich husband to pay plane fare, she would never see that southern island. "Lisa, what if my smile was crooked or the mascara smeared in those photos?" Doubt gnawed like a toothache. "What if I'm not perfect enough to be chosen?"

"*Ano ka ba?* Stop worrying. I turned you into a beauty queen!" Lisa squeezed Beverly's arm. "Someone will write soon. I'll tell Lydell's friend Hank to write you. *Malay mo*—who knows, maybe one day we'll be neighbors in Naples."

"Inay would like that." Beverly smiled at the thought of her mother. Perhaps Clara could persuade Saint Joseph to find a rich, handsome American husband for her daughter. Perhaps he would even be under forty.

CHAPTER 16

Falling

Amparo left the InterContinental Hotel with a suntan and a secret: Matéo would be her very first lover. This was not a decision made lightly, for after a dozen years in convent school Amparo still bore residual inhibitions about sex.

But today's date at the InterContinental had convinced her that Matéo was a cut above all her other suitors. As he stowed her bag in the trunk, Amparo settled into her seat, languorous as a cat from hours in the sun. She straightened the hem of her shorts, admiring the contrast between the creamy linen and her newly bronzed thighs.

"Did you forget to strap yourself in?" Matéo looked over at her as he fastened his seat belt. "I know seat belt laws aren't enforced in Manila, but indulge me. Let's pretend we're in the States. Better safe than screwed, I always say."

"If you say so." Amparo smiled, knowing they might as well have been in another country for all the freedom anonymity granted her. All day she had played at being a grown woman—an elegant, vaguely European woman—beguiling her beau under the disinterested gaze of waiters and tourists who did not know her or her parents. After today, sex appeared to be the only reasonable conclusion to their avid flirting. She had already moved a few steps closer to that notion after Ditas Tijeras's sly confession some weeks earlier.

The two had sprawled out on Ditas's bed that Sunday afternoon, browsing through American fashion magazines, when she held up a provocative photo spread for Amparo to look at. "Do you ever wish you could do *this* to a guy?" The model challenged the camera with a brazen stare, corseted breasts caught in midheave, arms akimbo. She straddled a shirtless man on a rumpled bed, locking him between her knees, a lioness interrupted before the kill. Across the page the headline blared: *Ten Ways to Dominate and Delight Him.* "Wanna bet I could do that to Rico?"

"You wish," Amparo snorted, flipping through a shoe pictorial. A second-string player on the varsity basketball team, Rico Gatmaitan looked like an eight-year-old on stilts, his full-cheeked face and snub nose not having matured as quickly as his gangly limbs. Ditas had only recently tweezed away his unibrow. "Do you even own a corset?"

"Props are beside the point. I've always delighted Rico. But now I also dominate him." Ditas sat up, adjusting the bra strap that peeked out of her tank top. Her eyes widened and she looked ready to explode with some delightful secret. "Guess what, 'Paro. We did it. We went all the way last Saturday."

"No way you had sex with *Rico*!" Amparo stared at her best friend. She'd known Ditas since infancy; their mothers had shared the same pediatrician. This was the first milestone Ditas had passed ahead of her. "I can't believe Rico talked you into it."

"Who said he talked me into it?" Ditas fished into her makeup pouch and puckered up for a fresh coat of Italian Nude. Amparo watched Ditas paint her lips, her newly curled hair arranged in careful tousles around her shoulders. She looked suddenly like a full-grown woman. Did all girls who'd relinquished virginity gain such a knowing look?

"*Ayyy*, Ditas . . . if Sister Mary Joseph only knew . . ." Amparo tried to erase the image of Ditas seducing Rico, to the utter mortification of their high school Christian Family Life teacher. "Where did you do it?"

"In his car, in front of A.S. around midnight. The parking lot was empty. We started fooling around and well"—Ditas sighed, eyes gazing skyward—"we just kept rolling along. . . . You know, it's true what *Cosmo* says about guys and sex. Now if I want anything from Rico, all I do is offer him—you know—and he folds, like *that*." She snapped her fingers.

"You are shameless! Who'd have thought you'd lose your virginity before I did?" Amparo imagined Ditas sprinting ahead, brandishing carnal knowledge like an Olympic torch. "Aren't you scared you'll get pregnant?"

"Nope. After that first time, Rico put a travel pack of condoms in his gym bag."

Amparo shuddered at the thought of condoms sharing space with Rico's tube socks. "So . . . did it hurt, that first time?"

"Maybe a tiny bit, I really don't remember. . . ." Ditas twisted a lock of hair, tightening its corkscrew curl. "It was definitely more fun than putting in a tampon."

Amparo clocked her friend with a pillow. "But did you have to do it in his *car?* Couldn't you have at least held out for a real bed?"

"Hey, it's not like there's a Tiffany's Place on every block! Rico's allowance wouldn't cover dinner *and* short-time at a motel. Besides, it doesn't matter where you do it." Ditas tugged at the gold crucifix she wore round her neck. "When you find the right guy . . . magic happens. That Matéo Madrigal—he could be The One. You never know."

Amparo considered the notion of surrendering to Matéo. She had been on the verge of doing so, the first time they'd kissed in Tita Carina's meditation garden. What might have transpired, had his brother Richard not interrupted them? Amparo had pondered that question for weeks, replaying their tryst in a continuous reel, remembering where his hands had wandered, where his lips. And yet how could she know for sure that he was The One?

By the end of their day at the InterContinental, Amparo knew. She glanced at Matéo, drumming long fingers on the steering wheel as he waited for the light to turn green. She remembered those fingers smoothing suntan lotion between her shoulder blades, teasing out the tightness around her neck, sliding down the cleft of her spine. They'd spent most of that Saturday in close quarters, practically naked. She had seen that his broad shoulders tapered to slender hips, that his legs were long and gently muscled, that he had surprisingly large feet. She'd heard the old adage about large feet. Blushing at the thought, she smiled out the window. Maybe Ditas had a point. He would be more fun than a tampon.

"Peso for your thoughts?" Matéo tapped Amparo's knee.

"Don't you mean 'penny'?" She took his fingers and held them on her lap.

"A peso probably equals a penny, what with devaluation."

"What do you know about exchange rates?"

"You'd learn about currency too if your family traveled as often as mine does. Dad tried to cut my allowance whenever we visited another country, but as long as I calculated the dollar equivalent for francs, marks or lire, he could never fool me."

"Who knew you were so shrewd?" Amparo shook her head. There it was again, another reminder Matéo had spent so much time abroad that he was practically a foreigner. Perhaps growing up European had made him more proficient at courtship than other boys. All that day, Matéo had spoiled her with small gestures, draping a towel round her shoulders, ordering mango daiquiris at lunch, feeding her spoonfuls of Death by Chocolate. How different he was from others with whom she'd dallied, all thumbs and bungling tongues. Amparo did not want to simply roll into sex the way Ditas had, like a runaway car whose brakes had failed, but today Matéo had proved himself worthy of becoming her first lover. Was she ready to make that leap? If Ditas had survived the fall, why couldn't she?

Matéo reached over and stroked her nape as they pulled up in front of her home. Amparo arched her neck, all but purring.

"Want to come in and say hello to my mom?" Amparo hung on to the car latch, reluctant to get out. "She likes you—she said your dad still makes her feel like a debutante."

"Do I make *you* feel like a debutante?" Matéo's lingering gaze raised the fine hairs on Amparo's arms.

"Sorry, but I had my debut three months before we met." She wanted to smooth Matéo's sun-streaked bangs away from his forehead, but desire made her suddenly shy.

"Too bad, I bet it was some party. Wish I could stay, but I need to get home. A friend of my parents is retiring from the foreign ministry and they're throwing a dinner in her honor. I went to school with her daughter in L.A.; our families go back a long way."

"You're having dinner with an old girlfriend?" Amparo raised an eyebrow.

"We're not playing that game, now, are we?" Matéo squeezed her shoulder. "I'll see you in class next week. Maybe we can have barbecue at the Beach House again." Before Amparo could reply, he pulled her in for a kiss that tasted of mangoes and rum.

"Lunch after class, then." Amparo stepped out of the car and pushed the door shut. She felt warm and short of breath, as though sparklers had ignited in her chest, tickling her skin with a thousand delicious pinpricks. "Don't forget we're discussing *Pride and Prejudice* on Tuesday."

"Have you always been so studious?" Matéo raised an eyebrow. "I didn't know you were vying to be teacher's pet in Valoria's class."

"Don't need to be teacher's pet, I've made the dean's list every semester since getting into U.P." Amparo leaned in through the window, the neckline of her blouse falling away to reveal the deep tan of her bosom. "Besides, Austen could teach you a thing or two about love. The romance is in restraint."

"Handcuffs? Austen used handcuffs?"

Amparo shook her head in mock despair and waved him off.

Marcela was in the driveway, winnowing rice with a wheel-sized *bilao,* when the houseboy opened the gate for Amparo. Afternoon sunlight slanted down through the acacia branches, turning chaff into gold dust each time the cook tossed the rice and caught it in the shallow basket. Amparo watched silently for a moment, loving the rhythmic shush-shushing of falling grain, loving Inay Marcela, steadfast as trees, loving every last part of her magical day.

"*Anak,* why are you still standing there?" Marcela crunched rice husks beneath her slippers, bemused by the distracted smile on Amparo's face. "Where have you been all day? Your mother will be upset when she sees how dark you are!"

"*Ay, Inay,* stop nagging." Amparo threw an arm around her nanny's shoulders. She took a deep breath. "Can you keep a secret, *Inay*? I think I'm in love."

"*Jesu-u-u-smaryosep.*" Marcela sang the lament, laugh lines deepening around her eyes. "It's that new boy, isn't it? The mestizo?"

"*Inay naman,* there's more to Matéo than his being mestizo. Promise me you won't tell Mama. She'll run straight to Tita Carina; then all of Manila will know." Amparo bit her lip. "Promise not to tell?"

"*O sigé na nga*—all right," Marcela clucked, pleased that Amparo still confided in her. "But if that boy breaks your heart, he will have to answer to me."

"I'll tell him you said that." Amparo turned on her heels and skipped to the house, wondering how long she'd have to wait before Matéo seduced her.

As it turned out, seduction was not as easy to orchestrate as Amparo had expected. A week after their date at the InterContinental, she met him on the steps of the Arts and Letters building. Amparo found Matéo there after her last class of the day, and welcomed a slow hour with him before the family driver came to take her home. The wide flights of steps spanning the front of the College of Arts and Letters building offered the closest thing to café culture at the university and students gathered there every day to sit and watch the campus world roll by.

"Hey, stranger." She set her notebook on the step and sat on it, nudging his shoulder.

"Ciao, bella." Matéo smiled but seemed preoccupied. "Sorry I haven't been around lately. Richard enlisted me to help campaign—you know, show up at more of Dad's speeches. Mostly I go along to keep my mom company." He poked at his knee through a frayed hole in his jeans. "If Dad wins a seat in the Senate, I don't know if she could stand to live here permanently. She misses Europe."

"Who wouldn't?" Amparo gazed at the file of jeepneys crawling along the street, at the frat boys smoking in the parking lot beyond. That was where Ditas had first sampled sex, she recalled, with a start. She imagined Ditas and Rico half-naked and horny, bumping against door handles and cup holders in his tiny hatchback. She assumed Matéo had lost his innocence much earlier, but in what country and with whom?

"Do you miss it? Living abroad, I mean."

"Now and then. Living here has its perks"—Matéo glanced sideways at Amparo—"but I got around a lot more when we lived abroad."

"What do you mean—you have your own car here, don't you?"

"I'm talking about freedom, 'Paro." Matéo rested elbows on

knees. "When my dad was ambassador, we were foreigners wherever he was posted. Foreigners can get away with pretty much anything because the locals assume you don't know any better. But now that we're back in Manila, we *are* the locals. People expect certain things of my family. Suddenly I have to worry about the family's reputation. It's all Richard talks about these days."

"What could you possibly do to harm your family's reputation?" In an innocently provocative gesture, Amparo twisted her hair and pulled it over one shoulder, baring her nape to the afternoon breeze.

Matéo reached over to trace the moist length of her neck, his finger lingering at the rim of her blouse. "I don't know, 'Paro. Do you have any ideas?"

A familiar giggle interrupted their conversation. "'Paro! I didn't know you were still on campus." Ditas Tijeras waved from the bottom of the steps, dwarfed by a tall boy in khakis. "Is that Matéo? Come down and introduce us."

Offering Matéo an apologetic shrug, Amparo got up and led him down the stairs.

The final weeks before Christmas break drained away in a deluge of schoolwork that kept Amparo too busy to daydream about trysts. That last Friday the campus thrummed with frenetic festivity, as students rushed to class with papers typed scant hours before deadline. Having extracted all they could from their students' intellect, professors dismissed class early in preparation for the Christmas Lantern Parade. The sixty-six-year-old event marked the beginning of Christmas holidays and was the university's most beloved and staunchly held tradition, and had been canceled only twice: the first time by World War II and once more upon the imposition of Martial Law. It was one of the few things Amparo had seen before Matéo, and she was pleased he would be watching it for the first time with her.

As the day crept away, red and yellow star lanterns flickered on, casting twin constellations upon the hundred-foot-tall pillars that flanked the entrance to the College of Arts and Letters building. The scent of boiled peanuts and frying fish balls suffused the balmy air, their vendors temporarily sidelined by the raucous procession. Scores of parade onlookers had already massed on the building's front steps, forcing Amparo and Matéo to seek an alternative vantage point.

"There's a free spot up here." Matéo hoisted himself up on the rim of a chest-high concrete box planter, ignoring bougainvillea thorns that scraped his back as he reached down for Amparo's hand. The ledge was just wide enough for her to squeeze in front of Matéo, their feet splayed like ballet dancers. It was not the most stable perch, and she was glad Matéo hooked his thumb into her belt loop, anchoring her. More students scrambled up on either side, forcing them to stand so closely together that Amparo could feel the rise and fall of Matéo's chest against her back.

A band of elves in scarlet caps, cotton beards and red high-tops marched past just then, their deflated Santa Claus bringing up the rear with a trombone.

"This is your first Lantern Parade, isn't it?" Amparo hollered over her shoulder to Matéo. "That makes you a Parade Virgin."

Matéo laughed and bowed his head alongside Amparo's to avoid yelling. "First time anyone's ever called *me* a virgin. But you're right, this is my first Lantern Parade; we spent last Christmas in D.C. Tita Carina said one of her cousins was crowned Queen of the Lantern Parade in 'sixty-nine, just before running off to the hills to join the insurgents."

Matéo's lips brushed against Amparo's ear as he spoke and she leaned into the crook of his neck, heady with the scent of aftershave. "She told me that story!" Amparo spoke into Matéo's cheek. "When they finally caught her, Marcos kept her in jail for two years. She was the last Lantern Parade Queen. After that, feminists killed the pageant. These days only gay students hold beauty contests, and all of them are queens."

Cheers drowned out Matéo's reply as a troupe of eight-foot-tall papier-mâché puppets trundled up the road. Children darted out on the street, dancing around the puppets until their mothers chased them back to the curb.

"The Fine Arts students work on their parade entry for weeks—I used to go to their studios and watch them. No one would tell me what those puppets were supposed to represent." Matéo leaned his head against Amparo's so that she could hear him. "They must've been smoking something good; I've never seen anything like those puppets."

"They weren't stoned, silly—those are monsters from the old folktales. See what you missed, growing up abroad? Look, that's the *kapré*." Amparo pointed at a tobacco-skinned giant with a Dalí moustache. In place of a lantern, the *kapré* carried a yard-long cigar, whose smoke wafted back and up the long black snout of a horse-headed man who snorted indignation. "That second puppet's supposed to be a *Tikbalang*—sort of like a centaur, only the other way around."

Matéo snickered. "So tell me, is that *Tikbalang* hung like a stallion or is he just a man from the withers down?"

Amparo would have turned to pinch Matéo had she not been afraid of falling off the ledge. She was acutely aware of his arm wrapped round her waist, nestling their bodies together snug as spoons on a tray. Luckily, the parade provided a reason for chitchat, distracting her from the intimate stance.

"Look, that's Juan Tamad." She pointed at a squat puppet with a little boy's outsized head. Folklore's beloved Lazy Boy waved a tiny *parol* in front of his mother, who stooped beneath the much larger star lantern she bore on her shoulders.

"I'm sensing a pattern." Matéo's breath tickled Amparo's earlobe. "Do guys have all the fun in those folktales? So far the best costumes are worn by men."

"That's why it's called *fantasy,* Matéo. Men play out the fantasy, and women pull them back to the real world."

"I bet girls have their own fantasies too. Don't you?"

With Matéo nuzzling her hair, Amparo exhaled a slow breath, trying to calm her popcorn heart. "That's for me to know and you to find out."

"I see you've been reading Austen again."

Crowds normally made Amparo uncomfortable and she would have skipped that year's parade had she not decided it made a good pretext for a date. To her great surprise, she found the event genuinely enjoyable. Swaddled in Matéo's arms, she cheered along with everyone else, feeling as though Christmas had already arrived.

"That's my brother Javier!" She pointed at a stocky figure in a safari vest, rifle propped on one shoulder, cigar clenched in his teeth.

"Is he playing the great white hunter?" Matéo asked, choking back a chuckle.

"Hemingway! Javier said the lit department chose a 'great authors and their characters' theme."

Sure enough, Amparo's brother walked with a curious assemblage of students and professors, variously attired in togas, trench coats, cloche hats and fringed flapper dresses.

"So would that be Cervantes?" Matéo pointed to a goateed man in a white neck ruff, brandishing a sword at the windmill that preceded him.

"Yes, but—how did they persuade Professor Valoria to come as Dulcinea!" Their literature professor strolled beside Cervantes the windmill, virtually unrecognizable in a tiered red skirt and peasant blouse, a scarlet carnation tucked behind her ear.

"Looks like she needs a good tumble in the hay," Matéo joked. "A little tumble never hurt anyone, wouldn't you say?" Matéo tickled Amparo's waist.

"You have a one-track mind." Amparo wiggled away. She would have tripped off the ledge but for Matéo's tight grasp.

"Whoa, steady." He pulled her close. "I can't let you fall—what would your mom say?"

Amparo felt his laughter on her cheek. If she turned a fraction of an inch, their lips would meet, but she could not kiss him in front of hundreds of spectators.

"Tell me, which writer would you have come as?" Matéo's question startled Amparo.

"Isak Dinesen, perhaps."

"Aha—the tragic writer. Her husband gave her syphilis and her great love crashed his plane. Couldn't you have chosen someone with a happier life?"

"My favorite female writers either committed suicide or drank themselves to death," Amparo retorted. "Tragedy is the price writers pay for love."

"So would you rather be happy and alone, like Professor Valoria?" Matéo teased.

"Too soon to tell, Matéo, too soon to tell." Amparo cupped his cheek. "Let's go. There's got to be a less crowded way to celebrate Christmas." Amparo peeled away from Matéo's embrace and leaped off the planter, confident she would not stumble.

The couple walked to the quiet street behind the parade route where Matéo had parked his car. Amparo relished the companionable silence until a low growl interrupted it.

"Excuse my stomach, I'm starving." Matéo laughed. "Look, this is one of the rare nights my dad isn't speaking at a fund-raiser. How about I take you to dinner?" Matéo opened the car door for Amparo.

"Sounds good." Amparo got into the car, giddy with the notion that dinner could well be merely the first course of the evening. "I told my parents there would be a party after the parade, so we'll be fine as long as I'm home by midnight."

"No problem, Cinderella. And since you took me to the Lantern Parade, I'm going to return the favor and show you a side of Manila you've probably never seen." As Matéo drove away from the university, Amparo glanced back at the statue of the Oblation, the naked man's arms raised, as though saluting her farewell. They sped down streets brightened by star lanterns and turned on Timog Avenue, ablaze with garish neon marquees of honky-tonks and beer gardens, where a man's fortitude was measured by the number of empty bottles on his table.

"You're right, I've never really seen this part of Manila." Amparo gaped at a billboard of a woman clad in sundry scraps of leather and sequins. "My mom would be mortified if she knew we came here."

"Then let's not tell her." Matéo winked. "My parents took us to so many fancy restaurants that I avoid them whenever I can now. Shawarma Heaven's food is way better than anything you'll get at a white-napkin joint." Turning down a side street, Matéo pulled up by an open shack fronted by four oilcloth-covered tables. He helped Amparo hop over the open sewer and led her to the counter, where a heavyset man stood by a ham-sized cone of meat. Amparo inhaled the potent bouquet of roast lamb, cardamom and allspice.

"Ahh, Matéo." The man's teeth gleamed white beneath his curled moustache. "Haven't seen you in a while."

"Blame the family. This is the first time I've gotten away from my dad's meetings." Matéo nudged Amparo. "Babak makes the best shawarma in town, and he's open till midnight. This is where the fine arts students come whenever they work late."

"Do you and your girlfriend want the dinner special?"

Matéo draped an arm round Amparo's shoulder. "Nothing but the best for her."

Amparo blushed. She and Matéo hadn't had that conversation yet, but if she wasn't his girlfriend now, she sensed she would be by night's end.

With surgical slashes, Babak slivered meat off the cone and

stuffed it into pita pockets, piling on cucumber, tomatoes and thin red onion rings.

"But those raw onions will make my breath smell," Amparo protested.

"If you both eat onions, you cancel each other out." Babak wagged his cleaver at Matéo. "Do me a favor, Matéo, and kiss your girl after dinner to prove it, eh?"

Matéo twisted a lock of Amparo's hair, his palm warm against her collarbone. "I was planning to do that anyway, with or without onions."

"In that case, eat quickly." Grinning, Babak handed them plastic plates laden with shawarma, tabbouleh and paper tubs of tahini.

Dinner proved to be a messier enterprise than Amparo had anticipated, the yogurt sauce dribbling through her fingers, tomatoes tumbling to the dirt, yet she found it deeply satisfying to eat with her bare hands. It evoked her earliest memories of serving pebbles and leaves in tiny clay pots to Nanay Marcela at play. Since childhood she believed the best meals were those eaten with people she loved. After Amparo had consumed every last bit, she let Matéo wipe her chin clean, then kiss her for the first time that night.

"It's not the Ritz, but I thought this would be more comfortable than my Corolla. Is this okay?" Matéo idled his car by the driveway of a low-slung building on a street heavy with the fragrance of *dama de noche.* At intervals, pink neon flared the name in rococo script: *Tiffany's Place.* After dinner they had left Timog's spangled storefronts and driven on to a silent street with small homes and a flower shop whose blooms stared through dark windows like orphaned children. Matéo dimmed the headlights, waiting to see how the evening would end.

"I didn't think we'd be going to a motel," she murmured.

"I could take you home, but I don't turn into a pumpkin till midnight."

Amparo looked through the open driveway at the windowless two-story building that stretched back from the street, a row of garage doors yawning open, each one offering private access to the bedrooms above. She had heard the jokes about the motels and their "short-time" rates. Would she become a "short-time" girl if she gave in to Matéo?

From the ivy walls that surrounded the motel, crickets played their Zen refrain, filling the silence between Amparo and Matéo. Waiting. Another car drove past just then and slid into a garage; a valet emerged from the shadows and shut the garage door. They could be anonymous here, Amparo mused, just as they had been at the InterContinental.

Matéo reached for Amparo's hand, massaging the flesh below her thumb. "I didn't realize you had such a prominent Mount of Venus." A dimple deepened on his cheek, sweetening the question in his eyes.

"So now you want to read my palm?" Amparo's voice was calm, but her heart thumped to Tiffany's neon pulse.

"I'd like to read all of you." Leaning over, Matéo caught Amparo in a kiss that stopped both her breath and heartbeat for an eternal moment. When they at last pulled apart, Amparo stared at him, afraid he would continue. Afraid he would stop.

"How about it, Cinderella?"

Amparo's fingers closed tightly over his and she released the breath she'd been holding. "Let's go before I lose my nerve."

If there was something Amparo learned that first night, it was that the rhythm of passion was deeply satisfying for its simple circularity. Mouths making pillows of opposing lips, the call and response of interlocking sighs, a passel of caresses, cascading one into the other as waves folding into sea foam. Afterward, they gathered the thin sheets about them and curled into each other, chin to forehead, chest to breast, dozing twins in a cotton womb.

CHAPTER 17

A Falling-out, 1989

Marcela should have suspected something was up when she caught a whiff of Beverly's new, intensely floral cologne when they met at the mall.

"What's that smell? You wasting money on imported shampoos now?" Marcela pulled away from their hug, startled to see her niece wearing lipstick for the first time.

"It's the cologne Lisa sent from Florida. A Christmas present she forgot to mail last year."

"It's already September. If she waited, she could have sent it for this Christmas." Marcela wrinkled her nose. "I prefer the one your mother used to wear."

"*Ninang, naman*, I was fifteen when I started wearing Inay's baby cologne." Beverly linked arms with her godmother and steered her along their usual *paseo* down the noisy gallery of the large mall. "I've worn Nenuco for eleven years; she'd have told me to try something new."

"Would she also have said you needed lipstick? That color makes you look so old."

"But I'm turning twenty-six in two months. Isn't it time I looked my age?"

"*Ayyy*, but how time flies." Marcela gazed ahead at a little girl, plump arms windmilling as she toddled away from her nanny. "You will always be a baby to me."

"For you, always." Beverly rubbed her godmother's back, gone meaty in middle age. "But for the rest of the world, I must grow up." She paused before launching into the careful announcement she'd spent weeks rehearsing. "Ninang, could you get an extra Sunday off in the first weekend of October? My boyfriend and I want to take you to lunch."

"*Aba!* Since when did you have a boyfriend?" Marcela stopped so suddenly that the shoppers behind them had to swerve. "Where did you meet him?"

The questions sounded like accusations. Marcela had to raise her head to look directly into her godchild's eyes, but she managed to make Beverly feel like a naughty child.

"Don't be angry, Ninang." Beverly nudged her godmother to resume walking. "I met him through a pen pal service. We've been writing each other since January." Beverly smiled, remembering how their letters had progressed from cautious introduction to teasing flirtation to the wistful longing she now felt whenever she looked at his photograph. Would Josiah's touch be as warm as his words? "I'm finally going to meet him this month. Will you come to lunch with us while he's in Manila?"

"What do you mean 'while he's in Manila'? Where is he usually?"

"He's from California. That's in America." Beverly faltered, made nervous by the sudden sharpness in her godmother's voice. "His name is Josiah Stein."

"He's American?"

"Yes, Ninang." Beverly pulled an envelope from her backpack. "Here's his picture."

Marcela stared at a pallid man with hair the color of faded asphalt. The slightly flared nostrils made his nose resemble an arrow pointing to pale lips that were parted in a wide smile. The gap between his teeth lined up exactly with a deep cleft in his chin. If she squinted, he would resemble Kirk Douglas, whose movies she had never liked. She handed the photo back to her godchild, her mouth a thin line of disapproval.

"*Sira ulo ka ba*—are you crazy? What woman in her right mind would send letters to a stranger? You've never met this Josiah Stein in person, so how can he be your boyfriend already? How do you know he is not a criminal, a murderer, even?" Marcela's shoulders rose like the ruff of an angry rooster as she harangued her niece loudly enough to turn heads.

"Ninang, calm down, you're embarrassing me."

"I will not calm down! *Susmaryosep*, your mother would be scandalized if she knew you were writing to a strange man."

"Inay wanted me to have a husband and children. It's what she wanted for herself."

"You don't know what she wanted, what she tried to do! You have no idea what she sacrificed to give you a life." Breathless with indignation, Marcela scowled at the statue of the red-haired clown in outsized shoes standing in front of a fast-food chain. "Why do you want to live in America? You don't even like hamburgers."

"Please, Ninang 'Cela. Mama wanted me to be happy. This is my chance. At least come to lunch and meet him. We'll go to your favorite restaurant, no burgers. We've not eaten at Max's since your birthday. Wouldn't you enjoy that?"

Marcela's shoulders sagged. After she'd devoted so many years to mothering her orphaned niece, Beverly's announcement felt like a betrayal. Even so, she remembered being that young and yearning for a man, any man, hoping she could one day find a husband. Marcela realized she could not begrudge Beverly this good fortune merely because she had gone without.

"*O sige na nga*—all right, then. I cannot protect you forever. You are old enough to make your own mistakes." Marcela buried old regrets in a sigh, and allowed Beverly to wrap an arm around her shoulder as they continued their walk through the mall.

Two weeks later Marcela was still brooding. The more she thought about it, the more indignant she became. To think that her goddaughter had kept this pen pal correspondence secret for over half a year, that Beverly would actually abandon her and move to America. How could Beverly abandon her?

She glared at the bowl of rheumy egg whites. She'd been flogging them for the last half hour, but they refused to rise into the stiff peaks she needed for the *canonigo.* In all her years making the rolled meringue cake, she'd never had this much trouble. Remembering the instant dislike she'd felt upon seeing Josiah's photo, she resumed whipping the egg whites with renewed ferocity. Five minutes later, she poured the slop down the drain, yet another misstep in a week's distracted cooking. In the last few days she had oversalted her chicken *adobo,* burned an entire batch of *okoy* fritters and forgotten to add shrimp paste to the squash and okra in her *pinakbet.* Her cooking had been so off the mark lately that even Señora Concha had asked her at breakfast the other day if she was going through the Change, if hot flashes had perhaps addled her sense of taste.

By now Marcela was almost relieved that the lunch with Beverly's American boyfriend was just a few days away. She could hardly afford to ruin any more meals if she wanted to earn an extra day off in October.

Chapter 18

I Shall Return

Josiah Stein's plane touched down at Ninoy Aquino International Airport on September 29, 1989, as the first of three cyclones that would slam Manila in quick succession brewed over the Pacific. Rain drummed on the Jetway, which shuddered in the gusting winds. As the American emerged from the plane's air-conditioned cocoon, humidity enveloped him in a damp embrace that smelled of wet cardboard. He wrinkled his nose, shrinking from other travelers who pressed up against him in the line to the terminal.

A persistently helpful porter pulled Josiah's bags off the carousel and ushered him past customs and immigrations to the arrival lobby. Josiah noticed how every Filipino he met smiled widely as soon as they locked eyes, as though wanting to sell him something. But on this trip he sought to acquire only one thing, had already paid good money for it. His most immediate concern was finding Carmelo Capulong, the Filipina Sweetheart manager who had arranged this visit, his first time back in Asia since leaving Vietnam. Just then Josiah spotted a tall man by the tourism information desk, holding a placard with *MR. STEIN* printed in bold letters. A purple heart encircling an *F* and *S* for "Filipina Sweetheart" embellished the sign just above his name. Josiah waved at him. Leading with his spatulate chin, the man strode toward Josiah, flashing a smile so wide that his eyes all but disappeared into his full mango cheeks.

"Welcome to Manila! Are you Mr. *Stain*? Josiah *Stain*?"

Josiah frowned to hear his surname mangled with such enthusiasm. "Yes. But you need to say *Stein* like Steinbeck, not *Stain* like pain."

"Oh, pardon me, I'm sorry, so sorry! I should know better; we get so many German guests." The man sounded overly eager to make amends.

"The first Steins were German when they farmed Wisconsin fields a hundred years ago, but I'm as American as they come. Are you Carmelo *Cahh*-pull-ong?"

"Ah, my name always sounds better with an American accent. Carmelo Ca-*poo*-long at your service, Mr. Stein." Carmelo shook Josiah's hand with exaggerated vigor.

The few times they'd conversed on the phone to discuss travel arrangements, Carmelo had spoken with a musical, vaguely feminine lilt, calling to mind a slight young man who sang Boy George in the shower. In reality Carmelo stood nearly as tall as Josiah, but unlike the American, he moved with balletic grace.

Yup. Clearly a queen. Josiah had a few gay acquaintances—in the Bay Area they were unavoidable—but none he would have trusted to set him up on a blind date. Clearly he would have to keep an open mind in the Third World.

"How was your flight?" Carmelo crooked a finger at the porter to follow with the trolley of bags, as they made their way to the exit.

"Fine until the last hour or so. Then we went through a bad stretch of turbulence." Josiah glanced at the gray curtain of rain beyond the glass walls. "Is it always this stormy? I was expecting tropical weather."

"So sorry, you arrived in time for Typhoon Angela. She's due to hit Luzon by Monday. The monsoon should have ended a month ago, but the weather is changing so much that now it seems to last all year round." Ushering the American through the glass doors, Carmelo signaled for an airport taxi. When it slid to a stop, he opened the back door with a Vanna White–like flourish. "Please make yourself comfortable while I tip the porter."

As Josiah folded his long frame into the backseat, he spotted a laminated sign with the driver's photo on the dashboard; it declared the cab was registered at the Department of Tourism and deemed safe for tourists. He noticed security guards patrolling the terminal with rifles slung over their shoulders, and thought of the handgun tucked under his Bible in the nightstand back home. He wondered if it had been a mistake to leave it behind.

Carmelo slid into the front passenger seat and consulted the driver on the quickest route to the hotel before turning to Josiah. "You know, I spoke with your lady friend last night." The matchmaker winked. "Beverly is so excited to meet you. If you're not too tired, she can meet you for dinner this evening. It's only two in the afternoon, so you'll have a few hours to freshen up. What do you think?"

"I suppose I can stay awake till dinner. Does she live far from the hotel?"

"Nothing's far in Manila, but traffic can be a problem." Carmelo peered through the windshield at the driving rain. "If this rain keeps up, she might have a hard time getting to the hotel by six."

"Let's do eight o'clock, then. I don't enjoy eating alone in a new town."

"Don't you worry, Mr. Stein, we take excellent care of our guests. In *this* town, I promise you'll never have to eat alone."

Ten minutes before eight that evening, Beverly stepped through the revolving doors of the Hotel InterContinental. The last time she'd been there was to see Lisa and Lydell off to the airport, nearly a year ago. She glanced at the concierge's desk and was relieved that the haughty Felicidad was not on duty that evening.

"Beverly!" Carmelo waved from an armchair at the far end of the lobby. She knew from the tilt of his head that the Filipina Sweetheart manager was sizing her up as she approached. She wondered if he was ticking off the checklist he called the "pointers for self-improvement": *hair worn long and flowing; tasteful makeup; elegant jewelry; a dress, never pants, hem no longer than knee length; pedicured toenails; open sandals.* That last edict would have been hard to pull off with the heavy downpour, but she had carried her sandals in a plastic bag and put them on in the taxi.

"Ano ba yan, may supot ka pang dala—why are you carrying that plastic bag?" Carmelo stood up, eyebrows raised as he looked her over. "Ah, good *naman*, you remembered to pluck those eyebrows. Aren't you glad I made you take lessons at Shear Beauty Salon?"

"*Opo*, Mr. Capulong." Beverly blushed. A weekend ago, Esperanza Datung, the salon's glamorous transsexual Aesthetic Directress, had used Beverly's face as a blank canvas for a painter's palette of shadows, creams and rouges. After demonstrating how to use each cosmetic, Esperanza directed Beverly to buy it "for practice at home." In two hours, Beverly spent a fourth of her month's salary on a handful of beauty in matching pink jars. "Até Esperanza taught me everything I need to know about makeup."

"Good, good. That's why I insist all my girls see her before meeting the guests. Best investment you'll ever make." Carmelo put a finger under Beverly's chin to lift it. "I see you're using Esperanza's fave lipstick: Maiden Mauve. Very nice, very nice."

He glanced lower and frowned. "Next time wear a strapless bra with that bateau neckline, *ha?* Only certain women—*yung mga mababa ang lipad*, those low-flying doves—expose their underwear. None of my girls are like that." Carmelo straightened her blouse, tucking the straps underneath its rim. *"Ayan!"* His hands spread wide as though presenting a magician's trick. "See how much prettier it is when you show off those collarbones? Trust me, *hija*, I've been doing this forever. Now, when I introduce you, don't be nervous. Just give him your best smile, yes? *SMILE* like your heart will explode through those pretty lips."

And like an obedient child, Beverly smiled, despite the chill numbing her bare toes, the gnawing emptiness of her belly, and the cramp between her shoulder blades that came from standing beauty-queen straight as Esperanza had directed. She had come this far to claim happiness, and by God she was going to smile, even if it killed her.

Carmelo stood arms akimbo, his underbite growing more pronounced as he assessed Beverly's tight grin. "*Ay naku*, just practice, practice, practice till that feels natural, *ha hija*? Now give me that *supot*. The only thing a lady should have on her arm is a handsome man."

"*Opo*, Mr. Capulong," Beverly murmured, passing the rain-spattered plastic to Carmelo, who rolled it into a tight cylinder and stuck it under his arm like a clutch. No one had fussed over her appearance this way since Lisa had prepped her for the Filipina Sweetheart photos. Carmelo's badgering attention was almost maternal, making her feel like one of the coddled eighteen-year-olds at whose debuts she had often waitressed.

"All right, *hija*. Ready to meet Mr. Right?" Carmelo looked over her shoulder, his face brightening with a beatific smile. "Here he comes!"

Beverly turned to see a whippet-thin man striding toward them. The gray hair was so severely trimmed as to make a bullet of his oblong skull, but his smile seemed genuine.

"Beverly, at last we meet in person!" Startling both Filipinos, he buried her in a tight hug.

"Nice to meet you, Mr.—I mean, Josiah." Beverly leaned away to reply, dismayed by the smudge of Maiden Mauve she had left on his collar. She had dreamed about this meeting hundreds of times, but could not now recall any of the greetings she had rehearsed. She took a step back and gazed at the man with whom she'd been exchanging love letters for the better part of a year. Josiah was taller and broader than he'd appeared in the few photos. She noticed that the tops of his ears angled away from his head like soft pink horns, that his lips were the same color as his cheeks, that the cleft in his chin resembled a scar.

But what most impressed her about Josiah was that he *smelled* rich. His clothes bore that newly arrived-from-abroad scent suitcases released when first opened. Voltaire the caterer once had her unpack his luggage after a linen-shopping trip to California, and she had never forgotten that odor of crisp, vaguely metallic *newness.* "Essence of America," the caterer called it in jest.

She was still staring at Josiah when Carmelo nudged her, murmuring in rapid Tagalog, "*Ano ka ba naman*, don't just stand there, say something!"

"Are you hungry?" Beverly was barely breathing, dazed.

Rolling his eyes, Carmelo rushed to salvage her attempt at chitchat. "You must be absolutely famished, Mr. Stein. Shall we have dinner?"

"Yes, of course. I made reservations at the Prince Albert Rotisserie."

"Oh my *Gad*." Carmelo clapped a hand to his heart. "Prince Albert is only the fanciest dining destination in Manila, *noh*!" He had originally planned to treat the couple to a modest bistro, but since Josiah had chosen the hotel's most opulent restaurant, the bill was going on the American's tab.

"Only the best for my girl. Besides, at twenty-one pesos to the dollar, I can afford to burn cash."

"See how lucky you are?" Carmelo tapped Beverly on the shoulder. "This is just the first date, and already he treats you like royalty!"

"Shall we?" Josiah held out an arm and Beverly took it, marveling at the surprising amount of hair that carpeted the freckled skin.

Carmelo ushered Beverly and Josiah down a hall, slowing as they passed the Boulevardier Lounge, where a sequin-drenched singer belted "It's Raining Men" to an undulating throng. Beverly stood transfixed. Apart from Bar Bibliotek she had never seen a live musical show.

"What a racket!" Josiah pulled Beverly along. "Good thing I'm on the seventh floor."

Farther on, the corridor ended at the restaurant's grand entrance, fronted by a mahogany podium. Prince Albert Rotisserie's old-world elegance stood in sharp contrast to Café Jeepney's cheerful Filipino kitsch, thoroughly intimidating Beverly. A maître d' in a wine-colored jacket checked the reservations book and nodded at Josiah. "Good evening, Mr. Stein. You requested a table for three, yes? This way, please."

Beverly followed the waiter past porcelain-skinned women and men in bespoke suits, their muted conversations mingling with chamber music and the clink of silverware on bone china plates. The room glowed with rich tones of amber, ruby and gold from the stained-glass mosaic that lit the ceiling to the gilded medallions on the wallpaper and carpet. It was as though she had stepped into a jewel box.

The waiter led them to an alcove in the far corner. With a brief nod, he indicated that Beverly would sit between the two men, pulled the armchair out for her, then eased it back as she sank onto claret damask. She stared at a daunting array of cutlery, plates and glasses laid out for her own use. She had waitressed at many sit-down dinners catered by Voltaire, but even he had never employed this multilayered table setting. Taking cues from Carmelo, she unfolded a snowy napkin upon her lap.

Another waiter arrived to fill their water goblets, but as he reached for Josiah's, the American held up a hand to stop him. "You'd better set out a clean glass before expecting me to drink from it." Josiah pointed to a barely visible smudge.

"Yes, of course, sir. I apologize for the oversight. Let me bring out a new one." The waiter bowed his apology and hurried off.

"Can't be too careful in a foreign country." Josiah smoothed his napkin on his lap and leaned back in his chair. "I've got more important things to do than catch a stomach flu." He reached for Beverly's hand and set it on the table under his, in a gesture that was both affectionate and proprietary. "I hope you saved up vacation days, babe. I expect to spend as much time with you as possible on this trip."

Beverly stared at her fingers, smothered beneath Josiah's heavy palm. "I worked double shifts for three months so I could take all next week off."

"Smart planning," Carmelo interjected. "You see how industrious this girl is?"

Carmelo's crowing reminded Beverly of a *sabungero* touting his champion rooster in a cockfight. She knew he was egging her on. *First impressions count,* the matchmaker had said over and over again during that first interview. It was time to make an impression.

Beverly tried one of the conversation openers she had practiced. "I am so happy you came to visit, Mr. Josiah. What would you like to do while you're here?"

"Honey, don't call me 'Mister.' It makes me feel like an old man." Josiah ran a hand over his sparse ash-colored hair. "I'm open to suggestions. What's Manila got to offer?"

"Hopefully not any more rain than we got today!" Carmelo joked.

"I can take you to the mall. . . ." Beverly's voice trailed off. She had seen fairly little of the city, having never had the spare time or money to visit museums, and had never been to the beaches that lay a few hours outside Manila. Suddenly she remembered her godmother. "I'd like you to meet my godmother Marcela, if you don't mind."

"Remind me who she is." Josiah squeezed Beverly's hand.

"Ninang Marcela is my mother's younger sister. She is the only family I have here." Beverly's hand was falling asleep, but she feared Josiah would take offense if she pulled away. "I thought we could have lunch with her on Sunday."

"Sure—as long as it's not one of those 'traditional' Filipino restaurants where they make you eat with your hands." Josiah cocked an eyebrow at Carmelo.

"Oh, Mr. Stein, those places are too déclassé for you." Carmelo tittered. "Beverly would never to take you to a place like that, *noh*, Beverly?"

"No, of course not." Beverly's face was on fire. She didn't know what "déclassé" meant, but at the same time, she was sure Ninang Marcela would never set foot in the Prince Albert Rotisserie. She prayed her godmother would make a good impression on Josiah, even at a place like Max's Fried Chicken.

"All this talk about food is making me hungry." Josiah finally released Beverly's hand to crook a finger at the waiter pushing a large silver domed cart by their table. "I hear the prime rib is the house specialty. Let's have some, shall we?"

As one waiter carved roast beef, another set a basket of warm dinner rolls in the center of the table. Beverly reached for a piece and set it on the bread plate to her right.

"You realize of course that this is *my* bread plate?" Josiah reached across Beverly to set the roll on the dish to her left.

"You must excuse Beverly; we Filipinos usually put all our food on just one plate. But Beverly can learn better table manners from you, *noh*, *hija*?" Carmelo nudged Beverly's foot.

"Yes, I'm sorry, I wasn't thinking." Beverly blushed. She was famished, but embarrassment prevented her from eating the roll.

"You need to put things in the proper place if you want an orderly life, babe." Josiah winked at Beverly. "Eat up, everyone!" He waved a knife. "I don't know about you all, but I'm starving!"

. . .

After his second glass of wine, Carmelo dropped all pretense and unleashed his inner queen. "*Hayy*, Mr. Stein, but you cannot imagine how hard I work to orchestrate these evenings. All worth it, for the sake of love!" Carmelo leaned back in his chair, steepling fingers under his chin. "Not everyone finds true love, but believe me, those who do always write back after the wedding to tell me how happy they are with their Filipina Sweethearts."

Josiah swirled the wine in his glass and inhaled deeply before sipping. "Does anyone ever write to say they're getting a divorce?"

Carmelo cocked an eyebrow at the waiter to signal his glass needed a refill before replying. "*Awa ng Diyos*—merciful God, no. Catholics do not believe in divorce. Besides, Filipinas are much more tolerant than Western women of, *ehem*"—Carmelo cleared his throat delicately—"conjugal challenges, because the truth of the matter is, they are historically inclined to love American men." Carmelo raised his glass in a spontaneous toast. "When General Douglas MacArthur uttered his immortal words 'I shall return' in World War II, how could we not fall in love with the Great White Hope?"

Beverly stared at Carmelo, who was gazing misty-eyed at his goblet. She recalled the general from a poster of MacArthur Park at the tourist agency next to the Filipina Sweetheart offices. A larger-than-life bronze statue of the American general posed midstride in ankle-deep water, overshadowing the figures of Sergio Osmeña and Carlos P. Romulo. The Filipino president and his aides were positioned slightly behind General MacArthur, mere supporting actors to the American's dramatic return, the moment enshrined in a memorial above the Leyte beach on which they had actually landed.

But what did that have to do with her and Josiah? She noticed Josiah trying to keep a straight face as he clinked glasses with Carmelo.

"Now, isn't that the nicest fairy tale." Josiah tipped his glass at Beverly. "If it works out between you and me, we'll have General MacArthur to thank, won't we?"

"And Kuya Carmelo, of course." Beverly smiled back.

"You're most welcome." Carmelo dabbed at his mouth with the napkin. "Well now, I myself could stay in this mah-velous hotel till the end of days, but you've had a long flight, Josiah. Perhaps Beverly and I should leave you to catch some sleep."

"You mean you're not spending the night, babe?" Josiah feigned surprise.

Beverly looked at Carmelo, perplexed. "But I did not expect to—"

"Ikaw naman, masyado kang tweetums," he murmured, chiding her naïveté. "Oh, Mr. Stein, let's not rush things, shall we? We Filipinos are a very romantic culture. After all, courtship comes before surrender. I think General MacArthur would agree with that." Carmelo leaned across the table, his voice dropping to a stage whisper. "You know, MacArthur was married, but he kept a Filipina *querida* in Manila Hotel's presidential suite during the war."

"Did he really?" Josiah's eyebrows rose.

"Ay, but of course! In those days, all great men did. My grandmother used to do the woman's laundry before the general moved her to Manila Hotel. *Lola* Consuelo swore she knew from smelling sheets when the general had spent the night. She said, *You can always tell a man's provenance from his sweat. Filipinos reek of vinegar, and Americans smell like milk.*"

"Are you sure you're not just making this all up?" Josiah glanced round the restaurant, which had gradually emptied out. Theirs was the only table still occupied. "Babe, is this what kids learn in history class?"

"I don't remember." Beverly flushed. Her mother had died midway through her last year in high school; she'd just barely managed to stay in class till graduation.

"Oh, but it's the truth, I swear on Lola Consuelo's grave!" Carmelo laid a palm over his heart. "The *querida* was a Scottish-Filipina film actress named Elizabeth Cooper; everyone called her Dimples. She was a trailblazer: first on-screen kiss in Philippine cinema. You might say Dimples Cooper was our very first Filipina Sweetheart."

"Never heard of her." Josiah pursed his lips, unconvinced.

"That's because historians always care more about war than love. But in fact this was a *historic* love." Carmelo spread his arms, just missing a waiter who had sidled closer to eavesdrop. "MacArthur took Dimples back to America, gave her an apartment in Washington, D.C. He never bought Dimples a raincoat but showered her with negligees . . ." Carmelo paused for dramatic effect. ". . . because he expected her to lay in bed all day and wait for him to arrive."

"Even if that's true, I'm no general. My woman would have to get a real job." Josiah chuckled, patting Beverly's hand.

"Didn't the general want to marry Dimples?" Hope warmed Beverly's heart like the lowest blue flame; Josiah seemed to be thinking about taking her to America.

"Wives hang on to their husbands long after the marriage is dead." Carmelo shrugged. "When someone threatened to expose the affair, the general gave Dimples a plane ticket home."

"So, did she come home?" Beverly couldn't understand why this was so important, but she needed to know.

"*Ay pobrecita*, no. The story goes that Dimples opened a beauty salon in the Midwest. When that failed, she moved to L.A. and committed suicide." Carmelo cast a mournful gaze at his empty wineglass. "This is why I insist all my girls get married. Nothing good can come from being the Number Two."

"Well, the visa you'd arrange for Beverly requires us to be married within three months." Josiah squeezed Beverly's hand. "When you board that plane, honey, it'll be with a one-way ticket to Oakland."

Beverly held her breath. Marriage was on the table and it was only their first date.

"*Talaga naman*, when Cupid takes a shot, he never misses his mark." Carmelo then smoothed his napkin into a neat square by his plate. "But why think about Oakland, when you are in Manila? I will give Beverly a few sightseeing ideas to keep you entertained. Now, Mr. Stein, you really must excuse us. We both need our beauty sleep."

"Next time I won't let you off so easily, babe." Josiah winked at Beverly as he signaled the waiter to bring the check. "I'll need all Saturday to recover from jet lag, but how about we meet back here for brunch on Sunday?"

"Yes, Mr.—yes, Josiah. Brunch on Sunday."

Beverly followed the two men back to the hotel lobby, tipsy from her first glass of merlot and intoxicated by the notion that she had found, at long last, love. Everything she'd seen indicated that Josiah was the man who would lead her to a happier life, an ocean away from this city of poverty and grief. Throughout dinner he had acted as though they were already married, correcting her when she picked up the wrong fork, pointing out a smear of gravy on her chin, insisting she would enjoy crème brûlée more than chocolate cake. What more could a woman want than an attentive suitor?

Each time he called her "babe" she felt a visceral thrill, as though bubbles coursed up her spine and popped in an effervescent fusillade against her nape. Before this night, no man had ever used such a seductive endearment on her. It made Beverly feel like a movie star, like Olivia Newton-John in *Grease*, the last film she'd watched a week before Clara's train accident. She and her mother had cheered at the movie's finale when, after a final frolic on sunny fairgrounds, the lovers flew away in their enchanted red convertible.

It occurred to Beverly that this pet name was no less than a portent—one at least as reliable as Ninang Marcela's favorite omen, where a fork fallen to the floor presaged a male visitor; a dropped spoon, a female guest. Yes, Beverly decided, "babe" was an augury of joy, of her mother's promised happy ending, just like in the movies. Beverly watched the men shake hands and whispered gratitude to heaven: *Salamat, Inay.*

Noticing the dreamy look in Beverly's eyes, Josiah pulled her into a tight embrace. "I'm glad we finally met, baby," he murmured into her forehead. "Maybe next time you can pack an overnight bag and stay over, instead of going home."

"Thank you for dinner." Beverly adjusted her blouse to cover her bra straps before raising her gaze. "I shall return."

Wind and rain assaulted Carmelo and Beverly the moment they stepped out of the hotel.

"*Naku,* you'll never find a bus in this rain." Carmelo cupped her elbow. "Let me take you home in a cab. You cannot afford to get sick during Mr. Stein's visit."

The taxi slushed through flooded streets, past several stalled cars, taking detours to avoid knee-high waters. The extended trip hardly dampened Carmelo's jubilation over a successful night. Dropping his carefully enunciated English, Carmelo reviewed the highlights of her date with the exuberance of a sportscaster, switching between gay patois and Tag-lish that made Beverly's head spin.

"*Tignan mo yan*—you see? You will be Filipina Sweetheart's latest, sweetest Mango Bride, and we did it all in one night! *Waging-wagi!* Winner *ka 'day*! *Basta* from now on, just be charming twenty-four/seven and make Josiah enjoy your company *hasta sa* he cannot live without you. Beauty *ka dapat* for two weeks, then *garantisado* he will bring you to California. Green-card-jackpot-spin-a-win *kaching-ching!"* Carmelo pulled an imaginary slot machine lever, whooping loud enough to distract the cabdriver from the road he was trying to navigate.

"But where should I take him while he's here, Kuya Carmelo? I only know the mall."

"Well, if not for this terrible *bagyo,* you could have taken him to Pagsanjan Falls or even Puerto Galera." Carmelo pouted. "*Sayang,* those places are no good in the rain."

Beverly was secretly relieved that she would not have to take Josiah anywhere that required a bathing suit, for she did not own one, nor had she ever learned to swim. "Is there anywhere indoors that I can take him?"

"The Ayala Museum is close to his hotel. They have dioramas there about, you know, history. Only students on field trips and rich people ever go there. *Por lo menos* it's more tasteful than the mall."

Carmelo drummed his fingers on the plastic bag, realized he was still holding her shoes and passed them back to her. *"Ayan,* put your new sandals away, you don't want to ruin them in this rain. *Para ka namang* Cinderella—but then I make the best Fairy Godmother!" He cackled. "Speaking of clothes, whenever you are with Mr. Stein, I want you to be especially careful with what you wear. *Alam mo,* some people say rude things when they see a Filipina with a foreigner. If you don't dress well, they think you're just a bar girl from Olongapo. So if you don't want to be called unpleasant names, you must always dress like a lady. In fact, you should behave like you are already married. Do you have a ring?"

Beverly shook her head.

Carmelo thought for a moment, then pulled off his pinkie ring and handed it to Beverly. "If it fits, you can borrow it for two weeks. It's only fourteen karats, Chinese gold *lang naman.* But make sure you give it back: if you don't, *kukurotin kita sa singit*—I will pinch your vagina!" Carmelo laughed out loud at the scandalized look on Beverly's face. *"Lambing lang."*

Biting her lip, Beverly slipped the ring onto her finger. It fit perfectly.

"Good. Now just act like a wife. If he wants to hold your hand, let him. If other people stare, just keep looking only at him, because no one else matters but Josiah. *Konting cariño lang*—a little affection goes a long way with these men. They wouldn't look for love so far from home if they were not lonely to begin with."

As the taxi slowed to a stop for the red light, a street urchin ran up to Beverly's window pleading for alms. *"Até patawarin*—have pity!"

The girl's chin barely cleared the sill, hands splayed like small brown starfish on the wet glass, imploring gaze fixed on Beverly. Rolling down her window, Beverly handed the child a few bills. With Carmelo footing the cab fare, she could well afford to give away her bus money.

As the beggar scampered off, two other children darted out from the underpass beneath which they'd been sheltering, grabbing at the bills.

"Masyado kang mabait," Carmelo chided Beverly's kindheartedness. "Whoever runs that street gang will just take the money from her. I know—I grew up hustling on the streets. *Kung hindi lang ako sinuwerte.* If I had not gotten lucky . . ." Carmelo gazed out the window at a view only he could see.

"And your luck rubbed off on me." Beverly patted Carmelo's shoulder. "It is only right that I share it with someone else."

"*Santa Santita ka talaga*—what a little saint you are!" Carmelo exclaimed, shaking off nostalgia. "I hope Mr. Stein gives you as good a life as you deserve. *Nonovenahan kita kay San José*—I will make a novena for you to Saint Joseph. *Garantisadong winner yan.*"

Beverly nudged him with an elbow. "If Saint Joseph grants your novena, you can visit me in California."

Saturday morning, Beverly awoke to the roar of a waterfall that seemed to have sprung outside her window. The torrential rains and gusting winds heralding a monster typhoon had intensified overnight. She drew the blanket over her head, recalling how she'd had to slosh through ankle-deep water flooding the walkway to her apartment. This weather must have made a terrible impression on Josiah. She, however, had fared much better than this Angela, or Rubing, as the weathermen called the typhoon that was set to arrive later that week.

Slipping into her mother's threadbare bathrobe, Beverly walked out of the bedroom, hoping to make some instant coffee for breakfast, but stopped on the stair landing. Her landlady was wading around the first floor in a half inch of dirty water, tying her polyester curtains up high and muttering sundry curses.

"Did the sewers overflow again last night?" Beverly leaned on the banister.

"*Ano pa nga ba*—what do you think? If people would stop throwing trash in the canals, this would not happen, but every year . . . *Putrés . . . magapatuka nalang ako sa ahas!*" She threw up her hands, declaring she might as well be bitten by a snake—she was so fed up.

"*O, 'wag ka na ma-high blood.* Don't get so worked up—I'll help you." Beverly took off her robe and ran downstairs. An hour later, the two women had mopped up most of the water and plugged the gap between the floor and the front door with a rolled-up towel.

"*Ay salamat naman,*" Manang Charing thanked Beverly. "*Halika,* after working so hard, we deserve a special breakfast." She threw open her kitchen cabinet and pulled out a prized can of SPAM. As her landlady minced garlic for fried rice, Beverly fried thin slabs of SPAM. She smiled at the thought that after dining on the finest prime rib Manila had to offer, she still preferred canned meat. Carmelo was right: she really was Cinderella.

"I hope you don't have to work this weekend, *hija.*" Manang Charing stirred day-old rice in the wok with her browned garlic. "I heard over the radio that buses have stopped running. Most of EDSA is flooded."

"*Buti na lang,* I'm on vacation this week," Beverly murmured, troubled by the news that the main highway to Makati was all but closed. "Do you think it will still be flooded tomorrow? I have to meet a friend in Makati."

"What friend would make you go out in this weather?" Manang Charing groused. "Can't you postpone your date until this storm clears?"

"But he's only going to be here for two weeks. . . ." Beverly stopped, but not soon enough.

"He? Is this your boyfriend?" Manang Charing turned from her wok, wooden spoon upright like a question mark. "Is this that *J. Stein* who's been sending you those letters from the U.S. all these months? Even the mailman was asking me about that. Is he your pen pal?"

"Opo." Beverly's cheeks burned. "Josiah just flew in from California. We had dinner last night at the Hotel InterContinental."

"Aba!" Manang Charing clapped her hands, spraying rice grains with her wooden spoon. "I suspected as much, but you know me—I always mind my own business." She hurriedly piled rice onto a serving dish and gestured for Beverly to sit down. "Is he handsome? How old is he? I always tell my friends, the best men are those with the four *M*s—*matanda, mayaman, madaling mamatay*—old, rich and quick to die!" Manang Charing shrieked with laughter, while Beverly swallowed her irritation with a mouthful of SPAM. She would never admit that Manang Charing was right about the first *M*.

The next few days went by in a tempest of sightseeing and rapidly intensifying flirtation. As Typhoon Angela raged like a rejected *querida*, drowning Manila in an ocean of tears, Beverly became ever more determined to secure Josiah's affection. Each morning she set out in rubber flip-flops through murky water, covered chin to shin in a plastic raincoat, hoisting an umbrella like a shield against the pummeling wind. Classes on all levels had been suspended because of the storm, so there was less competition for seats on the few buses that continued to creep along the freeway. Unlike the gray-faced commuters steeling themselves for another workday, Beverly seemed energized by the storm, touching up her lipstick and smiling into her compact mirror during the long ride. She kept a small towel in her backpack, using it to dry her feet before slipping on her one good pair of sandals.

Mindful of Carmelo's instructions, Beverly overcame her innate reticence and smiled at everything Josiah said. Walking around the Ayala Museum, she nodded—without really understanding—at his opinions on the Allied forces' tactical mistakes during World War II. The couple wandered through the diorama exhibition, oblivious to the well-heeled matrons who looked askance at the middle-aged American with the televangelist voice and the young Filipina clinging to his arm as though it were a lifesaver.

Even the stormy weather conspired to facilitate instant intimacy. Gusting winds forced the couple to huddle tightly together as they walked under her inadequate umbrella along the streets of Makati. Rain gave Josiah a pretext for brushing drops off Beverly's hair before pulling her into their first kiss at the deserted InterContinental poolside bar, where she had been showing him the backdrop for her Filipina Sweetheart pictures.

A week later, Josiah declared he was done with museums and suggested they go shopping instead. Beverly was only too happy to take him through more familiar territory.

"Could you come out of the dressing room, babe? I want to see how each of those dresses look on you." Josiah stood by the women's dressing room, ignoring the salesgirl standing by with more dresses in hand.

"I think it might be too short. . . . Doesn't it look tight?" Beverly emerged in a mint-hued sundress, an Empire waistline cupping her high breasts, the bottom of the flounced skirt brushing the tops of her kneecaps. She had never gone shopping with a man before. He motioned for her to turn around and she did so, smiling self-consciously at the salesgirl.

"Fits like a glove. I like it." Josiah beamed at her, then turned to the salesgirl. "You have that in blue and pink, don't you? We'll take all three."

By the time they were done, Josiah had bought Beverly a new dress for every day of the week. The rain had abated momentarily, and they decided to brave the five-minute walk back to the Inter-Continental Hotel. They were nearing the foot of the hotel's curving driveway when the clouds opened up with sheets of rain. Beverly let out a little shriek, struggling in vain to unfold her flimsy umbrella. Within seconds they were both sopping.

"Come on upstairs to my room so you can dry off." Josiah pulled her along, up the driveway, through the revolving doors and straight to the bank of elevators. One opened as if on cue, and Beverly stared at her sodden sandals, waiting for a group of tourists to walk out before following Josiah into the elevator.

"Aren't you glad you have a new wardrobe of dry clothes to change into?" Josiah squeezed her wet shoulder. "How 'bout I take you someplace nice for dinner tonight?"

"You always take me to nice places, Josiah." Beverly followed him down the hall.

"That's what I love about you: always so grateful." Josiah unlocked the door. "Now, let's get out of these wet clothes and freshen up. This is going to be a night to remember." Holding her bride-price of shopping bags, Josiah opened his door and welcomed Beverly with a wide, gap-toothed smile into the dark bedroom.

Chapter 19

The Deluge

Beverly stood beneath a steaming downpour, reveling in the first hot shower of her life. She washed herself with care, wondering if the bleeding had stopped. Lisa had said that eventually the pain would go away, that certain women actually enjoyed sex. She was determined to become one of those women. Beverly lifted her face to the gushing showerhead, smiling as though newly baptized.

It was not a dream. She really *had* spent the night at the Hotel InterContinental.

The sound of the door opening interrupted her reverie.

"Beverly, didn't you say we're meeting your aunt at eleven? It's ten fifteen." Josiah poked his head through the shower curtain, his gaze lingering on Beverly's nakedness. "Are you sure we can't move it back to noon? I wouldn't mind starting with appetizers." He slapped her bare bottom.

Beverly turned off the shower, unnerved by the mention of her godmother. Though Marcela had never raised Beverly as a Catholic, she would nevertheless have been scandalized to know that Josiah had seduced her goddaughter on the mere promise of marriage. The night before, Beverly had accepted Josiah's proposal in a rush of delight and confusion, less reluctant to lie with Josiah after he had made his intentions clear.

"Whaddya say, babe? Maybe move the lunch back another hour?" Josiah ran a finger down her spine, making other intentions equally clear.

"No, Josiah, please. I cannot call her now, she is already on her way. Ninang Marcela always arrives early." She wrapped herself in a towel before stepping out of the tub. Beverly had hung her panty on the towel rack after washing it the night before; she was relieved to see it looked dry enough to wear this morning. She balled it up in her fist, embarrassed that Josiah might have seen it there. "Which dress should I wear to lunch?"

"It doesn't matter. They all look nice." Josiah wrapped his arms around her, hugging so tightly she had to take little half breaths until he released her. "Why don't you wear the blue one, to match my eyes?"

"Okay. I'll come back in to dry my hair after you finish your shower." Beverly quickly shut the door behind her as Josiah dropped his boxers. Even after spending the night with him, the idea of such casual intimacy unnerved her.

Marcela was already sitting at a table when Beverly and Josiah arrived at Max's Fried Chicken. She wore her fanciest outfit: a brown short-sleeved shirtdress in a vaguely floral print, which skimmed forgivingly over a torso that had thickened in middle age. She scrutinized Beverly's companion as they approached. The American followed her niece across the restaurant to Marcela's table, swinging his shoulders wide of passing waiters and bearing the constipated grimace of someone who preferred less crowded spaces.

Marcela noticed the other diners watching as well, their gaze glancing off Josiah, lingering on Beverly. She recognized the question in their eyes; it was the same one she asked whenever she saw white men with a Filipina: *Whore or wife?*

"*Ay, Ninang, kumusta?* I'm sorry we're late." Beverly stooped to kiss her godmother's cheek before taking a seat.

"It's okay. I come early always." Señora Concha had made the cook learn enough English to serve guests at dinner parties, but Marcela felt awkward using it on her goddaughter.

"Good to meet you, Marcela." Josiah leaned across the table to shake Marcela's hand, then sat beside her niece. "Beverly tells me you're like her second mother."

"Her mother died when Beverly was very young." Marcela offered the American a wary smile, taking in the military cut of his gray hair, the almost unnatural blueness of his eyes, the way he leaned both forearms at wide angles on the table as though marking out his space.

"And what about her father? Beverly never talks about him."

"She never knew him." Marcela caught Beverly staring at her with the usual curious anticipation. "He is also dead." She pretended to pore over a menu whose contents she knew by heart. "You look hungry. Beverly, *anak*, call the waiter so we can order already."

Through lunch, Marcela watched Josiah with increasing irritation. The man behaved as though he knew more about her niece than a week warranted. He finished Beverly's sentences, put a chicken breast on her plate unbidden (*Not her favorite part*, Marcela tsk-tsked) and signaled the waiter for another glass of iced tea as soon as she had emptied hers. How could her niece be in love with someone so overbearing?

"How do you like Manila, Mr. Stein?" Marcela disjointed a wing and nibbled at the mini drumstick. So far she was enjoying her meal much more than this stiff white man who insisted on eating chicken with a knife and fork.

"Can't say I've seen much of it with all this rain. I don't know how you all manage." Josiah eyed Marcela's greasy fingers. "We've had a drought in California for some years now. Who'd have thought Oakland would be sunnier than the tropics?"

"It is the monsoon, Mr. Stein. It rains this time of year." Marcela sent Beverly a *who-does-he-think-he-is* glance, but her niece was too busy spooning more rice onto Josiah's plate to notice. Why was Beverly acting like a wife so early in the relationship? She stifled her irritation with a tight smile. "How long are you staying?"

"Just long enough for Carmelo to get a visa ready for my baby here. As soon as Beverly gets her work permit, she can start looking for a job in Oakland." Josiah took a fresh paper napkin to wipe off his mouth, refolding it and adding it to the neat pile beside his plate. "There're always jobs for hard workers, and I'm told Beverly works hard." Josiah stretched an arm around the back of Beverly's chair, pale fingers spidering around her bare shoulder. "Isn't that right, babe?"

"Yes, Josiah." Beverly blushed, aware that Marcela was not the only one watching this public display of affection.

"What do you mean?" Marcela dropped the chicken wing. "Why is Beverly going to Oakland?"

Beverly bit her lip, upset that Josiah had blurted out this news so clumsily.

"Ninang, Josiah and I are engaged." She put a hand on Marcela's forearm, the amethyst on Carmelo's ring sparkling in the fluorescent light. "He proposed last night. We're flying to California in ten days."

"Why only now you tell me? How can it be?" Shocked to see her godchild flashing what looked like an engagement ring, Marcela gave up on her meager English, her low voice crackling in indignant Tagalog. "How can you have decided so quickly? He arrived just last week and already he asked you to marry him? *Sira ulo ka ba*—have you lost your mind? Merciful God, did he seduce you? Is that why you're in such a hurry? *Papatayin ko siya*, on your mother's grave I swear I will *kill* him if he takes you away!"

"Now, look here, I don't know what you're saying, but you'd better not be giving Beverly grief just 'cause we're getting married."

Josiah set down his fork. He stared at Marcela with the cautious disapproval of someone stepping away from a lunatic. "Beverly can make her own decisions."

"Not a decision about marriage." Marcela pinned a murderous glare on the American. "My niece has never even had a boyfriend. She is a child when it comes to love." She looked at Beverly and continued in Tagalog. *"Ano'ng klaseng lalaki*—what kind of man is he, talking back like this! Will you be as disrespectful to your *ninang* Marcela as your *novio*?"

"Patawarin, Ninang 'Cela." Beverly begged pardon, frantic to make peace. "Can't you be happy for me? This is what *Inay* wanted for me—a good husband."

Marcela pulled her arm away, shutting Josiah out with Tagalog. "Just because he buys you new clothes doesn't make him a good husband. *Para ka namang puta kung mag-isip*—you think like a whore."

Beverly stiffened. She would have been no less hurt if her godmother had slapped her. She turned to Josiah with a placating smile, her eyes bright with the threat of tears. "My godmother is very sad to say good-bye, but she gives us her blessing."

Before Marcela could contradict her, Beverly picked up the chit the waiter had left on their table. "It is raining harder, Josiah. If we don't go now, no taxi will want to take us back to the hotel. Why don't we pay the cashier up front?" Beverly turned a cold glare on Marcela. "Thank you for coming to lunch, Ninang. If you do not see me before we leave, I will write you from Oakland and send the letters to my landlady. You can pick them up if you want to see how I am doing in America."

Marcela was too stunned to reply. She watched the couple make their way back across the restaurant, her heart torn apart like the chicken bones on her plate.

It was a keen irony that PAGASA was the Tagalog word for "hope," for the Philippine Atmospheric, Geophysical and Astronomical Services Administration did not offer much in the way of that sentiment during the catastrophic monsoon season of 1989.

On Sunday, October 7, PAGASA's senior meteorologist Amado Pineda delivered a televised storm update in his famously baroque English: "In the nine days since Super Typhoon Rubing's rains began pummeling this country, the monster storm has claimed nearly a hundred lives in mud slides and catastrophic flooding throughout central and northern Luzon. Over thirty-five thousand families have been made homeless, even as torrential rain continues to wreak havoc on Metro Manila and surrounding provinces. Unfortunately there is no silver lining in these clouds, for a second tropical depression has been sighted five hundred kilometers southeast of Hong Kong. Typhoon Saling is expected to make landfall on October tenth, even as Typhoon Rubing continues to spread a relentless path of destruction through northern Luzon."

The meteorologist turned from the large map of the archipelago and smiled into the camera. "Typhoon Signal Number Three remains hoisted over Metro Manila. The Department of Education, Culture and Sports has announced that classes on all levels will be canceled for the better part of next week. And that's the latest from PAGASA!"

Fico Guerrero usually welcomed typhoons, if only because floods added credence to his excuse of being held up by traffic. After attending Sunday morning mass, he had skipped lunch with his family, explaining that an emergency Monday deadline compelled him to work that afternoon. He suspected Concha saw through his flimsy pretext, but would not postpone what he and his mistress called their "afternoon delight." This sort of weather called for a day spent in bed.

The trysts had settled into a comforting rhythm: early-afternoon sex followed by a late lazy lunch. The lovers dallied over the meal, but when rain began hitting the bistro's windows like buckshot, they decided to leave. It was just past five o'clock when Fico drove out of the covered parking structure, but the storm had forced an early dusk upon the city. Rain was coming down in such solid sheets that Makati appeared to have sunk beneath the sea, cars and trucks crawling like bottom-feeders on its silty floor. Floodwaters blocked Fico's usual route and he grew increasingly aggravated by the many detours he was forced to make. *"Putrés naman,* someone should improve the drainage system in Manila. This is going to ruin my engine." Fico squinted through the windshield, swerving around stalled jeepneys and pedestrians.

"Why are you driving so fast, honey? I'm in no hurry to get home." Candida batted improbably long lashes at him.

"Maybe you aren't, but Concha's been bitchier than usual lately. I think she knows about us. *Ay, puta!"* Fico leaned on his horn and sped by a car trying to cut into his lane from an alley. Flipping a finger at the other driver, Fico zoomed past the intersection. Just then he felt a sudden cramping in his chest, the sensation of bile rising in his throat. Fico belched long and loud to relieve what felt like excess gas from their meal of deep-fried pork knuckles.

"Excuse *you*!" Candida giggled.

"Sorry, luv. I shouldn't have eaten so much." Fico thumped his chest with a fist to loosen the knot twisting just below his collarbone. Buendia Avenue was miraculously free of floods, and Fico dashed down the rain-slick road, trying to ignore the pressure in his chest, which had grown into a cramp in his left shoulder. "I'm sweating like a pig. Are you as hot as I am?" He adjusted the air-con vents to blast cold air on his face.

Far ahead, Fico saw the traffic light turn yellow and sped up, yet even as the car hurtled toward the intersection, he had the overwhelming sensation that his car was sputtering, decelerating, slithering to an inexplicable stop. The windows on either side of him darkened as a movie unfurled in slow motion across his windshield. Transfixed, he watched a monstrous octopus fall away from the clouds like a gray balloon and drop with a mossy plop on the hood of his car. Egg-sized onyx eyes stared impassively through the windshield, as tentacles slithered in through the air-conditioning vents and encircled his chest, a multitude of suction cups making small *fffffthupthup* noises upon his skin, eight arms embracing tentatively, then tightening with growing resolve, squeezing, squashing, steadily crushing the breath out of him so that his mouth opened in a soundless scream as the movie ended with a lap dissolve of the car hurtling full speed into the lurid red hearts painted on the bus that ended Fico Guerrero's mad dash home.

Makati Medical Center was a scant five-minute drive from Fico Guerrero's mangled car, but the traffic policeman who might have summoned an ambulance had ended his shift early that night to seek out a belly-warming bowl of tripe congee and the saucy waitress who served it. It was a good ten minutes before someone in a passing car thought to call for a doctor, another hour before the ambulance forced its way through the traffic that had clotted like blood around the wreck. By the time paramedics pried open the door with a borrowed tire jack, Fico Guerrero and his *querida* were long dead.

Señora Concha might not have heard of her husband's fatal accident until the next day, but for the fact that the pathologist on duty had recently married into the Guerrero clan. Concha had been sulking all afternoon over Fico's absence, irritated by his inexplicable compulsion to work during the worst weather. Fico's overtime hours generally increased with rainy days and it had been storming for over two weeks now. She answered the phone herself, walking up to the living room's windows, through which she could see the palm trees thrashing about in the gale.

"Hello, Tita Concha? This is Girlie Guerrero, *Doctora* Girlie Guerrero, Iñigo's wife. You came to our wedding last year, remember?"

"Yes, of course I remember you, *hija*, Girlie, the doctor." Señora Concha cradled the cordless phone between ear and shoulder as she lit her predinner cigarette. She stared through the glass, wishing the rain away. She missed her nightly smoke in the garden. "How is Iñigo? I haven't seen you two since the wedding. Are you pregnant yet?"

"No, Tita, not pregnant yet." Dr. Guerrero cleared her throat. "Tita, I'm calling with some bad news. Tito Fico was in a car crash—" The sharp gasp on the other end gave her pause. "Can someone take you to Makati Med right now? If Javier isn't home, I'll call Iñigo to pick you up."

Señora Concha put a hand to her throat. "*Madré de Diós.* How is he?" She imagined her husband arguing with a jeepney driver over a fender bender, his blood pressure rising dangerously. Perhaps he had suffered a heart attack; the doctor had warned he was at risk. "Give me a moment so I can pack an overnight bag. Fico insists on wearing his own pajamas, he cannot stand those tacky hospital gowns. . . ."

"No, Tita, there's no need to pack pajamas—" Girlie sighed. "Tito Fico did not make it."

Señora Concha leaned her forehead against the cold window, suddenly faint. Rain striking the glass felt like tiny fingers tapping on her skull, drumming counterpoint to the pounding in her chest. "How did it happen?"

"I was told his car ran into a bus. Neither of them were wearing seat belts."

"What do you mean 'them'? Are you talking about the other driver?"

"No, Tita. The bus he hit was stalled and the driver had left. But Tito Fico had someone in the car with him." There was a pause. "She was also killed."

"I see." Señora Concha took a long drag on her cigarette, seeking false solace in the mentholated fumes.

"We're still trying to reach Candida Immolación's family. Did you know her?"

"Miss False Eyelashes." The phrase escaped Señora Concha's lips before she realized she was speaking.

"What was that?"

"Nothing. I don't know that woman. Don't bother your husband. Javier will take me to Makati Med." Señora Concha hung up and stared unseeing through the window, ash from her cigarette drifting to the floor.

Over the next nine days, Fico Guerrero's wake and funeral kept Marcela busy cooking for an unending stream of mourners. In her rare moments of idleness, she wondered what Beverly was doing, but was still too hurt by her niece's betrayal to consider calling. In either case, it would have been impossible to ask for a day off, given Señora Concha's condition. The widow spent most of her husband's wake cocooned in a daze of alcohol proffered by Carina Madrigal and sedatives prescribed by Señora Concha's son Miguel, who had taken an emergency leave from his internship in San Francisco. With a mother so devoid of affect that she seemed to have been lobotomized, the younger Guerreros huddled around their *nanay* Marcela like bewildered children, crippled by grief.

Surprisingly, Marcela felt sorry even for Señora Concha, for she had seen the widow's self-control crack just once in the beginning, before sealing up completely. On the night of her husband's death, the new widow had returned from the morgue and instructed Marcela to set up a cot outside her bedroom door, close enough to hear her scream if Fico's ghost dropped in for a final visit.

Leaning against her bedroom door, a whiskey tumbler in one hand, a bottle of Johnnie Walker Black in the other, Señora Concha watched Marcela stretch a sheet across the foam mattress. "*Doctora* Guerrero tells me Fico had a passenger. It was her. Miss False Eyelashes."

Marcela looked up at her employer with sudden pity. "That earring I found in Kuya Fico's car last year?"

Señora Concha nodded. "Probably. *Doctora* Guerrero said Fico died instantly." She sagged against the doorjamb. "I hope the woman suffered longer."

"It's bad luck to speak ill of the dead, señora." Marcela watched Señora Concha take a long swallow of scotch and wondered what comfort it could offer to someone who'd so long ago chosen to be unhappy

"How much worse can my luck get?" Señora Concha raised her hand to look at her wedding ring, which hung loose on her thin finger. "Promise me one thing, Marcela. Promise you will never tell the children about Miss False Eyelashes." Señora Concha's voice broke, her eyes drowning in unwelcome tears. "They don't need to know their father was a bastard."

Fico Guerrero's body took five hours to burn down to gravel on October 18. Señora Concha, her three children and the cook waited at the crematorium, exhausted from nine days of prayers and the meaningless chatter of a society wake. Karen Carpenter was crooning "Rainy Days and Mondays" on Marcela's transistor radio when she was interrupted by an emergency weather alert. Stroking Amparo's hair as the girl dozed against her shoulder, Marcela listened, unimpressed, to Cipriano Nuqui's latest weather forecast. It was hard to worry about Typhoon Tasing, after two consecutive monster storms had already besieged the country for twenty days. After all, what harm could a category three hurricane do to a city already submerged?

Later that evening, in the foothills of the Cordillera Mountains far north of Manila, a farmer woke to the rumble of an approaching train, confused by the fact that his home was nowhere near the railroad tracks. As he sat up to rouse his wife and three children, a wave of sludge, tree limbs and one squealing pig exploded through the windows of their thatch hut, pulverizing furniture into a muddy stew and engulfing the family in a nightmare from which they would never wake.

The next day, those who had survived the mud slide picked through the wreckage, hoping the family had escaped in time. Not far from where the farmer's hut had stood, a woman cried out at the sight of a small fist poking out of the mud, fingers curled around a plastic doll whose blond hair had gone gray with mud.

Thirty thousand feet above them, meal service had just commenced on Continental Flight 117 bound for San Francisco. Relaxing into the first plane ride of her life, Beverly smiled at the flight attendant pushing the beverage cart up the aisle.

"What can I get you to drink, ma'am?" A blond stewardess beamed at the pretty young Filipina.

Beverly stared at the array of sodas, juices and bottles of wine, stunned silent by the sheer range of choices.

"She'll have a coffee, no cream, two sugars. I'll have the same, thanks." Josiah squeezed her knee. "Just wait, babe. Your life is going to change big-time from here on in."

Chapter 20

Elephant in the Room

In the months following her father's death, Amparo became increasingly dependent on Matéo for solace and—to her great surprise—sex. Grief-ridden, Amparo grew addicted to lovemaking, as though Matéo's caresses could somehow compensate for the loss of her father. Once the initial shyness had passed, she loosened up, giving in to the wordless urgings of his body, of hers, happily shedding residual Catholic guilt like clothes on the floor. Ironically, Fico Guerrero's death made it even easier for Amparo to steal away with her lover, for once the social whirl of the wake and novenas died down, Señora Concha sank into a full-blown depression and no longer cared whether her children came home to dinner every night of the week.

As their trysts at Tiffany's became more frequent, Amparo realized she could bring Matéo—teasing, unflappable Matéo—to the point of such fevered urgency that it was she who led the dance. It was a rare power to wield, and Amparo felt invincible as only a nineteen-year-old can. Until her own body betrayed her.

Amparo stared at the plastic strip on which she had just peed, willing the second line, the one that mattered, to go away. She shut her eyes, sending an urgent prayer to Saint Jude, Saint Anthony and the Virgin. The line remained. This was the third test she'd tried in the last half hour, and the answer had never varied. She was pregnant.

"'Paro, what's going on? What did the test say?" Ditas's high-pitched voice rang shrill through the bathroom door.

Amparo zipped up her jeans and opened the door. "My mom will kill me."

Ditas took a step backward, as though pregnancy were contagious. "Positive?"

"All three of them." Amparo nodded. "What am I going to do?"

"Obvious *ba?* You and Matéo have to get married." Ditas tugged on a curl, as she watched Amparo crawl onto her bed. "So what if it's *pikot*? People have shotgun marriages all the time."

"You mean like Colleen Capili?" Amparo hugged a pillow to her chest.

"Good thing she was a freshman at UP when she got knocked up; the nuns would have kicked her out of high school the minute she began to show." Ditas smiled at the memory of their former high school classmate strolling through hallways when classes let out, the swollen belly parting crowds like a ship's prow. "She was so brave, staying in school until her due date."

"So they had a quickie wedding to avoid having a bastard; what does it matter?" Amparo cocked an eyebrow. "I hear they split up after she caught Nimrod kissing a girl in the UP parking lot."

"Talaga?" Ditas frowned. "They've been married less than a year. *Punyeta naman*—to think I spent all that money on bridal- and baby-shower presents."

"Who even knows if Matéo would marry me?" Amparo scowled. "They probably don't have *pikot* weddings in Europe."

"You're not *in* Europe." Ditas stood arms akimbo. "He got you pregnant in Manila, no? It's the right thing to do."

"For who, Ditas? Matéo and I are a year away from graduation." Amparo raked fingers through her hair. "How do we fit a wedding into the school year?"

"How would I know? One thing's for sure: you need to talk to Matéo soon as possible. You'll need to present a united front when you tell the parents."

A united front was the last thing on Amparo's mind as she and Matéo watched an elephant sidle up to an old acacia on Morato Avenue. Flapping parasol-sized ears at the chorus of car horns and hollers, the elephant coiled its trunk round the nearest branch and shoveled leaves into its mouth. Drivers inched their vehicles forward to get a better view until dozens of cars and jeeps wedged against the sidewalk, tight as Lego cubes. Matéo's car was trapped behind a beat-up Honda two cars down the street from the animal. "Damn. Looks like we may not make it to Gene's Bistro after all." Matéo leaned back in his seat. "I'd try to pull over and park, but that taxi's not going to budge." He drummed fingers on the steering wheel. "Looks like we're stuck for now."

Amparo fumed. She had planned to tell Matéo about the pregnancy over coffee at their favorite bistro. The short, carefully worded speech she'd rehearsed made no provisions for escaped circus animals. "Where did that elephant come from anyway?"

"Let's find out." Matéo rolled down Amparo's window and called out to the taxi driver on their right buying a cigarette from a young vendor. *"Boss, saan galing yung elepante?"*

The driver leaned over the boy's lighter and sucked on his cigarette before answering. "*Sa* Elephant World." He pointed at the taxi's radio with the long nail of his pinkie finger, recounting events in the terse Tagalog favored by AM radio DJs. "Escaped this morning. Crushed the trainer's foot and galloped out of Araneta Coliseum. Jaywalked on EDSA, ran red lights all the way up Kamuning.

Now he's on lunch break." Smoke drifted out of his mouth as the driver chuckled. "He may be from Bangkok, but that elephant's got some Pinoy in him."

"*Tama ka diyan*—got that right!" Matéo grinned. "That elephant's not going anywhere anytime soon, 'Paro. We might as well relax and enjoy the show."

"All right, then." Amparo smiled thinly. The chortles of street urchins cavorting about the beast were infectious, but she resisted the impulse to jump out of the car for a closer look, for the noonday heat would be doubly intense in the growing crowd. She had lately been fighting off morning sickness, and heat usually triggered nausea. The elephant looked in their direction just then, its serpentine trunk swinging languidly from side to side as though wagging a finger: *You naughty naughty girl.*

"What the hell is Elephant World, anyway?" Feeling queasy, Amparo fanned away the cigarette smoke that drifted into Matéo's car.

"Don't you read the newspaper?" Matéo rolled her window back up, sealing them off from the noise of the spontaneous carnival erupting around them. "They've been advertising for weeks. It's one of the circus acts at the Araneta Coliseum. 'Amazing Thai Elephants Paint Watercolor Portraits,' the ads said."

"Who has time to read the paper?" Amparo held a handkerchief to her mouth as an ominous sourness formed in her belly and welled in her throat, teasing the edge of her palate. "I've got other things to worry about."

"You okay?" Matéo cast a sidelong glance at her. "You look pale. That barbecue we had at the Beach House wasn't rancid, was it?"

A barrage of sirens interrupted Amparo's reply as three squad cars, a fire engine, a pickup truck and a van emblazoned with the face of TV anchorwoman Marlu Makil roared up Tomas Morato, only to stop fifty yards distant from their target, blocked by the tangle of traffic that walled in the placid fugitive. Trying to clear the space for a vet and circus handlers, policemen banged on car hoods and snarled commands, threatening recalcitrant drivers with billy clubs.

The taxi driver began inching his car forward, only to be blocked by a vendor who rolled his cart bearing a drum of boiled peanuts into the street. The vendor had sold most of his peanuts to bystanders, who littered the street and sidewalk with their unsuccessful attempts to feed the elephant. As the taxi driver yelled at the peanut peddler to get back on the curb, a police officer approached, brandishing a truncheon.

"Someone's about to get busted," Matéo muttered.

"Can't say I care." Amparo rubbed her clammy forehead. "Mind if I roll down the window again? I need some fresh air."

By then the policeman was standing between Matéo's car and the taxi, haranguing the driver about an expired license. Hoping to escape the policeman's notice, the peanut vendor slid in front of Matéo's car, only to be blocked by a jeep that had wandered up from behind and into the opposing traffic lane.

"We could be here for hours." Matéo turned off the air conditioner.

Amparo began to feel acutely claustrophobic in the morass of heat and noise and traffic. People ran across the street and up the sidewalk, jostling for a better view, a flurry of hands reaching out to stroke the elephant's massive torso. Amparo shuddered to think that in a few months other hands could well be fondling the pregnant orb of her own distended belly.

She leaned her head out the window hoping for relief, but was immediately assaulted by a thick humidity rank with diesel fumes and elephant dung. The stink enveloped her head like a damp towel, making her choke, convulse and finally hurl what looked to be both breakfast and lunch onto the shoes of the surprised policeman.

"'Tangina . . ." The policeman waved his billy club, cussing at Amparo. "What you do that for? You trying to piss me off?"

"Pasensiya na po," Amparo begged for consideration, reflexively switching to her most obsequious Tagalog. Like many who'd grown up under martial law, she'd been raised to treat men in uniform with a deference born of fear. "I can't help it—I'm pregnant."

"*Buntis?* If you're pregnant, why are you staring at that? You want your baby to come out looking like the elephant man?" The policeman waved his truncheon at the elephant, which was now rubbing its back against the tree trunk. Bystanders mugged for the TV camera as Marlu Makil began filming her segment, the wings of her Farrah Fawcett do wilting under the noonday sun. Unimpressed by the TV crew, the policeman glared at Amparo. "*O, eh ano ngayon?* What are you going to do about this?"

Amparo turned pleading eyes on Matéo, bungled pregnancy announcement forgotten in her terror over a possible arrest.

"Let me handle this." Matéo eased his wallet out of his back pocket. "Throw enough money at them and they go away," he muttered, leaning across her to call out the window. "Sorry *po,* Boss. *'Di niya sinasadya.* She didn't mean to vomit on you."

Matéo pulled out all the cash he had and rolled the bills tight as a cigarette. "Why don't you buy yourself a new pair of shoes? Sorry *talaga, naabala pa kayo.* We didn't mean to inconvenience you."

The policeman pocketed the money with practiced smoothness and pointed his billy stick at Amparo's forehead. "*O sige. Kung hindi ka lang buntis*—if you hadn't been pregnant . . ." He made as if to wallop the windshield.

The elephant trumpeted just then, and even the policeman turned to look. A man in a safari vest and construction worker's hat held up an outsized syringe as though cocking a rifle The crowd cheered, anxious to see if and how soon the animal would pass out from the sedative the man had just administered.

Seizing on the moment's distraction, the jeepney driver idling in the wrong lane dashed forward to squeeze into a spot four cars up ahead, leaving a clear path for the peanut vendor to scoot across the street. Matéo revved his engine and made a run for it, speeding in the jeep's wake and swerving left to Kamuning Road, where another traffic jam ended their escape. They had driven barely five hundred yards, but at least they were out of the policeman's line of sight.

"Good save, that pregnancy excuse." Matéo grinned. "Remind me not to take you to the Beach House for lunch again. Today's barbecue might have been left over from yesterday."

"It wasn't an excuse, Matéo." Amparo swallowed hard, grimacing at the lingering sour taste in her mouth. "I really am pregnant."

Matéo turned to stare at her. "You're kidding. That's unbelievable."

"You know what's unbelievable, Matéo? An elephant on Morato. You getting me pregnant after all those nights we spent at Tiffany's? Not so hard to believe." Amparo's eyes filled. She swept a finger across her eyes to stanch the tears and took a last look at the elephant, which had somehow lumbered farther up Morato, as though trying to keep up with them. The behemoth swayed unsteadily as a man prodded it with a pole. She wished she had a pole to poke at Matéo. "What are we going to do now?"

Matéo revved the engine, slapping the horn, suddenly losing patience with the traffic. "If you're pregnant, we're going to need help. This isn't something we can handle alone."

Amparo remained silent as Matéo followed the file of traffic through Kamuning, then made a right on the freeway. This was what she had hoped to hear: that they needed help to deal with her pregnancy. Would it be better if they told both sets of parents at the same time? She knew her mother would immediately turn to Tita Carina. Tita Carina had a knack of finding solutions to the thorniest problems; she better than anyone would know just how to set up a hasty wedding. "Who should we tell first, my parents or yours?"

"Neither. We're going to my brother's office." A vein Amparo had never noticed before throbbed in Matéo's forehead as he drove silently to Makati.

"Good thing my two o'clock was canceled or I couldn't have seen you. Can you believe it? My client couldn't get across town because some elephant jammed traffic on Morato." Fingers steepling beneath his Vandyke beard, Richard Madrigal looked at the couple who, like all his visitors, seemed instantly diminished by his imposing desk. Richard had installed a platform behind his table that raised his seat several inches higher than the chairs in front of him. "To what do I owe this surprise visit?"

Matéo glanced at Amparo, then plunged in. "We need your help figuring something out."

Richard set an elbow on his desk and stared at Amparo, who had turned a deep red. "Help with what?"

"Can you promise to leave Mom and Dad out of it?"

"Not till you tell me why you need my help. You've never come to me for anything. Spit it out."

"Amparo is pregnant."

"Are you sure it's yours?" A knowing smile spread across Richard's face.

"What do you mean by that?" Amparo began to get up. "Why did we even come here? Let's go, Matéo."

"Calm down, my brother was just asking a question." Matéo's tone turned sullen.

Amparo glared at her boyfriend but sat down, wondering why his hand on her arm felt more like restraint than support. "Don't you care that I was offended by the question?"

"This is the wrong time to be thin-skinned. Especially around the one person who can figure this out." Matéo turned back to Richard. "Can you help us?"

"First of all, your timing sucks." Richard rocked back in his chair. "A shotgun wedding would be disastrous for Dad's campaign—he's been trying to get Cardinal Sin's endorsement for weeks. The last thing he needs is a rumor that his son is having premarital sex."

Matéo released Amparo's arm and stared at a photo on Richard's desk. It showed his father and Richard's late mother on their honeymoon, lounging in a gondola under the Bridge of Sighs. When he finally replied, his voice was low and uncertain. "I wasn't thinking of getting married."

"I'm not giving birth to a bastard—" Amparo turned to Matéo, indignant.

"Who says you have to give birth at all?" Richard looked at Amparo through lowered lids. "If you want my help, you'll do things my way." Richard flipped through his Rolodex, picking up a fountain pen. "There's a doctor in Mandaluyong who owes me a favor. He normally sees patients at Makati Med, but he maintains a clinic at home for special cases." Richard scribbled an address on the back of his business card and handed it to Matéo. "I'll arrange an appointment for you. If we're lucky, he'll be able to fit us in next weekend."

"But how much will it—" Matéo faltered.

"I'll pick up the tab on this one. But you'll owe me big-time." Richard leaned elbows on the desk, looking at Amparo. "Dr. Tiao is very busy, so you'll have to take the first appointment he offers, whatever time that may be."

"But I've only ever been examined by a female doctor. Why should I—"

"'Paro, stop." Matéo held up a hand, the business card pinched between two fingers. "Richard's just offered us a way out of—" He sighed. "—a solution to this problem. Come on. We're too young to be parents. I planned to spend next year at Oxford before starting law school and—"

"Bottom line: marriage is out of the question." Richard sliced through his brother's plea. "I suggest you deal with it and get on with the rest of your life: a career, grad school, whatever your little heart desires. Then who knows?" He shrugged. "Maybe in a few years you'll be in a better position to plan the wedding of your dreams." Hands clasped, Richard looked upon his supplicants like a stern but just God.

"It's the only way, 'Paro." Matéo stared at the card.

"Aren't we going to discuss this before—" Amparo reached for Matéo's hand, but he leaned ever so slightly away. Amparo looked at her lover with slowly filling eyes, realizing that somewhere between Morato and Makati, Matéo had cut loose from their relationship and was now drifting away to a future from which she was evidently excluded. Staring at the Madrigal brothers, she felt the oxblood walls of the office closing in, pinning her to the chair like a moth under glass.

One week later, on a moonless night, Richard drove Matéo and Amparo down a street where the houses hid behind blank walls. Phil Collins yowled about lost love on the stereo, but maudlin ballads could not melt the icicle in Amparo's heart. At the blind end of the street, a uniformed guard opened the creaking iron gate and waved Richard up a wide driveway. An ancient banyan tree stood opposite the front doors of the mansion, aerial roots forming a leafless forest, which blocked Amparo's view of the lawn beyond. Marcela had raised Amparo and her brothers on stories about *lamang-lupa*, dwarfs who lived in balete trees just like this one. The little people tempted children with enchanted sweets that, when consumed, imprisoned them forever under the earth. Amparo wondered if a part of her would be eternally trapped on that nameless street, in the house with a bewitched tree.

A slim young man, his long hair bound in a Chinaman's queue, opened the front door and nodded, his gaze lingering on Amparo. "*Gandang gabi po*—good evening. Dr. Tiao is expecting you. Please let me show you to his clinic."

They walked past a dim-lit living room and down a hallway lined with yellowing photographs of carnival queens in butterfly-sleeved gowns from the 1930s. As she lagged behind the men, Amparo caught a whiff of something tropical, a pineapple on the cusp of spoiling, the insistent sweetness obscuring a metallic disinfectant scent. She held her breath, trying not to gag.

Dr. Tiao's assistant ushered them into a room lined with white tile, occupied by an examining table with stirrups, a wheeled stool, two steel chairs. "Please wait here while I call the doctor." His voice sang high and musical, like that of a child.

Moments later, an elfin man in a lab coat and white slacks appeared at the door, nodding at Richard and Matéo, offering Amparo a knowing smile. "Ahhh, Richard, is this our patient?"

"Her name is Amparo." Matéo put a hand on Amparo's shoulder, but she jerked away.

"I've seen your tests, young lady." Dr. Tiao's smile was paternal, his voice soft and conciliatory. The balding doctor stood an inch shorter than Amparo, but his hands seemed disproportionately large. "You're about fifteen weeks along at this point. The fetus is smaller than your thumb."

"Is that supposed to make me feel better?" Even with the sedative Richard made her take, Amparo could still tell when she was being patronized.

"She's feisty, isn't she?" Dr. Tiao smiled at Richard. "Hormones seething, no doubt." The doctor startled Amparo by taking her hand in his. His cool fingers were those of a concert pianist, long, slender and immaculately groomed. "*Hija*, let's not be unpleasant," he cooed, as though placating a sulky child. "Everyone here is trying to help you feel better." He motioned to his assistant. "Oliver, why don't you take the little lady to the dressing room and help her into a gown while I set things up."

As Amparo undressed in the adjoining room, she heard Dr. Tiao chatting with the Madrigal brothers. "Why don't you two wait in the sala—make yourselves comfortable. My assistant set out a bottle of Johnnie Walker and refreshments. Oliver discovered the best *chicharones* in Manila, infinitely better than Lapid's. We'll be done in under an hour."

Amparo returned, barefoot and vulnerable in a thin hospital gown. While Dr. Tiao prepared his various instruments, she turned pleading eyes on Oliver. "Is this going to hurt? Is there going to be cramping?" *Will I burn in hell?* was the question she could not bear to ask.

"Relax *ka lang*, Miss Amparo, you're in good hands. Dr. Tiao has been doing this for years." Oliver shushed her with his placid murmuring, humming an old *kundiman* as he slipped a needle into a vein in her arm. The anesthesia swiftly took effect, doubly potent on her empty stomach. Soon after following Dr. Tiao's directions to hoist her heels into cold metal stirrups and just before he slid the cannula between her legs, Amparo surrendered to a fitful twilit half sleep. Fleeting memories twirled through her mind like images in a revolving shadow lamp, retreating ever backward in time: waltzing at her debut, skipping through water sprinklers across the family's wide lawn, scratching at the lace on her First Communion dress. Amparo smiled, no longer terrified of enchanted sweets as she fled to a simpler, uncompromised past. As Dr. Tiao suctioned up the remnants of careless passion, Amparo wandered to the edge of darker dreams, stepping off the precipice, tumbling through a continuum of regret: the inconstant Matéo, the nameless sweethearts of puberty, her absent father and finally, mercifully, Nanay 'Cela, catching her and catching her and catching her again.

Chapter 21

Expulsion

A dwarf had escaped the balete tree and was running amok in Amparo's gut, stomping on her insides with hobnailed boots, whacking her pelvis with a mace, beating her awake in the blue hours of dawn. She moaned in bed in a fetal curl, wanting to pee but in too much pain to get up. How could she be cold and sweaty at the same time? She remembered being driven home the night before, numb and sedated, waving off Marcela's scolding about the lateness of the hour. She would have slept forever but for these cursed cramps. The urge to urinate intensified. Irritably pushing aside her blanket, she flicked on the light and gasped: crimson streaks mapped her fevered tossing on the white sheets.

In a fog of pain, Amparo's first impulse was to clean up any evidence of the previous night's events, but she had never stripped a bed in her life, much less laundered sheets. She stumbled downstairs seeking the one person who always made things better. Tiptoeing past the hallway that led to her mother's bedroom, she followed the scent of coffee to the kitchen. "Nanay? Are you awake?"

Marcela leaned against the sink, staring out the window at the rumor of daylight. She turned at the sound of Amparo's voice. "*Aba naman, 'Paro*—for goodness' sake, you startled me. Why are you shivering?" Setting her cup down by the sink, she pressed cool fingers against Amparo's forehead. "Your forehead is burning. You looked only a little drunk when you got home. How on earth did you get sick so quickly?"

Amparo leaned into the cook's arms as another wave of cramps silenced her reply. The dwarf had been replaced by a circus elephant, stabbing her gut with sharpened tusks.

"And why aren't you wearing slippers, or even a robe—" Marcela stopped midsentence when she saw blood trickling down Amparo's leg like a crooked stocking seam. "*Madré de Dîos.* I'm waking your mother. You need a doctor right now."

"Please don't tell Mama I messed up my bed," Amparo whispered, just before passing out.

"*Santa Maria,* Concha, you look like death. Here, put on some makeup, will you?" Carina Madrigal handed her friend a tube of lipstick. "*A ver?* Better. Your cook called me to go to the hospital, but all she would say was that Amparo was bleeding. Do you know what caused it?"

"*Ay,* Carina, if I knew that, don't you think I'd tell you? She looked fine yesterday. I have to wonder if she caught the stomach flu or some other virus—she was out till very late."

"Did she tell you what she was doing last night?"

"I was asleep when she got back, but Marcela said she was brought home by someone in a black sedan. Matéo's car is blue. Who could she have been with?"

"His older brother Richard drives a black car; maybe Matéo borrowed it. I'll call Vinchy and find out."

Amparo cracked open an eye. A flak-jacket-clad reporter murmured from some nameless war zone on a TV just beyond the metal frame of her bed. On the wall above it a mournful Madonna gazed upon her Child, cherubs hovering above the pair's dull golden halos.

From the sound of it, Amparo's mother and Tita Carina were somewhere to the left of the bed. She tried to sit up, only to discover that she was tethered to an intravenous line.

"*Por Díos*, Amparo, be careful or you'll rip the vein out of your arm."

Amparo inhaled the familiar scent of cigarettes and Chanel No. 5 as Señora Concha leaned over her bed, a diamond crucifix dangling from her throat. "How are you feeling? You must have eaten something bad last night. Where did you have dinner?"

"Now, Concha, don't start on her yet, the poor girl's barely awake." Carina Madrigal tapped her friend's shoulder with a fan. Tita Carina's lips stood out on her pale face like scarlet poppies, reminding Amparo of her godmother's prescription for grace under pressure: *The bigger the crisis, the redder the lipstick.* "I'm sure Dr. Chien is in a better position to explain what's going on."

"The doctor couldn't tell us what she did last night, now, could she?" Señora Concha folded her arms and fixed her daughter with a disapproving gaze. "Tell us, Amparo. You were not sick yesterday afternoon. Who were you with last night?"

Amparo was mentally riffling through a list of alibis when a knock interrupted the interrogation. A tall woman, her face a symmetry of sharp angles, walked into the room. "Good morning, ladies. I'm Dr. Chien." The doctor shook hands with both women before turning an impassive gaze on her patient. "How are you feeling today, Amparo? The emergency room doctor briefed me and I've reviewed your chart. You lost quite a bit of blood last night; you're lucky we got to you in time." She glanced at the clipboard. "May I ask if you've had a procedure done recently?"

"I don't know what you mean." Amparo avoided the doctor's eyes, crumpling a fistful of bedsheet.

Dr. Chien folded arms across her lab coat. "You were bleeding from a perforated uterus and cervical lacerations. Had this progressed, you could have gone into endotoxic shock." Her gaze shifted to Señora Concha and she lowered her voice. "These injuries are consistent with a poorly executed abortion. I'd like to know where . . ."

"Abortion? That's not even legal." Indignation crimped Señora Concha's face. "Are you saying my daughter was pregnant?"

"The hormone levels in the blood samples we took certainly indicate—"

"*Santisima,* Amparo, were you having sex with Matéo?" The memory of a pregnant Clara surfaced through the red fog filling Señora Concha's mind and she lunged at her daughter, sunk now to the level of a promiscuous maid.

"*Por Dias,* Concha, calm down!" Carina flung an arm round her friend's shoulders, restraining her as Amparo shrank into a far corner of the bed, the IV tube taut as piano wire. "I'm sorry, Dr. Chien, you must forgive my *kumadre,* but this is a big shock. We did not even suspect my niece was sexually active."

"It was that nephew of yours," Señora Concha gasped, trying to wrench free. "If my husband were still alive, he'd have gone after that low-life *bugoy* with a gun and—"

"Shut up, Mama! You can't talk about Matéo like that." Amparo's outburst silenced the older women. For a moment she hesitated, mortified by her incivility. She yearned for her father, for Matéo, for anyone other than these women with the accusing eyes. Then the clouds over her heart exhaled, releasing long-held anguish that spilled through her fingers, dribbled down her chin, watered the flowers on her hospital gown.

"Let's give your daughter a chance to compose herself, shall we?" Dr. Chien put a firm hand on Señora Concha's elbow, turning her to the door. "It's best we pursue this conversation in my office. I'm sure Ms. Madrigal can keep Amparo company while we chat."

"We'll continue this later," Señora Concha hissed at her daughter, then stalked out of the room.

When the door clicked shut, Carina dragged a chair to the side of Amparo's bed, poppy red lips mirroring the Madonna's sad smile. "*Ay naku, hija.* If you want me to help you out of this one, you'll have to tell your *ninang* everything."

An hour later, Carina Madrigal and Concha Guerrero walked out of the hospital to compare notes over a much-needed smoke. Turning her back on the late-afternoon sunlight, Carina took a long drag, lipstick leaching into the fine lines that radiated from her mouth. "I tried everything, but Amparo wouldn't tell me who performed the—"

"*Calla te*—be quiet," Señora Concha snapped. "I cannot bear to hear that word. "I don't care who did it, as long as no one learns about this abomination, this scandal. *Qué barbaridad.*" She blew a plume of smoke, rage percolating through her very pores. "To think, all those years I pretended Fico was the model husband, and finally—*finally*—I was free of that adulterer. Who knew our only daughter would inherit his moral deficiency?"

Señora Concha paced back and forth, bitterness billowing like smoke. "I could kick myself for welcoming that Matéo into my home. How could that *cabrón* take advantage of us? *Por Diós*, this is more than I can bear." A nurse pushing an amputee in his wheelchair narrowly missed being poked in the eye with Señora Concha's cigarette as she flung her arms skyward.

"You have every right to be angry, Conchitina, but can't you at least be grateful the doctors saved her?" Carina flicked ash to the curb. She was used to her best friend's histrionics, having endured them each time Fico took up with a new *querida*. "If it makes you feel better, I will talk to Matéo and make sure he stays away from Amparo."

"What for?" Señora Concha's cigarette slashed across the dying sun. "The damage is done."

"Come, now, Conchitina, let it go already. Amparo is young. She will recover completely."

"Not quite." The matron tossed her cigarette in the gutter. "Dr. Chien said the procedure may have caused permanent damage to Amparo's cervix. An incompetent cervix means she will be unable to carry a pregnancy to term." Señora Concha's shoulders sagged, her face fissured in defeat. "*Ay*, Carina. I've been cheated of grandchildren. She could not even give me a bastard."

Carina rubbed her friend's back, murmuring consolatory words that were drowned out by the siren of an approaching ambulance.

Shaken out of her depression by the threat of scandal, Señora Concha busied herself with crisis control. Swearing Javier to secrecy, she directed him to file papers for Amparo's leave of absence from the university. Complying with her mistress's instructions, Marcela blocked Matéo's calls. Amparo barely noticed the protective walls rising around her, for after her discharge she withdrew into a brooding isolation. Every now and then a phone rang downstairs and she would come out of her room to eavesdrop on the maid's conversation. *Sorry po, Señorita Amparo cannot come to the phone, she is asleep*. Then she would wander back to bed too enervated by sorrow to protest.

She sought distraction by rereading favorite books, only to be dismayed by *Anna Karenina* and *Tess of the D'Urbervilles.* Had she always been fascinated by calamitous love?

While Amparo buried herself in old novels, Señora Concha was busy composing a suitable denouement to her daughter's dilemma.

Shortly before noon that Monday, Marcela walked into Amparo's room, freshly ironed clothes in hand. "I hope this skirt still fits, *anak*, you've become so thin. Your mama said you must put on some nice clothes for a change; your *ninang* Carina is coming to lunch."

"She hasn't visited in weeks." Amparo set down her book. "What's the occasion?"

"Who knows? Those two have been on the phone almost every day since you came home from the hospital."

"Did Matéo call today?" Amparo's eyes begged for an honest answer.

The older woman sat on the bed, reflexively smoothing out the blanket as she had done since Amparo was a child. "He's called every day since you came home. But I can only do as your mother tells me. You're lucky I was able to sneak in those flowers he sent."

"But Mama had them thrown away as soon as she saw them." Amparo picked up her book with an exasperated sigh.

"Enough reading, *anak*. You must get dressed for lunch now." Marcela smoothed hair back from Amparo's pronounced widow's peak, marveling at how closely it resembled Beverly's. "Sounds like they have something important to tell you. Your mother had me make all your favorite dishes."

"I'm not hungry."

"Just come downstairs and see your *ninang* Carina. It will make your mother happy. We just want you to recover."

Dragging leaden limbs, Amparo eased off the bed. "No one recovers from this."

Carina and Señora Concha beamed ladies-who-lunch smiles when Amparo approached the dining room.

"So nice to see you dressed well, for a change." Señora Concha leaned back, elbows perched on the arms of her chair. Since Fico's death, she had taken over his place at the head of the table.

"How are you feeling, *hija*?" Carina allowed her goddaughter to brush lips against her cheek, noting the pallid skin, the lank hair. "You look like you've been in prison. A bit of sun would do you good. Your mother tells me you don't get out as much as you used to."

"Amparo hasn't done anything but read lately." Señora Concha began pulling a cigarette out of her pack but set it down when Marcela arrived with a tray of *pochero* stew, pickled papaya and dumpling soup. "Perhaps today you'll surprise us by actually eating, no?"

Marcela stiffened at the sharpness of Señora Concha's tone.

"*Heto, kain na*—eat up," she murmured to Amparo as she set the serving dishes down with exaggerated slowness.

Carina offered her godchild a coaxing smile. "I don't know how anyone could resist Marcela's cooking. Shall I serve you some *pansit molo* soup, Amparo?"

"Yes, thanks." Amparo kept her eyes on her plate, hoping her godmother would distract her mother. In the last week Señora Concha had subjected her to so many mealtime lectures that Amparo would have preferred to shred her brain on a mandoline over enduring yet another rant against the repercussions of promiscuity and the duplicity of men.

Señora Concha watched Carina ladle soup into Amparo's bowl, then resumed lighting her cigarette; her mother-in-law's old cook had taught Marcela the Ilonggo recipe Fico loved, but she herself had never cared for dumplings. She blew a jet of smoke at the chandeliers. "Now that we're all here, I'd like to discuss how we're going to deal with"—Señora Concha regarded the nebula of smoke—"with the *consequences* of your recklessness."

Amparo looked up from her soup. Señora Concha had assumed what the Guerrero children called the executioner's gaze, a frigid glare she fixed on her husband whenever he came late to dinner. Bolstered by her godmother's presence, Amparo sat up straighter. "I don't know what you mean, Mama. Haven't I already paid for my mistake?"

"Not in my book you haven't. Matéo has made a complete nuisance of himself since you came home from the hospital, and I am tired of fending off his calls." Señora Concha waved off Carina's attempts to interrupt. "Then there is the matter of restitution."

"What are you talking about?" Amparo snorted. "Twenty-four acres and a mule?"

"Don't be clever with me, Amparo." Señora Concha flicked her cigarette in the ashtray. "That's how you got into trouble to begin with."

"Please, Conchitina. Let me explain this part. After all, this involves my family too." Carina looked at her goddaughter, who seemed on the verge of bolting from the table.

"Since you refused to tell me anything in the hospital, your mother and I had it out with Matéo's father and brother." Carina watched Amparo shrink in her seat. "Vinchy nearly had a heart attack when Richard coughed up the whole story."

"No need to mince words, Carina. Amparo was seduced and then forced to be complicit in murder. The scandal would have derailed Vinchy's campaign. You know, our parish priest at Santuario has the ear of Cardinal Sin. When I told him I needed to go to confession and clear my conscience, it was all over." Señora Concha waved her cigarette like a gavel. "That's when he offered to recompense us for your—for *our*—pain and suffering."

"You asked Matéo's dad for *money?*" Amparo dropped her spoon.

"I asked him to make amends." Señora Concha unfolded the napkin on her lap. A small nerve in the corner of one eye twitched, faint as hummingbird wings beneath the pale skin. "It was the least Vinchy could do, especially in an election year."

"I can't believe you blackmailed Matéo's father." Amparo gripped the edge of her chair, feeling blood surge up her neck, coloring her cheeks. "How could you be so crass?"

"*Hija*, it wasn't like that at all." Carina gave Señora Concha a warning glance. "Vinchy *wanted* to make up for Matéo's indiscretion. In the end we all agreed you two needed to spend some time apart. To heal." Carina reached across the table to her godchild, crimson nails hovering above the casseroles. "After much discussion, we decided since Matéo is spending a year in Europe, you should also go away for at least that long. So my cousin Vinchy bought you a ticket to California."

"He's paying to make me go away?" Amparo glared at her mother, too angry for tears.

"*Por Díos,* must you always act like your life is one big *telenovela*?" Señora Concha ground out her cigarette in the ashtray, mouth crimped with irritation. "Vinchy Madrigal has only your best interests in mind. With both you and Matéo abroad, the gossip will have nowhere to go and will eventually evaporate. You get to spend some time with your older brother Miguel, maybe even look in on your *tito* Aldo." Señora Concha leaned toward Carina, lowering her voice. "Last I heard, that useless brother of mine was just about to enter rehab—again."

"In that case he wouldn't be allowed visitors. Makes one less dysfunctional man she has to deal with," Carina murmured. She sipped ice water, looking at the food that lay cooling between them. "*Hija,* think of this next year as your chance to make a fresh start. No one cares about the past in America. It's where people go to reinvent themselves."

"And if you decide you like it, perhaps you can even finish your studies there," Señora Concha added. "Besides, it's already the beginning of July—too late to enroll at the university; classes started three weeks ago. Javier has asked the registrar for copies of your transcript. They should be ready by the time you leave."

Amparo sat completely still, a mouse trapped between twin Cheshire cats. "When do I leave?"

"Two weeks from today." Señora Concha swirled the ice in her glass, grimacing at her watered-down cola. "The school year there begins in September, so you'll have plenty of time to sign up for classes. Miguel says you can enroll as an international student. It will be hard in the beginning." She gazed down the table at cutlery, food and linens, all laid out by other hands. "But life without servants builds character. God knows you need that."

On Amparo's penultimate Sunday in Manila, Marcela paid a special visit to Quiapo Church. She hated having to squeeze through the perspiring faithful, but Sunday was her only day off.

Unable to wedge into the packed basilica, worshippers spilled out into the plaza to watch the midafternoon mass projected onto a large screen high on its west wall.

Marcela was uninterested in begging favors from the Black Nazarene, the centuries-old ebony-skinned statue of Jesus Christ that reclined in a glass coffin inside the church. Like everyone, she too believed the icon could work miracles if one came within stroking distance of his sacred foot, but the Black Nazarene's feast day was long past. Marcela needed help now. She held her breath against the stench of open sewers and made slow progress through the praying masses, taking special care to step around palsied beggar children with their coin bowls and exhausted eyes.

Planted like toadstools around the church plaza were dozens of merchants hawking novenas, candles and sundry accessories for the folk religion that fed on Catholic superstition. From previous visits, Marcela knew the amulet vendor liked to station himself beside the sloe-eyed herbalist whose malformed roots and homemade unguents claimed to cure everything from ulcers to infertility. Marcela found him sitting beneath a tattered umbrella, in an ancient wheelchair that cupped his shriveled lower half.

At her request, Télesforo Lumpó held up a large steel ring from which safety pins dangled dozens of bronze talismans. Marcela flipped past horseshoes, the Eye of God and Christopher, former patron of travelers before his demotion from sainthood. She had seen them all before, but the naked child with an erect penis gave her pause.

"It enhances virility," the vendor whispered, scratching an atrophied thigh. Finally Marcela found the one she wanted: a Santo Niño figure in his fan-shaped king's cape, crown surrounded by a halo; it was still small enough for Amparo to take to America.

"*El Señor* is my best-selling *anting-anting*," the cripple cackled, detaching the child Jesus from his ring of amulets. "It brings good luck to whoever holds it. *Garantisado suwerte!*"

The cook didn't waste any time haggling; she had to be back in time to roast a chicken for Sunday dinner. Pushing through the crowds once more, Marcela dipped the figurine in a font of murky holy water by the basilica's doors. Then she tucked the charm into her bra and held it next to her heart until the day Amparo left. She only wished Beverly could have received the same protection before leaving, the year before.

Years later, Marcela would swear that the Santo Niño began working magic the moment she handed the amulet to Amparo. Had it not been for the argument that erupted just before Amparo had to leave for the airport, she would never have had that extra hour in the car with her ward. It had begun as such arguments usually did, with one of Señora Concha's cutting comments.

A week after Marcela's trip to Quiapo Church, Señora Concha walked into Amparo's bedroom that afternoon to offer her own going-away present. "Here. I don't want you to look penniless in America."

"Thanks." Amparo felt the weight of the gold bracelet in her palm, but delayed putting it on, preferring to watch Marcela wedge shoes, belts and brushes into every free crevice of the suitcase. She resented her mother's refusal to allow a final visit with Matéo, but at this late date the sole weapon available was a sullen silence.

"I can only hope you will not be like every other person who moves to America," Señora Concha said, as Marcela folded the last of Amparo's clothes into the suitcase.

"I'm not like every other person." Amparo picked up an old teddy bear, wondering if she could still squeeze it into her luggage.

"You would think. Everyone I know doubled her weight after moving to America. They don't call it the land of milk and honey for nothing."

"Is that all you care about, Mama? How I look?" Amparo

looked at her mother, unbelieving. "Don't you ever worry about anything beyond appearances?"

"At this point, that's all you have going for you." Señora Concha regarded her daughter with the dour indifference of a sentencing judge. "You've dropped out of school and disgraced your family. For all we know, you may never bear a child. And for what—a few moments of immoral pleasure?"

"You wouldn't know pleasure if it kicked you in the face." Amparo threw her teddy bear on the bed. "I loved Matéo, how is that immoral? But of course you wouldn't know the answer to that because you never loved Papa."

The slap hit Amparo square across the jaw, knocking her to the floor. Her mother continued to rant far above her, but shock muffled Señora Concha's voice so that indistinct phrases drifted down to Amparo like pebbles through pond water.

At some point Marcela gathered Amparo up, stroking her heaving back, rocking her as though she were a little girl.

Watching her cook soothe her weeping daughter, Señora Concha felt vaguely nauseated; so unaccustomed was she to remorse. "I'm going to lie down now. Marcela, take Amparo to the airport; I'm no longer interested in taking her, but she cannot ride with the driver alone." With a last brief look at her daughter, Señora Concha turned and left the room.

Marcela remained silent through most of the drive, waiting until the car was ascending the departure ramp before pulling a small pouch from her pocket.

"Keep this close to you always, *anak*." The cook held up the Santo Niño.

As the Guerrero sedan slid into an open space by the curb, Marcela helped Amparo thread the *Santo Niño* onto the gold bracelet that Señora Concha had given her daughter. "Promise you will never take it off. *El Señor* will protect you wherever you go." Marcela's heart rose to her eyes, threatening to spill over. Amparo was the second child she was losing to America. All she knew about that province called California was that Beverly lived there too.

The driver opened the door, ending their hug.

Amparo rolled her suitcase to the end of the millipede line shuffling through security with the slowness of a funeral cortege. *My funeral*, Amparo mused. She might as well have been dead; so terrified was she by the notion of this newly solitary life.

Staring at the anonymous travelers, Amparo remembered a morbid game she used to play as a child: on nights when sleep eluded her, she composed a list of friends and relatives who would attend her wake, each mourner offering a fond memory from what Amparo imagined would be her long and happy life. Who would come to her funeral if she died in America? Would anyone reminisce on her tawdry past? *No one cares about the past in America.* Finding cold comfort in her godmother's words, Amparo hoisted her suitcase onto the conveyor belt and turned her back on Manila.

PART III

Truth and Consequences

Chapter 22

Oakland, 1995

Dear Ninang 'Cela,

Look how big Claire is now! We took this picture just before she started preschool. I am still waiting tables at the Japanese restaurant, saving up for our plane fare so we can visit you. Josiah will not let me travel without an American passport, so I must apply for citizenship before we can make definite plans. He says he is too busy now to take me to the INS, but I will keep reminding him. I hope you are well.

The photo showed Claire in a romper suit staring at the unseen photographer with the intensity of innocence. The four-year-old stood just tall enough for Beverly to sit on her haunches, chin perched upon Claire's shoulder, arms wrapped tight round the pretty child. Claire had inherited her mother's dark hair, widow's peak and full pink lips; only the blue eyes were Josiah's. They posed on a blanket the color of sunshine, the park a green blur in back.

The snapshot offered little more than the banal charm of a postcard, for after six years Beverly had learned to disguise the bleak landscape wrought by her marriage. Jeans hid the cumulus of bruises that darkened her thigh after Josiah had shoved her into a coffee table; the cardigan concealed a crescent scar seared into her left forearm by a hot skillet. Clasped hands disguised the crooked pinkie finger, misshapen by a poorly mended fracture in its middle joint.

With each successive altercation, new marks overlaid those that had come before, so that over the years Beverly's skin took on the appearance of pentimento, her suffering reworked time and again by a mercilessly exacting artist.

The day this photo was taken had begun on a hopeful note. Josiah had worked the graveyard shift at the drugstore the night before, and insisted Beverly and Claire be quiet while he slept. By noon the child was restless. Wanting to make the most of Claire's last weekend before school began, Beverly tossed toys and a box of animal crackers into her backpack and left a note for Josiah on the kitchen counter saying they had gone to Willard Park.

The small park had been her refuge whenever Claire became too rowdy for their little apartment. Beverly left the Sunday papers unread while she watched Claire roll a ball around with three other children, displaying her grandmother's charm. Josiah had resisted naming the newborn Clara, claiming it sounded "too Mexican," but for once Beverly had stood her ground, arguing until they compromised on the anglicized "Claire." Beverly leaned back on her elbows, her eyes half-shut to the afternoon sunlight. She was daydreaming about her mother meeting Claire when a shadow fell across her face.

"How's it going? We haven't seen you at the park in a long time." The woman standing over Beverly shifted her caramel-skinned infant to the opposite hip. "Not working tonight?"

"Hitomi! I should have known you would be here." Beverly grinned at the slender woman whose black hair fell to her waist like a curtain. One of the park regulars, Hitomi was one of Beverly's few friends in Berkeley.

"I switched shifts so I could put Claire to bed early tonight.

Tomorrow's her first day at preschool. Come sit so I can see your big boy." Beverly swept Claire's toys aside, clearing a spot on the blanket for the baby. "I can't believe how big Isaac's grown; will he cry if I take him?" She held up her arms.

"Where's that charming husband of yours?" Hitomi handed her son to Beverly, casting a wary glance around the park. "How did you get away from Josiah on a Sunday?"

"He's sleeping off the night shift. I couldn't keep Claire quiet, so I took her here."

"Good thinking. Jamal had to work the Sunday shift at Berkeley Bowl, but he'll come, soon as he's done. Why don't we get an early dinner at the Smokehouse? You shouldn't have to cook on Sunday night."

"I would love to." Beverly hesitated. "But I'll have to ask Josiah first."

"Since when does Josiah decide what you eat for dinner? You wait tables all day at work—don't you get a break from that on your day off?" Hitomi asked testily, as she stroked Isaac's tight black curls. "You deserve a life too."

"This *is* my life." Beverly wiggled Claire's sock monkey in front of the baby, avoiding her friend's gaze. Hitomi would never know that the price of disagreeing with Josiah was set by the amount of pain Beverly could endure on a given day. "In my life everything goes through my husband first."

"I guess you drank the Kool-Aid on that one."

"What are you talking about?" Beverly laughed. "I never drink Kool-Aid."

"Never mind, honey, never mind. Sometimes I need to remind myself that you didn't grow up in Berkeley."

"But my daughter will." Beverly shrugged. "In the end, that's all that matters." Putting the baby on the blanket, she pulled a camera out of her backpack. "Before I forget, can you take a picture of me and Claire? It's that time of the month again."

"Sending another update to your aunt?" Hitomi's smile was sympathetic. She had never met her own grandparents, who lived in Osaka and were now too frail to travel.

Beverly nodded. "It's the only way we keep in touch. Josiah says it's too expensive to call long-distance." Beverly rubbed her crooked pinkie finger, remembering all the celebrations Marcela had enjoyed vicariously through the monthly photos: Claire smiling with her first tooth; grabbing for Snow White on her birthday cake; dressed as Tinker Bell for Halloween. "Don't take more than a couple of shots. I can't spend too much money on film; he checks all our receipts."

"Give me a break. You have a right to spend at least some of the money you earn."

"It's not worth another argument." Beverly offered her friend a rueful smile. They had talked about this many times before, although she never discussed the violence, ashamed her marriage was unhappy. "I'm not fierce like you."

"And Jamal's nothing like Josiah." Hitomi peered through the camera's viewfinder. "Gotta drag that husband of yours out of the Middle Ages, girl."

Ignoring the dig, Beverly waved her daughter over. "Claire, come take a picture with Mama." Beverly held Claire in front of her, staying seated so Marcela could see how tall the child had grown. "Smile for your *Lola* 'Cela," she whispered in the little girl's ear, leaning against the small warm cheek.

"Too cute. Like peas in a pod, you two are." Hitomi snapped two photos and handed the camera back to Beverly.

Isaac began to fret, rolling forward on pudgy knees to crawl to his mother. Hitomi gathered the baby up and lifted her T-shirt just high enough for him to latch on to her breast.

Beverly settled Claire down in her lap. "Ready for a nap, Clarita?"

"Yes! Sleepy time, Mama." Claire nestled into the cradle of her mother's arms, twirling a lock of Beverly's hair round her finger. Beverly hummed an old Ilonggo lullaby Clara used to sing; she could no longer remember the lyrics. She envied the dreamy look that softened Hitomi's eyes as she fed Isaac. The same sense of hermetic peace had come over Beverly whenever she nursed Claire those first weeks, wrapping them in a cocoon that excluded her husband entirely.

"I wish I'd been able to nurse for longer." Beverly traced little circles on Claire's forehead, easing the child into sleep. "Josiah made me switch to formula when she was just three months old."

"If I'd known you then, I'd have raised a stink about that. What's his problem?" Hitomi's eyes narrowed. "Not a fan of breast milk?"

"He thinks breast-feeding is indecent. That only women in Third World countries suckle their babies—just like animals, he told me."

Hitomi threw her head back and whooped. "Where does that man come up with these things? Wait till I tell Jamal he married a cow."

"Better a cow than a monkey!" Beverly giggled. "That's what Josiah calls Claire whenever she acts out." Dropping her voice an octave, she mimicked her husband. "What's wrong with you, Claire? You some kind of Philippine monkey?"

"Daddy's silly!" Claire squealed.

"He is, isn't he? Give Mama an Eskimo kiss." As Beverly pulled Claire close to nuzzle noses, she missed the flash of anger in her friend's eyes.

"Son of a bitch," Hitomi muttered. Isaac's mouth went slack and she eased him off her nipple, curling the infant into the crook of her arm. She looked up at Beverly. "Jamal should be here in an hour or so. Maybe we can get a burger to go for your grumpy old man."

The women slipped into a companionable silence, heads drooping like spent blossoms over their napping babies.

As the two friends basked in the cool autumn sunlight, a pale blue car cruised slowly up Telegraph, its driver searching for a parking spot. The car squeezed into a space by the restaurant a block away. A middle-aged man with a steel gray crew cut slammed his door and headed for the park.

Josiah scanned the park, his gaze landing on a familiar yellow blanket halfway down the wide square of grass. The women had their backs turned to him, and sat side by side, fat baby feet poking out from under their elbows. He recognized the woman sitting by Beverly by her long black hair. "Goddamn Jap." He quickened his pace.

Walking quietly, he came round to stand directly over Beverly and Claire. He poked his wife's knee with a slight kick, startling her awake. "Were you planning to leave me alone on my one day off?"

Beverly flinched at the sight of Josiah. "*Ay naku,* I'm so sorry, Josiah. I lost track of the time. I was planning to go home earlier, but I must have dozed off. I'm sorry, I didn't mean to make you drive."

"I didn't have a choice, did I? If you were going to sneak out, you could have at least left the Sunday papers behind."

"I'm sorry, Josiah. I only meant to take the magazine, but Claire was making so much noise that I just rushed out the door." Beverly covered Claire's face with one hand. "I was afraid she'd wake you. It was silly of me to be so careless."

"Is this what you were looking for?" Hitomi held the newspaper up to Josiah. "We didn't even touch it, we've been so busy catching up."

"I'll bet." Josiah ignored the paper she offered. "Pack it up, Beverly. With any luck I'll be able to read while you cook dinner."

"Oh, don't worry about dinner." Hitomi forced a smile. "I suggested we just get burgers at the Smokehouse."

"I much prefer a home-cooked meal." Josiah glowered at Hitomi, taking in the milk-stained T-shirt, the infant drooling into her chinos. "Beverly cooks dinner every night she's off work. I insist on it." Leaning over, he pulled Claire out of Beverly's lap, jostling her awake. She began to whimper, but he clamped a hand on her back, keeping a tight hold on the squirming child. "Girl, if you don't get up right now, you'll have to walk home." Without another word he turned and strode away.

Hitomi scrambled up after Beverly. "Look, Bev, we can easily drive you home if you want to stay. Jamal should be here any minute."

"Thanks, but I really need to get going." She turned pleading eyes on her friend and whispered, "Please don't argue, you'll only make things worse." Beverly crammed toys and juice boxes into her backpack and threw the blanket over her shoulder. Josiah was already at the edge of the park, Claire shrieking from his shoulder. "Wait, Josiah, please. I'm coming."

Hitomi stared after her, holding Isaac close. The noise had wakened him and he rooted around her neck, hungry for comfort. She shushed him, watching Beverly's retreat.

Claire's wails caught the attention of a couple sipping coffee on Le Bateau Ivre's patio in front of whose curb Josiah had parked his car.

"*That's* a guy who needs to get his yoga on," the man whispered to his date.

"Yoga can't save everyone, Seamus." Amparo tugged playfully on his ponytail as they watched the man march up the sidewalk, the flailing child held tight against his chest.

A woman lugging a picnic blanket, a backpack and the Sunday paper scurried after them. "Josiah, please give her to me, you're scaring her."

Having reached his car, the man turned and thrust the child into the woman's arms with such force that she staggered backward. "Don't you ever let me catch you with that bitch again," he hissed, jabbing the woman's shoulder with the point of his car key.

"Aray!" Quick as the word escaped, the woman looked around, fearing someone had heard her cry, and for an eternal second, she locked eyes with Amparo. Recognition passed between them, each one wondering how the other Filipina had come to be there, so many miles from home.

The man opened the rear door. "Get the hell in."

The woman fumbled with the child's car seat latch, then scrambled into the front seat, barely managing to shut the door before the car screeched off.

Amparo exhaled. "Seamus, she's Filipino."

"And her husband's a dick." Seamus lifted his cup of tea. "Looks to be just another vet, screwing the spoils of empire. You were right. Even yoga couldn't save that dude."

CHAPTER 23

Kill the Wabbit

"Claire, honey, why don't you watch TV while I make dinner?" Beverly led her sniffling daughter into the bedroom and put on a video, turning the volume up and hoping the Looney Tunes would drown out the storm brewing in the next room.

"Is Daddy mad at me?" Claire clutched her sock monkey tight to her wet cheek as she crawled into bed.

Beverly was desperate to make good on her mother's promise of a better life, for Claire's sake. She smoothed away the frown squinching her daughter's brows. "Daddy's cranky because he's hungry. That's why I have to hurry cooking dinner. Don't come out until I call you to eat, promise?"

"Okay, Mommy." The little girl leaned back against the pillows, drew her knees up to her chest and began sucking furiously on her thumb, a small anxious version of her grandmother Clara. Beverly paused after shutting the door, trying to calm her rising apprehension. The heavy stillness in the apartment felt like the ominous lull that blanketed Manila just before a storm: a sticky heat that smelled of rotted plants rose from the soil and the wind dropped, as though heaven were holding its breath until the onslaught began.

Josiah was reading the Sunday newspaper at the dining table; a breakfast counter just beyond his seat marked the borders of the small kitchen. Holding her breath, Beverly slipped past him to the one place she felt was all her own.

Josiah's sole concession to Beverly's pregnancy had been to move her into the one-bedroom apartment, when morning sickness made her unable to tolerate the scent of food in the cramped studio where they'd lived as newlyweds. During those first months in their new home, Beverly would sometimes stand in the center of her kitchen with both arms stretched out, touching the refrigerator with one palm and the stove with the other, measuring the borders of her domain. It pleased her no end to think that after years of being a transient in other households, she finally had her own kitchen. Five years ago it had felt womblike in its smallness. That night it felt like a cage.

Josiah looked up from the sports page as she tied on her apron. "What the hell were you doing with that woman all afternoon?"

"Her name is Hitomi." Beverly took a packet of ground beef from the refrigerator, speaking low to hide her unease. "I didn't plan on seeing her. She goes to the park almost every day—they live just around the corner."

"I could care less where she lives." Josiah shook out his paper, the pages making a brittle crackle. "I don't want you wasting any more time with that woman."

"But why not? She's one of the few people I talk to." Beverly glanced at Josiah's knuckles, the knobbly heft of his hands. How many times had he used his fists as wrecker's balls on her face? She looked to the window above the kitchen sink, yearning to leap out. "I don't know who else I can spend time with. You never like any of my other friends."

"What friends? Those Mexicans you chatted up at the Ashby Flea Market?" When Josiah took off his reading glasses, tiny red dents on his skin showed where they'd pinched his nose. "They didn't care about you. They were trying to con you into buying their junk."

"Okay, then, Josiah. You're right, they were not sincere." Beverly resisted being drawn into an argument. Hoping to distract him with dinner, she struggled to pull a cast-iron skillet from the cupboard above the stove. In her rush she miscalculated its weight and dropped it with a loud clatter on the stove burner.

"Banging pots now, are you?" Josiah set down his newspaper. "Trying to tell me you're too upset to cook dinner?"

"I didn't mean to drop it, I'm sorry." Beverly swabbed sweaty palms on a dish towel. She stared at his scalp, gleaming under the sparse gray hair, pale as gravestone marble. Her voice grew shrill, sounding like a child on the verge of tears. "I should have been more careful, but I always forget how heavy it is."

Josiah's chair rasped on the wood floor as he got up. "I don't believe you. I think that Jap's been feeding you her feminist crap again, trying to turn you against me." With slow, deliberate movements, he folded the Sunday paper, rolling it into a club thick as his forearm. "I'm sick of these Berkeley hippies, with their pickaninny kids and brown rice. They think they're better than regular people because they're so frickin' PC." The club made dull slapping thwacks against Josiah's palm. "I can always tell when you've been talking to those people because you start assuming things; making dinner plans without consulting me. I won't have my own wife taking on that holier-than-thou attitude. Turning all feminist. You're going to drop that PC bullshit, if I have to beat it out of your thick skull." He rounded the counter, swinging the club with an ominous slowness.

"Please, Josiah, I swear, Hitomi didn't tell me anything. I never listen to her advice." Beverly backed away until the sink ended her retreat. Her husband loomed over her, rage sucking all the air out of her small kitchen.

"She was giving you advice? You telling her problems instead of coming to me? What the hell were you whining about?" Josiah's cudgel slammed into Beverly's cheek. "What're you complaining for, Beverly?" The club struck her neck. "I gave you the good life, you ungrateful bitch. Yanked you out of that Third World ghetto. Gave you a frickin' green card." He stuck the end of his makeshift truncheon under Beverly's chin, leaning so close she could feel his breath on her eyelids. "You owe me big-time. Is this the way you repay me?"

The counter pressed into Beverly's spine as she tried to block a hailstorm of blows with thin forearms. She fought to stay upright to avoid being kicked, and endured the assault in virtual silence, gasping only when Josiah's club rammed into her belly. The explosion of pain knocked the breath out her and she doubled over, giving Josiah the fresh flesh of her back to work on. A savage whack across the shoulder blades brought Beverly to her knees; she crumpled to the floor, sobbing into scuffed linoleum.

The newspaper had begun to shred by the time Josiah stopped to catch his breath. "Sunday's family day," he panted. "What the hell were you thinking, leaving me alone like that?" He tossed the newspaper in the recycling bin.

Beverly cowered, too frightened to respond. She heard a rustle of plastic, then curds of cold ground beef showered down on her hair.

"I'm eating dinner out. This place is a sty." Josiah tossed the Styrofoam tray on the floor. "This better be cleaned up by the time I get back."

When she heard the dead bolt click shut, Beverly slowly raised her head. The floor was littered with pink maggots and torn newsprint. From the bedroom down the hall, Elmer Fudd chanted *Kill the wabbit* with murderous zeal.

A door opened and Claire peeped out. Venturing no farther than the edge of the dining table, she stared at her mother. "What happened, Mommy? Did you fall down again?"

Beverly bowed her head and wept.

Chapter 24

Two-Part Harmony

Day one at Harmony House Preschool began with a traffic jam of strollers. Harried mothers crowded into the yellow cottage to cram lunch boxes into cubbies, pry tiny fingers off their knees and dispense farewell kisses to the anxious angels they were leaving with a teacher for the first time. In the front classroom, a little girl bawled by the Good-bye Window, smudging the glass with snot and tears, as her mother walked out the gate.

Beverly walked into this commotion dressed like a celebrity in disguise. Large sunglasses covered her blackened right eye, a baseball cap hid the bump on her forehead, and vermilion lipstick obscured the cut on her lip. She led Claire by the hand into Harmony House, smiling vaguely, murmuring *Good morning* when anyone glanced her way. Her preternatural calm amid this chaos was born of simple exhaustion.

Josiah came home past eleven the night before, long after Beverly had mopped up the kitchen, nuked macaroni and cheese for Claire and done what she could to salve her injuries. She pretended to be asleep when her husband stumbled in, hoping he was too drunk to demand reconciliation sex. Even after he began snoring,

Beverly remained awake, railing at her dead mother. *You promised my life would be better. Why is it worse?*

She finally gave up on sleep at dawn, and got up to fry eggs, brew coffee and set the Monday paper next to Josiah's plate, before rousing Claire and escaping to Harmony House.

That bright September morning Beverly wanted more than anything to be like all the other moms, with little more than a nervous child to soothe before returning to the office, the gym or the harmless chores of home. Beverly would gladly have spent all day in that room of rainbow posters and knee-high tables, but Miss Vanessa was already murmuring good-bye to the mothers, gathering her querulous flock to the rug for Circle Time.

"Mommy stay, Mommy stay," Claire pleaded, turning tearful eyes on Beverly.

"I'll be back soon, sweetie." Beverly winced as the little girl clutched her bruised neck. She pulled away to stand, but Claire grabbed at her jeans with a loud wail.

"Claire, honey? We can't start Circle Time without you." A redheaded teacher's aide squatted down so her face was level with Claire's. "Do you need help letting Mommy go or can you do it yourself?"

"Do it myself." Ignoring the aide's outstretched hand, Claire folded her arms and trudged off to the rug.

Beverly whispered her thanks and walked out of the classroom without looking back, displaying a nonchalance she did not feel. She paused at the front door and readjusted her scarf, making sure it covered her bruises. Beverly was the last mother out the garden gate, and even there she took her time folding up the stroller. With the restaurant closed on Mondays, the morning stretched before her like an open road. Unwilling to indulge the false contrition Josiah offered after each fight, she decided to stay away from home until he left for work, killing time with a leisurely detour to Berkeley Bowl. Beverly never tired of visiting the grocery, browsing through its painter's palette of vegetables and lingering by bulk bins of grain and jellied candy. Berkeley Bowl reminded her of market day with Marcela: her godmother would have been dumbstruck by the abundance of produce laid out like art under a celestial dome.

A few minutes later, she was dragging her stroller toward the grocery's fruit section, drawn to a mound of golden fruit. *Manila Mangoes,* claimed the hand-lettered sign atop the pile. The familiar sweet fragrance lifted Beverly back to long-gone childhood Sundays when Marcela would visit, bearing home a basket of carabao mangoes. Beverly would eagerly peel the mango like a banana and feast on honeyed flesh until all that remained was a bare seed sucked dry and forearms sticky with nectar. Taking off her sunglasses, Beverly picked up a mango and breathed in the scent of home.

"Here you are again! *Pilipina ka ba?* Are you Filipino?"

The voice startled Beverly out of her nostalgic reverie. A young woman in a pumpkin-hued sweater smiled at her from the other side of the fruit bin. The grin faded as Beverly turned to reply; embarrassed, she raised a hand to cover her blackened right eye. "*Oo, Pilipina ako.* Pardon my face, I was in an accident yesterday."

"*Sabi na nga*—I knew you were Pinay." The woman rolled her grocery cart around the bin chattering in rapid Tagalog. "I saw you on Telegraph yesterday. When you yelled *Aray,* I swore you were Filipino." The woman pushed long mahogany hair back from her forehead, revealing a distinct widow's peak nearly identical to Beverly's. "My name's Amparo."

"Beverly Stein." Beverly remembered now the restaurant in front of which Josiah had parked, the patrons staring as he yelled at her. Embarrassed, she gestured at the fruit. "Mangoes are so expensive here. But I want my daughter to have one."

"The little girl you were carrying yesterday? She looks just like you. *Saan ka sa atin*—where are you from, back home?"

"Manila. But I've been here since 'eighty-nine." Beverly smiled.

After years of Josiah criticizing her English, it was such a relief to lapse into Tagalog.

"I don't see a lot of Filipinos at Berkeley Bowl. They prefer to shop in Oakland Chinatown, it's cheaper there." Amparo gestured in the general direction of Oakland, revealing a Santo Niño charm dangling from her gold bracelet. "Do you live near here?"

"We live on Fairview Street."

"That's two blocks away from us. We just moved into an apartment on Alcatraz." Amparo checked her watch. "*Ay naku.* I need to start work in twenty minutes. But we should meet for coffee sometime. Want to trade phone numbers?"

Beverly hesitated. Her back still ached from last night's beating. "I'm sorry, my husband told me never to give out our home number."

"*O sige*—all right, then." Amparo remembered the man with a face like death and thought it wise not to insist. She piled a half dozen mangoes into her cart. "Have to hurry to work, but maybe we'll see each other here again. We're practically neighbors, you know."

Beverly watched Amparo walk off, sorry she'd turned away a potential friend. There were a good number of Filipino-American students at the university, but much fewer of what Josiah jokingly called the "native strain." She turned back to the fruit bin and selected two of the fattest mangoes she could find. Claire loved mangoes as much as her mother did, but Beverly felt she deserved to have one all to herself.

Half an hour later, Amparo let herself into the small apartment she shared with Seamus, panting from the three flights she'd scaled, loaded down with grocery bags. The phone began ringing as she kicked the door shut and sprinted for the receiver.

"Hello, this is Amparo, Tagalog interpreter number 2268. How may I help you today in Tagalog?"

"Hi, this is Daphne from National Domestic Violence Hotline. I have a mother by the name of Cristeta on the other line. She's yelling something about her child that I can't understand. Can you find out what the problem is?"

"Ang anak ko! Kinuha niya ang anak ko!" The frantic voice on the other line faded in and out of static, as though the woman was walking in and out of some distant dead zone.

"She says someone took her child." Amparo dropped her keys on the table and kicked off her clogs, reaching for the whiteboard and a dry-erase marker.

"How's that possible?" Daphne inhaled sharply. "Mrs. Fisher and her son were right about to be admitted into a shelter in Fremont. Ask her if she knows who took the child."

Before Amparo could translate the question, Mrs. Fisher replied, undeterred by her broken English, "My husband kidnap Miguel. He just lie to the schoolteacher after I drop off my son. He tells Miss Amanda we have family emergency, then he take my son away. I don't know where they are. *Awa ng Diyos,* merciful God, please, help me find my son."

"Tell Mrs. Fisher I'll get the police to put out a kidnap alert on your son. If she has a picture of Miguel to give them, that would really help. I'll also have them send an officer out to the school to interview the teachers and escort her to the shelter. Look, I know she's upset, but please remind her that she can't tell anyone, not even her son's teacher, where this shelter is. It's for her own protection."

Amparo's hands turned cold and she felt light-headed as she translated the terse instructions. She suspected the scowling man on Telegraph had caused the "accident" that blackened Beverly's eye. Had he ever harmed their little girl? As she ended the call, Amparo looked out the window, over the maple trees and shingled roofs that filled the space between her apartment and Fairview Street, wondering if she'd ever see Beverly again.

Amparo's pensive mood lasted all day, through calls for two bankruptcy court hearings, three car insurance collision claims and an indignant mother yelling about the two-hundred-dollar bill for porn her teenage son had purchased on cable. By the end of the final call she was slumped on the living room futon, a dull headache pulsing through her temples. Seamus walked in the door as she was signing off. She looked up at him through crosshatched fingers. "I'm so tired even my hair hurts."

"Rough day?" He settled next to her on the couch, stretching an arm around her shoulders.

"Just the usual. I'm worried about something else that happened today." Amparo nestled her head on his chest, entwining her fingers with his. "Remember Angry Man on Telegraph? I ran into his wife at Berkeley Bowl this morning. You'll think I'm crazy, but she even sort of looked like me. Problem is, she looked like she'd been hit by a truck. Or maybe a fist."

"You think Angry Man worked her over?" Seamus massaged her temples, long fingers still carrying the faint scent of cardamom from the Ayurvedic clinic where he worked. "He certainly looked capable."

"Turns out he was her husband; I didn't want to pry. She lives in the neighborhood, but when I suggested we hang out sometime, she said her husband didn't allow her to give out their phone number." Amparo sat up, turning to face Seamus. "That's classic controlling behavior—I hear about it all the time on those domestic violence calls. It wasn't just a black eye. A good third of her face was bruised."

"You going to try to help her?" Seamus pulled off the elastic that held his hair and shook out the wavy brown locks.

"I don't know how. Maybe I shouldn't even interfere. Maybe the child keeps them together." Amparo stroked his jaw, loving the rough cat's tongue feel of stubble beneath her thumb, loving the celadon eyes gazing at her. "Who even knows how anyone decides on a partner anyway? Sometimes I think the person you get depends on the luck of the draw. I could have ended up in Beverly's shoes."

"Ahh, but there's where you're wrong, luv." Seamus pulled her close till their noses touched. "You have much better taste in men."

A long moment later, Amparo pulled out of the kiss and gazed, bemused, at Seamus, wondering how she had lucked out.

Three years earlier he had been just another person doing downward dog beside Amparo. Her uncle Aldo had persuaded her to take up yoga to alleviate the chronic back pain she'd developed from sitting hunched over the telephone all day. Had she put any stock in her mother's opinions, Amparo might well have ignored advice from the black sheep of the Duarté family, but she had grown fond of her fellow exile.

Six months into her yoga practice, Amparo found a ponytailed man with the lean lines of a swimmer sitting in her usual spot in the front row of the room. Miffed, she took the space beside him, noting the worn patches on either end of his sticky mat, the runes tattooed down each bicep, the claddagh ring on his right hand. *Just another sensitive ponytailed dude, seeking salvation in yoga. Probably gay.* Assuming she had nailed the type, she focused on her *vinyassas*, without another glance at him.

A week later, she arrived ten minutes early to snag her favorite spot, but was surprised to find Ponytail Dude meditating cross-legged in the teacher's spot. He opened his eyes and smiled as Amparo rolled out her mat. "How's it going? You were in class last week, weren't you? I'm Seamus Delaney." He touched folded hands to his forehead for *namaste*.

"Amparo." She nodded at the greeting. "What happened to the regular teacher?" Amparo tied up her hair, watching him watch her. *Definitely not gay.*

"Heather asked me to sub for all her evening classes while she leads a five-day yoga retreat in Tahoe. Don't worry. I taught yoga for years. Tried changing my name to Sunesh once, but my folks are from Boston and wouldn't stand for it."

"Oh." Amparo sat cross-legged, suddenly sorry her favored spot happened to be directly in front of his mat. Their faces would be inches apart during Cat and Cow. She bit her lip, but it was too late to move.

"Hey, don't look so bummed. I teach a mean *vinyassa.*" Laugh lines crinkled round Seamus's eyes as he smiled. "I guarantee you'll be just as tired after my class as you are when Heather teaches it."

"Sure I will." Amparo blushed. *Relax. It's only yoga.* Yet she was relieved when other students began to arrive. While Seamus was handing out straps and blankets, she pulled her mat backward a few inches, closed her eyes and focused on breathing.

The class was as rigorous as Seamus had promised, made more distracting by his habit of grinning through the most difficult poses. As he urged students to rise from a low lunge into the one-legged bird of paradise, he looked directly at Amparo. "Try straightening that bound leg and point your toes to the sky."

Amparo wobbled and fell off-balance, red with embarrassment.

"There's no shame in falling out of a pose. That's just your ego getting in the way."

I'd kill him if he weren't so damn cute.

By the end of the ninety-minute class, Amparo was only too grateful to relax in the corpse pose of *savasana.* Dimming the lights, Seamus put on Heather's favorite end-of-class music: the solitary sitar exploring a melody slow and even as a heartbeat. Relaxing into her mat, Amparo inhaled lavender from Seamus's palms as he cupped hands above her face. Then firm fingers stroked the space between her brows, lifting away the frown and circling wide across her forehead before pressing into her temples. She breathed voluptuously as his fingers reached under her hair and kneaded the back of her neck, stretching it straight and long before moving lower to tug each shoulder blade back so that her heart rose in her chest. He was simply adjusting her spine; it was something all teachers did. But that evening Amparo felt something else realigning, falling into place. One was supposed to keep the eyes shut through *savasana*, but at that moment, she opened hers. Seamus gazed down at her, a half smile on his face.

Yes.

Chapter 25

Shrimp Paste

Envy began to fester in Beverly's gut as she paid for her mangoes. How was it possible, she wondered, for Amparo to have piled so many mangoes into her basket without a thought to the expense, as though she didn't care that a whole roasting chicken could be had for the same price, as if she never worried about money? Had Amparo simply chosen a better man? Feeling cheated, Beverly turned homeward on Shattuck Avenue, jeans chafing her bruised thighs, her two mangoes tucked into the stroller like treasured twins.

She checked her watch: nine o'clock. Josiah would be leaving the apartment right about now, but just to be sure, she slowed down, lingering in front of La Peña's sprawling mural. She had always loved the community center's wall-long painting of tawny musicians playing trumpets and panpipes, bongos and guitars. Hitomi once told her that the mural was named *Canción de la Unidad*, "Song of Unity," that the minstrels stood for all countries of America, but to Beverly they could well have been Filipino, brown faces upturned, flinging joyful sounds to heaven.

She no longer remembered when she last felt like singing.

Beverly's throat constricted as she approached the run-down two-story house, the shabbiest sister on the treelined street. The forty-year-old cottage had been rather clumsily divided into two separate units, its low rents attracting a retired firefighter and the Stein family. Beverly had wanted to ask their landlord to replace rotting planks on the swaybacked porch and shear the ivy that crawled over the house like unkempt whiskers, but Josiah refused to pursue the matter, fearing such improvements would cause the rent to rise.

Jiggling the knob as she shouldered open the misaligned door, Beverly walked into a house that was blissfully empty. Sunlight streamed through the window by the dining table and squirrels chittered from the neighbor's maple tree. She looked forward to the coming weeks, when the tree's scarlet leaves would bring some color to the unadorned white walls and beige sofa in their living room. Floorboards creaked underfoot as she crossed the sitting room to the island of linoleum that marked her kitchen, her personal space if only by default. Josiah had declared early on that cooking and dish washing were woman's work, and rarely ventured there except to pour a cup of coffee or wash his hands.

Beverly put the mangoes on the counter. She would share them with Claire as a treat for getting through the first day of school, then toss the seeds in the dumpster before Josiah came home. She smiled at her small act of rebellion, as she opened the pantry door. Out of habit, Beverly looked over her shoulder and scanned the dining room windows before reaching behind tubs of flour and rice. From the very back corner of the pantry she pulled out a squat jar that could have once held mayonnaise. The faded label on it displayed a clay pot of saffron-colored *kare-kare* stew; a jaunty script spelled out *Neneng's Bagoong Guisado.*

The jar no longer smelled of the shrimp paste it had once held, for she had boiled it, rinsed it out with vinegar and scrubbed the insides clean of every last speck of its pungent contents. Now it contained her other act of defiance: a cache of dollars in small bills and loose change. One day she would have enough cash for two plane tickets to Manila. It had taken her two years to save this money, pulling a few dollars out of her tips at the end of each waitressing shift, throwing in stray coins she found while laundering Josiah's jeans. Over time, putting the money away had turned into a ritual: she would smooth out the creases, then press each bill flat against the inside of the glass like a thin brick, so that over time the jar appeared to be papered with dollars. It was the one thing that Josiah knew nothing about, would never control, the escape route she would take when things became truly unbearable. She had nearly reached that point the night before, but decided to stay through Christmas. Diners always tipped generously during the holidays.

Beverly dropped three quarters into the jar and screwed the lid back on tightly. The coins clinked soft as distant bells, as she rolled the jar back and forth on the kitchen counter, remembering how it had arrived, two years earlier.

Beverly was hanging the last trinkets on the three-foot-tall Christmas tree during Claire's nap when the mailman came to the door with a shoe-box-sized package. Beverly's name was scrawled on the letter taped upon the box, and she recognized Marcela's childlike script. There was no letter, but within the box sat a jar of *bagoong*, nestled like a dark egg in a bed of shredded newspaper. Its maroon contents quivered seductively as Beverly unwound the multiple layers of packing tape that sealed it shut. When she lifted the lid, the familiar odor of fermented shrimp rose into the kitchen, evoking memories of banana hearts and long beans, of bok choy and oxtails, all anointed with annatto seeds. Beverly shut her eyes, inhaling the scent of remembered feasts. The aroma of sautéing shrimp paste suffused their home whenever Marcela came to cook. Staring at the jar, Beverly realized what she most wanted to do just then: re-create one of Marcela's meals.

Rummaging through the kitchen, she found a butternut squash and some frozen green beans left over from Thanksgiving. They would make a meager *pinakbet,* but now that Marcela had provided the stew's crucial ingredient, she was happy to improvise. Beverly had just stirred a heaping spoonful of *bagoong* into the simmering pot of vegetables when Josiah walked in the door.

"How's it going, babe? You know I dodged a bullet today—another pharmacist got laid off this afternoon; that makes two since January." He rubbed his nape, stretching his neck first left, then right; a vein throbbed green beneath pallid skin. "Without seniority, I could've been fired as easily as the other guy."

"You will never get fired." Beverly looked up from the pot she was tending. "Are you hungry?"

"I could eat. But what the hell's that smell?" He paused, wrinkling his nose at the intense odor that permeated the apartment. "Did the septic tank bust a leak again?"

"No, honey." Beverly offered Josiah her brightest smile. "That's *bagoong*—you know, Filipino shrimp paste. I haven't had any since Manila, but my godmother, Marcela, sent me a jar of it for Christmas. Wasn't that nice? I'm cooking her special *pinakbet* stew for dinner tonight." She held out a spoon. "Want to taste?"

Josiah threw his baseball cap on the dining table, exasperation souring his face as he stared at Beverly over the breakfast counter. "You're kidding, right? You expect me to eat that fermented shrimp crap? How many times have I told you I don't like Filipino food?"

"I know you don't mean that." Beverly set a lid on the pot, speaking slowly, as though to a naughty child. "You always ate my *lumpia.*"

"Spring rolls don't count—they're Chinese." Josiah waved his hand dismissively. "I don't even know why you bother making them, I've always preferred the ones they sell in Chinatown." He leaned over the counter and grimaced at the bubbling pot. "What else did you make for dinner?"

"We still have the chicken potpie from last night. I can heat it up if you're hungry." Beverly's voice faded under her husband's scowl.

Rounding the counter, Josiah picked up the jar of *bagoong*, thin lips pursed in disgust. "I just don't get it. I crawl through a shitty day peddling drugs to senile seniors and all I get for dinner is left-overs? Why, because you wasted the afternoon cooking that swill?" Stepping behind Beverly, he shook the jar upside down over the sink, flicking on the garbage disposal and pouring its contents into the gurgling maw.

Beverly watched him rinse the jar out with hot water and felt a wave of heat rise through her cheeks and into her forehead. She wanted to smack him, to break her wooden spoon on that disapproving nose, but she could only stand there, frozen by rage. "How could you do that? My *ninang* Marcela spent a lot of money to mail it to me."

"Waste of money. Tell your aunt I won't have my house smelling like a damn sewer." Josiah turned and saw the fury in Beverly's eyes, the spoon she clutched like an ax. "Oh, so now *you're* mad? You want your damn Christmas present back? Here, take it, it's all yours." Josiah shoved the empty jar at her, grinding it into her chest.

"Okay, Josiah, I'm sorry, I didn't think the smell would upset you so much." Beverly dropped the spoon on the counter and grabbed the jar's rim, watery shrimp paste soaking the front of her shirt. "I just wanted to make something that we used to eat at home."

"This is your home now. And in *this* home we don't eat that crap." Josiah jerked away and went to the dining nook to open the windows. A chilly December wind whirled through the apartment, whipping about the red star Beverly had hung from the ceiling as a Christmas *parol*. It banged against the ceiling, denting its card-board points. Josiah slapped it away with his hand. "And there's another one of your idiotic ideas. Don't you see the ceiling's too low for hanging things? That star of yours damn near poked my eye out. Can't you be satisfied with a simple tree?" He saw her pick up her wooden spoon. "What are you doing now? Toss that slop in the dumpster. I already said we're not having it for dinner tonight."

From the bedroom, Claire began to whimper.

"Y'see? Even Claire hates the way this place smells." Josiah clapped his baseball cap back on.

"But you woke her, Josiah." Beverly wrung her hands on a dish towel. "She was sleeping fine until you started yelling."

"Can't help being pissed when my home reeks like a frickin' cesspool." Josiah threw up his arms. "What were you thinking? Jesus, it's like you never left the damn islands." He zipped his jacket shut. "I'm taking Claire out for pizza tonight. Go toss that out in the dumpster; I won't have it stinking up our trash. I don't care how cold it gets in here, but you keep those windows open till this place smells decent again, understand?"

"Okay, Josiah." Beverly glared at her husband's back as he went to take their daughter.

"Putangina." Son of a bitch. The word hissed like steam from a boiling kettle. Josiah's tantrums these past two years had always terrified her, but for the first time, rage overcame fear.

"Come on, honey, Daddy's taking you out for pizza." Josiah helped Claire put on her tiny pink coat, gently easing the hood over her head. He and Beverly had an unspoken agreement never to fight in front of their daughter, though the child had heard many arguments from behind closed doors.

"Mommy?" Claire reached arms over her father's shoulder as he picked her up. She wiggled chubby fingers at Beverly.

"No, baby, Mommy has to clean up the mess she made in the kitchen." Josiah glared at Beverly, but his voice softened as Claire wrapped her arms around his neck. "We'll bring pizza home for her, okay?" He nuzzled the child's round cheek and reached for the door.

Beverly waited until they left before tasting the *pinakbet.* The squash had not stewed long enough to soften, but the frozen beans were turning to mush. Even then she could not bear to throw away what remained of Marcela's gift. Shivering in her frigid kitchen, she scalded her tongue on hot mouthfuls of half-cooked squash, tears mingling with *bagoong* brine.

When she could eat no more, she poured the stew's remnants into a plastic bag and carried it out to the dumpster behind their apartment. A raccoon shuffled off, slowing as it rounded the corner of the recycling bin. Beverly knew it was loitering somewhere in the shadows, waiting to dive into the dumpster as soon as she left. She recognized that unreasoning hunger. But the thought of a furry scavenger devouring her failed stew outraged her—Ninang 'Cela's food deserved better. She tossed the bag into the trash, then strode up to the recycling bin and kicked it so hard she jarred her kneecap. The raccoon skittered away.

"*Putangina walang hiya*—he has no shame, that son of a bitch." Beverly grabbed the bin's plastic rim and shook it, jiggled it so violently that the bottles within clattered against each other, creating such a racket that a lamp turned on in the second-floor apartment and a sliver of light speared the alley. Beverly did not startle at the screech of a window pushing open, but she was done dissembling, done apologizing, done explaining why, where she was from, shrimp paste trumped pizza, and she fled to the shadows like the raccoon before her.

She hurried back to the apartment, her stomach roiling, already spurning the half-cooked stew she'd gulped down. She managed to reach the bathroom before seizing up, doubling over and clutching the toilet seat to keep from falling in. After the cramps had passed and her breath slowed to normal, Beverly scrubbed the spattered bowl and floor tiles, wringing out the sponge till her hands were raw from bleach.

Any other person would have thrown the *bagoong* jar away at that point, but Beverly had inherited her mother's superstitious nature, and saw portents in everything. Discarding the empty jar would have been disrespectful of her *ninang* Marcela, she surmised. It had come for a reason. After cleaning the bathroom, she returned to the kitchen and hid the jar beneath the sink.

She began putting money into it the next day.

CHAPTER 26

Checkmate, 1995

A cold wind flung its withering embrace round Amparo as she rode the escalator up from San Francisco's Powell Street BART station. It was the last Friday afternoon in October and she had a standing appointment to visit Manong Del at his chess tables, a tradition they'd begun since meeting six months earlier. Señora Concha would have been mortified to hear that her wellborn daughter was consorting with a retired valet, but Amparo had grown fond of the old man and treated him like a surrogate grandfather who, together with Uncle Aldo, helped feed her need for family in America.

The brick-paved concourse at the corner of Powell and Market was a locus for street performers, vendors and tourists on their way to the cable car turnaround. Amparo could see why Manong Del had chosen to set up shop there: it was the closest thing to the bustling town plazas he'd known in the old country. She walked up the wide curb to the row of folding tables where old men plotted silent conquest, deaf to the clamor of traffic on Market Street.

"There you are, Amparo! Ready for your chess lesson?" A man with a leathered face and a mane of silver hair waved at her from the nearest table. "I am just about to beat Aguinaldo, so you can take his place."

Aguinaldo Tan cocked his head at Miguel. "Look at this Magnaye: nowhere near checkmate and already he is crowing." Grooming for their pretty visitor, he readjusted the frayed red scarf around his wattles.

"I don't have to be psychic to know I will win." Miguel Magnaye wagged a pawn at his opponent. "Why don't you go back to cutting hair? Make more money than betting on chess."

"Maybe I cut your hair first," Aguinaldo snapped. The retired barber made scissor motions with his fingers, jowls quivering with feigned indignation. "You look like some kind of beatnik. Why you have to grow it so long?"

"Because I still *have* all of mine." Moving with a quickness that belied his years, Miguel reached across the table and swiped off Aguinaldo's cabbie hat, revealing a completely bald head.

"By golly, you give that back or I tell Del to kick you out." Aguinaldo rubbed his mottled scalp and sought sympathy from Amparo. "You see the clowns I have to play with?"

"You don't fool me—you act up like this every time I come to visit." Amparo smiled indulgently at the two old-timers. Manong Del liked to joke that the retired barber and former waiter were the only married couple among his players, aging bachelors to a man.

"Go ahead and finish your game, I want to say hello to Manong Del." Amparo rubbed Aguinaldo's shoulder, specks of his ancient leather jacket flaking off on her palm. She spotted Manong Del whispering advice to another player at the farthest table. When the old man heard Amparo's greeting, his face creased into a wide smile. "So, here you are. I was afraid you forgot it was our Family Friday."

Amparo walked straight into his hug, inhaling the rich tobacco scent that suffused his old leather bomber jacket. He even smelled like her family. "How've you been, Manong?"

"Could be better. Remember Gaudencio? He always played at this table for good luck. Not so lucky after all: he fell in the shower and broke his hip yesterday." Manong Del pulled out a pack of loose tobacco, and sat down on a low stool to roll a cigarette on his lap. "We passed the hat this morning and I gave Gaudencio's roommate, Orfeo, half my week's earnings to help with the medical bills. All those other guys, they gave what they could."

Amparo remembered a cheerful codger with cheeks pocked like pomelo rind. Manong Gaudencio had often regaled her with tales of playing for a band at taxi dance halls before the war. Even arthritis-gnarled fingers did not dissuade him from plucking on the ukulele he carried everywhere. "Didn't Manong Gaudencio have health insurance?"

"Sure he did—but no one on social security can pay those deductibles. The doctor told us he would be in bed for a long time, that he should move into a nursing home. Who can afford that?" Manong Del tapped ash from his cigarette, frowning as the gray snow drifted in the breeze. "Me and my buddies, we going to take turns bringing food to his place, poor guy."

"Doesn't he have family?"

"This is all the family we have." Manong Del blew a stream of smoke down the row of old men huddling over chess.

"Didn't any of you ever want to marry?" Amparo squinted, trying to imagine each of the old-timers in their youth.

"Of course, of course." Manong Del's smile was weary. "But there were no Pinay women in America back then, and the white ladies were off-limits." He sucked on his cigarette and winked at her. "On the bright side, you are like a daughter to me now! So I did not do too bad, no?"

"Hoy!" Farther up the sidewalk they heard a scuffle, the soft patter of chess pieces falling. "Give me that, *tarantado ka*!" Through the bustle of pedestrians walking by, Amparo saw Manong Orfeo's red baseball cap bobbing in the distance as he ran after someone.

Manong Del pulled his whistle out, blowing a long blast as he gave chase. Six other chess players stood up, but remained rooted by their tables as Manong Del and Amparo dashed by.

Amparo quickly caught up with Orfeo, who panted, "That *bugoy* picked my pocket! I had all the donations for Gaudencio in my wallet, almost one hundred dollars."

Half a block up she could just make out a tall figure zigzag quickly through the crowds. He was too far ahead to catch. The whistle blasted one more time but was cut short by a cry of pain.

She turned to see Manong Del sprawled on the sidewalk behind them. He rolled over on his back, clawing at his chest.

"Orfeo, forget your wallet, call 911." Amparo ran back to Manong Del, kneeling to cradle his head on her lap. She was wild with panic, having never before had to deal directly with a medical emergency. The old man was breathing in shallow pants through his mouth, eyes shut against pain. Stroking his clammy forehead, Amparo prayed the ambulance would come soon.

An hour later, Amparo pulled curtains shut around the bed in the semiprivate room they had wrangled for Manong Del.

"When can I go home?" Manong Del looked like a wrinkled child, dwarfed by large white pillows and tethered to a heart monitor.

"Maybe tomorrow. The doctors want to do an EKG and monitor your heart overnight before they discharge you."

"I can save them time and just tell them." Manong Del waved impatiently with his hand.

"A doctor told me I had cardio—what is that blasted word?" He scowled, forming his mouth around the syllables as though it were a voodoo curse: "Car-dio-myo-pathy."

Amparo was stunned. For someone with such a serious heart condition, Manong Del seemed defiantly unconcerned. "And what did he do to treat it?"

"He wanted to put in a pacemaker. Heck—who has money for that?" Manong Del glared at the heart monitor he'd been hooked up to. "I told him I just take my chances. That was last year. I was fine until that *bugoy* stole our money. Better if I just blew my whistle instead of trying to catch him."

"The doctor said you needed a pacemaker and you said no?" Amparo clenched the bed railing, speechless with frustration, imagining the full regiment of labor—doctors, nurses, servants and drivers—that she could have summoned to help sustain his rebel heart. If only he had collapsed in Manila.

"Manong Del, you can't just ignore something as serious as heart disease. You should be seeing a cardiologist regularly, taking medicines every day." Amparo sputtered random bits of medical advice she remembered her brother Miguel dispensing whenever their elder relatives came to him with their various aches.

"And who would pay for all that?" Manong Del crossed his arms upon his chest, belligerence darkening his face.

"You fought in World War II, didn't you? Don't you get veteran's benefits?" Amparo was clutching at rhetorical straws now, working off her scant knowledge of American history.

"HA! Yes, I am a veteran, and yes, I deserve veteran's benefits." Manong Del's voice rose as he waved an angry arm. "But do I GET those benefits? No!" A vein dissecting the old man's forehead pulsed like a brown root. He sat rigidly erect in bed, more enraged than Amparo had ever seen him. "Why don't I get veteran's benefits? Why, you ask? Because that gaddamn Harry Truman signed the Rescission Act after the war. That's why I don't get no gaddamn veteran's benefits! None of the *manong* get them." He fell back against his pillow heaving with indignation. The red line zigzagged on the heart monitor screen; fearing she'd brought him close to a heart attack, Amparo stroked the old man's shoulder.

Amparo had never heard that word and the way Manong Del

pronounced it confused her. "You lost your benefits because of the recession?"

"Re-sci-ssion." Manong Del rubbed slow circles on his chest. "Congress passed it right after the war ended. They said Filipino veterans could not get the benefits we were promised. Sixty-six countries helped America win the war. All those other veterans got their benefits. Except us Pinoys." He stared sorrowfully at his heart monitor. "Fifty years we *manong* been waiting for Congress to repeal the Rescission Act. Soon it will not matter. We are dying, one by one."

"Maybe it won't be repealed. Maybe you should stop waiting." Amparo laid a cool hand on his brow, stroking away the scowl. "Why don't you go home to the Philippines, Manong? When you are this sick, wouldn't it just be easier to be home?"

"But I *am* home." Manong Del exhaled a sorrowful sigh. "Long, long ago, I learned the heart cannot live in two places. I had to choose. My heart is in America. Where is yours?"

Amparo was stumped. No one had ever asked her such a question. She had always considered Manila her true home, Oakland as the necessary substitute. After so many years in America, after Seamus and Uncle Aldo and Manong Del, perhaps it was time to reconsider. The day's events descended on her shoulders like an anvil and she shut her eyes against the sudden threat of tears. Could this really be home, so far from Nanay 'Cela?

Manong Del patted Amparo's hand, as though she were the one who needed sympathy. "Do not think so hard, *hija*. You can find *kababayan* everywhere in America. You only have to look."

CHAPTER 27

Turkey

Thanksgiving 1995

Amparo wrestled the turkey onto the roasting pan, frowning. Her bird didn't look anything like the burnished masterpiece displayed in the magazine. She doubted that roasting would prettify the bird she had haphazardly stuffed and trussed while doing phone interpretation for a bankruptcy court hearing, but Seamus's parents were arriving at dusk and it was too late to buy a roasted turkey. Two nights earlier she had argued that there was no shame in eating out for Thanksgiving, but he had been adamant about a home-cooked feast.

"They've never seen our new place and this is the first time you're meeting them. If we take them to a restaurant, they'll think you can't cook."

"And I would agree with them—I can't. At least not anything larger than a chicken thigh." Amparo pouted as Seamus hoisted the fifteen-pounder on the table beside a daunting lineup that included fresh cranberries and what appeared to be a complete sampling of Berkeley Bowl's produce section. If Manong Del were not still ailing, she would have invited him to come over and walk her through this culinary ordeal.

"Sweetheart, it's not rocket science." Seamus shrugged. "I brought home Martha Stewart's Thanksgiving issue. Just look at the pictures."

Amparo had evaded making turkey the year before when her uncle Aldo invited her to the fellowship dinner hosted by his rehab facility. *Believe me, Amparo, when I tell you that alcoholism is the very least of my sins, but somehow it is the only one I have not escaped.* She wondered if an aversion to cooking could be considered a lesser sin as well. Now that she and Seamus were living together, she could no longer evade the turkey task, particularly since his parents were flying in from Boston for the holiday.

That morning, she'd followed the prep instructions as closely as possible, still sulking over the fact that in Manila she would have been free of such chores. It was these times when she most missed Inay Marcela. Señora Concha would no doubt have seen the grim humor in her domestic struggles. Amparo imagined her blowing a plume of smoke into the dining room and declaring, *That's what you get for living in a country that believes it's too good for servants.*

Brushing aside thoughts of her mother, Amparo slid the roasting pan into the oven and set the timer. Amparo had seen Señora only once since being sent away, when she had been summoned home for the double funeral of her grandparents, tragic casualties of the 1990 Baguio earthquake. Doña Lupita and Don Rodrigo Duarté had been sipping afternoon coffee in the hotel atrium when the first tremors hit. The pyramid-shaped Hyatt Terraces had shuddered, and collapsed, burying them beneath crumbled concrete and shattered glass. Her brother Javier had traveled to the crippled mountain city and identified his grandparents' remains, two broken bodies among a thousand others whose lives had been snuffed out by the powerful quake.

Upon hearing the news, Miguel and Amparo had flown home

immediately, only to find their grieving mother wrapped in a hermetic cocoon of Valium and vodka. Señora Concha welcomed her expatriate children with the same distant civility with which she greeted all other mourners, and seemed indifferent to the news that her only brother, Aldo, had declined attending the wake. Consequently Amparo was startled by her mother's almost remorseful response upon learning she'd accepted an interpreter's job and planned to remain in Oakland indefinitely.

"I suppose congratulations are in order," Señora Concha had said, laying out a fresh row of cards for her perpetual game of solitaire. "At least you can use the good English we taught you to help those low-life immigrants stay out of trouble." Señora Concha looked up at her daughter, her gaze softened by sedatives. "*Desgraciadamente*, there is no future for you in Manila. Your reputation here is ruined. Despite our best efforts, malicious stories about you and Matéo kept gossips busy all through last year. *Malasuwerte*—it's unfortunate, but none of the young men *de buena familia* will ever want you."

Amparo had come away from her fortnight's visit convinced she was right to abandon Manila. She had become, as her mother said, one of those people with nothing to lose.

Now, five years later, she was determined to prove her mother wrong: not only had she found a young man from a good family, but she would also make them a memorable turkey on her first attempt. After setting the oven timer, she decided to log back on to work. Phone interpretation would distract her from the rising nervousness she felt over meeting Seamus's parents for the first time. As directed, she dutifully basted the turkey every half hour, braving the blast of sage-scented steam that greeted her each time she opened the oven door. Amparo made a mental note to take a quick shower just before Seamus returned. He may have turned her into a cook that day, but she refused to smell like one when she met his parents.

As dusk approached, she picked up what would be her longest and final call that Thanksgiving.

"Interpreter, this is Miss Younger from the National Suicide Prevention Hotline. Will you ask the caller what his name is, and where he is right now?"

A rush of static that suggested brisk winds momentarily obscured the caller's voice, but eventually Amparo made out enough of his reply to translate it. "He says his name is Manolo de los Santos. He's sitting in a children's playground somewhere in Golden Gate Park, but no one else is there right now."

Ms. Younger sighed. "Well, it is Thanksgiving afternoon, after all. Everyone else is home with family. Now, I know Manolo speaks some English because he was trying to tell me earlier that he felt sad about being alone on Thanksgiving. Can you ask him please if he has any friends or relatives in the area?"

As soon as Amparo translated the question, Manolo replied in a manic monologue she could not interrupt.

"I am alone today. Alone, all alone, only myself here alone! My wife, Monica, she left me last night. We were married ten months only, but last week she say she does not love me anymore. She say we do not have good future together, she say better she go home to Minneapolis, her parents have a bigger house there. *Ay bakit naman ganyan siya*—why is she like that? You know, I cannot afford a bigger apartment here in San Francisco—it is too expensive for what I earn. I want to go with her back to Minnesota, but she refuse. 'No, Manolo,' she say. 'You stay here. I need my space.' Space—what space? There should be no space between husband and wife! Oh, my Monica, why you have to go? Can you call her for me? *Sige na*, please *lang*. Her last name is Kawilihan. You can find her in the phone book, how many Kawilihan can there be in Minneapolis, *ha*? But maybe she does not want to talk to me, she call me *loko-loko*, she say I talk crazy, I act crazy. But I am really not crazy, you know? Not crazy. It's only because I hear voices. Yes, the voices. She complains I am always talking to other people even when I am alone. But always I have to answer the voices if they ask me something. Sometimes she catches me talking when there is no one in the room and then she calls me *loko-loko.* I do not mind she calls me *loko-loko,* she think I'm crazy, I love her just the same, but now maybe I will really go crazy because my Monica is gone! *Ay,* Monica, why? Why she had to leave me? Leave me behind for a bigger house, a bigger house in Minneapolis? It snow all the time there! Is that not *loko-loko*? And then yesterday I come home from work and the apartment is empty, she took her clothes but not the wedding pictures and the plates and pots we bought together. I did not want to stay in an empty house on Thanksgiving, so I come here, I just come here in the wide-open park, where the voices can talk to me. But now even the voices are gone and so I have to call you. Can you call my Monica please, please can you tell her Manolo will die if she does not come back? Please *naman,* you bring my Monica back. *Awa ng Diyos, awa ng Diyos.*"

Manolo let out a low, keening moan as he called out for God's mercy and Amparo rushed in to interpret what she remembered of the rambling speech. She imagined Manolo shivering on a bench in the deserted playground, while rope swings creaked in the wind. Seamus had taken her for a walk in Golden Gate Park the week before. The park had emptied out by dusk, but Seamus insisted on detouring through a trail lined by tree ferns whose tendrils stretched high above their heads in the twilight. Amparo clung to Seamus's hand, imagining dwarfs peering at her from behind every frond. No, she thought now, the park was not the best haven for a suicidal depressive.

"Holidays are really tough on people with depression; it's not safe for him to be alone. Ask him if he has friends he can call to come get him, someone he can stay with tonight." Ms. Younger sounded calm but deeply concerned.

"*Wala, wala akong kilala*—I know no one," Manolo replied, his voice leaden with grief. "I left them all behind in San Diego when I married Monica. She is my wife, why she has to leave me?"

The call continued for another half hour, Manolo swinging between grief and anger. Suddenly he wondered aloud about the Golden Gate Bridge. "*Baka doon ako tatalon*—maybe I can jump from there. How long you think it will take to walk there?"

Without thinking, Amparo burst out in Tagalog before translating the question. "*Diós ko naman, maawa ka sa pamilya mo*—my God, have pity on your family! They'll never find your body if you jump off that bridge. How will they hold a wake?" Realizing her outburst violated company policy, she rushed to tell Ms. Younger what Manolo had asked, leaving out her own reply.

"Tell Manolo to stay where he is, I'm calling 911." Ms. Younger snapped out of her professional calm; her voice sounded almost stern. "Someone will be there soon to take him to a shelter."

When Amparo translated these instructions, she heard a muffled gasping, as though Manolo had covered his mouth with his hand.

"*Kabayan, ano'ng ngalan mo*—countrywoman, what is your name?" he asked. "Amparo, is it? Amparo, there are angels flying above the big slide. Big, big wings, silver robes, hair like clouds. They are beautiful creatures. One of them is also named Amparo."

Over his sobs Amparo discerned the sound of sirens.

Miss Younger sighed. "Looks like someone's come for the poor guy."

The call wrapped up moments later, but Amparo continued to hold the handset against her cold cheek. She wondered how long Manolo would be able to live at the shelter. How many others like Manolo were out there on this cold holiday night—discarded by family, far from friends, adrift in a land not their own? Had her brother Miguel not helped enroll her at a community college, had she not met Seamus, she might well have been wandering the park at dusk, while everyone else in the city sat down to turkey.

Turkey. She glanced in the direction of the kitchen and gasped at the sight of smoke billowing from the oven door. "*Punyeta*—I forgot to baste the damn bird."

The bird was a sordid mass of blistered black skin, legs splayed to reveal a pile of bread cubes that seemed welded to its cavity. Amparo checked her watch. Less than an hour remained to do damage control before Seamus and his parents walked in the door. Her mind still heavy with thoughts of Manolo, Amparo turned for help from the one thing she hadn't had to make from scratch: a box of instant gravy mix. It seemed idiot-proof. Putting the gravy on to simmer, she peeled off the turkey's scorched skin and began carving. After discarding the still-bloody flesh by the bone, one dried-out drumstick and both desiccated wings, she had just enough fillets left to fan out on a platter. She was just pouring gravy all over the dried-out meat when she heard Seamus's key turn in the lock. Slipping out of her grease-smeared apron, Amparo turned to the door with her brightest smile.

CHAPTER 28

The Reckoning

Black Friday 1995

It was a twisted blessing that holidays brought out a mossy melancholia in Josiah, dampening his temper and turning him quietly morose.

"Daddy, why didn't Grandma come to Thanksgiving?" Claire's innocent question broke through the heavy silence at Thanksgiving dinner.

"I haven't seen Grandma since she left home, honey." Josiah frowned, sawing at the wedge of white meat on his plate.

"Can you call her to come next year?" Claire pushed stuffing around on her plate.

"No, Claire, I will not. Grandma left when I was eight years old." Josiah took a long swallow of beer. "*She* left. She might as well be dead for all I care."

"Don't bother Daddy with questions, Claire." Beverly cast a nervous glance at her husband. "Please don't be mad at Claire. Teacher Vanessa says they've been talking about family all week at school. That's the only reason she asked."

"I answered, didn't I?" Josiah snorted, pouring gravy over his mashed potatoes. "No point pretending my family was perfect." He chucked Claire's chin. "Claire, honey, you tell Miss Vanessa this is all the family you have—" Josiah spread his arms. "Me and Mommy. Far as I'm concerned, we're all you'll ever need."

Josiah drank more than he ate, then retreated to the bedroom to watch TV.

Though Beverly welcomed the peaceful reprieve, she could not help wondering about Josiah's enduring resentment toward his family. While holidays brought other families together, their austere celebrations seemed only to commemorate the many ties Josiah had severed, all the bridges he had burned. By Black Friday, Beverly was only too happy to set Claire down for an afternoon nap and enjoy a few hours of solitude while Josiah went off to watch the latest Bruce Willis action film in an Emeryville theater.

From fragments of stories she'd assembled over the years, Beverly had learned that Josiah's mother fled her abusive marriage when he was eight, leaving him to be raised by an alcoholic father. Josiah had enlisted at eighteen, gladly trading the certainty of his father's fists for the undefined menace of the Vietcong. After surviving Vietnam, he had moved to California. Josiah returned to Wisconsin only once, to bury his father two decades later.

At first Beverly could not conceive a marriage so intolerable that a wife would abandon her only child, but after enduring the blunt trauma of Josiah's temper for six years, she constantly fought her own impulse to flee. When she finally gave in to that urge, she vowed, Claire would leave with her.

Beverly was putting away the dishes when she remembered she needed to add Wednesday night's tips to her jar of savings. She tiptoed past the love seat where Claire napped and fished the bills out of her coat pocket. On a whim, Beverly decided to count how much money she had saved in the last months. The task took some time, since most of what she had was five- and one-dollar bills.

"Nine hundred and sixty-three dollars." A satisfied smile lit her face as she set the last dollar upon the neat pile on the kitchen counter. She split the money into two thick wads and curled each to push through the mouth of the jar, then sat back on the barstool, contemplating a crinkled Abe Lincoln, pressed tight against the glass.

"Mommy, what are you doing?" Claire poked her head up over the back of the love seat, squinting through the late-afternoon sunlight.

"I'm counting dreams." Beverly beamed at her daughter, imagining how pleased Ninang 'Cela would be to finally meet the child who so resembled Clara with her widow's peak and wide brown eyes.

"I want to count too!" Claire clambered onto Beverly's lap.

"No, there's no time. Daddy will be home soon." Beverly lifted her daughter's chin to look Claire in the eye. "This jar is going to be our secret, okay, Claire? You cannot tell anyone about it. I want it to be a surprise, especially for Daddy. Promise you won't tell him?"

"'Romise." Claire reached out to touch the jar, her hand making a pale starfish across its width. A lifetime ago in Manila, on the night of Beverly's first dinner with Josiah, another child had splayed fingers across the taxi window, begging alms in the rain. Beverly had given the little girl all her coins, happy to share her good fortune. But how far had she really come, these last hard years?

Claire drummed fingers on the jar. "What will you do with the money, Mommy?"

"I'm saving to buy something for Christmas."

"What?"

"It's a surprise. Can you keep the secret for me?" Fear pricked like a needle at Beverly's heart.

"Mhmm." Claire twirled a lock of dark brown hair and nodded solemnly at her mother. "It'll be our secret, Mommy."

Beverly helped Claire off her lap, then went to the pantry to hide her dreams behind tubs of rice and red beans.

. . .

December 15

Beverly and Claire sang *"Feliz Navidad"* all the way home after the hour-long festival of cute that marked the Harmony House Christmas pageant. A ponderous load of books, rain boots and accumulated stuffed toys from Claire's cubby weighed down Beverly's backpack, providing ballast against the wintry gale that swept them along the sidewalk like snowflakes that Friday afternoon. They opened the front door with a rush of cold wind, Claire giggling, scarf spread like wide red wings, as she pranced into the room.

"Looks like I missed a great show." Josiah's voice cut through Beverly's laughter. He sat at his usual spot by the window, hands clasped on the dining table. "Seems I've been missing out on a lot lately."

"I don't know what you mean, Josiah. I told you about the Christmas pageant two weeks ago, but you said you couldn't get to Harmony House in time to catch it after your shift." Beverly scanned the living room, wondering if she'd forgotten to pick up after Claire. Josiah habitually beat her whenever he tripped over stray toys left on the floor.

"That's not what I'm talking about." The dining room lamp shone upon the crags of Josiah's face, heightening fault lines on his forehead, deepening the fissure that was his cleft chin. "I thought we promised there'd be no secrets between us. Now I realize you've been holding out on me all this time." Josiah unclasped his hands and rapped a knuckle on a familiar jar. "How long have you been stashing cash in the pantry?"

Beverly paled at the sight of her jar trapped between Josiah's large hands on the dining table. "How did you find that?" Fear shriveled her voice to a hoarse whisper.

"Claire showed it to me. She found a dime on the sidewalk the other day and said she wanted to put it into Mommy's dream jar."

Josiah picked it up, feeling its heft. "Looks like you been saving up for some pretty big dreams."

"Daddy, you promised not to tell." Claire shifted from one foot to the other, a small, uncertain axis between quivering poles. "You're not supposed to take the jar out. I *told* you."

Beverly stooped to come level with her daughter's face, tamping down terror with the pretense of calm. "Claire, go into the bedroom and turn on the TV. Mommy and Daddy need to talk."

"I didn't mean to spoil the surprise, Mommy." Claire's bottom lip quivered.

"Don't cry, it's not your fault. Now go and shut the door behind you."

The little girl skittered into the bedroom.

"Oh, so it's a surprise now, is it?" Josiah rolled the jar back and forth, the heavy glass making soft slapping sounds against his palms. "What kind of surprise were you saving so much money for? Did you forget our rule about discussing all purchases? You weren't planning to surprise me with a new stove, were you?"

"No, of course not, Josiah." Beverly bit her lip. "I was saving for a trip."

"I see." Josiah's eyebrows rose. "So you were planning to surprise me by leaving? Is that what you're saving up for—plane fare?"

Beverly stared at the jar and sensed a door swinging shut, a lock sliding into place. Somewhere within her chest flapped a sparrow, wings beating frantic against her ribs. "You're right, that's what the money is for. When you said you would work on our passports, I started saving for plane fare. I wanted to help pay for the trip." Beverly straightened her shoulders. "My *ninang* Marcela has never met Claire; she's getting old. I wanted to buy plane tickets as soon as you got our passports."

"Is that right?" Josiah raised a skeptical brow. "You know what my mother said, the night she left? She said she was just going to visit her cousin Molly in Milwaukee. Not to worry, she'd be back in time to tuck me into bed. Never saw her again." Josiah looked out the window at the neighbor's leafless tree, peering at a childhood nightmare. "Dad was so mad he damn near broke the wooden spoon over my head." Josiah ran fingers over his thinning hair, as though feeling for old fractures.

"But it's not like that, Josiah. I'm not leaving you. I just want Claire to meet Ninang 'Cela."

"Why waste money on that old crone?" Josiah scowled. "She hated me, I could tell."

"She was just worried about me moving to California, that's all." Beverly glanced down to the hall to make sure Claire had shut the bedroom door. "Ninang 'Cela knows we're doing fine now." She watched her jar of money rolling back and forth between Josiah's leathery palms, wishing she had the courage to rescue her dreams before they shattered.

"Fine? Is this what you call 'fine'?" Josiah sneered. "You hide all this money from me, you make our daughter lie about it and you think we're doing okay?"

"I just wanted to visit my family, Josiah." Beverly slid her backpack off her shoulders and clutched it like a shield over her chest. "I haven't seen Ninang 'Cela in six years."

"I haven't seen my mother in fuckin' forty-seven years, you don't see me crying over it, do you?" Josiah slammed his palm on the table. "Get over it. My daughter stays in America, understood?"

"No. I do not understand. She is my daughter too." Beverly stepped toward the table, but stayed just beyond Josiah's reach. "And after all, that is my money."

"Your money? What if I said you owed me for giving you that green card? Wouldn't this money just be a drop in your bucket of debt?"

"Maybe I owe you for bringing me to America, but you do not *own* me, Josiah." Pride stiffened Beverly's stance so that she stared defiantly at her husband. "You married me, you did not buy me."

"Same difference. You know what that manager at Filipina Sweetheart was, who set up the pen pal matches? That faggot was a pimp with stamps. Nothin' but a pimp with stamps."

Beverly flinched. She remembered the child at the Café Jeepney, chanting a word his parents could only whisper: *puta*. "I am your *wife*, Josiah. Don't you call me a whore."

"Again, same difference." Josiah laid thick fingers upon the jar and eased his wallet out of a back pocket. Flipping it open, he pulled out a card. "Remember this?" He held up the alien immigration card, an unflattering photo of Beverly, dazed by camera flash. "It's all you need to travel anywhere in this country, no need for passports. Long as I keep your green card close, you're not going anywhere without me."

"*Putanginamo*. You son of a bitch." As Beverly realized Josiah's deception, fury overtook fear. "You told me my citizenship application was pending. You promised to work on our passports."

"And you were dumb enough to believe me." Josiah began to laugh. "After all these years in Oakland you're still just a stupid Filipino. Always were, always will be." Throwing back his head, Josiah bellowed glee, delighting in the payoff on a ruse he had maintained for months.

Josiah was still laughing when Beverly's backpack smashed against his temple, knocking him off his seat. As he was momentarily blinded by a large Hello Kitty zipper charm that had grazed his eye, it took him a few seconds to get up, but by then Beverly had already run to the bedroom and locked the door.

"What's wrong, Mommy?" Claire looked up from her TV show. "Is Daddy mad again?"

"He's just upset." Beverly tried to sound calm, but the bird in her chest now fluttered in her throat, choking her with panic, as she scanned the room for an escape route. The bedroom windows were sealed shut from the landlord's last bad paint job. She'd have to break the glass, but Josiah could run outside before she and Claire could climb out. Her gaze landed on the night table by Josiah's side of the bed. Opening its drawer, she tossed out a Bible, a garland of Trojans and an eyeglass case before grasping cold steel. Not wanting to frighten Claire, she slid the handgun into her coat pocket. On the table, the cordless phone's screen glowed green: six p.m.

"Beverly, open the damn door!" Josiah pounded on thin plywood.

"Daddy said a bad word." Claire snuggled her sock monkey under her chin, turning wide eyes on Beverly.

"Sssh, it's okay, sometimes Daddy forgets. That's enough TV. Turn it off, Mommy needs to make a phone call." Struggling to keep her hand steady, Beverly dialed 911.

Chapter 29

A Gathering of Crows

Friday, December 15, marked the eve of *Misa de Gallo* season, and Amparo found herself waxing nostalgic for a Manila Christmas. Growing up, she had not always succeeded in attending all nine dawn masses that led up to Christmas Day, but whenever they made it to church, the Guerrero children always came home to the traditional Christmas breakfast Marcela prepared: batons of purple yam showered with sugar and grated coconut, palm-sized *bibingka* studded with salted duck eggs, bowls of gingered chicken congee and steaming mugs of pudding-thick hot chocolate. Curled up on the window bench, Amparo daydreamed of those early-morning feasts, while Seamus puttered around the kitchen, humming something vaguely Leonard Cohen.

"Thanks for cooking." She looked over her shoulder at Seamus, piling ingredients for a stir-fry on the counter. "I'm too distracted to deal with a hot stove tonight."

"I know. We've been through three Christmases, but you still get all nostalgic for home this time of year." He set a head of emerald leaves on the chopping board. "Ever wish you could go back to Manila for the holidays?"

"No." Elbow on the windowsill, palm cradling her chin, Amparo gazed at the periwinkle sky and remembered the flamboyant sunsets of her youth, heavens ablaze with coral clouds, crickets chanting the day's demise. "This is my home now."

A gravelly caw broke the evening's silence, drawing Amparo's gaze to a trio of black birds swooping through twilight. "I wonder how crows decide where to congregate. Do you know?"

"Nope." Seamus sliced the bok choy with deft movements, long fingers retreating from the advancing knife. "But I read somewhere that a flock of them is called a 'murder.' Isn't that weird?" He smiled, looking like one among thousands of Berkeley's grad students in his ponytail and UC sweatshirt.

"I remember learning that in lit class." Amparo watched the shadows circling a house in the distance.

The phone rang. "Rats. I forgot to sign off."

"Make that your last call." Seamus crushed a garlic clove beneath his knife. "Dinner will be ready in five."

"Interpreter, this is 911. This caller is so upset she keeps switching to Filipino and I can't make out what's going on. Can you get her name, what the emergency is and where she's at?"

"Beverly Stein. *Dito kami sa* 613 Fairview Street. *Awa ng Diyos, tulungan niyo kami!"*

Amparo froze, recognizing the voice that begged the mercy of God. *Beverly with the blue bruised eye, caressing mangoes at Berkeley Bowl.* Breathlessly, she translated Beverly's plea for help. A relentless banging in the background made it hard to understand the woman's whispered pleas.

"What's all that racket?" The 911 operator's voice sharpened with irritation. "Can you ask her to turn down the TV or move to a quieter room?"

"That's not the TV." Amparo's heart hammered her ribs as she translated Beverly's reply. "She's locked the bedroom door and her husband is trying to break it down."

"Open the door, Mommy!" a child's voice shrilled. "Daddy's really mad."

"Beverly, *si Amparo 'to—"* Desperate to calm Beverly, Amparo went off script.

"*Sino*—who?" Beverly was too panicked to think beyond the monster at her door.

The operator intervened before Amparo could reply. "Interpreter, ask Beverly if her husband has a weapon—a gun or a knife."

"No. But I do." Beverly continued in English, her voice suddenly calm. "I have a gun. My husband's gun."

There was the briefest of pauses as the operator registered a sudden game change. Then: "Translator, tell Beverly she needs to put the gun away and wait for the police to arrive."

"Ayoko." Beverly refused, replying before Amparo could translate. "I need to protect—"

A loud crash cut her off. A man's voice rang out with frightening clarity. "Goddamn it, woman, don't point that gun at me. Give it back."

"No, Josiah." Fear shredding her voice, Beverly screamed, "*Labas!* Go out or I will shoot you."

"Not in front of our kid you won't—"

"I said get out!"

The child's frightened wails combined with her parents' enraged voices, and Amparo clutched the phone, hearing the family shatter into a hundred anguished shards.

The operator's voice pulled Amparo back. "Interpreter, make sure Beverly stays on the line till the police get there. Could you get her to put the gun away?"

Again Beverly replied before Amparo could translate. "I will stay on the phone. But I am keeping the gun." Her voice became less distinct, as though she had turned away from the phone. "Claire, baby, come here. You go under the bed with Minnie Monkey. We pretend to play hide-and-seek, okay? Mommy and Daddy need to talk outside."

"Mommy stay!" The child's whimpering rose to a wail.

There came a rustling, as if of sheets, and a few muffled sobs. When Beverly spoke again, her voice sounded diffused, and Amparo imagined the woman clutching the phone in one hand at her side as the other held up the gun. "Look what you did to the door. What will Mrs. Bucher say, ha, Josiah?"

"Fuck the landlord. Come out to the living room so we can talk. I don't want that gun anywhere near Claire."

In the brief pause, Amparo shuddered to imagine Beverly in striking distance of her enraged husband. *Why are the police taking so long to get there?*

"Don't come near me, or I will shoot you." Beverly's voice turned shrill.

"Sure you will. You don't even know how. You want your piggy bank back? Here, it's all yours." There came the brittle sound of glass breaking.

"Putanginamo," Beverly screamed. *"Papatayin kita!"*

"Operator, she says she's going to kill him." Amparo turned terrified eyes on Seamus. He stared back, oblivious to the garlic burning in the wok.

Just then a distant firecracker popped. Amparo startled at the sound, confused for having heard it simultaneously on the phone and from somewhere out the window.

"Did you hear that?" Seamus turned off the burner, waving away acrid fumes of burnt garlic. "Sounded like gunshot."

"Hello, Beverly? Nine one one, are you there?" Amparo yelled into the receiver, but the call had gone dead. Amparo dropped the phone, numb with shock. "I need to find Beverly." Not bothering to grab a coat, she ran out, frantic to get to Fairview Street.

CHAPTER 30

Dead Presidents

Josiah hurled the money jar at the pantry door just as Beverly stepped out of the short hallway. She had the odd sensation of time slowing down as the jar left his hand, hurtled in a wide arc over the counter and crashed into the bead-board panel, spraying broken glass and dollar bills on the kitchen floor. She howled rage, her Tagalog stretching into long syllables like an echoing lament. *Tanginamo papatayin kita.* I will kill you.

She squeezed the trigger and the gun went off, its recoil kicking her shoulder back. Josiah flung himself on the floor as she ran to the kitchen, falling to her knees upon all her dead presidents.

"Wala na, wala na, wala na," Beverly cried, dropping the phone and gathering up the bills like so many fallen leaves. Her fingers curled around a shard of broken glass, long and slim as a pocketknife. She hid it in her palm.

Thick fingers clamped round her forearm. She turned to see Josiah reach for the gun. He stooped over her, his face a purple mask of rage. "You trying to kill me?"

"You broke my jar."

"And you shot at me. I bet somebody's already called 911. When the cops get here, I'll say you stole my money, then turned my own gun on me."

"I will tell them the truth."

"You think they'd believe you?" Josiah's pale eyes burned rage. "After I destroy your green card, you'll be just another illegal alien. They'll keep you in jail till your teeth fall out. Now give me my gun." He yanked Beverly up.

Beverly glared at Josiah but barely saw him, for her mind burned with the image of Marcela. Ninang 'Cela, who loved her like a daughter. Who could not protect her now.

"Fuckin' give me the gun already." Josiah had both hands on the gun now, crushing her fingers. He was slowly turning the barrel away from him, pulling the gun out of Beverly's hands, but wrath gave her uncommon strength and she resisted with the tenacity of a bull.

Through a red haze, Beverly stared at the pale vein pulsing on the side of Josiah's neck. She was clenching the glass shard so tightly that a drop of blood ran along its edge, quivering from its point like a scarlet pearl. Suddenly she heard Marcela speak as clearly as though the old cook were standing in the kitchen: *To kill a chicken, you must cut quickly and with great conviction.*

Beverly released the gun so abruptly that Josiah stumbled forward. As he fell, she raised her left arm, and in one swift movement slashed his throat, the glass dagger sinking deep into the soft flesh, slicing the vein like a flower stem, blood speckling the floor with warm red rain.

The gun went off again, and Beverly felt a punch to the ribs that rammed the breath from her, an explosion of pain, of flames engulfing her chest, consuming a heart long ago broken.

Mama.

Marcela.

Claire.

Dreams.

Wala na. All gone.

CHAPTER 31

Revelation

Amparo had just turned the corner on Shattuck when the second shot cracked sharp above the shushing of passing cars. She stumbled as though she'd taken the bullet, then rushed on, panting small clouds into the chill night air. Two squad cars zoomed past her and swerved right on Fairview Street, sirens screeching a 110 decibel alarm. Doors opened along the treelined street and people hung out of windows to watch two police officers get out of the car, handguns drawn. The retired firefighter who lived above the Steins stood on the yard's dying grass, a beanpole in droopy jeans and red flannel, pointing the policemen to the front door.

"Amparo, slow down!" Seamus caught up with Amparo as she reached the squad car, and threw a coat over her shoulders. "The police won't just let you walk in on a crime scene."

"I have to find out if Beverly's okay." Amparo hurried up to the lawn in time to see one of the policemen kick in the door and peer inside, handgun drawn.

"Whoa, where do you think you're going?" A policeman tall as a sapling and nearly as narrow stepped in Amparo's way as she approached the porch. "Step back, miss, this is a crime scene."

"But I'm a witness. I heard everything happen," Amparo gasped, sweat beading on her forehead.

"Sure you did." The policeman waved a large hand at the neighbors gathering on the street. "See all those people? They heard the gunshots too."

"You don't understand. Beverly's husband was threatening her, but she said she had a gun. I just want to make sure she's okay." Amparo tried to step around the policeman, but an arm thick as her thigh parried the move.

"I said step away," the policeman barked, looming over Amparo.

"Please just hear me out." Amparo swallowed hard, trying to slow her breath. "I work as a phone interpreter and took a 911 call just now. The operator needed me to translate because Beverly kept breaking off into Filipino. I could tell she was terrified. You can't think in another language when you're that scared. We could hear her husband yelling in the background. Then the gun went off and we lost the call." Amparo squeezed her eyes shut briefly, palm pressed to her forehead, willing herself not to cry. "I live nearby, so I ran over. Please, just please can't you find out what happened to Beverly?"

"Who is this Beverly?"

"Oh for God's sake, weren't you listening? She's the woman in that house, the one whose husband was threatening her. She called 911—*punyeta naman*, don't you get it?" Amparo gestured like an agitated moth, too distraught to realize she had turned incoherent.

"Look, I get that you're upset about this person Beverly, but I can't let you in there. Sorry." He spread his arms wide, backing her away from the front porch.

"He's right, Amparo." Seamus squeezed Amparo's shoulder. "Let the cops do their job."

Amparo turned pleading eyes on the policeman. "Please, can't you just tell me if Beverly's okay?"

The policeman's partner called out just then. "I got two people down, male and female. Stab wound to the man's neck and gunshot to the woman's chest. No vital signs."

"Oh God." Amparo staggered back, eyes brimming over. "Officer, Beverly has a young daughter. I heard her crying during the call. Could you find her?"

"We'll do what we can." He stepped up on the porch and called out to his partner. "I got a lady out here who says there's a kid in the house. Check the other rooms, will you? The ambulance should be here soon."

Amparo sagged against Seamus. She would have sunk to the ground but for his arm around her shoulders.

"The paramedics should be here soon; until then, nothing's certain. Why don't you wait over there." The policeman gestured to the side of the house. "The lead detective will want to ask you about that 911 call when he arrives."

Amparo and Seamus waited on the driveway flanking the lawn, its asphalt blistered by the roots of a large maple tree. Silhouetted in the high beams of a squad car, they watched policemen wrap yellow tape around the house. Sirens from an arriving ambulance drew more neighbors outside. Amparo felt as though she were stuck in the wings as actors entered and exited an unseen stage, acting in a play whose end she already knew.

Just then the scream of a child rose above the hushed conversations of neighbors. A female police officer emerged from the front door, struggling to keep hold of Claire, who hung over the woman's shoulder, arms flailing at the apartment. "Mommy! I want Mommy!" the little girl wailed, pigtails askew, a wrinkled red party skirt ballooning out from under her white parka.

Amparo cautiously approached the pair as they reached the squad car, hoping she would not be rebuffed. "Officer, where are you taking her?"

"Child Protective Services will put her in a safe home while we contact her relatives." The policewoman rubbed Claire's back. "Poor kid. She must've heard everything. Did you know her mother?"

"We were friends, sort of." Amparo clutched Seamus's handkerchief, already sodden with tears. "I don't know if she had any family here."

"Let's hope she does. If not, she goes to foster care."

"Where's Mommy?" Claire looked around at the crowd of people standing on the curb. "What are they doing here?"

"Come on, honey, let's take you someplace warm. I bet you've never ridden in a police car before." The policewoman carried Claire away to the squad car.

"Did you hear that, Seamus? Beverly's daughter could end up in foster care." Amparo turned to Seamus, who wrapped her in a hug. She was shivering as much from grief as from the unforgiving breeze. "Can't we do something?"

"Excuse me, miss. Officer Reeves told me you were one of the last people to talk to the deceased before she died. Can I ask you a few questions?" A tall, slightly stooped man held up a police badge as he walked up to Seamus and Amparo. With his trim moustache, navy windbreaker and dark slacks, he looked more like a college professor than a cop. He held out his hand. "Name's Jack Fujitani. I'm the lead detective conducting the investigation. Could you tell me what Beverly told you, why her husband was threatening her?"

Amparo offered him everything she could remember of the 911 call.

"Can I call you if we need more information? The neighbor from upstairs told me Beverly was Filipino. If she doesn't have any family, we might have to call the Philippines."

"Of course. I'll do whatever I can to help you out." Amparo scribbled her phone number on his pad. A blast of icy wind blew hair into her eyes and she swayed, feeling light-headed.

"Let's go home, Amparo." Seamus pulled her close. "You can't do anything more for Beverly or her daughter tonight."

"He's right. Go on home." Detective Fujitani took a step back toward the house. "We've got a few hours' work ahead of us. I'll call you soon as I figure out what happened back there."

Unable to think of an argument for staying, Amparo reluctantly walked home with Seamus, feeling she had lost a part of herself that would never be recovered.

Officer Fujitani's call came two days later. Amparo and Seamus had just gotten home from a late lunch when the phone rang.

"Hello, is this Amparo? Detective Fujitani calling. I hate to bother you on Sunday, but could you come to my office this afternoon? Turns out Beverly Stein's only direct relations are in the Philippines and every time I call this one number, all I get is some lady yelling at me in Filipino. Could you come in and interpret for me?"

Amparo didn't think twice before replying. "I'll be there as soon as I can."

Fifteen minutes later, Seamus rolled to a stop in front of the police headquarters on Seventh Street. He offered an apologetic smile. "Mind if I walk around Chinatown instead of going into the station with you?"

"Sure. I'll meet you over by the Chinese bakery on Eighth." Amparo hopped out of the car.

Detective Fujitani ushered Amparo into an office sparsely furnished with a desk and two chairs. Its sole window looked out on a scaffolded building across Broadway. He pulled out a chair behind the desk and gestured to the one on the other side. "Have a seat." He handed her a cordless phone and leaned over his phone, squinting at the number he'd taped to the keypad. "You might have to raise your voice; last time I called, the connection to Manila was terrible. It's morning over there now, isn't it?"

Amparo checked her watch as she sat down. "Manila's fifteen hours ahead of us, so it should be around seven a.m. on Monday."

She worried over how Beverly's mother would take the sad news, who would be there to hold her while she wept.

"Too early for bad news?" Detective Fujitani's fingers were poised above the keypad.

"Most people are up and about by that time, but thanks for asking." Amparo smiled.

"All right, then." Detective Fujitani punched in the number. Moments later a phone rang on the other side of the world.

"Hello?" The line hissed static. Amparo remembered how phone reception worsened on stormy days and wondered if it was raining now in Manila.

"Gandang umaga po. Tumatawag kami galing California." Amparo automatically launched into professional interpreter mode, trying to disarm the person on the other line with a cheery good-morning and the announcement that they were calling from California.

Her charm fell on deaf ears. *"Bakit, sino ba to?* Why, who is this anyway? I know only one person in California." The woman's voice crackled shrill and petulant, bristling with the sharp *r*'s of a northern dialect.

Amparo glanced at Detective Fujitani, who put his hand over his receiver and whispered: "Ask if she's related to Beverly."

Amparo conveyed the question, steeling herself for anticipated grief.

"*Naku hindi*—of course not." The woman's voice turned suspicious. "*Ulila si Beverly*—Beverly is an orphan. I was her landlady: Manang Charing. Why do you ask?"

Despite Amparo's best attempts, Beverly's old landlady stubbornly refused to divulge any more information. Realizing they were getting nowhere, Detective Fujitani put his hand over the mouthpiece and whispered to Amparo. "Tell her what happened to Beverly."

"Sorry po—" Amparo took a deep breath and used her most for-

mal Tagalog to deliver the bad news. "Manang Charing, yours was the only phone number we could find. Beverly was killed last Friday and we need to inform her family. Can you help us find them?"

"*Diós ko*—my God, *kawawang* 'Cela. *Sandali lang*—wait a moment while I get her aunt's phone number." Moments later, Manang Charing read out a phone number that seemed oddly familiar to Amparo. Jittery with nervous excitement, Amparo assumed she had misheard the number. *No way Beverly could have family in Mama's house, that's just some wild coincidence.*

"Got it!" Detective Fujitani scribbled it down. "Thank you very much, ma'am." He hung up and began dialing the other number. "I don't know how things work in your country, but bad news travels awfully fast here. I need to reach Beverly's aunt before that landlady calls her and ties up the line."

"Hello, good morning, Guerrero residence."

Amparo recognized the voice and instinctively called the other woman by the nickname she had used since childhood: "Nanay!"

"Amparo, *anak ko!* How good to hear your voice, you never call anymore. Why are you calling so early in the morning? What time is it there?"

"*Kumusta na*—how are you?" Hearing Marcela's voice, low and soothing as a pigeon's coo, Amparo felt like a child once more, and she chattered happily in Tagalog as though her old nanny were sitting in the next room. "I'm at the Oakland police station, Nanay. We're looking for the family of someone named Beverly Stein. Here I am, I just wanted to help the police and we reached you. Isn't that funny?" Cupping the mouthpiece, she whispered to Detective Fujitani. "You just called my mother's home. I'm talking to our cook! Are you sure you wrote down the right number?"

Marcela spoke up before Detective Fujitani could reply. "How do you know Beverly? Who told you about her? She is my niece, the daughter of my sister, Clara. Beverly lives in California just like you. She is married to that *tarantado* American, Josiah."

Detective Fujitani raised his brows, listening intently as Amparo translated this exchange, euphemizing the slur Marcela had cast on Josiah.

"Why are the police asking about Beverly? Did they arrest her?"

Amparo bit her lip. "No, Nanay. Beverly was killed Friday night—"

"Ano? Pinatay siya? She was killed?" Marcela gasped into the phone, breathing so heavily Amparo feared her old nanny was having a heart attack.

"Imposiblé," Marcela cried. "I just got a letter from her last week. *Mali ka*—you are mistaken, that must be someone else."

"But it's true, Nanay. The police found her green card in their house." Amparo stared out the window, unable to find adequate words of comfort. "They identified her body."

"How did she die?"

Amparo shut her eyes, wishing she were there to hold her *nanay*'s hand while someone else answered the question. "They think Josiah shot her."

"Ahayyyyy Diyos ko. Anak ko. My God. My child." Marcela's wail stretched across an ocean. Amparo choked, struggling to interpret their exchange for Detective Fujitani. He reached for a bottle of water on the shelf behind the desk and passed it silently to her.

"Patawarin—I'm so sorry, Nanay. I did not know you had a niece, or even a sister." Amparo took a quick swallow of water, but her mouth still felt dry.

"How could you?" Marcela's voice was thick with grief. "Your grandmother Lupita swore me to secrecy."

"Why would Lola Lupita care? It's none of her business."

"But it *is* her business." Marcela's voice turned sharply bitter. "Ask your *Tito* Aldo."

For once, Amparo was unsure she could interpret everything correctly, for nothing Marcela said made any sense. Detective Fujitani waved to get her attention, but Amparo shook her head, needing to understand before she could translate.

"Ask if she knows who can take care of Beverly's daughter." The detective would not be put off. "If the kid has no next of kin here, juvenile court will send her into foster care."

Marcela exploded when she heard the translation. "*Hindi ako papayag*—I will not allow it. Why should my sister's grandchild be given up for adoption when she has a family?" Marcela drew a ragged breath. "That *inutil* uncle of yours, he has avoided responsibility long enough. Make him bring Claire home to me."

"But why should Tito Aldo help Claire?"

"Because Claire is his grandchild." Marcela hurled the words like stones.

"Paano 'yan?" Amparo fell back against the chair, shock leaching all color from her face. "How can this be?"

"What? What did she say just now?" Detective Fujitani rapped a pen against the desk.

Amparo raised a hand to beg patience, for Marcela's story was tumbling out in a rush, as though it had pushed all these years against a locked door, a door that just now swung open. "Clara and Aldo were about the same age back then, barely eighteen. My sister loved Aldo and they carried on for months in your grandmother's home. But after Clara became pregnant with his child, he abandoned her. When Doña Lupita discovered the affair, she banished Aldo to America to avoid a scandal."

Amparo stared out the window at the shrouded building as Marcela spoke, feeling layer upon layer of scaffolding fall away from the pedigree her mother and grandparents had worked a life to uphold. The exalted Duarté image had been no more than a scrim for years of deceit. Now she understood why Marcela never served at table when Doña Lupita came to dinner, why Aldo refused to attend his parents' funeral. "*Inay*, I'm so sorry."

"*Ay, kawawang anak ko.* My poor child. My Beverly is dead."

Marcela's keening wove a cord of despair around Amparo's heart, tightening into thick bitter knots until she could scarcely breathe for listening.

"Please, Nanay, tell me how I can help." Amparo wanted to crawl through the phone lines all the way to Manila and gather Marcela in her arms, just as her nanny had consoled her infinite times through childhood.

Finally Marcela coughed and cleared her throat. When she next spoke, it was with the calmness born of the deepest sorrow. "You must tell Aldo. Force him to be a man. Too many lives have been ruined by these secrets."

"He had a daughter." Amparo crushed the sodden tissue in her fist, thinking of years lost to subterfuge, of the cousin she had never known. Would never know. "How could Tito Aldo have kept this from us?"

"I would have told you, had I not loved you and your brothers so much." Marcela sighed. "It is too late now for Clara and Beverly, but I will not allow your family to spurn Claire. Go now and find your *tito* Aldo. I need to speak with Concha."

Amparo flinched. She had never heard the cook refer to her mother without the respectful "Señora." Before she could reply, she heard a click and Marcela was gone.

"Mind telling me what that was all about?" Detective Fujitani watched Amparo blow her nose. "I expected you to translate as we went along."

"This is going to sound crazy, but I just found out that Beverly and I are related." She recounted Marcela's revelation, still grappling with what it meant to her family.

Detective Fujitani pinched the broad bridge of his nose, eyes shut tight for a moment. Then he fished a notebook out of the drawer and scribbled on his pad. "This sounds more like a soap opera than a murder investigation."

"It's not like that." Amparo flushed. "I never even knew this side of my family, but I have to believe Marcela. She would not lie."

"Way I see it, hiding that story about her sister and your uncle counts as lying. What do Catholics call it? A sin of omission." Shaking his head, the detective scribbled on his notepad, tore off the page and passed it across the desk. "Since your uncle Aldo had nothing to do with Beverly, we don't need to interview him for the murder investigation. I'm not saying I believe your cook, but let's assume he's Beverly's father. That makes him the closest blood relative to Claire, because Josiah himself has no known family. If you want to keep the kid out of foster care, your uncle better get a DNA test done. Have him call the lab in Oakland and take that test as soon as possible."

Chapter 32

Deliverance

Marcela walked into the empty kitchen and leaned against the sink, running cool water over her sweaty palms. She stared out the window, taking deep gulps of air until her sobs subsided. Then she wiped away her tears and prayed to Santo Niño for strength. A gentle rain wept upon the bougainvillea hedge by the garden walls, but the large Christmas star hanging from the acacia tree sparkled in the morning sunlight. Marcela smiled bitterly, recalling the old superstition about rain on a sunny day: somewhere in the land of fairies, a witch was getting married.

Moments later, she walked out to the dining room with a platter of sliced mangoes. Señora Concha was already sitting at the head of the table, sucking on her first cigarette of the day. It was too early in the day for makeup and Señora Concha's unpenciled brows and wan cheeks made her appear somehow diminished, vulnerable, even.

Marcela set the tray on the table and smoothed down her apron before speaking. "Señora, Amparo called this morning."

"*Talaga*—really? And why did you not wake me?"

"Because she wanted to speak with me." Marcela raised her

head, looking through lowered eyelids at Señora Concha. She drew herself up, standing taller in her blue-checkered uniform. "Amparo called because she had bad news about Clara's daughter—*our* niece, Beverly."

Señora Concha scowled at the impertinent pronoun. "Don't take that tone with me, Marcela. How would Amparo know about Clara? And why should she care about Clara's child?"

"Because however much you want to deny it, Beverly is her cousin." Marcela noted with scant pleasure that Señora Concha paused midway through an exhalation. "Beverly was shot dead by her husband in California last Friday. She has a daughter just four years old. Amparo said that if no relatives come forward, Claire will be sent away for adoption. You must speak with your brother, Aldo, and tell him to claim her as his grandchild."

"*Sira ulo ka ba*—are you mad? I will do no such thing." Señora Concha gesticulated irritably, weaving wreaths of smoke above the dining table, indignation painting spots of pink upon her pallid cheekbones. "After all these years, why should we concern ourselves with your problems? It is not our fault Clara and her daughter made such poor choices."

Marcela stared at the woman for whose family she had sacrificed her own, on whose husband she had spied, whose children she had raised. Rage flared in her heart as she thought of Clara and Beverly and Claire: three generations of Obejas women turned invisible for the greater glory of the Duarté clan. She could no longer remain complicit in the service of secrets, not at the risk of losing Claire.

"I cannot believe you have the nerve to ask me this. For years we put Clara's sister through school, gave you work, a bed in our home, and still you want more. No, this is too much, my mother, rest her soul, would never—" Señora Concha was on a roll now, listing every favor her family had bestowed upon Marcela these last thirty years, to avoid conceding to this one. "And to think we bought that cemetery niche for Clara, gave you a day off every two weeks, even paid for your trip home to Banaté two years ago. . . ." Caught up in her recitation of benevolence, Señora Concha gazed heavenward and did not notice Marcela step up to the table and reach for the knife on the plate of mangoes.

CHAPTER 33

Twelve Steps

Amparo ran. Dashing out of the police station with secrets writhing like Medusa serpents round her head, she bolted past noodle houses and fish markets into the heart of Oakland Chinatown, seeking Seamus, the one person who had never lied to her.

She spotted Seamus standing in front of Sam Yick's Filipino-Oriental Foods, a few storefronts beyond Sun Sing Pastry.

"Look who's finally here," Seamus called over his shoulder to the diminutive figure in a scuffed leather bomber jacket picking over the orange bin. The old man tuned to Amparo, his face lit up with a Christmas morning grin.

"Manong Del," Amparo gasped, breathless from the run. She tried to say more, but grief had stolen her voice. Shuddering, she pressed palm to forehead and wept.

"But why is she so sad?" Manong Del exclaimed. He and Seamus huddled protectively around Amparo as Sunday shoppers jostled past, weighed down with large bags and loud with holiday cheer. The scent of roasting chestnuts hung in the air and storefronts shimmered with tinsel, yet Amparo sobbed as though Christmas itself had died.

"Breathe, honey, just breathe," Seamus murmured, kneading her nape. "I'm sorry, Del. Amparo had to translate something for the police this afternoon. Looks like it didn't go well."

"But why must she work on Sunday?" Manong Del was incredulous. "Even I don't work that hard."

As the tears subsided, Amparo recounted Marcela's revelation and the daunting task her nanny had charged her to carry out. "What if Tito Aldo refuses to take the DNA test? What if he denies it all happened? And how could my mother be so coldhearted?"

"And risk breaking rules eight and nine of the twelve-step program?" Seamus's tone was wry. "That could drive him right back to alcohol."

"What steps you talking about?" Manong Del folded arms across his chest. "A lie is a lie. Has her uncle not broken one of the Ten Commandments?"

Seamus shook his head, remembering the many uncles and cousins he'd grown up with in Boston, God-fearing, hard-drinking Catholics to a man. "The twelve-step program is sort of like the Ten Commandments for alcoholics. Steps eight and nine have you write a list of all the people you've hurt and make amends to every one of them."

"It's too late to make it up to Clara and Beverly." Amparo dabbed at her eyes with Seamus's handkerchief. "But we need to make sure he does right by that little girl."

She stared at a toddler jouncing by on a man's shoulders, plump as a partridge in a scarlet jacket, small fists clutching his father's hair. She looked up at Seamus. "If Tito Aldo rejects his grandchild, maybe I could—"

"One thing at a time, Amparo. We'll cross that bridge when we get there." Seeing her shiver in the stiff December wind, Seamus wrapped an arm round her shoulder. Grocers along the street were closing shop and voluptuous aromas of anise and roasted meat beckoned from the Chinese restaurant next door.

"It's too late to drive into the city now. Why don't we go home?" Seamus looked over Amparo's head to Manong Del, begging support. "You can visit Aldo tomorrow morning."

"Seamus is right." Manong Del nodded. "Sleep on it tonight. Big news, just like babies. Best delivered in the morning. That way you have all day to fuss over it."

"But Tito Aldo lied about Clara all these years." Amparo twisted her scarf. "How can I persuade him to own up?"

"Something you don't know about men—" Manong Del picked up his bag of vegetables. "We drink to forget. Forget wives. Forget jobs. Forget all things we regret. So many years your uncle drank to forget that child." Manong Del raised a righteous finger. "Now he is sober. Maybe he will want to remember."

"All right, then. I'll take the day off and visit him tomorrow." Amparo allowed Seamus to steer her toward the car. "But I don't know if I'll be able to sleep at all tonight."

Seamus was clearing away the dinner Amparo did not eat when the phone rang, brittle chimes jangling in the quiet apartment. She picked up and, even though it was Sunday, instinctively opened with the professional interpreter's greeting. But when her vowels flattened out, Tagalog peppered her English and her voice rose and fell like a cork on waves, Seamus knew she was speaking with someone from Manila. Given recent events, a call from Manila did not bode well. He hummed an old Leonard Cohen song and turned back to loading the dishwasher.

"Don't play English professor with me, Javi. I meant what I said." Amparo's voice turned sharp. Hanging up without so much as a good-bye, she pulled the phone from her ear, holding it careful as a loaded gun, and laid it facedown on the table. Minutes passed and Amparo continued to sit, staring at her hands. Silence circled the room like a cat on stealthy paws, flicking its tail at Seamus till his curiosity overcame apprehension.

"Everything all right?" He leaned against the sink, noticing the phone's pink imprint on Amparo's cheek.

When Amparo raised her eyes to his, they were dark as the windows of a bombed-out building. "I don't care what Manong Del said about bad news and babies, I need to see Tito Aldo tonight. Marcela stabbed my mother this morning."

CHAPTER 34

Family Feud

Anger flared in Amparo's gut, roasting her innards in a murderous heat so that by the time they drove into San Francisco's festival of lights, she was fairly quivering with rage. "What a hypocrite my mother was," she said, for the eleventh time. "After what her family did to Nanay's sister, how could Mama call me morally deficient? No wonder Nanay attacked her."

"Come on, Amparo. None of that matters now." Seamus glanced uneasily at Amparo, unaccustomed to this fury. "You should be figuring out what to say to your uncle."

"Nothing to figure out, I'm just going to tell him."

When Seamus pulled up in front of Aldo's home, Amparo all but leaped out of the car and ran up the stairs, pressing long and insistently on the doorbell.

The chime touched off a cacophony of domestic noises: the sudden flushing of an upstairs toilet, windows screeching open, sundry bangs and clatters and, finally, the shuffling of steps on creaky floorboards. A shard of light slashed the dark stoop as Aldo opened the door a crack.

"Good Lord, Amparo, you nearly caused a panic. My housemates thought we were being raided by the police." He called over his shoulder to someone down the hall. "Relax, Fleming. It's not the pigs. Just my niece come to visit." Reknotting the belt of his bathrobe, he stood aside to let Amparo and Seamus in. "Do you realize what time it is?"

"I'm sorry to bother you, Tito Aldo, but this couldn't wait till morning."

"Everything can wait till morning." Aldo flicked on a light in the parlor left of the hall. He gestured at the sofa, but Amparo refused to sit. "Clearly you've never heard that saying: the only emergency is death."

"In that case, I have an emergency." She skewered her uncle with an unforgiving stare. "Your daughter, Beverly, is dead."

Aldo fell back as though he'd been struck. One hand sought the crook of his neck and his mouth fell open, but he seemed unable to draw breath. "Who told you about her?"

"Marcela. Beverly was shot dead last Friday and the police needed to find her next of kin." Amparo cudgeled her uncle with words, remembering Marcela's pain. "The only number they had was one in Manila. I translated the call."

"What I would do for a drink just now." Aldo reached blindly for the nearest chair and eased himself into it. "Tell me everything."

As she described Beverly's death, a sea change came over Aldo. His eyes, usually crinkled in an ironic smile, now sank into their sockets; a cleft appeared between the heavy brows, and deep furrows drew marionette lines from either corner of the mouth to the edges of the fine Duarté nose. Even his hair seemed faded. Looking at him crumpled into the large armchair, Amparo realized her uncle was old. *Just a helpless, lonely old man.*

"I just need to know why, Tito Aldo," Amparo found herself pleading. "How could you abandon your child?"

"It was another time, another world; you could not possibly understand." Her uncle stared into the middle distance, unearthing the old nightmare. Some parts of the story he had discovered after the confrontation: Marcela had filled in the details, going by what Clara had told her, and later that morning he had overheard his mother telling Carina Madrigal about it in a phone call laced with sundry profanities. Over the years he had tried to drown the event in an oblivion of alcohol, but dredging it up now from deepest memory, he could still see that day, clear as a fossil in amber. And when he spoke of that morning, the entire Duarté household came ferociously alive.

In the summer of 1963, Aldo and his family had traveled to California to celebrate a cousin's wedding, and over those hot summer months, Clara's belly swelled. She endured the discomforts of pregnancy in stubborn isolation, refusing to confide in her younger sister, ignoring the pointed remarks of Manang Pipay and Isabel. As the weeks passed, she affected a stoop, shoulders and spine curving over her midsection like a parenthesis, as though pregnancy were an unfortunate afterthought of her failed affair. She was midway through the ordeal when the family returned late one night in June. Marcela hauled luggage upstairs, trailing after Don Rodrigo and the children, but Doña Lupita lingered in the living room, checking if everything was as she had left it.

"*Santisima*. Manila always feels like a sauna after America!" she exclaimed as Clara walked into the living room, balancing a hatbox atop Concha's sweater, a duty-free bag dangling from one hand. "Set breakfast out on the patio tomorrow; it will be cooler. Digoy wants the works—eggs, chorizo, *sinangag*, *tinapa*."

As instructed, Clara set the coffee and breakfast dishes on the patio table early the next morning. She was on her way back to the kitchen for the food when a flutter of wings caught her attention. A maya bird flew off the low coffee table to her right, leaving a small wet turd on the glass.

"*Ay buwisit*," Clara cursed, pulling a dish towel from her apron.

As she leaned over the table, she heard someone approaching. Out of habit she shifted, turning her back on the other person to obscure her belly.

Doña Lupita strolled out to the terrace, pleased to see her maid hard at work so early in the day. She walked to the rim of the patio and surveyed the perfectly pruned hedges that bordered the lawn. A smile teased at thin lips as Doña Lupita enjoyed a moment of smugness. Toni-Mae may have landed a green card, but she had to cook, clean and launder clothes like a common servant; Doña Lupita's older sister was barely fifty, but already she had the hands of a crone. Each visit to America only strengthened Doña Lupita's conviction that there was no place like home, with servants to spare ladies from the drudgery of life.

Doña Lupita turned back to the patio and was about to light her breakfast cigarette when she spied something on the floor beneath the coffee table that Clara was wiping down.

"Clara, you missed a spot under the table." Doña Lupita gestured with her lighter. "Clean it up, will you?

"*Opo,* Doña Lupita." Clara squinted at the object. "It's just a button." The maid squatted on her haunches to grab the button, but only pushed it farther under the table. Trying to ease the strain on her lower back, Clara genuflected, leaning her cheek on the table's edge to reach as far as she could. Her fingers were just curling around the button when a sharp kick to the inside of her ribs threw her off-balance.

"*Susmaryosep!* Can't you be still?" Clara muttered to her unborn child. She leaned her free hand on the table to stand up, only to hear the unmistakable pop of a second button, which had finally surrendered the battle to contain her considerably larger breasts. Clara snatched it off the floor before it rolled away, mortified to see that her uniform now gaped open at the bust. Sitting on her haunches, she pulled a barrette from her hair and threaded it through the buttonhole, hoping it would hold her top shut until she could flee to the kitchen.

Doña Lupita gazed idly at Clara, wondering at the maid's clumsiness and the unusual girth of her hips. "*Naku,* Clara, how fat you've grown! Did you eat all our food while we were abroad? You'd better lose that weight. If I have to buy you a new uniform, the money is coming out of your salary. Didn't your mother ever tell you gluttony is a sin?"

Clara stood up, her back stiffening with anger. After another sleepless night she was in no mood to discuss sin with Aldo's mother. "There was never enough food for us to risk turning into gluttons."

"*Huwag kang bastos*—don't be rude," Doña Lupita scolded. "Turn around so we can see how much weight you need to lose. *Sayang ka naman*—it's such a waste for someone so young to let her figure go the way you have."

Clara threw her shoulders back and did as she was told, swiveling slowly to face her employer. Doña Lupita gasped at the sight of her belly.

"*Madré de Díos!* What foolishness were you up to while we were gone? Did Dencio do this to you? *Punyeta naman*—didn't you know that driver already has a *querida*? I'll be damned if I lose another maid to that *cabrón!*" In her indignation, Doña Lupita forgot to light her cigarette. She paced the length of the patio, the Marlboro twitching between her fingers.

Clara flushed, biting back the impolite retort itching to fly out of her mouth.

"How could you have slept with that cretin?" Doña Lupita demanded. "Had you no care for the three other maids in that room . . ." Her voice faded away, as she turned, eyes narrowed at Clara. "But maybe you had more privacy. Did you seduce him in my bedroom?"

The suggestion that she would pander to a balding, potbellied driver twice her age tipped Clara over the edge of caution. "*Mang* Dencio had nothing to do with this, Doña Lupita. I am carrying Aldo's child."

Time stopped and the world fell silent, frozen in the vacuum of Doña Lupita's rage. Fault lines rose on the matron's forehead and lightning flashed in her eyes. *"Madré de Diós,"* she hissed. "I have a *puta* living in my own home." She crushed the unlit cigarette in her fist, scattering tobacco flakes like sawdust to the floor. "Tell me the truth. Lying now would make you both a whore and an *oportunista*."

Feeling a gentle roll beneath her navel, Clara put a palm on her stomach, determined to defend her baby. "Ask your son. I told Aldo I was pregnant last April, but he did not have the courage to tell you himself."

"Santisima, but you have some nerve! Who do you think you are, *puta ka*, dragging my son into your perversion . . . ?"

The fusillade of profanity that Doña Lupita showered on Clara startled Marcela, who arrived just then with a tray of garlic rice and eggs. As she stepped through the sliding doors, she saw Doña Lupita lunge at her sister, hand raised as though to strike.

"Doña Lupita! *Huwag!* Please don't hurt Clara. We did not forget breakfast, here it is!"

"I could care less about your lousy food." Doña Lupita turned demon eyes on the younger maid. "You. Make yourself useful. Wake up my husband and children and bring them here. I want everyone to hear what I have to say to your shameless sister. *Go*."

Marcela set the tray on the nearest table and fled, pounding on bedroom doors until Don Rodrigo, Aldo and Concha yelled back, aggravated but awake. Then she ran to the kitchen, hollering for Manang Pipay and Isabel to follow her to the patio. In her panic she imagined that four servants would be an even match for four Duartés in the coming scuffle. The three maids got only as far as the living room when theatrics on the terrace stopped them in their tracks. Kinetic as a dragonfly in her scarlet robe, Doña Lupita waved her arms as she hectored Clara. Marcela gaped at the sight of her older sister, standing straight for the first time in months, distended stomach in high relief.

"What's all this noise, so early in the morning?" A familiar growl caused the maids to shrink back against the damask drapes bordering the sliding doors. Don Rodrigo walked out to the patio, frowning in the morning glare. Nothing seemed amiss. He could smell fresh-brewed coffee, and a tray of eggs and chorizo sat on the table, waiting to be served. His wife stood on the patio, smoking her morning cigarette. "What's the emergency, Lupé?" He poured himself a cup of coffee. "Breakfast could have waited another few hours."

"This isn't about food, Digoy," Doña Lupita retorted. She stared at her son, who shuffled out in shorts, knees wrinkling upon pallid legs.

"Aldo, do you know why I called you down here?"

Aldo stood perfectly still, unable to take his eyes off Clara's stomach.

"No, Mamá," he murmured. "But I'm sure you plan to tell me."

"Clara claims you got her pregnant," Señora Lupita said, looking from her son to the servant. "Tell me she's lying."

Aldo ran a hand through his hair. "I can't."

Clara sought his eyes, hoping for some sign of affection, but his gaze had already slithered to the floor.

"Putangina naman." Don Rodrigo pinched the bridge of his nose as though suddenly beset by a migraine. He looked wearily at his son. "What's wrong with you? Couldn't you wait till you left the house? Did you have to seduce our maid?"

"At least I stayed home." Aldo attempted a show of bravado. "*Por lo menos*, Mamá didn't have to stay up all night wondering where I was."

"We're not talking about your father, Aldo." Doña Lupita's tone was caustic, but she cast a triumphant glare at her husband.

"Didn't anyone tell you not to shit in your own backyard?" Don Rodrigo chided. "How long did you think you were going to get away with this?"

Clara watched the Duartés argue, one hand shielding her belly, afraid to breathe, much less speak up in defense of Aldo, for whom she felt a surge of unexpected pity. With his sleep-tumbled hair and forlorn gaze he looked a mere boy, too young to be the father of her child.

At that moment the last Duarté arrived. Concha was surprised to see the three maids huddled in the living room and wondered why her family had gathered around the fourth servant out on the patio. "What happened? Did Clara steal something?"

"Just our good name." Doña Lupita blew a jet of cigarette smoke at Clara. "Congratulate your brother, he's going to be a father." She jerked her head toward the maid. "There's the slut he knocked up."

Concha was not in the habit of looking at servants, but her eyes widened when she noticed Clara's belly. She poked Aldo's shoulder. "You must be joking. You and Clara? Of all the girls you could have had, did you have to sleep with the maid?"

"You think any of your friends would have taken me, Concha?" Aldo sneered. "With the guilt those nuns lay on you, do you really think they would have screwed around with me?"

"Watch your tongue, Aldo." Don Rodrigo poured himself another cup of coffee, trying to push away a memory. "You can't talk that way around women."

"It's a bit late for civility, don't you think, Digoy?" Tiny lines fissured Doña Lupita's lips as she sucked on her cigarette.

"So if Aldo really did get the maid pregnant, what are you going to do about it?" Concha spoke as though the maid in question were not standing a few feet from her.

"We'll send her away, of course." Señora Lupita shrugged. "She deserves to be put out into the streets."

Realizing that Aldo was not going to oppose his mother, Clara stepped into the breach. "But what about the baby I am carrying? Would you abandon your first grandchild?"

Before either parent could reply, Concha shoved Clara, the force of her assault causing the maid to stumble back against Aldo.

"*Walanghiya ka!* You are shameless! Mamá took you into our house and gave you a life. Is this how you repay us?"

"Don't touch me. I more than earned my keep." Cornered by the three Duartés, Clara erupted in rage. "I don't owe you anything."

"Don't you take that tone with me, *punyeta ka*!" Concha raised her hand to slap Clara, triggering a ripple of unexpected responses. Dropping his cup of coffee, Don Rodrigo grabbed Concha's wrist; at the same moment Aldo flung an arm across Clara's shoulder and stepped between her and his sister. Exploding with curses, Doña Lupita attacked her husband, showering his back with cigarette ash as she pummeled his shoulder blades.

"*Putangina*, let Concha go, Digoy! The maid deserves a beating."

Still clutching Concha's wrist, Don Rodrigo turned unbelieving eyes on his wife. "For God's sake, control yourself! There's no need to behave like uncivilized people."

"Don't talk to me about self-control, Digoy. This is what you get for whoring around Manila all these years! Did you think Aldo wouldn't notice? Can you blame him for fucking a servant?" Doña Lupita sank long nails into her husband's hand, trying to pry his fingers off Concha's wrist. Don Rodrigo was a head taller than his wife, but he was no match for her vengeful tenacity.

"My God, this is the first time I've seen them touch," Manang Pipay whispered to Isabel as they watched the soap opera unfolding before them. Marcela ignored the other maids, for her eyes were fixed on Clara, who had burst into tears the moment Aldo's arm brushed her shoulder.

"*Calla te*, Lupé. That's enough." Don Rodrigo released his daughter so suddenly that she fell backward, clutching her sore wrist. "It's too late for blame. What matters now is how we deal with this."

"You're a fool to play into her hands, Digoy," Señora Lupita thundered. "If you acknowledge the bastard child, you will regret it. I swear on your father's grave, you will live to regret this day."

Don Rodrigo stared aghast at a wife who had suddenly metamorphosed into his mother. His mother had been seized by this same frenzy decades earlier, when a *querida* disrupted the final day of his father's wake. The woman strode up the church's center aisle, veil askew to reveal vermilion lips, one hand pulling along a child who looked to be about Rodrigo's age. The boy had his father's eyes, the narrow Duarté nose. His mother had come unhinged by her husband's mistress and bastard son, and her shrieks echoed through the cathedral's eaves, startling doves, bats and a hundred members of Manila's high society, who suddenly realized they were mourning an adulterer.

Now it was apparent his wife had reached that same point of unbridled rage, a snarling, spitting hysteria that threatened to sunder his already shaky marriage. And yet he was determined not to repeat his father's sin.

"Servant or not, Clara is carrying our grandchild. We cannot abandon our own blood."

"Over my dead body, Digoy. I refuse to raise a bastard in this house. *Qué scandalo!*" Doña Lupita shot a murderous glance at Clara. "She must leave immediately."

"And so she will. Nevertheless we must ensure Aldo's child is supported." Don Rodrigo gazed at his son, who stood now as though an invisible wall had risen between him and the weeping maid. "My father should have done the same thing."

"What did your father—" Concha's curiosity withered under Don Rodrigo's stern look.

"We all pay for the consequences of our actions, Concha. Even you will learn that eventually."

Doña Lupita recognized the resolve in her husband's voice and shifted gears. Wrapping pride around herself like a shroud, she devised a compromise that she could live with. Her gaze lit upon Marcela. "*Bueno,* this is how we will arrange it.

"You." Doña Lupita crooked a finger at Marcela. "Come here so that you understand exactly what we will do for your sister." Marcela crept into the patio, keeping a healthy distance between herself and Concha. "You, Marcela, will continue to work here for as long as you want us to support Clara's child. You will deliver the money every month to your sister. You, Clara, must promise never to return to this house or seek work as a servant anywhere in this neighborhood. I must have your word that neither of you will gossip with anyone about this—" Her eyes flickered over Clara's belly. "—this disgraceful situation. Now take her away and gather her belongings. I want her gone before noon."

"*Opo*, Doña Lupita," Marcela whispered to the floor, still dazed by all that had transpired. She put an arm around Clara and led her sister out of the patio.

As the servants retreated, Doña Lupita called out after the cook. "Pipay, search Clara's bags before she leaves. Make sure she doesn't steal anything."

"Are we done now?" Don Rodrigo looked from his wife to his children.

"Almost." Doña Lupita ground her cigarette butt on the floor and pulled out another one, taking time to light it as she considered her son's fate. She looked out at the garden, so serene in comparison with the disarray before her. Finally she turned to her son.

"Aldo, you have disgraced this family. Your father and I are disappointed, but we will get over it eventually. *Gracias a Díos* you still have a whole lifetime to put this behind you. I'm calling Toni-Mae today. You liked L.A., didn't you? I think a year in California will do you good."

"You're sending me back? But we just got home!" Aldo turned pleading eyes on his father. "Pa, you won't let her do this, will you?"

Don Rodrigo rubbed his forehead. "You can't be serious, Lupé. There's no need to—"

"We need to nip this in the bud, Digoy. I want to ensure that the young lovers"—Doña Lupita shuddered delicately—"don't reunite when the bastard is born."

Don Rodrigo nodded, too exhausted to protest.

"Tita Toni-Mae will help you enroll in a junior college. After a year we can decide what to do next."

"But, Ma, what about my classes? I only have a year left at school," Aldo argued.

"You should have thought about that before seducing the maid," Doña Lupita snapped. "At this point you don't get a say in the matter."

"That's it? He gets the maid pregnant and you give him a year in the States?" Concha sputtered. "I don't see how that's fair."

"Ahh, Conchita, everyone gets what he deserves." Doña Lupita offered her daughter a dead smile. "Life in America is no picnic when you have to live there." She rubbed at a stiff spot on her nape; a thin blue vein pulsed along the side of her neck. "I think this is all we need ever say on this matter. The subject is closed. Now. Shall I have Isabel serve us breakfast?"

"I'm not hungry." Shoulders sagging, Don Rodrigo left the patio. Aldo and Concha followed silently, each one returning to the sanctuary of separate rooms.

Alone once more, Doña Lupita contemplated the detritus left by the morning's chaos—a broken coffee mug, a dirty floor, a pregnant servant. As long as they followed her lead, everything would be cleaned up by day's end.

Aldo sat back, weary from talking. "What I would give for a drink just now," he muttered again, running a finger across dry lips.

"No wonder you never went back." Amparo slumped against Seamus. "I can't understand how Mama could be so heartless, even back then."

"When I look back on it now, I think she was afraid." Aldo sighed. "Afraid the scandal would ruin her prospects."

"What prospects?" Seamus stretched an arm round Amparo's shoulder.

"Americans care so much about the future they forget it rides on the past." Aldo leaned back in the armchair, rubbing his forehead. "Manila is all about provenance. If word had gotten out that I had sired a child"—he held up a finger—"with a *maid*, the scandal would have haunted our family for generations. And it would almost surely have ruined Concha's chances to make a good marriage. She would no longer have been *de buena familia*—from a good family." He looked at Amparo. "Your mother has always been very concerned about the family's good name. All she wanted was to live exactly as our parents did: to marry wealth." Aldo shrugged. "Should have been careful what she wished for. I heard she got it in spades."

"And you, Tito Aldo? What did you get?" Amparo leaned into Seamus's warmth, feeling suddenly weary.

"A boatload of regret in an ocean of gin." Aldo offered the old ironic smile.

"But now you have a grandchild," Amparo whispered.

"And a murdered daughter. God forgive me for waiting so long to deal with the damn ninth step." A solitary tear slid down Aldo's cheek, but he looked back at Amparo, unblinking.

PART IV

Reunion

CHAPTER 35

Homecoming

Marcela was cooking the dinner of her life. *Pansit molo* might well have been Fabergé eggs, for all the care she took dropping each dumpling into a pot of simmering, garlic-scented chicken broth. She smiled over the steaming soup, remembering how she'd taught a pigtailed Amparo how to pinch the square noodles around marble-sized balls of shrimp and pork so many years ago. Javier's prized paella sat tented under foil on the counter, next to the ten-yolk flan that his late father had loved. She had even made a pot of Aldo's beloved *kaldereta,* but only after haggling vigorously at the market for the freshest cuts of goat meat.

She almost wished Doña Lupita were still alive. How the grande dame would have howled to see the son she'd banished come home. But this was one reunion that was hers alone to savor.

Distracted by old ghosts, she searched for the wall clock, but saw only a row of frosted glass cabinets. Six months after switching kitchens, she sometimes forgot she no longer lived in Señora Concha's home.

"Come stay with me, Nanay, you don't even have to cook,"

Miguel had pleaded, two days after she'd stabbed Señora Concha. "We won't let you leave, you are family—you always have been."

"You would have me simply switch employers? I have cooked for two generations of your family. Must I cook for a third?" Marcela folded arms over her chest, but the heart within lifted with new hope. If she could escape Señora Concha without losing touch of the Guerrero children, whom she considered her own, it would ease the pain of losing Beverly.

"No, Nanay. As I said, you would not have to cook unless you wanted to," Miguel coaxed, sensing a softening in her defensiveness. "In any case, Amparo and Seamus are bringing Claire to stay here with me during their visit. Wouldn't you like to be just down the hall from your only grandchild?"

"Is it true, then, that Amparo is adopting Claire?" Marcela clasped her hands. She had heard rumors of it but needed confirmation.

"They are fostering her for now," Miguel spoke with cautious optimism. "But since Amparo is, after all, a blood relative, I imagine that it will not be too difficult for her to eventually adopt Claire."

"Then my answer is yes," Marcela cried, blinking back sudden tears. "I cannot wait to meet my grandchild—and her new parents."

Señora Concha had been livid over Miguel's offer, but after Amparo's phone call, the three younger Guerreros would not be dissuaded. Marcela caressed the marble countertop: she had raised her children well.

The timer went off just then; grabbing two mitts, she pulled a tray of golden *ensaymada* out of the oven. Clara would have laughed if she knew her sister now made them better than those bought at the store. Marcela knew Amparo could eat several buns easily, but wondered if young Claire would like the bun's sweet purple yam filling; one never knew about children born in America. And what would that man with the strange name think of her food?

"If he is smart, he will have second servings of everything," she said aloud, painting the swirled bun tops with sugared melted butter.

As she showered the *ensaymada* with grated cheddar, she worried the guests might be too tired from their twelve-hour flight to eat the feast she'd spent all day preparing. *Hayaan mo na*—never mind, she thought. She would have many more chances to feed them during their monthlong visit.

Three long beeps blared and a uniformed maid scampered out to open the gates for Javier's car.

"Nanay, leave that stove and come outside." Miguel swung open the kitchen door, smiling at the woman he called mother. "They're here."

Holding wide the door, he gestured toward the living room, where Amparo stood, young Claire perched on her hip, next to a tall ponytailed American with gentle eyes.

"Nanay! Come meet your grandchild," Amparo sang, her smile bright as the Manila sunlight slanting through the windows.

Slipping out of her apron, Marcela walked out of the kitchen, eager to welcome her family home.

Photo by Nancy Kwak

Marivi Soliven has taught creative writing at the University of the Philippines, Diliman, the Ayala Museum and the University of California at San Diego. Short stories and essays from her fifteen books have appeared in anthologies and textbooks on creative writing. She was awarded a Hedgebrook writing residency in August 2012 for her work on *The Mango Bride* and its advocacy of women's issues. Prior to publication, this novel won the Grand Prize for the Novel in English at the 2011 Carlos Palanca Memorial Awards for Literature, the Philippine version of the Pulitzer Prize. Her short story "Talunang Manok" was adapted for a short film in December 2011, and is set to participate in independent film festivals in 2013.

CONVERSATION GUIDE

MARIVI SOLIVEN

A CONVERSATION WITH MARIVI SOLIVEN

Q. The Mango Bride *delves into fascinating questions about immigration, exile, and where and how we define home. Both of the main characters, Amparo and Beverly, come from the Philippines to America, but for different reasons and in different ways. In fact, you yourself also came from the Philippines to America and settled in California. Are there echoes of your own story in theirs? Where do they depart and what does the process of creating fiction allow you to do when examining your own past?*

A. Beverly's and Amparo's moving to America contains details drawn from my personal immigration experience. I came to California for marriage, not as a mail-order bride as Beverly did, but because my husband was working on his doctorate at UC Berkeley. The Oakland neighborhood in which these two characters lived was ours for many years.

On another level, my parents' view of America reflected that of Señora Concha. But people migrate for any number of reasons and I wanted to portray the many facets of our diaspora. Having spoken with other immigrants over the years, I've learned that each person's perception of the United States is somehow affected by the circumstances under which he or she left the Philippines.

Q. Although much of the current story of The Mango Bride *takes place in America, there are also long sections set in the Philippines. Those sections are so rich in imagery and sensory detail that the reader is immediately transported. What sort of research did you need to do to create another place with such richness and depth?*

A. I simply needed to remember what it was like growing up in Manila. I moved to California as an adult, so I have very clear memories of most of the places mentioned in novel. I drew on memories of studying and teaching at the University of the Philippines to describe Amparo's undergrad life. And a circus elephant really did escape from the coliseum and walk two miles down to Morato Avenue. I hung on to that story for a good decade, knowing I'd use it somewhere.

Q. In The Mango Bride *an omniscient third-person narrator dips down to follow the stores of both Amparo and Beverly. Was it difficult for you to create the distinct characters of each woman and to go back and forth between them as their stories unfolded?*

A. My family more closely resembled the Duarte-Guerrero clan, so I was already familiar with that milieu, but I also drew on Manila's rich trove of gossip to develop the backstory for that family and Amparo's character. As for Beverly's provenance, the story of poor girl meets rich boy is a recurring theme in soap operas, so imagining Clara and Aldo's affair was challenging but not insurmountable.

Q. Between the two, did you have a favorite character and story line? Who was your favorite character in the entire novel?

A. Beverly, if only because I had to work harder at filling out her character. Conversely, I'm fond of antagonistic personalities because they are so much fun to write. Even though Doña Lupita and Señora Concha were not appealing people, I enjoyed writing their dialogue, particularly during the fight scenes.

Q. Food becomes a metaphor in the story and a source of both connection and servitude between characters. Do you yourself enjoy cooking? Do you have favorite dishes you like to cook?

A. Food is the central metaphor in this story because I love to cook! The food writer M. F. K. Fisher is one of my favorite authors, and I've seen the film version of Isak Dinesen's *Babette's Feast* multiple times. Some of the dishes I most enjoy cooking are mentioned in *The Mango Bride.* This fascination with food happens to be a cultural thing. Among Filipinos, one way to say "How are you?" is *Kumain ka na?*—Have you eaten?

QUESTIONS FOR DISCUSSION

1. The question of motherhood is examined closely in *The Mango Bride*, and nowhere is there more ambiguity than in the roles Marcela and Señora Concha play in the lives of Amparo, Javier, and Miguel. What makes someone a mother? And is Marcela's opening act understandable once you have heard her full story? Is it defensible? Is it right?

2. Amparo and Beverly both come to America seeking a better life than what they can have in the Philippines—but they find very different results. Why is this? Do they each deserve what they find here? In general, do you believe people get what they deserve in life?

3. Early in the book, Amparo recalls that when her mother heard she had to do laundry, Señora Concha cried, "My daughter was not raised to wash her own clothes!" What does Amparo lose by coming to America? What does she gain? Do you think the move was worth the price? In what ways is *The Mango Bride* a book about class?

4. Amparo has two lovers through the course of the book—one in the Philippines and one in America. Yet these men are very different

from each other. Has Amparo's view of love changed as she traveled? If so, what has facilitated this growth?

Beverly's experience of "love" in America is quite different from Amparo's. Why do you think the women had such different outcomes?

6. Manong Del seems like a minor character in this story—but why is his presence important? What issues does he allow the author to explore?

7. Uncle Aldo and Amparo form a bond as two expelled members of the family clan. In the beginning of the story we are told: "Curiously, neither one ever talked about the reasons for their expulsion. Amparo's reticence was borne of shame, Aldo's, of guilt." How has this changed by the end of the story? In what way is this a story about secrets and the way they affect relationships?

8. The concept of shame recurs throughout the novel and directly affects way the Filipino characters make crucial life decisions. Would someone from another culture respond differently to the situations in which Amparo, Clara, or Beverly felt shamed? Discuss how a woman in this country might respond if she were faced with an unplanned pregnancy, single motherhood, an abusive relationship, or an adulterous husband.

9. The author's original working title for *The Mango Bride* was *In the Service of Secrets*. Who has secrets in this story? Who eventually reveals his or her secrets? And does this telling bring harm or does it bring help?

10. The story opens with Marcela picking up a knife from a plate of

mangoes and ends with her cooking a special meal. What role does food play in the story—and how does it tie into the title *The Mango Bride*?

11. The ending of the story is somewhat open to interpretation. What do you think happens next to Amparo, Seamus, Claire, Marcela, Señora Concha, and Aldo?